Love P

Also by this author

Who Will Love Polly Odlum?
Dancing Days
Something Sensational

And in this series:
The Love Detective

For more information, visit: www.annemarieforrest.info
or email Anne Marie at am_forrest@hotmail.com.

Love
Potions

Anne Marie Forrest

POOLBEG

Published 2008
by Poolbeg Press Ltd
123 Grange Hill, Baldoyle
Dublin 13, Ireland
E-mail: poolbeg@poolbeg.com
www.poolbeg.com

13 5 7 9 10 8 6 4 2

A catalogue record for this book is available from the British Library.

ISBN 978-1-84223-335-1

Typeset by Patricia Hope in Bembo 11.3./14.5

Printed by
CPI Cox & Wyman, Reading, RG1 8EX

Note on the Author

Anne Marie Forrest began her writing career with the publication of her first novel, the bestselling *Who Will Love Polly Odlum?* This was followed by *Dancing Days, Something Sensational* and *The Love Detective. Love Potions* is her fifth novel. Anne Marie's novels have been translated into French, German and Spanish.

Anne Marie lives with her husband, Robert, and her two young daughters, Lucy and Sylvie.

To my parents, John and Claire

"Fetch me that flower, the herb I show'd thee once;
The juice of it on sleeping eyelids laid
Will make or man or woman madly dote
Upon the next live creature that it sees."

From Shakespeare's, A Midsummer Night's Dream.

1

The thing is, I don't feel comfortable. I should have known better. I should never have allowed Caroline persuade me. I should never have let her talk me into wearing her navy Paul Costello suit. For starters, it's too big, the skirt especially, and despite her assurances (and the presence of a couple of discreet safety pins) I worry it might go sliding down over my hips without notice – most likely at some inopportune moment, like when I'm crossing the room to shake hands with the interviewers. I did try voicing my worries to Caroline last night when she was doing her Trinny and Susannah on me but she just waved my concerns aside and told me the suit could have been made for me. Made for me? Why, yes – *if* I were a stone or two heavier, a couple of inches shorter and was shaped and proportioned altogether differently. Made for me? No, but the sad truth is, it is so much better than anything I own.

And, because it is so much better, I've been terrified all morning that I'll spill a cup of coffee on it or rip it on something sharp. Caroline must have mentioned a dozen times how very expensive it was and how privileged I am to be getting a loan of it. What with the prospect of being humiliated by a panel of interviewers hanging over me, this additional worry of doing hundreds of euros' worth of damage is one I could do without.

Another reason I don't feel comfortable is because I simply don't feel like me. This power-suit-wearing me is a false me; it's me playing at being a Caroline type – sharp, in control, the kind that looks like she could juggle a budget of millions with one hand while applying blood-red lipstick with the other.

And that's another thing. I should never have let her persuade me to wear her blood-red lipstick. It makes me feel like a hooker which isn't quite the look I was aiming for and, now, even at this late stage, I have the urge to find the Ladies' and go wipe the scarlet gash from my face. Only the worry of having my name called out in my absence keeps me in my seat.

Despite my preoccupation with my too-loose skirt and my too-tarty lipstick, I get the feeling that someone is staring at me and I look up to be met by the haughty gaze of a haughty-looking woman, early twenties I'd guess, who's sitting across the waiting-room and who heretofore has been at pains to haughtily ignore me. Now that she's caught my eye, she arches one of her thinly plucked eyebrows and stares pointedly at my foot. I follow her gaze and look down. My foot is tapping like crazy, powered by my nervousness.

"Nerves," I explain, smile apologetically and force myself to still that errant foot. She looks at me stony-faced, like she has no comprehension of this word. "What is this 'nerves', you speak of?" I half-expect her to ask in (for some reason) a heavily accented voice. I struggle to keep my foot still while she sits there, coolly studying me, deciding whether I'm a worthy opponent, all the while managing to look utterly composed as if being here in this sterile room, waiting for a head to pop around the door, call out a name and then the owner of that head to lead one of us candidates, one of us condemned, down a corridor to face a panel who'll look us up and down, judge us, ask us to explain our life, or at least that portion and version of it outlined in our CV and then, most likely, reject us – *me* – is, well, no big deal. No big deal! Oh God! God!!!!!!! My stomach lurches. I think I'm going to get sick. I think about making a dash for the toilets but again the fear of being called in my absence keeps me where I am.

Across the room, Ms Cool, Calm and Collected, having now dropped me from her stare in the manner a child might drop some bug after examining it to his or her satisfaction, picks up her expensive-looking leather satchel. She unfastens it, extracts what I guess is a copy of her CV, then relaxes back in her chair, opens it, and begins to read. Maybe I should take my lead from her and study my own CV but no, I would find no comfort there – it would make me even more anxious: the poor science degree that took longer than it should, the lack of any relevant work experience, and – yes – the lies. Was I right to listen to Caroline? Was I right to take her advice and omit the fact that I'd spent my time since graduating working in the unrelated area of fashion to put it in lofty terms or, more prosaically, as a shop assistant in a Dublin city centre boutique? I'd probably still be there but for the fact that months back it closed its doors permanently to the city's shoppers who failed to come through those doors in numbers sufficient to keep it viable, lured as they were by trendier, brighter, brasher and much cheaper shopping opportunities in the city. All that I left out. Caroline argued that to tell the truth would show a lack of interest in my field. Far better, she maintained, to say I'd been travelling. They'd like that, Caroline said. They'd like the idea that I'd wanted to broaden my mind and now that it was sufficiently broadened, I was ready to settle down and apply myself to this new job, ready to become a productive member of their team and society at large.

Now the door slowly opens. I look towards it, holding my breath – has my time finally come? But no, instead a nervous-looking human beanpole sidles in, eyes firmly focused on the ground. His fresh-from-the-shop suit but even more so his nervousness suggest he's here for the same reason I am. But how can this be? He looks fifteen – tops. Nervously he glances around the room but manages to avoid eye contact with either me or Ms Cool, Calm and Collected. Then he takes a seat exactly equidistant from me and Ms CCC so that we're like three magnets repelling one another. For what seems like an age he sits there, head bent, not daring to look up until, finally, he garners the courage, raises his eyes nervously, catches mine and, when he does, I smile, hoping to put him at ease but instead I guess I startle him, my own nerves having strangulated my facial muscles, doubtlessly making my smile more like a wolf-like grimace. He promptly drops the A4 pages he's been clutching – his CV? – and, unstapled, they flutter to the floor.

Both he and I jump from our seats and bend down to pick them up.

"Ms Rosie Kiely?" a voice calls out from behind my back.

From my disadvantaged squatting position, I turn my

head around and look up to see a friendly, bubbly young woman looking down.

"Yes, that's me."

"Can you please come with me, Ms Kiely?" She beckons with a nicely manicured nail but to me it's as menacing as the long gnarled finger of the Grim Reaper.

I get up from my haunches. My time has come.

In Renaissance times, nightshade and foxglove were often combined and then applied to a sleeping man's eyes to make him propose upon awakening.
Since both plants are poisonous, I wonder just how many poor men suffered before the link between cause and effect was made.

2

There they are. All five of them sitting in a row: a long desk in front of them, a big picture window behind them opening onto a bleak little carpark bounded by a two-metre-high unpainted concrete wall. Why, I wonder, did the person who designed this modern building bother to put in such an enormous window only to have it looking out onto such a dreary scene? But I'm not here to critique the building. No. I'm here to persuade them, these five strangers, to want me. I remind myself to focus. I need to impress them from the outset. As Caroline has told me repeatedly, I need to dazzle them from the word go.

"Hello," says the man in the middle, his dark eyes looking out at me from beneath a pair of Brillo pads. He has a matching head of thick, steel-grey hair and a florid face. Thickset, I think would be the word to best describe his physique, and this thickset body of his is just about contained in a brown suit — a size or two bigger wouldn't have gone amiss. Especially about the chest. Why doesn't he unbutton the jacket? It can't be comfortable. The cream shirt he's wearing isn't a great fit either and folds of his pinkish-purple neck bulge over the collar. Maybe he lives on his own and has no one to advise him on what looks good on him. Poor man.

"Rosie Kiely, isn't it?" he says.

I nod, and answer. "Yeah, hi."

Oh dear! Far, far too informal – Caroline would not be impressed. This man with the thick eyebrows and the too-small suit who maybe/maybe not lives on his own is probably not impressed either. This is not good. Studies show, so Caroline claims, that interviewers make up their mind about a candidate within five seconds of first meeting them.

"Please, won't you sit down?" says the man. I guess, even if he has made up his mind, he still has to go through the motions. "Thank you for coming," he adds.

Thank you for inviting me, I'm about to answer but that doesn't seem the right thing to say. Instead, I remain mute and smile again, do what I'm told and take a seat. Once sitting, I notice that all five interviewers are studying me. I fight back my nerves and smile in turn at each of the miscellany of faces staring so intently at me. On one side of Eyebrows sits a youngish man with a clean-shaven face and rimless spectacles with lens that make his eyes look enormous, or maybe they are enormous. I'd look a little closer but I don't want him to think I'm staring. Beside him there sits a serious-faced Asian woman who would be quite beautiful but for an ever-so-slight squint in her left eye. On Eyebrow's other side sits the fourth member of the panel, another woman who could be the older sister of the woman in the waiting room (same haughty stare, same self-assurance). That leaves the final panellist, an elderly man so wizened he could be Old Man Time himself. He's dressed in a conservative well-cut suit as might be expected in the circumstances but, rather surprisingly, it's teamed with a shocking-pink shirt and a cheerfully coloured tie which make me warm to him a little. This pink shirt and the jazzy tie suggest to me a colourful past and, age aside, this old man does look like someone who has a lot of history, like he might very well have been something of a lady's man in his day. Maybe he still is. But then, wouldn't that make him a dirty old man? But, if it were ladies his own age he was interested in, I guess not. Lecherous old men are only considered lecherous if it's young ones they lech after. I think. But why am I thinking any of this? I'm meant to be focusing, I remind myself, and I remind myself that these are the five people who, in the next half hour or so, will determine my fate, will decide if they want me as part of the team. Or don't want me. And do I really want them to want me? But now is not the time for such reservations. Caroline says interviewing panels can sniff out doubts like dogs can sniff out fear.

Eyebrows is talking to me now. I tune in. He's introducing himself, telling me about his position within the company. Then he goes on to introduce the other members of the panel. All the while I nod like I'm taking all this in but I hardly hear let alone retain a word of what he's saying. I'm all a-jitter. I realise my foot is tapping again. I still it.

"So, Rosie Kiely, you're interested in working with SciEire," says the man with the eyebrows.

"Yes, very much so." I wonder if I should add anything else to make it sound convincing. ("You've got to sell yourself, Rosie! Believe in yourself! Believe you're a winner, not a loser!" The words of Caroline naturally, consumer of – in my opinion – an unhealthy number of self-help books.)

Maybe I could tell them how it's been my life's ambition to work for SciEire, that to work for them was my very reason for going into science in the first place (even though I'd never heard of them until my mother spotted their ad in a journal) but I know I'd lack the necessary conviction. Instead, I repeat, "Yes, yes, I am," and, with nothing better to add but still wanting them to see that I am an enthusiastic person, I add another, "Yes." And then I smile in what I hope is an enthusiastic way. "Yes, indeed. I am *very* interested in working for SciEire." I smile again – for good measure.

There's a pregnant pause but I have nothing else to add. Instead, to fill it, I smile once more.

"And I see you graduated last year?" Eyebrows goes on.

"That's right."

I notice the crop of hairs peeping out from both his nostrils. They're pretty gross but somehow oddly impressive; they're just so very, very thick and, further evidence, I think, that he lives alone. Had he a wife or partner she'd surely have urged him to shave them, or pluck them, or whatever method one uses to remove nostril hair. What is the best way of getting rid of nose hair anyway?

"From UCD?" he adds.

"Pardon?" I don't believe I've ever seen thicker.

"You graduated last year from UCD?"

"Yes," I answer. Not that I make a habit of examining or even noticing people's nose hairs but these are hard to miss. Are there special depilatory creams for such sensitive areas? I don't know.

"With a degree in Science?" he adds.

"Yes," I answer again. Yes, yes, yes, it's all there on my CV. What more am I meant to say?

"But you've been travelling ever since?" he's asking now.

"Yes." Oh, why has he got on to *this* – and already! And how can I change the subject back to something safer, something I'd feel more assured talking about than my bogus gap time out? But, really, there is no area of comfort in my CV. "That's right," I say. Now move swiftly along, I silently plead.

"You spent some time in India?" the Asian woman comes in, one eye fixed upon me, the other otherwise occupied.

"Pardon?" I'm playing for time. I'm trying to remember the list of countries Caroline dreamed up when, instead of simply going and printing out my CV for me as the favour I'd asked of her, she decided to have a go at creative writing. I should have put my foot down when I saw her 'improvements' and made her change them back. Instead, I let her talk me into sending in her version and now I'm going to have to give voice to the lies she dreamt up to make me more, to use her term, marketable.

"You spent some time in India?" repeats the woman. She nods down at the copy of my CV she's holding in her hand. "You say here you travelled in India, Bangladesh, and Pakistan."

"Ah yes, that's right."

"My family is from India. I'm interested in your impressions. Were you there for very long?"

Great! What are the chances? Of all the interviewing panels in all the world . . .

"Just a couple of months," I mumble. Months! Months! Why months when I could have said weeks – or even days?

"And what parts did you visit?"

"Ah – all over."

"And did you like it?"

"Oh yes." There's a pause while they all sit there, waiting

for me to expand and I sit there, staring back while frantically searching through the part of my brain that stores all the Indian-related facts I've accumulated in my lifetime. It turns out to be quite a small part. It turns out I can fit all these facts into one convoluted sentence that I now blurt out in a nervous rush. "Yes, it was all very interesting and different and there were cows everywhere and of course I liked the food, you know, the naan bread and the curries and that and it was very colourful, very colourful, especially the women in their saris which were very colourful as I already mentioned and of course there's the Ganges –" I make a flowing motion with my two hands in case anyone is in any doubt about what I mean by the Ganges "– and the magnificent Taj Mahal which is just gorgeous and huge," again I use my hands to make a big sweeping gesture to demonstrate what I mean by huge lest there be any confusion, "and the spicy scents and the wonderful scenery and . . . and . . . ah –" I've run out of things to say "– and I loved it."

Considering I've never set foot in the place I think I've acquitted myself quite well but the woman's eye is upon me as if she expects even more. But what? That's it. I'm done. I couldn't come up with a single other thing to say on the subject of India, not if these five were an actual firing squad. What was Caroline thinking? India? Bangladesh? Pakistan?

But the woman isn't quite done just yet.

"Tell me, what cities did you visit in India?" she asks.

Oh sweetest hour!

"Well, ah, Bombay," I tell her, "and ah –"

"You mean Mumbai?" she interrupts.

"No, Bombay."

"Mumbai," she repeats.

What's with this lady? Why is she so keen that I should

have visited Mumbai? Maybe that's where her family are from. Maybe she likes hearing news of home. No harm, I guess, in humouring her a little.

"I think I may have passed through Mumbai on the way to Bombay."

Now she's staring at me with what can best be described as suspicion. But what have I said? She can't know I've never set foot in either city.

"But Bombay *is* Mumbai now," she finally tells me, "and has been for over ten years."

Has it? But I've never heard of Mumbai? It strikes me that she may be trying to catch me out but, apart from coming right out and asking her, I have no way of knowing for sure so I laugh to show that I made a silly mistake, a slip of the tongue, that *of course* I know it's called Mumbai now, doesn't everyone?

"Ah yes, of course."

"And where else?"

"Ah – Delhi." I hold my breath for a second, wondering if I'll be corrected again. Has Delhi too changed its name unbeknownst to me?

But it seems not, and she goes on: "Mumbai to Delhi? That's quite a distance. Tell me, how long did it take you to travel from one to the other?"

"Ahh – a day," I blurt out nervously.

"A day." She raises an eyebrow. "By train, was it?"

"Yes," I answer though already I know, I just *know*, I've given the wrong answer. Should I have said longer? Shorter? How far apart are these cities? I have no idea.

She's looking at me doubtfully but lets whatever suspicions she has go unvoiced. "And what were your impressions of Delhi?"

All five are sitting there, expectantly, waiting for me to answer. I mean, what *is* this? An interview for a position as travel guide?

"It was – ah – colourful."

"Ah yes, with all those women in their saris?"

Is that a hint of sarcasm in her tone?

"Yes. And it was very busy of course, but I liked it."

"And the naan bread and the curries were good there too?"

"Em, yes," I mumble.

The woman is looking at me keenly. I try not to look at her. She knows I'm lying but I hope good manners will prevail and she won't come right out and call me a liar. They're all staring at me now, waiting for me to go on. Silence drags until finally, the young man with rimless spectacles and the maybe/maybe not enormous eyes, takes the conch.

"So, tell us, Rosie, why do you want this position?"

Because I need the money, because I'm not qualified to do anything else, because my mother says I should get a job in science and not waste all the years I spent studying. But of course none of these is the right answer.

"Well," I begin – the sun has come out now and is flooding in through that huge picture window and shining directly into my eyes and I can't see his face as I answer – "I feel I'm qualified to work as a chemistry laboratory technician within your company. I have an excellent knowledge of laboratory procedures and practices and possess an ability to successfully resolve analytical issues. I also have excellent documentation skills and am able to work on my own initiative."

"Are you indeed?" comes the response – from the man in the rimless glasses, I think, but I can't be sure on account of the sun in my eyes.

Neither can I tell if my answer has found approval as he speaks in a monotone and, not being able to see the face that goes with the voice, I have no visual clues. I hope I didn't sound like I'd learnt this speech off by heart, which in fact I have – all of what I'm saying originates from their original advert.

"As you probably know, this position involves shift work," one of the men points out, but again, with the sun blinding me, I can't be sure which one. "Have you any objection to working at night?" he – whoever – asks.

"No, not at all," I lie in an attempt to please. "It suits my lifestyle," I add, though why I'm not sure. I mean what kind of lifestyle am I suggesting by saying this? A vaguely nefarious one?

The sun goes behind a cloud again. Old Eyebrows coughs now before speaking and I turn to him. He begins reading out the list of hobbies Caroline concocted, not happy with what I'd put down. Deciding my personality didn't come across as well rounded enough, she deleted the list of hobbies I had written – reading, going to the cinema and running – and wrote out her own list. She wanted, she said, to give the impression that I was sociable, active, broadly educated, and had leadership qualities – seemingly under the impression that I was applying for the job of president of the country, and not that of a lab technician

Now Eyebrows reads:

"Film – founding member of the First Tuesday film club. The First Tuesday film club is composed of a group of ten friends and we meet in our own homes to view and discuss classic films" (to illustrate my leadership qualities and my interest in the arts), *"non-fiction – particularly works pertaining to historical figures"* (to suggest an educated and discerning reader), *"basketball"*

(team player), *"and cooking"* (creativity). He puts the CV down. "So tell me, Rosie, what are you reading at the moment?"

What am I reading? Nothing – at this moment. But I can't say that, not after the hyperbole of my CV. He's looking at me so expectantly I want to please him. Of all the panel I like him the most. And then, suddenly, a title comes to me.

"*The Diary of Samuel Pepys,*" I say.

It's a book Caroline's boyfriend Mick left behind him the last weekend he was staying and, ever since, it's been sitting on the coffee table in the living-room. I have been thinking about reading it. I will read it. I've just not got around to it yet.

"Really?" says Father Time, suddenly looking uncomfortably interested.

"Ah – yes."

"I find," says Father Time, "my wife hath something in her gizzard."

"Pardon?" His wife? What's he on about? Isn't it chickens who have gizzards? But then it occurs to me that – of course – he must be quoting from Pepys. Though what he means, I have no idea.

"My wife," he repeats again, "hath something in her gizzard, that only waits an opportunity of being provoked to bring up; but I will not, for my content sake, give it."

Had I really an interest in Samuel Pepys I might be able to throw a quote back at him. Had I taken the time to read him instead of just thinking that some day I might then I'd be able to discuss the context of it. All I know about Samuel Pepys is that he kept a diary and it's been sitting on our coffee table this past week. I know nothing about his wife and her gizzard. Never in my wildest imagination did I expect the interview to come to this! After all, what they're looking for is someone to beaver away in a lonely lab in the dead of night – not someone to sit on the panel of some late-night television arts show.

"Very good," I say lamely instead.

The old man is looking at me suspiciously now, as is the Indian woman (she has definitely got my number). I begin to think that, perhaps, I should just come clean, throw myself at his mercy, at the mercy of all of them and tell them how, after six failed interviews, a well-meaning if misguided Caroline took me in hand, dressed me up like a dog's dinner and embellished my CV (or rather falsified it) but, if they do give me this job, I'll work hard, be punctual, learn what I need to learn and be a team player, I really will. And I'll never lie again.

But I don't. I stay silent. I just want this whole thing to be over now.

Eyebrows puts my CV down on the table. He looks at his watch, and then, in an uninterested way, as if he's just filling in time, he goes through the motions of telling me about the company and the job.

"International contracts . . . an annual research and development budget of fifteen million . . . profits expected to double within ten years . . ."

Heartsore at the thought of flunking yet another interview, I sit there, pretending to listen.

"So," he finally winds up, "are there any questions you'd like to ask?"

I know I should have one. Good candidates are expected to have a question or two at the close of an interview but I'm not a good candidate. I think all of us in the room know that by now. What's the point in even trying to pretend otherwise at this late stage? I shake my head.

"Well then, Ms Kiely, I think that's about it for now."

He stands up. Interview finally over, I half-expect him to say, "Don't call us, we'll call you", but he's more polite than that. He reaches out a hand and I take it and shake it to find that it's warm and clammy, and limp too – there's no heart in it. It's certainly not the handshake of someone sealing the deal.

"Goodbye then," I say and I sidle out of the room. If I had a tail, it would be between my legs.

Aztec emperor Montezuma swore by chocolate.
Apparently he sustained his virility by drinking vast
quantities in liquid form, 50 goblets of it a day,
with an extra one for luck.
Hmm . . . how long was it before it had an effect on
his waistline? And did that have a subsequent adverse
knock-on effect on his pulling power which, in turn,
would have decreased his need to be so virile
in the first place?
A vicious circle . . .

3

I hurry down the corridor, anxious to put some distance between me and the scene of my shame. I'm not sure who I'm most mad with, Caroline or myself. Myself, I guess. After all, Caroline was, in her own fashion, just trying to help. She only interfered because she knew I was so down at not being able to get a job. I'm the fool to have gone along with her. I feel mortified. To think all those people on that panel are probably discussing me now, dismissing me as wholly unsuitable and not so much because of my poor academic qualifications or my dearth of relevant work experience but because I'm so evidently a liar. They may be strangers and I'll probably never set eyes on them again but I hate the idea that those interviewers know me as a fake. I think of some time in the future, some years from now, and I see them all sitting around the coffee room with the successful candidate who's now a much-loved colleague and they're all reminiscing about the time she (that woman in the waiting room, I just know it) got the job and that in turn brings them back to the interview and how dreadful some of the other candidates were, like the strange girl who unaccountably pretended she'd been to India and had read Samuel Pepys' diary.

Head down, I push through the front door and stomp down the steps of the building until I nearly collide with someone coming up.

"Sorry," I mutter and go to step aside, too disheartened to even bother to look up.

But then I feel a hand on my arm, and hear a familiar voice ask: "Going somewhere, stranger?"

I raise my head to see Finn, my boyfriend, smiling at me in his slightly lopsided but most lovely way.

"Finn! What on earth are you doing here?"

"I thought I'd come and see how you got on. Maybe take you out for lunch to celebrate." He considers my face. "Or to commiserate . . ."

"There was no need to come," I say but I am glad he did.

After my history of disastrous relationships, it's still quite strange for me to be in a normal and nice relationship with someone so very normal and so very nice as Finn. I still find it hard to believe that a man can be so nice and thoughtful and care about me enough to, say, come and surprise me like Finn has done today. I still find it hard to accept that it all can be so . . . well . . . very nice. Okay, I may be overusing it but 'nice' is a much underrated word. Nice is, well, definitely a very nice thing. I should know. I've come face-to-face often enough with 'not-so-nice' in Finn's sad, sorry list of predecessors.

"Rosie?"

"Sorry, what were you saying?"

"Do you want to go for lunch?"

21

"I don't know." I shrug. "I kind of just feel like running home and climbing under the duvet."

"Come on. It can't have been that bad!"

"You think?" I shake my head. "It was. I didn't get the job."

"They told you already?"

"Not in actual words, no, but they didn't need to – it was a disaster!"

Finn looks at me for a second. "There's an Italian place around the corner. Come on. Lunch will do you good. You can tell me all about it there."

"I'm not sure I could bear to."

"Was it really so awful?"

"Yes! But I *am* starving. I haven't eaten a thing all morning. I hadn't the stomach for it."

As we walk down the street, Finn takes my hand and, as he does, I look over at him and, I swear, my heart does a little leap. God, how I love this man, how I love everything about him! The gentle expression on his face. The curve of his cheekbone. His mop of curly black hair. His truly gorgeous deep dark-blue eyes. Despite what Caroline says ("Jesus! Rosie! They're blue, just blue. Now give it a rest!"), his eyes really are the most amazing shade. If paint manufacturers could do the impossible and replicate this miracle of nature, the tins would go flying off the shelves.

The thing is, I can't ever imagine not being with Finn. I can't ever imagine an end to me and him. I simply can't imagine a day when our relationship will finally run a natural course and we'll split up. I'm not saying I'm dead certain we'll be together for ever and ever – we have only been going out for a matter of months – but I like to think that it's a possibility that we could – that maybe – who knows – perhaps – we might – just might – be together forever. I smile to myself as Finn just happens to glance in my direction and, spontaneously, he picks up my hand in both of his, brings it to his lips, and kisses it. I swear I feel like bursting into song. Thoughts of the disastrous interview are utterly forgotten and momentarily replaced with the urge to go skipping down the street, hand-in-hand with Finn, both of us singing, "We Got a Groovy Kind of Love," as we throw sweet loving glances at one another and kick our heels high in the air before coming to a stop at the lights at the end of the path. But this is Dublin city centre. At lunch-time. We don't want to be hauled off by the men in white coats. And besides, I don't think Finn would go for it.

We reach the restaurant to find it's packed but the waiter tells us he can just about squeeze us in, that he has a single table for two left, and directs us to follow him. Strictly speaking, he isn't lying. It is a table for two but the tables on either side are so close that, really, he's splitting hairs, or tables. On one side are another couple who – apart from looking a little disgruntled when we squeeze in beside them – carry on talking and allow the etiquette of the circumstances to dictate by pretending we don't exist. On the other side is a solitary diner who stares at us as we take our seats. Not for him to furtively look away when caught staring. If he were subsequently to be questioned by the police or whoever, for some reason, whatever reason (I'm just saying *if*, I haven't worked out the exact scenario) I think they'd find that not a single aspect of our appearance or demeanour had escaped him. What a nosy little man!

"So, tell me about the interview," Finn begins once we've ordered.

"Oh Finn, it was awful, far worse than all the others. As

well as coming across as a total and utter idiot, it was obvious to all of them that I was a complete liar. I swear I will never pay any heed to Caroline ever again as long as I live."

Finn gives me a disbelieving smirk. "Yeah, you will."

"No, no, this time she went too far. I'd have been better off without her interference. I know she was only trying to help but she made it so much worse. You know she wrote down on my CV that I'd spent some time travelling in India amongst other places?"

Finn looks puzzled. "But why?"

I shrug. "She was trying to help. The thing is, one of the interviewers was from India. Can you believe that?"

I see Finn is smirking again.

"Stop! It wasn't funny. Like what was I supposed to say when she asked me what my impressions were of a country I'd never set foot in?"

"What did you say?"

"What could I say?"

"But what *did* you say?"

"I can't really remember," I lie. "I think I may have said something about finding it very colourful," I mumble, "and – ah – something about liking the cuisine."

"The cuisine?" he raises an eyebrow.

"I think I may have told her I liked the naan bread and the curries."

Finn bursts out laughing. "No doubt she was impressed by your keen grasp of the country's political, social, and economic past and present?"

"Stop! It's not funny!" A question occurs to me. "Tell me, have you ever heard of a city called Mumbai?"

He thinks for a second. "Isn't that what Bombay is called nowadays?"

I throw my eyes to heaven. "How can you possibly know that! I thought they were two different cities. I told her I'd been to both."

"Ah Rosie – you didn't!"

"It gets worse. They asked me about books, what I was reading, and I was so nervous by that stage I couldn't think of a single book I'd read lately but then I remembered one Mick left behind – *The Diary of Samuel Pepys* – so I pretended I'd read that but then I find out that one of the others on the panel is a huge Pepys fan. Can you believe that? He even began quoting from it – something about his wife's gizzard. But I mean really, what are the chances I'd have an Indian *and* a Samuel Pepys fan interviewing me?"

"Fairly slim?" he laughs.

Annoyingly, the solitary diner is still giving us his undivided attention. Hasn't he anything better to do with his time? I feel like pointing out we're not the floor show but settle for throwing him another dirty look. There's just no shaming him. I turn back to Finn.

"Anyway I don't care. I'm not even sure I want the job but it would be nice to be offered it. I'm sick of going for interviews. One's worse than the other. They're humiliating. How is it," I demand, quickly descending into self-pity, "how is it that everyone else's life is going so well?"

"Like whose?" Finn demands sharply. "Like mine?"

I could bite my tongue. I was thinking of all the others. I was thinking of the rest of our bunch of friends. Of Caroline with her high-flying career in marketing, of Dana who's completing her Master's degree in psychology, of Shane building his reputation as a solicitor and of his girlfriend, Loretta, working as a junior doctor. I was thinking of Caroline's boyfriend, Mick, who, for as long as we've all known him has played the real-life role of a struggling actor but who, with no small help from Caroline, has recently secured the lead in a feature film. I guess I wasn't thinking of Dana's Doug who's struggling to get work as a painter-decorator. And I definitely wasn't thinking of Finn.

"Well, no," I answer, a little shamefacedly, feeling like the self-engrossed cow I sometimes am though I've been trying hard to be less of one in recent months.

Finn looks upset.

"I'm sorry," I say. "I guess I was thinking of Mick and the others."

I struggle to think of something else to say, to lighten the mood but I can't. It seems Finn hasn't much to say either and I can't blame him. We both sit there in silence. Floor show over, our dining companion calls for the bill.

I try to eat some of my lunch but it sticks in my throat. When I look at Finn I see his head is bent over his meal and he's pushing his food around on his plate with his fork but he's not eating either. I could kick myself for being so bloody insensitive.

Poor Finn. Apart from the not inconsiderable worry of being jobless and therefore penniless which I like to imagine is temporary despite today's fiasco, I'm still probably happier than I've ever been in my life and that's all down to Finn. I've never felt about anyone the way I do about him. I know he feels the same about me but, the sorry truth is, I'm probably the only good thing in Finn's life right now. He doesn't bang on about it but every other aspect of it is pretty much in tatters. Looking over at the top of his curly hair, I want to reach out and stroke those curls but I hold back. I don't want to crowd him. I do wish he'd look up at me. I need to see him smile. What I wouldn't give to make everything all right for him!

Six months ago everything was all right in Finn's life – more than all right – his star was in its ascendancy, he was the man, his future was so very rosy. Finn and his band, Dove, were being hailed as the next biggest thing – there were even talks of recording contracts. Then, the band began falling apart but things didn't stop there and bad turned to so much worse when the lead singer, Mark, died in the most awful car accident. It's a very long and horrible story in which I had quite a big part to play. You see, before Finn I'd gone out with Mark for a short while. To begin with, everything was great. Mark was gorgeous-looking, talented and, so it seemed to me, the perfect boyfriend but underneath that shiny surface there was something not quite right as I began to realise. When I broke up with him, it became evident just how 'not quite right'. He became obsessed – sending me flowers, texting me all the time, showing up at my work, at my home, at my parents' house and even at the hospital where my dad was a patient. Looking back now I can hardly believe how awful it all was and the night Mark died was the tragic climax. He was following the taxi I was in when he lost control of the steering in his car. That night, Mark lost his life, Dove lost its lead singer, and Finn lost his best friend.

Finn and I don't really talk about what happened that night much any more but that doesn't mean we don't think about it. I know I do. I still go over the 'what ifs' of it all in my mind. I know I feel guilty about Mark dying. If thoughts of Mark frequently occupy my mind then they probably preoccupy Finn's. I know he misses Mark an awful lot. How could he not? They'd known each other since childhood; they were brought up together; they were more like brothers than friends. All Finn's early memories – learning to ride a bike, first day in school – are all tied up with Mark.

Plus they were living together and, until just before Mark died, working together in the band.

Since Mark's death, Finn has let his music slide. Right now, he's working full-time in one of his dad's hardware stores and is back living with him, having rented out his own house, the one he shared with Mark. Given how well everything was going for him last year, this is not where he'd have foreseen himself at this point in his life. So no, things are not going brilliantly for Finn.

The waiter comes to clear away our plates.

"Sir," he says, noticing Finn's barely touched plate, "was your meal okay for you?"

"Fine," says Finn. "I guess I just wasn't as hungry as I thought."

"Shall I bring you dessert menus?"

Finn looks over at me. "Do you mind if we get the bill? I should be heading back to work."

"No, not at all." I reach my hand across the table and he takes it and gives it a short squeeze, then stands up and begins putting on his coat. I follow suit.

We pay and leave and, once outside, we stand on the pavement buttoning up our coats. It's begun to drizzle.

"Fancy going to the cinema tonight?" asks Finn.

"I'd love to. Anything good in?" But then I remember. "Damn! I can't. It's our girls' night out, remember?"

"Oh yes, of course," he grins. "The long-talked about girls' night out."

"What so funny about that?" I ask but I'm glad to see him smiling again.

"Nothing. It's just that you've all talked about it so much, I hope it lives up to your expectations."

"Course it will."

"Where have you decided to go?"

"Not sure, some new place Caroline is keen on. I must give her a text later to find out."

"I'll give you a ring tomorrow to see how you got on. Look, I'd better get back to work."

"What are you going to do this evening?" I ask before he goes.

"Don't worry about me. I'll probably stay in and watch some telly. Anyway, have a good night."

I watch him walk away. Then I call his name. He looks back. I blow him a kiss. He smiles a smile that doesn't quite reach his eyes, gives a wave, then he turns and carries on walking, his hands deep in his pockets, his shoulders slightly drooped.

Pearls dissolved in wine did it for Cleopatra, or rather she hoped it would for Mark Antonius. Some say she created this expensive drink to show off her wealth to him (was she the Ancient Rome equivalent of the Elton Johns of today?). Others, however, say she dropped the pearl into wine because she believed it was an aphrodisiac.

A wine capable of liquefying a pearl? How palatable could that be? I hope Mark Antonius had a strong stomach.

4

"Do you mind if I take your table?" I ask.

The group of strangers, all standing around the afore-mentioned table in various stages of putting their coats back on, stop for a moment and turn to stare at me. Of course it would have been politer to wait until they'd actually left before attempting to grab their newly vacated spot but this place is so crowded – there's maybe thirty people at the bar with eyes trained like vultures looking for a place to sit – that ambushing this group is the only way I'm going to bag seats for myself and the girls when they arrive.

With little choice, one of the group nods and I slide in while they finish dressing for the outdoors.

A short while after they've left, the waiter comes and clears away their mess from the table. I look at my watch. I'm ten minutes early. By my calculations this means I have ten minutes to wait for Dana who is always bang on time and I've up to forty minutes to wait for Caroline. Dana is a stickler for time-keeping whereas Caroline's private code of

31

manners decrees that being anything up to a half an hour late is perfectly acceptable and should be considered as being on time. At least when it comes to herself – she isn't quite so flexible when she's the one doing the waiting.

For the next ten minutes I defend the table from the approaches of the many who covet the two stools I'm holding.

And then I see Dana in a gap through the crowd. She's standing at the doorway looking like a lost little soul in that truly ridiculously oversized overcoat she's so fond of wearing. She doesn't have her glasses on and from the way she's peering around myopically with those enormous eyes of hers I'm guessing she doesn't have her contacts in either. I wave to catch her attention but she looks right through me. Poor Dana, she really is as blind as a bat. I wave again and call her name and, this time, she squints over at me, waves back, then begins making her way across the room.

"Hi there!" she says when she reaches me. "I wasn't sure if it was you."

She sits down on the stool across the table from me.

"How come you're not wearing contacts?" I ask.

"I am but I think one of them has slipped." She leans forward and stretches out her neck until her face is inches from mine. "Can you see it?" she asks, making her huge brown eyes even more huge.

I peer. "Aaah – yes, I think, in the corner and no, don't even dream of asking me to try and shift it into place. Go find a mirror."

"Sure – in a sec." She sits back and then begins fanning herself. "God! It's roasting in here, isn't it?"

"Maybe it would help if you take off at least some of your many layers of clothes," I suggest.

So Dana begins the somewhat lengthy process of disrobing. She unwinds her scarf, removes her gloves, takes off her long navy overcoat but she's still not done. She unbuttons and takes off her woolly cardigan to reveal a further layer, an equally woolly jumper which, with some difficulty, she manages to pull over her head. While other women's dress is dictated by style, Dana's is dictated at this time of year by her overriding fear of being caught out at a wet windy bus stop with no sign of a bus anytime soon. Finally, with the sweater now removed, she's down to just a blue T-shirt and jeans which look really good on her. She has a lovely figure and the tiniest little waist ever, an inch of which is visible in the gap between jeans and T-shirt.

"I'd better go and fix that contact," she tells me. "I won't be a moment." And she hurries off.

"Dana!" I shout after her but she's gone too far to hear me. I guess as soon as she looks in the mirror she'll find out that her long mahogany-brown hair has come off worst in her struggle with the jumper and looks a mess.

Five minutes later she comes back. "You could have said something!" she berates me as she sits down again.

"I did try. But you were gone too far."

"You know, now that I can actually see it, this place is a bit trendy, isn't it? Maybe I should have changed before coming out."

Before – before Doug, that is – Dana wouldn't have noticed what anyone else was wearing and she certainly wouldn't have considered the need to change just to keep up. Nor, come to it, would she have gone to the trouble of wearing contacts but, ever since she started going out with Doug, she's become more conscious of her appearance which seems a little strange to me. Doug is so much in love with Dana that I really don't think it matters to him in the least what she's wearing. He just thinks she's wonderful – plain and simple.

Now Dana reaches into her bag and takes out her phone and checks it for texts and then she smiles, reads whatever message has come through and then smiles again as she thumbs out a reply.

"Doug?" I ask.

She nods. "He just wants to know if I got here okay."

"That's sweet."

She nods. "But it *is* the third time he's sent the same text since I left home!"

I laugh.

"You know, he can be a bit of a worrier at times," she tells me

I laugh. "You don't say!"

She puts the phone down. "So, tell me, how did your interview go?"

I shake my head. "Didn't get it."

"You heard already? That was fast."

"I don't need to hear to know."

"Ah, now, come on! No need to be negative."

"I'm not being negative. I'm being realistic. Faking positivity isn't going to change the odds. There isn't a snowball's chance in hell that I got that job. It was the worst interview in the history of interviews. I swear somebody writing a manual on the subject could use it as an example of what *not* to do in an interview. I cringe now just thinking about how awful it was, how awful I was."

Dana looks at me but says nothing. Dana's one of the kindest, most thoughtful people I know and I think she understands just how disappointed I am. She's also uncompromisingly honest as a rule but now even she resorts to platitudes in an attempt to cheer me up.

"Well, then, they just don't know what they're missing."

"I think they do."

"There will be others, you know."

"Other whats? Other excruciatingly embarrassing interviews where I'm ousted as a liar?"

"No, other jobs." Then, before I descend into a blubbering, self-pitying mess before her eyes, she changes the subject. "Have you looked at the menu?"

I nod. "Apart from olives and fancy cheese and hams, there's not a lot on offer. I wonder why Caroline chose this place? It's a wine bar, not a restaurant. I thought we were supposed to be going for a meal."

"So did I but clearly Caroline has a different idea of the night." Then something – or rather someone – catches Dana's eye. "Speak of the devil!"

I look and spot Caroline standing in the centre of the room, talking animatedly to an acquaintance I'm guessing she bumped into on her way over to us. She's clutching her phone in one hand and has an enormous cream leather bag draped over the other arm, but she's still managing to gesticulate wildly with both hands. The well-groomed woman she's with is clearly enjoying whatever it is Caroline's saying and is smiling back at her. Now she affectionately reaches out and touches Caroline on the arm. Caroline says something else and then I see her throw her head back and laugh. I notice the other woman looks momentarily startled as well she might. Caroline's laugh, on first hearing especially, always comes as a surprise. It's a full-throated, dirty laugh that's totally at odds with her rather polished appearance. It's the laugh of some gin-drinking eighteenth-century slapper in a Hogarth painting, not a twenty-first century urbane sophisticate such as Caroline most definitely is. The other woman, now having overcome her surprise, has joined in the laughter in spite, or maybe because, of its raucousness. It is an infectious laugh.

"Caroline looks great, doesn't she?" observes Dana.

I nod. She does. As always, she's immaculately, stylishly, expensively, most perfectly turned out from top to bottom. There's not a blonde hair out of place in her expertly styled blonde bob, not a speck on her cream, woollen, high-collared, three-quarter-length swing coat, not a crease in her black pencil skirt, not a mark on her knee-high black-patent stiletto boots. This despite the fact that she left our house, the house the three of us share with my old school friend Shane, at seven this morning and has characteristically spent the day rushing from one high-powered meeting to another before coming straight from work to meet us.

This could be what Dana's talking about but she could equally be referring to a certain sparkle, a certain frisson of excitement, a certain glow that emanates from Caroline these days and can be attributed to one thing and one thing only – her boyfriend, Mick.

"How does she do it?" muses Dana.

"Do what?"

"Wear boots that high all day long?"

I shrug. "Years of practice, I guess. And a steely will."

Caroline catches sight of us and gives us a wave. She says her goodbye to the other woman by way of a kiss on each cheek and then we watch as she crosses the floor towards us. Her progress is slow however. Caroline is one of those people who knows everyone and, once, twice, three times, she stops to briefly chat to various acquaintances and startle them with her laugh.

Finally, she reaches our table.

"Hello, hello, hello, hello! Sorry, sorry, sorry, sorry, I'm late!"

She plants a kiss on Dana's cheek, comes to my side of the table, does the same to me, then sits herself down on the stool beside me. She reaches out for my glass of wine and takes a mouthful, then gives a satisfied gasp.

"Ah, I needed that!" She looks around. "Isn't this place fabulous! Opened just two weeks ago. Involved in the marketing. Great crowd! Thought I'd never get here this evening! Work is mental! Was out the door when the MD of Fotomina rang. On and on about their campaign. Couldn't get him off the phone. Thinks he owns me – body and soul." Rat-a-tat-tat, that's the way Caroline talks when she's hyped up which is quite a lot of the time. She talks like she's far too impatient to be dealing with anything as cumbersome as a full sentence.

"For the money you're charging them maybe he's entitled to think that," observes Dana.

"Who? What?"

"Fotomina and the MD."

"Excuse me? For the money my campaign is going to bring in – *I'm* the one who should own *them*!" She takes another sip from my glass. "That wine is absolutely delicious!" She picks up the bottle and, as she's reading the label, the waiter comes back with our plates of olives, ham and cheese.

"Hello, Caroline."

"Hi, Alain."

"Nice to see you back again."

"Can't keep away from the place!" she laughs.

"Shall I bring you another plate?"

"When you have a moment. And another wineglass too."

37

"Certainly."

Once the waiter is gone, Caroline turns her attention to me.

"So, tell me, Rosie, how did you get on today?"

"Oh yes, the interview. You'll be pleased to know they offered me the job there and then."

"Really?" She looks surprised.

"Caroline! You could at least pretend you believe it could happen."

"And I do. Of course, I do." She reaches out and gives my hand a little squeeze.

I shrug. "I won't hear for a couple of days."

"Did you make sure to be enthusiastic like I told you?"

"So enthusiastic they thought I was half-mad. I'd a pain in my face from all the smiling. Tell me, do you know where Mumbai is?"

She shakes her head.

"No, neither did I. When you were making out my travel itinerary, couldn't you have come up with somewhere like France? At least then I might have been able to sound like I knew what I was talking about. That's the last time I'm using your version of my CV."

"But Rosie, you'll never get a job with your old one."

"Why thank you, thank you for that vote of confidence!"

"Sorry, Rosie, I didn't mean it like that."

"I don't get it. I don't see why I shouldn't be able to get a job."

"And you will," says Dana. "Just stick in there."

"You know, apart from the humiliation of nobody wanting me, I'm really sick of being broke."

"Welcome to the club," moans Dana.

Love Potions

"But you don't mind being broke," I point out.

"Don't I?"

"No," I tell her. "You know it's a means to an end and some day all the studying will be behind you and you'll be in exactly the position you want. You're nearly finished your Master's so all you've left to do is your PhD and then offers of lecturing jobs will come rolling in."

"You make it sound so simple," sighs Dana.

"And isn't it? I mean, sure, I know it will take a lot of work and a lot of time, but at least you do know exactly where you're going."

"Yes, well, I thought I did but things aren't going quite as smoothly as all that."

"What do you mean?"

"You know how my supervisor wasn't happy with my thesis?"

"Yeah, but isn't that all sorted now? I thought you made all the changes he wanted?"

"So did I. I rewrote the entire second half for him which took me months but he came back today and said he still isn't satisfied. He says my conclusions lack original insight and he's probably right. I guess I have nothing of particular note to add to the volumes already written on the topic."

"You're kidding!"

"I wish. The problem I have now is that I can't see how I can improve on it but, if I don't, then there's no question but that I'm going to fail."

"Fail? You? You're kidding?"

"No, he more or less told me as much."

"But, Dana, you worked so hard!"

"Who are you telling?"

"You've been holed up in your room night after night!"

Dana shrugs. "They don't give marks for effort."

"But Doug told me he thought it was great! I think he thinks you're some kind of genius."

Dana shakes her head. "No disrespect to Doug but he's hardly the most impartial party."

"What is the thesis on again?" asks Caroline.

"Does it matter? Anyway, I don't know how many times I've told you both before."

This is true and I guess it's not exactly to our credit that we have to ask again.

"Go on. Tell us," urges Caroline.

Dana sighs. "It's about how women and men internalise the power relations established in the gender order and how the structure of these power relations is based on assumptions of what it is to be male and female. It's about how this arrangement divides humanity into separate classes according to gender by attributing certain physical and psychological characteristics to each and it's about how, on closer observation, we can recognise these simply as a set of binary opposites."

"Right," I nod, thinking it's no wonder I forgot, while at the same time trying to appear like I now understand but then I catch a glimpse of Caroline's knitted brow and can almost see the cogs grinding slowly in her brain as she tries to make some sense of what Dana has said. Caroline catches me looking at her, shrugs her shoulders and gives me a 'I haven't the foggiest either' look that causes me to burst out laughing.

"Oh for God's sake!" snaps Dana. "Why are you even asking me if all you're going to do is laugh?"

"I'm sorry, Dana," I say.

"Yeah, me too," adds Caroline.

"You're not really interested, are you?" demands Dana.

"Course we are," I tell her.

"You're not and I can't say I blame you. Even I'm completely bored with it. I've spent months and months and months at it and now I've hit this enormous wall and for the first time in my life I don't know what to do. And it is true, I am sick and tired of being broke. I swear I feel like chucking the whole thing in and getting a real job."

"But you are going to get a real job," insists Caroline. "This is just a minor blip. You'll figure it out. You'll finish this thesis of yours. It'll be accepted, you'll graduate, start your doctorate and, then, in no time, you'll land yourself a nice lecturing job. Come on. You can't give up now. That's always been your plan."

"Always *was* my plan."

I've never really understood Dana's long-held ambition to be a college lecturer, especially given how quiet she is. She's so much quieter than either of us and yet I can't imagine a job more terrifying than standing at the top of a lecture theatre in front of rows upon rows of students. But, for some reason, however baffling to me, this is what she wants to do. It's one of the first things I remember her telling me when I got to know her and Caroline at the start of college when, as a stranger I turned up on their doorstep, hoping to rent the room they'd advertised.

Caroline can remember even further back – she's known Dana a lot longer than I have. "Remember first year in secondary you told the career guidance teacher you planned to be a psychology lecturer?"

"Did I?"

"Sure. I remember being impressed because none of the rest of us had a clue, we couldn't plan beyond deciding what to bring in for lunch the next day and there you were planning out the rest of your life. Come on, Dana, you can't give up now!"

"Can't I?" Dana sounds defeated. "Look at you, Caroline. You're making more money than anyone I know and —"

"Yes, yes, but money's not everything."

"What?" Both of us cry. These are words we never thought we would hear from Caroline.

"But Caroline, it's the mantra by which you lead your entire life!" protests Dana.

"That's not so."

"Yes, it is," insists Dana. "You may not have known what job you were going to do when you grew up but you've always, always known you've wanted to be rich. Remember when you were ten and you asked your mother if you could open a bank account because the pocket money you'd saved wasn't earning any interest in your piggy bank?"

Caroline looks like she's about to deny this but then her pride takes over. "Actually I was nine. And, for your information, I didn't keep it in a piggy bank, I had a special little metal box with a key. And of course I wanted it in a bank. It was over two hundred euros, you know. But, just because I've always been smart with any money I have, that doesn't mean I allow it to dictate my whole life."

"But it does!" insists Dana. "You wouldn't go out with Mick at the start because he was broke."

"Not so. I wouldn't go out with Mick for many reasons. I wouldn't go out with him because he's much older than me. I wouldn't go out with him because he has a country accent as thick as the ham sandwiches he's so fond of. I wouldn't go out with him because I was afraid he'd disappear back to Mammy and Daddy and the farm when he tired of the big smoke. I wouldn't go out with him because I was afraid he wasn't very dependable which is understandable given that he gave everything up to suddenly become an actor when he was thirty – I mean, come on! You can see why I was wary. And anyway, as it happens, he and I did get together *before* he landed the lead in *Fate Farm* so your argument is seriously flawed."

It's true. Caroline and Mick did get together just before he got the role in Kevin North's latest film. It's also true that, but for Caroline, he wouldn't be down in Wicklow now, working on the film. It all happened like this: our flatmate Shane has a girlfriend, Loretta, who's a doctor, and who just so happened to have Kevin North as a patient and when she mentioned this to Caroline and mentioned that North was in the middle of casting a film based on *Fate Farm* – that dark disturbing novel set in rural Ireland – Caroline was so convinced that Mick would be perfect in the lead of Lenny the farmer's son (who unfortunately gets his brains blown out in the end) that she persuaded Loretta to persuade Kevin North to audition Mick. Caroline's instincts were spot-on and Mick got the role – quite a coup for someone whose acting jobs had heretofore amounted to a couple of crowd-filling non-speaking roles in the Irish soap, *Fair City*, and a very small speaking role in one big-budget Irish-American movie. Sadly, his one scene in that movie didn't survive the cutting room as we discovered the night we all went to the cinema for the sole purpose of cheering him on in what should have been his debut on the big screen. But that was then. Now? Now is very different – and all thanks to Caroline. At this moment he's probably holed up in a pub somewhere in Wicklow with Kevin North and Audrey Turner, his gorgeous and extremely famous leading lady, reflecting on the day's shoot.

"So what are you saying, Caroline?" Dana persists. "That you're dissatisfied with your work?"

"I'm not dissatisfied. Well, not really, but I don't know, I guess I'm not as wholly satisfied as I was once. Sure I like my work, and I'm very good at it, and I like getting paid well for it but . . . but . . . I guess I'm getting to the stage where I'd prefer if I was working for myself, making money for myself and not for others."

"So it does all boil down to money then."

"No, you're missing the point. More than anything I'd like to come up with some brilliant idea, something that would make me a fortune but –"

"Wouldn't we all?" I interrupt, thinking of my last bank statement which did not make for comfortable reading.

Caroline ignores my interruption. "But more than that I'd like to come up with my own idea for a business, something that I would be responsible for setting up, for running, and for building into a success. Something that I would own. I mean, how hard can it be? People do it all the time."

Dana looks at Caroline then at me and then she laughs. "Look at us! Not one of us is satisfied. We're a sorry lot, we really are."

On the other hand, Casanova swore by oysters. The famous 18th century lover would sit down to breakfast and polish off a plate of fifty.

Fifty oysters? Surely all he'd be fit for after that lot would be another lie-down?

5

We leave the wine bar and stand huddled in the doorway. Or rather Caroline and I stand huddled in the doorway – only Dana is dressed to withstand such a bitterly cold night. I'm thinking we need to get a taxi as soon as we can and get home to our respective beds in double-quick time. I'm thinking I might make myself a cup of hot chocolate and bring it up with me to drink while I read a chapter or two of a book – maybe I'll even start Pepys' diary. I'm thinking it's a pity I didn't put on the electric blanket before coming out.

"Will we go to a club?" suggests Caroline brightly.

"Ah, no!" I moan. "Let's just go home."

"Home? Already?"

"What do you mean 'already'?" asks Dana. "It's gone twelve."

"Exactly. It's early yet. What are the pair of you like? I can't believe you've become that boring and settled."

"Who are you calling boring and settled?" protests Dana,

peeking out at us from the oversized hood of her overcoat, her arms crossed, each hand tucked cosily into the opposite sleeve.

"Ah, come on!" persists Caroline. "What do you say? It'll be a laugh."

"A laugh?" I look at her. "Queuing for ages in the cold and the damp with no guarantee that we will get in? Being scrutinised at the door by some bouncer who, on a whim or because his gastro has him feeling off-form, decides some aspect of our appearance displeases him and turns us away –"

"Excuse me!" Caroline interrupts. "I have *never* in my life been turned away by a bouncer and, as long as Dana here takes her hood down, we won't have a problem tonight either."

"What's that you're saying about me?" asks Dana, peering out from said hood.

I ignore her and go on: "And if we do get inside? Then what? What's so good about inside? What's so good about being squashed in a mass of sweat-secreting, beer-spilling, elbow-bumping, toe-treading people? What's so good about standing outside a cubicle bursting to go, waiting until the two giggling girls on the other side of the door finally decide to emerge? What's so good about being looked up and down by guys who, buoyed up by a bellyful of drink, suddenly develop the strangest notion that they're God's gift to women despite a lifetime of evidence to the contrary? What's so good about paying ten euros for a glass of wine that costs half that for a whole bottle in Super –"

"Enough!" Caroline interrupts. "I hear you. You know, there was a time when you thrived on all that. A time when you'd have considered a Friday or Saturday night *not* spent in a club as signalling a major crisis in your life. If the queue wasn't long enough, you'd have wanted to try somewhere else for fear of missing something better."

"Well," I shrug, "people are allowed to change, you know."

"Yeah, but not to morph into someone totally different. Now come on!"

"No!"

Caroline throws her eyes to heaven. "I don't believe I'm hearing this! I can't believe you've become so boring. Despite all your moaning, I know you'll enjoy yourself. Look, it's Saturday tomorrow. We can sleep in. This is the first night the three of us have been out together in ages. We can't just go home!"

Why can't Caroline ever take no for an answer? Why does everything have to be a battle with her? I can feel that cup of hot chocolate sliding further and further from my grasp.

"Caroline, we've had a nice evening," I say. "Why don't we just leave it at that?"

"Don't you want to spend time with your friends?"

"I've already spent the entire evening with you!"

"Do you want us to be the kind of friends who allow their closeness to disappear the minute they're in a relationship?"

"Hang on a minute," I protest. "We've all been in relationships for months now and nothing's changed between us. For crying out loud! We live together – it's not like we don't see each other every single day."

"Yeah, when we're rushing out in the morning or coming home exhausted in the evening from work, or at least those of us who have work."

"Thanks," I say.

"Hey, sorry, Rosie, I didn't mean that the way it sounded."

"I know."

"All I'm trying to say is that friendship is like a flower – one has to give it care and attention if it's to survive."

"What?" I look at her in disbelief, wondering where she came up with a line so un-Caroline-like when Dana pipes up:

"Ahh, Caroline, I didn't know you were such a softie."

Sensing Dana is the weak link, Caroline immediately pounces. "You can see I'm talking sense, can't you, Dana? You know how important it is to make time for one another. So what do you say? Are you on?"

"Well, I don't know that –"

"Tell you what," says Caroline linking Dana's arm, "we'll start walking. If we see a taxi we'll go home, otherwise we'll go to a club. All right?" She looks back to where she's left me standing, staring after them. "Are you coming, Rosie?"

I consider my options. To head off on my own and try to flag a taxi down to take me home. Or to go with them in the hopes that we'll spot a taxi en route and, if we don't, head with them to a club. If I go home now I know I'll be left feeling vaguely unsettled by the thought that I'm missing out.

"Yeah, I'm coming," I call and begin following them, just as I know Caroline knew I would.

We don't see a taxi but we do find ourselves outside the imposing, horseshoe-shaped doorway of a nightclub that's flanked on either side by matching torches with tacky fake flames (vertical strips of orange fabric illuminated by hidden orange lights and made to look like they're flickering by a breeze emanating from a fan, also hidden – at least that's what I figure). Underneath each torch stands a bouncer and this pair too match each other in terms of physique (proverbial brick houses), dress (black suit, white shirt, black tie) and hair (number ones). As predicted we queue for ages, we are scrutinised by the matching bouncers but we do manage to pass whatever standards they choose to judge us by (Dana has put her hood down, at Caroline's insistence), and then, finally, we pass through the horseshoe shape and quickly become part of the heaving mass of sweating humanity within.

Straight away, Caroline heads to the bar and Dana and I go to put our coats and a couple of other layers of Dana's clothes in the cloakroom. (Come to think of it, just why is a cloakroom still called a cloakroom given that it's been quite a while since people donned cloaks on a night out? And come to that, why do I use the word 'don' when talking about cloaks when I wouldn't dream about using it in conjunction with the word coat?) But anyway, so we're on our way back from the archaically named cloakroom when these two guys in their thirties appear in front of me and Dana, blocking our path.

"Hi there!"

"Hi!" says Dana.

One thing about Dana is that she's much too polite for her own good – she finds it impossible to be rude to anyone even in a situation like this, where rudeness is excused, where even a hint of politeness is seen as full-on encouragement.

"So, are you ladies having a good time?" one of them asks, eyeing me up leerily.

At least I think that, or something like it, is what he says. Given the noise level, it's impossible to know for sure.

In an attempt to convey to him that (a) I can't hear a word he's saying, and (b) I am not in the slightest bit interested in any case, I point to my ear, shake my head and shrug my shoulders in an offhand way.

He understands the (a) part of my mime all right but the (b) part eludes him and he takes a step in closer to me.

"I said, are you ladies having a good time?" he shouts into my ear.

"Fine, thanks," I answer and take a matching step back but not before I feel the spray of saliva hit my face as he roars:

"What?"

What's the point in answering? Aside from the fact that he's not going to hear me, I really don't want to give these two any encouragement and have them thinking that we actually want them hanging around all night, roaring into our faces and spraying us with their spittle.

"Would you like a drink?" his buddy shouts.

"What?" shouts Dana.

"I said — would you like a drink?"

I shake my head but Dana, ignoring the golden rule of only saying the absolute minimum unless you are actually interested, decides an explanation is necessary.

"Our friend is getting us one. She should be back in a minute. Although it does look very busy up there. There's a huge crowd here tonight, isn't there?"

One of them nods though who knows if he understood any of what Dana's just said. Maybe he thought Dana was inviting him to lay his hand on her arm for that's exactly what he does now.

"So, do you want a drink?" he shouts.

"No, thanks!" Dana shouts back but she doesn't just leave

51

it at that — oh no! No, instead she decides to do some more explaining so as — I'm guessing here — not to hurt his feelings. *"You see we both have boyfriends. We're just having a girls' night out. But thanks for asking!"*

"What did you say?" he roars back. *"I can't hear you with all the noise."*

"What?" shouts Dana back at him.

"I said, I can't hear you with all the noise!"

She repeats herself again but still he doesn't hear.

"What?"

Oh, Good Lord!

"I said we both (she gestures at the pair of us) *have boyfriends* (she gestures at the pair of them), *we're just having a girls' night out* (she does a little boogie with her hips), *but thanks for asking"* (she nods effusively).

To me, even though I know what she's trying to say, it looks like she's saying that the pair of us want the pair of them to dance, please.

I'm not alone in reaching that interpretation.

"I don't dance!" Dana's one shouts.

"No! No! No! I'm trying to tell you we both have boyfriends!"

This time they get the message. One shouts something back at us, something like, *"Jesus! Why didn't you say so in the first place!"* and, not wishing to waste any more time, they give us one last look, and not a very pleasant one either, then walk away. And that's that.

"Here!" Caroline's back again with our drinks. *"Grab these before I drop them!"*

"Thanks, Caroline!" Dana shouts, taking hers.

"What?" Caroline shouts back

"Thanks!"

"What?"

"I said, thanks for the drink!"

"What?"

Jesus! This could go on all night. I intervene. *"She's just saying thanks for the drink. All right? That's all!"* I bellow.

"Oh, right. No problem!" shouts Caroline.

"What?" shouts Dana.

Oh sweetest hour!

They finally give up their useless attempts at communication and the three of us now stand there, sipping our drinks. Caroline's right when she says there was once a time when I'd have preferred to be nowhere else but where we are now. Fridays and Saturdays were all about getting dressed up, going out, dancing our feet off, shouting and laughing ourselves hoarse – all the time feeling that underlying excitement at the possibility that we just might meet 'someone'. But things have changed. I have met someone. I don't need to meet anyone else and, with that need out of the equation, my enjoyment of a place like this isn't what it used to be.

I look around. At the groups of girls on the dance floor giving it their all – some dancing for the sake of dancing, some dancing for the sake of whoever's watching, hoping that maybe that 'someone' is looking at them right now. I look at the couples tucked away in cosy corners, engrossed in conversation or in each others' bodies. I look at the groups of men, standing, drinking their pints, having conversations about football or whatever it is groups of men, standing, drinking their pints, do have conversations about but, at the same time keeping an eye (as keenly trained as the premier leaguer they're discussing) out for any attractive female who chances to come into their field of peripheral vision. And, yes, I can see why I liked being a part of all this but equally so I'm happy to have moved beyond it. I'm happy not to find myself judging the potential of the men around me, and happy not to want so desperately to be judged favourably by them. Now when I look at them, all I see is they're not Finn, and don't even come close.

How quickly things change. Just months ago, Caroline, Dana and myself had the most pitiful love lives imaginable – so pitiful that Caroline used to joke about how at least we'd have each other in our old age. The minute we turned sixty-five, she argued, we should lose no time in applying for our free bus passes so that we could spend our autumn years going on day trips around the country. Not for us sitting around in day care, no, but with our little dayglo backpacks to hold our packed lunches, our flasks of tea and our pillboxes with our cornucopia of pills, we'd be free to hit the wide-open road – or at least any road that Bus Éireann travelled. Now, it's looking like there is a chance we might escape that fate.

Unexpectedly Dana, who'd never had a boyfriend in her life (and gave the impression of not being particularly bothered by this fact) was the first to fall. Doug, her Doug, is handsome I guess in a dark, brooding Heathcliff sort of way, and gives the unfortunate impression of being every bit as taciturn, but he's shy rather than bad-tempered which, to my shame, it took me quite some time to realise but then I've never been the best judge of character.

Dana and Doug first met at his birthday party thrown by his mum, Monica, who used to run the boutique I worked in until she decided she'd make more doing it up to rent out. I swear the first time Doug and Dana set eyes on one another at that party it was like a scene from a movie. They just stood there, staring at each other like they were looking at the most amazing person they'd ever seen in the whole of their lives. I don't think I ever really believed in love at first sight (like or lust – yes, but not love) so it was a little freaky to be witness to it that night because that's exactly what it was.

Ever since, they've been inseparable. Despite my (many) early reservations, I've really grown to like Doug. True, the fact that he's so quiet around me, and everyone else but Dana, means we're never going to be bosom buddies but I have grown fond of him.

I like how he makes Dana so happy, how he loves her so much and how he came up trumps when she really needed him. Dana was going through a pretty rough time back then. Her mother, having found out that Dana's father had had a brief affair and that a baby was a result of that affair, asked him to leave and then, after years of being sober, she descended into chronic alcoholism, refusing all care until Dana's father with Doug's help finally managed to persuade her to get the help she needed. Today things are better. Dana's parents are back together, her mother has come out the other side of rehab and the 'affair baby' has become Dana's much doted-upon baby sister, Cathy.

Next to fall was Caroline. Caroline likes to give the impression that she's a hard-headed businesswoman driven by money and the desire to be the very best at what she does. And it's not a false impression either – that is certainly a big part of who she is. So, over a year ago when Caroline was returning by train from a business trip to Cork and chanced to sit down beside a handsome if somewhat ruddy-looking, thirty-year-old farmer who was moving to Dublin to realise, what seemed to her, his quixotic ambition to become an actor, there was no question of Caroline taking a romantic interest in him. But during that journey they made enough of a connection to decide to keep in touch. As friends, of course, just friends. After all, Mick was the very antithesis of the sort of man with whom she envisioned sharing her high-powered, successful, urbane life. At least that's what she told herself then, and for many, many months to come. Dana may have fallen in love at first sight but Caroline's path wasn't so smooth and she fought and railed against it every step of the way, boring everyone – her friends, herself and even Mick – with her protestations that love played no part in their relationship. But for once in her ordered, perfectly planned life, Caroline was unable to plan or order her feelings to perform as she wished. By the time she finally came out and admitted those feelings, the only one she surprised was herself.

And that brings me to the third coupling – me and Finn – and I've already told you the story of us, at least part of it. I didn't fall in love with Finn at first sight when I saw him up there on stage, sitting behind his drum kit. I hardly noticed him. The only person I noticed that night was Mark, lead singer and best friend of Finn, who happened to be Hollywood good-looking with dazzling white teeth, cliff-like cheekbones, baby-blond hair and oodles of confidence – just my type. The dark, cute, curly-headed drummer didn't get a look-in. But while I was looking at Mark, Finn was looking at me. While I was plotting a way to get to know Mark, Finn was plotting a way to get to know me. When later Finn threw a party in the hopes that I would come, I went in the hopes that Mark would be there and he was, and that was the start of Me and Mark.

It didn't take long for me to realise that very little lay between Mark's perfectly proportioned ears. It took me a little longer to realise that what did lie there was a confused mess. He turned out to be a manipulator and a liar and tragically unbalanced – I don't use the word tragically lightly. The crazy infatuation he developed for me after I broke up with him was what prompted him to follow my taxi on that awful night he crashed his car.

It wasn't until after his death that I found out Mark's early interest in me was generated by the fact that he knew Finn wanted me, ergo he wanted me too. It wasn't until I came to terms with the guilt I felt over Mark's death, and with the guilt I felt at the growing closeness between Finn and myself that I was finally able to acknowledge (helped by some arm-twisting by my friend Shane) that these developing feelings were far too precious to fling away out of a misplaced sense of duty to the dead. And that's the happy ending (at least for Finn and me) to the sad story of how I got to be with this most amazing man.

"Rosie!" Caroline is shouting at me now.

"What?"

"We're going out to dance. Are you coming?"

I'm about to say no. But then I think, why not? Since conversation is out of the question, I may as well. So I nod and follow them. And as we're dancing, my mood begins to lift. I've never heard the song before but it reminds me a little of one Finn and Mark's band used to play and I let the music take over and soon I start giving it my all. After the tension of the last few days – the build-up to the interview, the interview itself – this feels good. I begin to really let go. I start shaking my head, stamping my feet, shouting out the song's repetitive and easily learned chorus at the top of my voice. I look over at Dana and Caroline and smile at them and they both beam back at me. I realise I'm enjoying myself. In the months we've been together Finn and I have become too settled – the cinema and a couple of hours in the pub are the highlight of our social life. True, it doesn't help that I'm so broke but that isn't the only reason we lead such a quiet life. We haven't felt like doing anything more. It occurs to me (and not for the first time) that part of Finn must miss the old buzz of playing in a band. Before, music was his life but now his drum kit sits amongst junk in his father's garage. I begin to think maybe Finn and I should start going out more, to clubs, maybe even to some gigs again. Maybe that would prompt him to climb out of the rut he's in, to unearth his drum kit, and to focus once again on his music career. He's wasted working for his dad. I think of the past few months and all we've been through and how it's time we started leaving the sad times behind. I begin thinking of the future and how much better it could be. I can make it better – for Finn and me, but especially for Finn.

I smile over at Dana again but this time she doesn't smile back – she doesn't even see me. She's staring over my shoulder into the distance with this odd look on her face. As I turn to see what she's looking at, she grabs my arm roughly.

"Come on!" she shouts. "I want to go home, now!"

"You're kidding!" both Caroline and I shout back.

"It's still early!" Caroline adds.

"No, I have a headache. I'm going right now! I have the tickets for the coats." And with that, she turns and storms off without another word.

Caroline and I give each other baffled looks but, with no choice, we follow her.

"What was all that about?" Caroline demands once we're out on the street.

"All what?" asks Dana

"The sudden departure? We were just starting to have a good time."

"You might have been but my head is killing me. I need to go home and take some Panadol. Look, there's a taxi pulling up. Come on!"

When the taxi comes to a halt, three men climb out and when one of them spots us close by on the pavement, waiting to get in, he gives a wolf whistle.

"Shut it!" snaps Dana and, shoving him aside, she clambers in.

After we've recovered from the shock of hearing Dana being so rude, we follow her.

Dana gives the taxi driver our address and the three of us sit there in silence as he takes us home. Sitting in the middle, Caroline has a face like thunder, mad, I guess, at having her night prematurely ended. I can't see Dana's face – it's resolutely turned to her window. I too turn to my window, try to ignore the reek of beer those three left behind and all the other underlying and worrying odours and begin to reflect on how much I enjoyed tonight despite our abrupt departure and, once again, I resolve that from now on, Finn and I are going to concentrate on having a little fun.

The Kama Sutra says, "If a man mixes the powder of the milk-hedge plant and the kantaka plant with the excrement of a monkey and the powdered root of the lanjalika plant, and throws this mixture on a woman, she will not love anybody else afterwards."

She may not love anyone else, but given the indignity he's put her through, is she really going to love him?

6

"Up! Come on! Up, up, up!"

I open my eyes – barely. The light hurts. I see a figure – Caroline – standing over me like some sergeant major. All she's lacking is a bugle. I close my eyes again.

"Come on! Up!" she barks.

"Go away!" I mumble.

"Come on, Rosie! It's time to get up!"

"Why? Who says?" I moan. "What time is it anyway?"

"Time to get up!"

"Oh, Caroline, go away! I need more sleep."

I try to pull the duvet over my head but it resists, like someone – Caroline – has got a firm hold of the end of it.

"You don't need any more sleep. You only think you do. You've had plenty already. Look at me!" she cries a little shrilly. "I've had no sleep whatsoever! Come on!" She begins tugging at my duvet but I hold on tight and pray she'll go away. My prayers go unanswered. She just keeps tugging and going on at me in this annoyingly high, excited tone. "I couldn't sleep a wink – not a wink! I swear, Rosie, my head is bursting with such brilliance you wouldn't believe it. I am an absolute genius. You have to come downstairs straight away. I've solved all our problems!"

"What problems?" I open one eye. "The only problem I have right now is you standing in my bedroom at the crack of dawn, screeching at me."

She throws my dressing-gown on the bed. "Get this on and come downstairs. I'm going in to wake Dana."

"Caroline!" I shout after her. "Turn off the light – please!"

"Come on downstairs – I'll be waiting."

Fifteen minutes later, having finally given in to her constant shouts from the bottom of the stairs, I make my way down to the kitchen and take a seat beside Dana who's looking every bit as grumpy as I feel.

"Here you go!" Caroline puts a mug of steaming coffee down on the table in front of me. "And here you are, Dana. Nice and strong, just the way you like it!"

She sits down opposite. Compared to us with our bleary faces, our hunched figures, our dressing-gowns wrapped tightly around us, Caroline is already showered, dressed and looking the picture of bright-eyed and bushy-tailed vitality. I uncross my arms and gingerly reach out for the coffee. I take a sip.

"Okay, I have a plan," begins Caroline, deciding we're now responsive enough to hear what she has to say.

"So have I," says Dana, her two hands wrapped around her mug. "To go back to bed and not wake up until it's morning."

"It *is* morning. It's gone past eleven."

"Okay, well, not wake up until it's lunch-time then."

"Come on now. You need to stop whingeing and start listening to my plan, a plan that will get each of us what we want."

"And what is it each of us want?" I ask.

"The comfort of our warm beds?" suggests Dana.

Caroline ignores her. "Can't you just listen for a moment? Don't you want to hear this most ingenious plan devised in my most brilliant brain while you were snoring your heads off, a plan that will get each of us out of these ruts we're in?"

"Excuse me? I never actually said I was in a rut," interrupts Dana.

"Well, you are."

"Now hang on a min —"

Caroline cuts her off. "It's the truth!" She points at her chest. "I'm in a rut." She points at me. "She's in a rut." She points at Dana. "And you're in a rut." Then she makes a big sweeping gesture that encompasses all three of us. "We're all in a rut!"

"Will you please stop saying that horrible word 'rut'?" I ask, suddenly annoyed, by the word, by the way she rudely refers to me as 'she', but mostly — I guess — because I recognise Caroline's speaking the truth, about me at any rate, and I don't like hearing it.

"How else would you describe our various predicaments?" she carries on. "Take me. I'm fed up working for other people — making fortunes for them. It's time I began thinking about myself and what I really want. It's time I turned my not inconsiderable talents to making my own fortune."

Next, she focuses on me.

"Take you, Rosie. You're flunking one interview after

another. There's no knowing if you'll ever get a job and, if you eventually do, if you'll manage to keep it and, if you do manage to keep it, if you'll be happy in it. I have my doubts. I think you have your doubts. Think about it. It's not by chance it took you so long to finish your degree or took you so long to finally decide to get a job in science, now is it?"

"Gee, thanks, Caroline. Thanks for reminding me how hopeless I am."

"You're not hopeless – far from it. You're just a round peg trying to squeeze yourself into a square hole or a square peg trying to squeeze yourself into a round hole. Whatever. That's you."

"A peg?"

"Yes – you're the peg and science is the hole you don't fit into. You don't have the interest in it – not really. You've got to find your own hole."

Done with me for now, she turns to Dana.

"As for you, Dana, the way I see it, you're feeling so down about your thesis that you're thinking about chucking it all in but you can't. You need to carry on your studies and become a lecturer but there are two stumbling blocks you have to overcome in order to do that. Firstly, you're getting too old to be still leading an impoverished student existence –"

"I don't think I ever actually used the word 'impoverished'," protests Dana.

"– and so this lack of money is your first problem," Caroline ploughs on. "Your second problem is your lack of a suitable thesis topic now that you've hit a wall with the one you've been working on for God-knows-how-long. But, if you don't have a thesis to submit, you don't pass your Master's, and if you don't pass your Master's, then it's bye-bye to eventually becoming a lecturer which – and you don't need me to tell you this – has been your ambition for so long. Now, if I said I could come up with one solution to both of your problems, Dana – your money problem and your lack of a thesis topic – I imagine you'd be pretty interested?"

"But –"

"No buts! Don't you want to hear what I have to say?"

"But –"

"No buts."

"Actually I do have a but," says Dana sounding annoyed. "Not meaning to be rude *but* I've managed to get this far in my academic career without anyone in this house knowing or especially caring much about what it is I do and, while I appreciate your sudden interest, couldn't you save it for a more opportune time and not first thing on a Saturday morning when we've all been out half the night?"

Caroline isn't listening. It looks like her mind is on the next stage of her presentation, for that – I'm beginning to see – is what this is. All she's missing is a flip chart. If she had one now she could summarize all she's said so far by flipping over to a clean page and quickly penning little sketches of all three of us, standing in our individual ruts, our eyes peeping over the top.

"Okay. Firstly," Caroline goes on, "you, Dana, are a psychologist."

"And – so?"

"And you are currently looking for a new thesis topic, yes or no?"

"Well – yes, I guess."

"Okay. Secondly, you, Rosie, are essentially a scientist. In the sense that you have a degree in science which gives you a certain gravitas – at least to outsiders who don't know you well."

"That's one way of putting it."

"And, as a scientist, you have acquired a certain set of skills such as an ability to carry out research and perform experiments. Yes or no?"

"Well, I do know my way around a pipette and a Bunsen burner."

"Okay. Thirdly – I am a marketing executive. I run campaigns that help make millions for others. You could say my job is to convince people they need things they never knew they needed." She looks at both of us in turn, as if she expects us to interject but how can we when we haven't the foggiest where she's going with all this? "Now," she goes on, "don't you think that a marketing executive, a psychologist and a scientist is an interesting combination of professions?"

"In what sense, interesting?" asks Dana.

"I'll come back to this again," she replies briskly, "but bear in mind our respective skills. Now, moving forward: what is the one thing everybody wants? The one thing everybody needs?"

We both look at her blankly. Is she speaking rhetorically, or is she expecting an answer?

"Come now. Give a guess," she demands.

"Aspirin?" asks Dana, rubbing her temple.

"Come on. You're not trying."

"Sleep?" I yawn.

"Oh come on. Think!"

"We shouldn't be asked to think so early on a Saturday morning," moans Dana.

"Try harder! What is it everyone needs?"

"Clothes?" I say.

"And?"

"Money?" tries Dana.

"And?" Caroline demands, exasperated that we're not coming up with the answer she's looking for.

She's not the only one who's exasperated.

"Fresh air, warmth, running water? What *is* it you want us to say?" I demand.

She gives a sigh, like she can't believe how dull-witted we're being.

"It's love – of course," she says.

"Love?" Dana repeats.

"Yes, that's what everyone wants. Last night got me thinking. All those people at that club – deep down, isn't that why most of them were there?"

Dana and I shrug.

"I guess," Dana eventually concedes. "Maybe."

"Of course, it was. Everyone wants love and for a business to succeed we need to find something people want and give it to them and so love . . ." she gives a pause long enough for a drum roll ". . . is the business I've decided we're going into."

"What?" I'm confused. "You're thinking we should set up a nightclub?"

"No! Don't be ridiculous. That market is too crowded already, the competition too fierce and the overheads would be enormous."

"So what is this business you're talking about then?" I ask.

"Good question, Rosie," she answers in her infuriating business-like tone. "Well, that's what I've spent the night mulling over. Now many people have already spotted that love is big business – think of all the dating agencies, all the lonely-heart websites, all the events like speed-dating and what-have-you. So, what we need is to come up with our own unique angle, to come up with something different to get our slice of the pie. And that something different is . . ." she looks excitedly at me, then at Dana ". . . is love potions."

"Love potions?" I repeat.

"Love potions?" Dana repeats.

"Exactly!"

There's a long silence

"You have *got* to be kidding!" I burst out. "And you thought I was being ridiculous when I guessed you meant a nightclub?"

"No, I'm deadly serious. *That's* the gap in the market we're going to fill. We're going to open a shop selling love potions."

"I see." But of course what I really mean is I don't see at all.

"Okay, Rosie, you're the scientist. It'll be your job to come up with the potions."

I burst out laughing. "What? What do I know about love potions?"

"You're a scientist, aren't you?"

"Excuse me for being so stupid but I don't see the link. As far as I recall Love Potions 101 didn't feature in our curriculum at university, or maybe I was missing that day."

Caroline isn't listening. "First, you do your research. Start by getting on the internet, find out about all the herbs and spices that have traditionally been considered aphrodisiacs. Research which ones are regarded as safe and which ones are readily available. Check to see if you can find old recipes. Make up your own combinations. Experiment. Isn't that what science is all about and you *are* a scientist, aren't you?"

"So you keep saying, and, as a scientist, I can tell you now I don't believe in any of this nonsense."

"Well, as a scientist, I'd have thought you'd wait until you had all the evidence in front of you before you passed judgment."

"But —" I begin but I'm at a loss for words. This is all so utterly ridiculous. "But —"

Caroline's done with me for now. She turns her attentions again to Dana. "You," she says, "you're looking for a research topic. Well, I have a suggestion."

"You have?"

"Yes. How about looking into the whole area of aphrodisiacs. Investigate if they really do work, if they do actually influence people's behaviour, something like that. You could use Rosie's potions to carry out some trials."

"Rosie's potions!" I interrupt. "Excuse me, I haven't agreed to anything."

Dana is shaking her head. "Nah, I'm sure studies like that have been done before."

"Yeah, but that doesn't necessarily have to stop you. You could add to the body of knowledge that's already in existence."

Dana looks doubtful. "I guess I could read up on this a little, see if there's an angle worth studying. Maybe."

"Never mind maybe. It's a great idea."

"Well, it is an interesting area and —"

"Sure it is. And definitely worth thinking about, yes?"

"There could be something in it." But then Dana shrugs. "I don't know. There's a lot of ethical issues to consider and —"

"Yes, but it is worth considering?"

"Maybe."

"Maybe's good enough for now. And, say," Caroline goes on at full trottle, Dana's 'maybe' already becoming a definite in her mind, "if it turns out that your studies show that love potions have an effect – great – then we use your findings in our promotional literature."

"What," I ask, "do you mean by our promotional literature exactly?"

"You know, our press releases, flyers, that sort of thing."

"Our press releases, flyers, that sort of thing," Dana repeats slowly, like this is an unfamiliar language she's hearing for the first time.

"Yeah, I'm thinking this idea is so novel we'll easily generate a lot of interest in the press if we go about it the right way. And of course there's the human interest side to it as well – three long-time friends with our diverse backgrounds going into business together – it would make a perfect magazine piece for the weekend newspapers. I've got a lot of contacts. It shouldn't be hard to generate the interest."

She looks at Dana again.

"So, Dana, you may get a suitable topic out of all this and, in the meantime, you have a job – helping to set up the shop and working in it. At the very least it's a steady income where you have control over your hours and can fit them around your studies. And if, when, things start taking off, you'd be in at the start of what could be a very lucrative business for all three of us. When it takes off you get a share in the profits which will be considerable, of course, for my role in all of this is to turn it into a very lucrative commercial enterprise. And just imagine what fun it could be! The three of us, working together in our own business, what could be better?"

I turn from Caroline to Dana to see her reaction. Her face looks confused, like there's a million questions struggling to be made into a form she can ask. She opens her mouth, closes it, opens it again.

"But how?" is all she manages.

"I'm thinking along the lines of that soap shop in town, you know the one – it sells nothing but soaps and other smellies for the bath. If they can make a business out of something as peripheral as soap then surely we can make a business out of something as fundamental as love."

"No, no, forget it!" I tell her.

"Wait a minute, hear me out. I can see it now. I'm thinking city centre location. I'm thinking fabulous pink façade. I'm thinking colourful bottles all twinkling in the window. I'm thinking –"

"I'm thinking," I interrupt, "that the thing about soap is it actually does what it's supposed to do. It cleans people. What do you expect these love potions to do?"

"Make people fall in love, of course. Or make people buy them in the hope that using them will help them fall in love. And who's to say our love potions won't really work? There's a whole history behind this sort of thing. Lots and lots of people believe in them, have done throughout history. Who am I to disagree? And we will only use ingredients that have long been considered aphrodisiacs already."

"But you don't think love potions really work, do you?"

"Who am I to say otherwise when so many others before me have thought so? That's not my place and, anyway, it doesn't matter what I think."

"But you don't really believe in them, do you?" I persist.

"It doesn't matter what I believe! What matters is what the buying public believe."

I'm staring at her. "Jesus! We might as well set up as psychics!"

"That market is already cornered," she jokes, or at least I think she's joking

"And just how are we going to find this city centre premises exactly?" I ask. "Not to mention finance it? What you're talking about will cost a fortune!"

"Don't worry about money. Leave all that to me, that's my job. But say I did find a premises and say I did raise the capital, would you be interested? What do you say, Dana?"

"I don't know. Maybe," says Dana tentatively, not realising she's walking right into the trap Caroline has set.

"Maybe?"

"Yes, but –" she breaks off, having noticed that Caroline is sitting back in her chair, grinning like she's the Cheshire Cat.

"What?" demands Dana.

"The good news is, I've already found us a premises!"

"No way!"

"Yes, I rang Doug's mum first thing this morning."

"Doug's mum? You rang Monica?"

"Yes, yes." And Caroline carries on, ignoring the look of astonishment on Dana's face. "You know that since Monica closed the shop she's been upgrading it, getting it ready to rent out again? Well, there's still some work left to do but, the good news is, when she's finished, she's happy to have us as tenants."

"But how did you persuade her?" demands Dana.

"Honey, believe me, I can persuade anyone to do anything. Besides, it wasn't hard. Monica just loves you, Dana – she thinks you're the best thing that ever happened to Doug. She's happy to give us the chance. I managed to convince her to rent it to us and for a reduced sum for the first six months until we get established. Then, once we begin turning a profit, she'll be in on a share because, not only did I persuade her to let us rent the premises, I think I've also persuaded her to come on board as an investor."

"You're kidding!"

"Nope!"

"You did all this without first talking to us?"

"I wanted to have something concrete to put on the table. I thought it would let you see how serious I am about all this and how possible it all is. And it is."

"But –"

She cuts me off. "What's more, I made a few other phone calls and I think I've interested a couple of other deep-pocketed individuals into coming on board."

"Like who?"

"Like some people whose accounts I've dealt with over the years – people with whom I've worked very closely and for whom I've made a lot of money, people who trust me. I reckon I can easily get all the finance we need."

"You really are something else!" Dana is looking at Caroline with something that looks worryingly like admiration.

"Is it only now you realise that?" Caroline laughs.

What's Dana saying? Surely she's not actually beginning to give any credence to this absurd plan?

"Hang on a second," I interrupt. "Finance has to be paid back. Suppose, just suppose for a moment, we're going to do this – thing – shouldn't we consider starting somewhere where the overheads wouldn't be so great?"

Caroline shakes her head. "No, we only get one shot at this. An appearance of success breeds success. We open in the city centre in a swish premises and, I guarantee you, it'll work. Monica already believes it could, as do the other prospective investors and they're not stupid people."

The implication is there, that we *are* stupid people if we don't see the potential when these other cleverer and wealthier people do. But it simply can't be as easy as Caroline is making out.

I put my one remaining card on the table. "But what about a business plan?" I demand, speaking the language Caroline understands. "Don't we need a business plan?"

Caroline goes to the counter and brings back a spiral notebook. "While you were sleeping . . ." She smiles and hands it to me. "I'll need to tidy all this up, of course, put some order to it, but most of the important stuff is in there somewhere."

I flick through it. It's a muddle – a mixture of sums with scarily large totals and of the ideas she's just presented to us. I see where she's listed the team – *Caroline Connolly, B.Comm – Dana Vaughan, B.A. (Psy) – Rosie Kiely, B.Sc.* I read what she's scrawled after my name. '*Rosie, a graduate of UCD, heads up our Research and Development.*' Head of Research and Development? I have to say seeing those words written down gives me a little thrill – for the briefest of moments – until I remind myself just what I'd be head of researching and developing.

She takes her notebook back and begins flicking through it herself. "The beauty of this whole enterprise is that we'll be making our product – the potions – ourselves so there'll be no middleman taking his cut. By my reckoning, they shouldn't cost us more than a euro each to produce but when it comes to selling them we can charge whatever we like, whatever we decide they're worth. The key is in the packaging. I'm thinking pretty little glass bottles would look really classy and, since we'll be buying them in bulk, I reckon we should be able to get them for 50 cents a pop.

Then we'll get eye-catching labels made up with an attractive name for each potion and a little spiel about the ingredients and their aphrodisiac qualities."

"You have given this some thought, haven't you?" remarks Dana.

"Yup! I'm thinking €9.99 is a good figure. Most people don't have to think too much before spending €9.99. And €9.99 means a profit of €8.49 before VAT and taxes and running costs. After VAT we have a profit of nearly six euros. Our running costs – rent, our wages, light, electricity – remain the same whether we shift one or a thousand a day, so the success of this whole enterprise depends on the number we sell and the number we sell relies very much upon how well we market this whole venture – which is where I come in again." She thinks for a second. "Of course, €9.99 might be too low – maybe we should charge more. The more we charge, the more people will value our products and the more desperate they'll be for them to work." She puts the notebook down. "I need to get all this in better order and type it up on the computer. But the bottom line is I believe I'm on to a winner here. This is the challenge and the opportunity I've been waiting for and I'd like all three of us to be in on it together. We could make a good team, a great team."

"But, Caroline . . ." I look at Dana, to see what she's thinking. She's usually the most sensible of the three of us but now I'm alarmed to see a worrying look in her eye, like she may actually be thinking Caroline's plan is a viable one. "Dana!" I say. "Don't tell me you think this is a good idea too?"

"Well," she hesitates, "I think it's worth considering. I'm not sure I'll get a thesis topic out of all this but I like the rest of what Caroline is saying. I like the idea of the three of us working for ourselves, together. I like the idea that it would leave me free enough to carry on studying. It all just sounds so exciting, doesn't it?"

"But, hang on – you don't actually believe in love potions, do you?" I ask.

Dana shrugs. "I don't think I really know enough to say yes or no. I'd need to read up on the whole area first but, as Caroline says, people have believed in them for generations. Many plants have great healing properties and, as I'm sure you, Rosie, with your background will know, pharmaceutical companies have exploited these properties for years – most of the drugs they sell are based on what were originally homeopathic remedies. I don't think it's such a huge leap to believe that some plants could have an aphrodisiac effect too."

"Just think about it, Rosie," Caroline resumes her hard sell "It *could* work, it *will* work and, when it does, just imagine the potential! And our Dublin shop could be just the start. First Dublin! Then London! Paris! New York! We could franchise this baby!"

"Whoa, steady on!" laughs Dana.

"It could happen!" Caroline's eyes are as bright and feverish as a televangelist.

But could it? Could it really work? She makes it all sound so plausible. Her enthusiasm is infectious. Despite myself, I can feel the tiniest bubble of excitement welling up inside but I quell it.

"And imagine, Rosie, when you arrive into your – say – five-year college reunion and someone asks what you're doing with yourself these days and you tell them you're one of the founders *and* a director of a multinational business, how cool would that be? Imagine how all those scientists will look at you with envy then!"

For a brief moment, I picture a room in a fancy hotel and I'm surrounded by my old classmates and (somewhat oddly, given this is a social occasion) we're all in our white coats and they're all hanging on my every word and looking on in awe as I show off a little glass bottle filled with some brightly coloured liquid. But I quickly dismiss this bizarre image from my mind.

"You think? Envy me because – what? Because I've become the modern equivalent of a quack doctor peddling snake-oils?"

But Caroline's not listening.

"Love Potions. How about that for a name?" she asks, looking from one of us to the other.

"Yeah, I like it," says Dana.

"So, come on girls. What do you say – are you in, or are you out?"

"Count me in!" Dana cries, sold by Caroline's Billy Graham act.

While I'm still dithering, trying to come up with reasons why this has to be the most hare-brained, doomed-to-failure plan ever, Dana (yes, Dana) and Caroline are high-fiving each other.

Now that she has one of us on board, Caroline turns her attention fully on the other, on me.

"What do you think, Rosie?"

I shrug – she's not going to reel me in as easily as all that.

"You have to have faith, Rosie," she says. "Anita Roddick wouldn't have got where she did if she didn't believe in herself. Nor would Ann Summers –"

"Ann Summers isn't a real person!"

"Body shops, soap shops, lingerie shops – why not love potion shops? Do you really want to spend your whole life testing water quality?"

"I only did that for one summer, it was a job placement but even so there's something to be said for that. People *need* water."

"Yes, people need water but they don't need bottled water. The first person who decided that they would take water from a spring, bottle it, and sell it irrespective of the fact that there's perfectly decent water coming out of our taps and for free is now a multimillionaire! There's no underestimating what people will pay for. You too could be that, Rosie. You could be that millionaire or you could spend your whole life working for someone else, working in a job your heart really isn't in. Come on, Rosie. It's a no-brainer!"

Someone here should be the sensible one. But that someone should be Dana. It's always been Dana. Not me, never has been. I stare at their two faces, all animated at this impossible dream Caroline's dangling before us.

"A millionaire?" I say.

She shrugs. "Sure – it's possible, anything is possible and, at the very least, you'll have a job which is more than you have now. First researching, then producing and, later, working in the shop as well, if you like. As I recall you're pretty good at selling. Monica was always saying it."

They're both staring at me.

What have I got to lose? My reputation as a scientist? But I don't have a reputation. As Caroline says, I don't even have a job. And it's true, I did like working in the boutique. I liked the contact with the public. I've always found lab work quite isolating. But love potions? Could I spend my life promoting something I don't believe in? But then I think of others I knew in college. I think of Eamonn who I went out with for a very brief time in first year. His childhood love of geology prompted him to study it. Did he ever imagine as a young kid poring over his rock collection that he'd end up working for an oil company? I think of Adrienne, another college friend, who studied archaeology. After graduating she found work with a property development company. Big businesses are the ones who can afford to take on so many of these graduates and do so to promote their own big business interests. In a way both Adrienne and Eamonn could be accused of selling out but everyone needs to work. If I say no to Caroline, then what? I carry on going for interviews and, if I do finally land a job, chances are it will be with some big multinational. But will I necessarily approve of everything that a multinational does?

So, no, I don't believe in love potions. But at least they won't do any harm – I can make sure of that. I can be meticulous in my research. Maybe that should be enough. That, and a chance to be in on the start of something, and a chance to work alongside my two friends.

"I think," I hesitate for a moment then take a deep breath, "I think you can count me in."

Caroline lets out a whoop. "That's my girl!"

The three of us look at one another. The excitement is palpable. Even in the middle of it, I realise what a special moment this is. It could all go belly-up, but it mightn't.

"Love Potions," I say aloud.

"Love Potions. Opening for business in three months' time!" says Caroline taking the opportunity to slip in this little detail, maybe hoping it will go unnoticed in the excitement.

"In three months' time!" I cry.

"The sooner we start selling, the sooner we start making money! So, I suggest you go and shower, and I'll cook up some breakfast. After that you, Rosie, can get down to work. The best place to start is probably the internet. All right, partner?"

Totonac lore has it that Xanat, the young daughter of the Mexican fertility goddess, loved a Totonac youth. Unable to marry him owing to her divine nature, she transformed herself into a plant - vanilla - that would provide him with pleasure and happiness.

Note: Flutes filled to the rim with champagne with an added vanilla bean make for a bubbly treat.

7

I look up from the computer and swivel around in my chair to see Finn standing there, leaning against the door frame, his hands in his pockets, one ankle crossed in front of the other.

"God! You gave me a fright! How long have you been there?" I demand.

"Not long."

He comes over, bends to give me a kiss, then looking for somewhere to sit he crosses the room to my bed. I say 'crosses' but that implies a degree of distance. What I really mean is he takes one truncated step to reach the bed as I am the unfortunate occupant of our house's short straw – the so-called boxroom. While Dana and Caroline and Shane reside in (comparative) spacious splendour, my domain is a space too impossibly small to keep any order to the elements of my messy life as now witnessed by the fact that Finn is pulling the duvet over some of those elements – crumpled sheet, cast-aside pajamas, upturned book, damp towel, hairdryer, clothes I considered wearing today but rejected – all in order to have somewhere to sit.

"So tell me, how did your girls' night out go?" he asks, having made himself comfortable in so far as it is possible.

"Good. The first half anyway."

"And the second half?"

"Well, you know what Caroline is like. We were all set to go home when she persuaded us to go on to a club instead. But then, even though I hadn't wanted to go, I was just beginning to enjoy myself when Dana suddenly announced she wanted to leave, said she had a headache, so we all had to troop off in search of a taxi. Anyway, what about you? Did you go anywhere?"

"Hmm?"

"What did you do last night?"

"Nothing much."

"Stayed at home and watched telly with your dad?" And then I remember my new resolution – about us two getting out more. "You know," I say, "I really enjoyed myself last night before Dana decided to drag us away. It got me thinking. All we seem to do is go to the cinema and the pub. I think we should start going to clubs more and going to see some live music."

"Sounds good to me," smiles Finn. "So, Caroline tells me you've got some big news."

I laugh. "I'm surprised she didn't tell you herself. Okay, you are not going to believe this but we've decided to go into business together."

"Really?"

"Yeah."

"What kind of business?"

"Selling love potions," I say, in a casual but confident way as if I were talking about something more conventional like, say, home insurance.

Finn looks at me, then laughs. "No, really, what kind of business?"

"Selling love potions," I repeat, somewhat defensively this time.

"Love potions?"

Okay, I see he is not too impressed but I remind myself of how I reacted when I first heard and so I begin telling him everything, starting with Caroline waking us, and I work my way through all of what she had to say. Evidently I don't share Caroline's powers of persuasion and as I go on I can't help but notice that Finn is sitting there, struggling to keep his expression neutral but the ever-so-slight raising of his brow manages to convey a lot – scepticism, amusement and a certain lack of enthusiasm, all of which I try to ignore.

"So," I say, coming to an end, "I'm going to spend the next few weeks researching everything, coming up with the actual potions." I nod towards the computer. "I've started already. It's amazing just how much information is out there." I pause. "So what do you think?" I ask, willing him to approve.

"What do I think?"

"Yes?"

"I'm not sure what I think."

"Okay, well, no fear you're going to bowl me over with your unbridled enthusiasm, that's for sure!" I snap.

"I'm just trying to get my head around the idea, trying to figure out how it could work."

"Work? Of course it will work. It's a great idea and we're a great team. Caroline says that –"

"Ah, yes, Caroline."

I look at him, waiting for him to expand but he doesn't.

84

"'Ah, yes, Caroline' – like what's that supposed to mean?" I demand.

"You know I like Caroline, a lot. She's fantastic. She's upbeat, enthusiastic, lively, clever, but –"

"But what?"

"Okay." He thinks for a second then begins tentatively. "Just because Caroline is good at her job, good at promoting other businesses, that doesn't make her a natural entrepreneur. It doesn't necessarily mean she'll be good at running her own business. And, yes, I know you've been friends for ages but it doesn't automatically follow that you'll make good business partners."

"No, but that we get on with one another, trust one another, understand one another, has to be a good start. And if it wasn't for Caroline there wouldn't be a business to begin with. She's the one who persuaded us that it was such a good idea."

"Yes, I can imagine," he says in a tone I do not like at all. Then he shrugs. "I don't know. The whole thing sounds . . . well . . . a little fishy to me."

"Fishy?" I'm annoyed.

"Well, yes, fishy."

"If you're talking about oysters, then yes," I point to the computer screen. "You know, oysters are considered an aphrodisiac, as indeed is kelp, or seaweed as we'd call it. Of course kelp isn't a fish as such but it smells fishy."

"Whatever are you talking about, Rosie?"

"Before you came in I was reading about the scientific basis as to why kelp is considered an aphrodisiac. You see, it's rich in vitamins and minerals including iodine which is interesting because a lack of iodine can result in excessive physical fatigue and that in turn can result in a lowered sex drive."

He looks at me, like he doesn't have a clue what I'm talking about and maybe he doesn't. I'm not sure I do myself, or have a clue why I'm babbling like this. Maybe I'm trying to impress him with my scientific knowledge to make the idea seem less wacky. Maybe I just don't want to give him a chance to tell me how he thinks Caroline has railroaded me into this whole thing.

"Macrocystis pyrifera," I erupt, like someone with Tourette's.

"I beg your pardon?"

"That's the scientific name for kelp, for your information."

"If you say so."

"I do."

"Look, Rosie, don't be cross. I just don't want you getting carried away. Don't you think that – maybe – Caroline has managed to talk you into something you'd be better steering clear of?"

I shrug. "I want to do this because *I* think it's a good idea. Caroline hasn't talked me into anything. I'm not an idiot, you know. I can think for myself."

"Yeah, sure, but we all know what Caroline is like."

"What do you mean?"

"I think you know exactly what I mean. Think back to yesterday and your CV?"

"Yes, well, that was different."

"Was it? Come on, Rosie, you're a scientist. What are you doing getting involved in something like this? You can't really believe in love potions."

"As a scientist I feel I have to be open to new ideas and maybe there's more to all this than I think." I point to the computer screen. "There's lots of interesting information out there." I begin scrolling. "Look, see here for example.

Research was recently presented to a meeting of the American Chemical Society no less which suggests that oysters and other bivalves can raise levels of sex hormones in both men and women. They contain high levels of zinc that stimulate and increase the blood flow. They're not stating that oysters and the like are aphrodisiac but at least they're open to the possibility. These people are scientists, like me. As I see it, my role is to do the research, consider the whole folklore behind what are traditionally considered aphrodisiacs, come up with some recipes that I know are safe to take and, then, reproduce them."

"I see."

"In a cost-effective way."

"Cost-effective way?" He looks around. "Hark! Do I hear Caroline?"

"Give over. Okay, I was sceptical too to begin with and, yes, if it wasn't for Caroline there's no way I'd be considering getting involved in something like this but I am finding a scientific basis to some of it; like oysters, like kelp. The iodine in kelp actually does improve people's well-being which in turn increases their libido. You feel good, you're more likely to feel sexy − it's as simple as that."

"Yeah, but feeding someone a bowlful of kelp isn't going to make them actually fall in love."

"I'm not saying it will but neither is it going to do them any harm. Anyway, we're not going to be doling out bowls of kelp. We'll be selling colourful potions in attractive dainty bottles."

"So that's it? You're happy to be persuaded by Caroline to set up in a business the basis of which is selling concoctions in pretty bottles to people, concoctions that don't actually do what they purport to do but at least they don't do them any harm either? You're happy to take people's money for products you don't actually believe work."

"Oh come on! You're making out we're complete charlatans!"

His look says it all – he doesn't have to use words.

"Come on, Finn – lighten up. It's only a bit of fun. It's not life-and-death stuff. Nobody's going to think that what we're selling really will change their lives. Most people are going to buy them for a laugh, to set the mood. Say, this couple, for example, have been going out together for a while. Lately, things have been a little stale between them. They're in town doing some shopping. They spot our shop. On a whim, they wander in and end up buying one of the potions. They go home, have a romantic meal and at the end of the evening they settle down by an open fire and pour out the potion, like they might a bottle of wine. Later, when they go to bed, they make love for the first time in months. Now, I'm not saying the love potion had any real chemical effect but it did have an effect. It changed their mindset. If they hadn't bought it earlier that day, their thoughts wouldn't have taken the direction they did and they wouldn't have rekindled their relationship. How can that be a bad thing?"

Finn shrugs. "Maybe they should have stuck to the wine – it would probably have had the same effect."

I shrug. "The potion isn't going to cost them any more and it'll taste as good – I can make sure of that."

He shrugs, doesn't say anything, but this lack of enthusiasm is deflating.

"You could at least pretend to be enthusiastic!" I snap.

"Is that what you'd really prefer, Rosie? Someone who'd tell you they think the whole idea is brilliant, even if they have reservations, even if they think you'd be better off hanging on until a real job comes up? If this fails, then what? What are you going to do then? Six months down the line you'll be back going for interviews except then you'll have the additional problem of explaining what you've been up to in the meantime. To be honest I couldn't care less about love potions and whether they work or not but I do care about you."

"If you do care about me then all I ask is that you give me your support."

"But Rosie —"

"Look, it's not like I've been inundated with job offers. In fact, this is the first opportunity that has come my way. I'm not doing this at the expense of some other prospect. The fact is, right now I don't have any other prospects. This is it, this is the one and only chance I'm being offered. Couldn't you try to be a little encouraging? Please?"

"But what if it all goes wrong?"

"At least I can say I tried."

He nods, thoughtfully. "Sure. Of course, I would like to see it work out."

"Thanks."

He stands up. "Come on, we'd better go."

"Go? Where?"

"Don't you remember? My dad asked us to come for lunch?"

"Oh God! I'd forgotten."

"We should go now."

Apart from asking him to stop off so that I can pick up a bottle of wine to take with me, I don't say much to Finn as he drives to his dad's. I guess I'm still feeling a little deflated by his lukewarm reaction to our plan. Now we turn off the main road into a quiet housing estate of several hundred identical semi-detached houses. The estate was built around the time Finn's parents married and most of the houses are still occupied by couples who also married around that time and have lived there ever since, raising their families.

I say the houses are identical but that's not quite true. When they were first built they probably were indistinguishable but the intervening years have seen families put their individual stamp on their own homes. The garages and attics of some of the houses have been converted to accommodate the needs of ever-increasing families. The original railings of some have been torn down and replaced by brick walls and fancier gates. Quite a few have conservatories now. A couple of the houses have been painted deep colours in contrast to the original yellow of the majority. Most of them look well cared for. But not Mr Heelan's house, or the house it's attached to, I notice as we pull up, as I do every time.

Just as the cobbler's children go unshod, Mr Heelan's house looks like it could do with a lick of paint though he's the proprietor of several hardware stores. As a widower bringing up a young son on his own Mr Heelan had, I guess, less time and inclination to spend his weekends pottering in the garden and the front is bare of any shrubs and the grass has been replaced by tarmac through which some resilient weeds have broken through.

In contrast, the front garden of the adjoining house is full of shrubs – evidence that someone once did put effort into it but the overgrown and neglected state these shrubs are now in would lead one to think that whoever planted them has since lost that interest. Actually, I'm not just guessing when I say this. This house and garden belong to Mark's parents. Finn says he hasn't seen Mrs McCarthy out in the garden since he died.

I like Finn's dad a lot and I like coming to see him but I don't come too often. I always worry I'll bump into Mark's parents. I know Finn has talked to them about me and him, and I know they're happy about us going out together insofar as they can be in the circumstances but Finn feels they're not ready to meet me, which is just as well – I don't think I'm ready to meet them either. Mark and I went out together for such a short time that I never got to meet them when he was alive and then, when he died, I was too upset to go to his funeral. I did write to them afterwards but, strange to say, I've still never met them.

As we're about to get out of the car, Finn leaves out a groan.

"What?" I ask.

"I think I just saw Mrs McCarthy at the window. Listen, I might pop in for a moment. I don't know if Dad told her you were coming around today. I guess I should have said something. Do you mind?"

"No," I say. "Course I don't." Which I don't. I don't mind that he's popping in to her but I guess I do mind his reason for doing so – that she might find the very sight of me so upsetting he feels the need to go and talk to her.

We climb out of the car. Finn hands me his bunch of keys.

"Let yourself in." He heads next door, calling back as he does: "I won't be too long."

As I walk up to the front door of Finn's house, I sneak a look next door and think I see the pink of a jumper through the nets. I quickly look away.

I put the key in the door. "Hello!" I shout as I shove it open. "It's me – Rosie!"

Mr Heelan appears in the hall wearing an apron with "*No 1 DAD*" emblazoned across the front in big letters.

"Ah Rosie, lovely to see you! Is the young fellow with you?"

"He's just popped next door for a minute."

"Oh?"

"He saw Mrs McCarthy at the window."

"Oh, right."

I see Mr Heelan doesn't need any more explanation.

"I guess I should have said something," he reflects. "Anyway, come on. I'm in the kitchen."

"I hope you didn't go to too much trouble." I follow after him.

As I say, I like Mr Heelan. He's in his fifties and looks like an older version of Finn. He too is stocky and has the same mop of curls except his is completely grey now. But Mr Heelan's eyes are brown not blue. Finn has his mother's eyes. I know this from the wedding photograph I've seen on the mantelpiece in the living-room on earlier visits. The photo shows her to be a beautiful woman, slim and tall, or at least taller than her husband, as I am taller than Finn. The last time I was here, I jokingly asked Mr Heelan why it was that all the Heelan men went for women who were taller than them and Mr Heelan laughed, said it was a case of needs must and there weren't too many women out there who were smaller. Yep, taller was fine, as long as they were beautiful – that's the way the Heelan men liked their women, he joked. Later, Finn said he was glad I talked about his mum like that, like she was a real part of the family. He said most people tended not to mention her at all. Mr Heelan may not be a talking-about-his-feelings sort of man but I know he likes me. Finn has told me so but I'd know it anyway.

Now, as Mr Heelan goes to the oven to check on what's cooking, I look around. The kitchen is as tired-looking as the outside of the house. Back in the eighties, the moss-green Formica units may have been the height of fashion but time and fashion have marched on since then. The flowery wallpaper is woefully outdated too. Whenever I see it, I always picture Finn's mum – young, beautiful, in tight leggings with an oversized shirt to accommodate her pregnant tummy, and I imagine her in the middle of hanging this flowery wallpaper, spurred on by the nesting instinct. But I imagine if she were still alive the wallpaper would have long ago been replaced. I know Finn is keen to do a complete makeover on the kitchen but his dad doesn't share his enthusiasm. I guess I can understand why he likes it this way.

Another thing I do understand is why Finn moved back in with his dad but I'm not sure it was such a great idea. I worry that the pair of them will become increasingly dependent on one another and it will be hard for Finn to move out a second time, back to his own house.

"So, you're keeping well then, Rosie?" says Mr Heelan.

"Fine," I answer. "And you?"

"Never better. The dinner should be ready soon."

I hand him the bottle of wine. "Just a little thank-you for inviting me around."

"Ah Rosie, you shouldn't have gone to the bother."

"It's only something small."

He puts the bottle on the counter then turns to me.

"So did ye have a good time last night?" he asks.

"Great," I say, thinking Finn must have mentioned I was going out with the girls.

"I thought so," he grins. "It was all hours when he got home."

"Pardon?"

"It was all hours when Finn got home from wherever the

93

pair of you went to. Not that it's any of my business – Finn's a grown man – but it's good to see him getting out and enjoying himself. He's been through a lot." He gives a little embarrassed cough before adding. "You're good for him, so you are, Rosie."

Am I? I want to ask. If I'm so good for him, then how come he pretended to me he was at home last night watching telly, and pretended to his dad that he was out with me?

"Hi, Dad," says Finn, coming into the kitchen.

"Hello there, son," says Mr Heelan.

They don't kiss or hug, that's not their way but Mr Heelan slaps Finn affectionately on the back.

Finn notices the apron. "Where did you drag that old thing out from?"

"I found it in the back of one of the cupboards."

Finn turns to me and grins. "In case you're wondering, I bought it for him years ago when I was a kid."

I guess he's expecting me to laugh or to slag him off or something but I don't care about the apron. I want to ask him why he lied to me. But I can't cause a scene, here, now, in front of Mr Heelan.

"Now," says Mr Heelan, "why don't the pair of you sit down? The dinner is ready." He pulls out a chair for me. "Here, Rosie, you're the guest. You sit there."

I sit down. Finn sits down opposite me. I look over at him. He catches my look and gives me a wink and mouths, "love you." I don't respond. I'm trying to figure out what reason there could be for him to lie to me. Why would he let me think he was sitting at home watching telly with his dad when clearly he wasn't? Instead he was out somewhere – somewhere he didn't get home from for all hours.

Mr Heelan brings the food to the table. "Now I never claimed to be the world's greatest cook," he says, putting my dinner down in front of me, "but I think you'll find this tasty – Finn told me you liked lasagne."

He's not lying when he says he's not the world's greatest cook. Despite the apron, the food in front of me is an individual supermarket portion of lasagne still in its container.

"It looks great," I say.

"Yeah, thanks, Dad," says Finn.

"I'll just get the salad and the garlic bread." He goes to the counter, brings them both to the table, then sits down.

"Well, tuck in."

I begin to eat as do the others. None of us say a word. I don't know what they're thinking but for a brief moment I forget about Finn and his whereabouts last evening and instead I imagine how different life would have been for Finn and his *No1 DAD* if Mrs Heelan hadn't died so young. I'm thinking Mr Heelan wouldn't be sitting there, in that apron. I'm thinking four of us instead of three would now be tucking into a nice home-made roast and not these containers from the supermarket. I'm thinking of how Finn once told me that he ended up eating with Mark's family next door most evenings because, as often as not, his dad was working late and, when he wasn't, this is what they ate, or something like it. I look over at Finn and picture him as a small motherless boy, sitting there with his dad, both not speaking, both eating this cardboard food. But then I push this picture from my mind. I don't want to feel sorry for Finn right now. I want to know why he lied to me.

Once we're finished, Mr Heelan clears the table and comes back with coffees, and dessert – bought too from the supermarket.

"So, Rosie, Finn was telling me you didn't get that job," says Mr Heelan.

"No," I shake my head.

"I guess you were disappointed."

"A little."

"I'm sure something will turn up soon for a bright girl like you."

I think of telling him about Caroline and Dana and the love potions and the shop and everything but decide not to, not after Finn's reaction. I wonder if Finn will say anything to him about it but he doesn't, and this annoys me.

Mr Heelan looks to the clock on the wall opposite. "Rosie, I hope you don't mind but the match is starting at three."

I laugh. "Course not! My dad would be the exact same except he and my mum are on holiday in the US. I'd say he's kicking himself for missing it. Or frantically scouring the place for an Irish pub with a telly showing the match."

Mr Heelan laughs. He gets up from the table and then goes into the sitting-room, taking his cup of coffee with him. Moments later, the telly comes on at top volume.

". . . *and the crowd here this afternoon is in mighty form despite the showers . . .*" Immediately the sound is turned down to a murmur.

Finn is looking over at me. He smiles. "I should have warned you about my dad's cooking – if you can call it that."

"No need to warn me," I reply snappily. "It was delicious."

"He says it saves on the washing-up if he leaves the food in the containers."

"That makes sense."

"Rosie, have I said something?"

"No."

"Or done something to annoy you?"

96

"Like what?"

"Are you annoyed over how I reacted when you told me about Caroline's plan?"

"*Our* plan, you mean."

"Your plan then. Is that why you're annoyed?"

I shrug.

"Look, Rosie, I care about you. If I didn't say what I thought then —"

"Why did you tell me you were at home with your dad last night, watching telly?"

He looks at me, surprised.

"Why did you lie to me?"

"I didn't lie."

"Really?"

"No."

"No?"

"I just never corrected you when you assumed that's what I was doing."

"Isn't that called lying by omission? So what were you doing? Where were you?"

"Look, Rosie . . ." he begins.

"Yes?"

"I guess I should have told you."

"Told me what exactly?"

"It's nothing really but do you remember Ashley from the band?"

"Course I do. The bass-player."

"Yeah. He called into work yesterday and we got talking about the band and then we went for a few drinks when I finished work. In the pub we happened to bump into some other musicians we know from around and we ended up in this club with them. I don't know why I didn't tell you. I guess

I just thought that if I mentioned meeting Ashley it would get you thinking about Mark and I didn't want to upset you."

"And that's the truth?"

"Of course."

"The whole truth, and nothing but the truth?"

"Yes. What did you think? That I was out with someone else?"

"No! Well, I guess, maybe." I shrug. "For a second."

"Rosie, you know I'm mad about you."

I nod. "Yes, I do, but men can be devious and –"

"Isn't that something of a generalisation? Aren't you perhaps judging me by the standards of some of your old boyfriends?"

I shrug.

"Rosie, I'm not like that. You know that. And you know that what we have is special. I love you."

I nod. "Sure. I know."

Finn reaches out and takes my hand. Then he leans across the table and kisses me. I close my eyes and keep them closed for as long as the kiss goes on, and that's quite some time. Only when we hear Mr Heelan coming down the hall do we pull apart.

"Ireland are playing brilliantly," he says as he comes in. "It's going to be one hell of a game."

Finn looks at me.

"Go on," I say. "Go watch the match. I should be getting back to my research."

"I'll drop you back."

"No, stay with your dad. I could do with the exercise."

I walk home and as I do I realise I'm feeling happy for all sorts of reasons. After six weeks away, my parents are due back from the States soon and, even though my mum drives me crazy at times, I have missed her and I'm really looking forward to seeing her and Dad again and to hear the pair of them telling me all about their travels, both trying to talk at once, both butting in on each other's account of the holiday because the other is not doing it justice. I'm happy too at the thought of getting back to carrying out more research on the internet. One of the worst things about not having a job is the boredom. Now I feel I have something to put my energies into. And I'm feeling happy that my ridiculous suspicion that Finn might be seeing someone else proved to be just that – a ridiculous suspicion. How could I have imagined it even for a moment? Finn? The nicest man I've ever met – so, so much nicer than anyone else I've ever gone out with? But maybe that's the problem. I'm not used to being with someone like him. I'm not used to the fact that he is so very different from anyone else I've ever dated. And that's why I love him.

Late that evening, Caroline comes into the kitchen to find me hunched over my laptop.

"Hiya," I say, looking up at her, a little square-eyed.

"How are you getting on?" She pulls up a chair. "Have you been at it all evening?" She eyes up the collection of cups I've emptied to break up the hours I've spent going through literally hundreds of sites.

I nod.

"So," she asks, "have you found anything useful?"

"Well, it's not as straightforward as you might think," I begin. "The problem with a lot of what's commonly considered to have aphrodisiac properties is that it's not exactly pretty."

"What do you mean?"

"You know how you have this vision of all these pretty bottles of potions all a-glinting in our shop window?"

"Yes?"

"Well, if you ask me, we're talking less of the pretty boudoir look and more of the butcher's-strewn-with-raw-meat-and-entrails look."

"What are you on about?"

"We're talking skink flesh. We're talking —"

"Skink flesh? What's that?"

"A skink is a little lizard found in warm climates. Skink flesh is — well — its flesh."

"Ugh!"

"Hold your 'Ughs!' a moment, there's worse to come. We're talking eel, we're talking fresh snake-blood, reindeer penis, shark fin. We're talking river snail, rhino horn, tiger testicle, bat blood —"

"You're winding me up?"

"Afraid not! Since time began humans have been gobbling up bits of animals in the hopes they'll restore their libido."

"God! People are weird!"

"So I'm finding out."

"But how do they decide?"

"Decide what?"

"How do they decide on one animal or on one part of an animal?"

"Lots of reasons. The sex organs of, say, rabbits are popular because — well — you've heard the term 'breeding like rabbits' so people think by eating them some of the effect will rub off. And what do eels and rhino horns have in common?"

Caroline shrugs.

"What do they remind you of?"

She thinks for a moment then shakes her head. "I don't know. Nothing in particular."

I indicate downwards with my eyes.

She stares at me blankly. "Rosie, I don't know what you're getting at."

"Rhino horns? Eels? Do they remind you of a particular part of the male body?"

Caroline bursts out laughing. "Oh my God, Rosie! I don't know what kind of men you know but I'm happy to say I've never been reminded of either a rhino horn or an eel!"

I shake my head impatiently and carry on over her laughter. "Their popularity is based on a thing called sympathetic magic."

"What's that?"

"It means that a rhino horn, for example, gets its reputation as an aphrodisiac because of its phallic shape."

"Come on, Rosie. You must be looking in the wrong places. None of this stuff is of any use. You need to start focusing on what's relevant. Who's going to want to leave our shop with a bottle of bat-blood in their handbag? That's not quite what I had in mind. You must have come across some recipes, some *herbal* recipes, that we could actually make and sell?"

"Well, I have come across one recipe that involves horsetail and —"

"Horsetail! Rosie, I said recipes with herbs!"

"Horsetail not horse's tail and it *is* a herb though I'm sure if I carry on looking I'll find some culture somewhere where an actual horse's tail is considered an aphrodisiac."

"Herb or no herb, we're not selling anything called that. There is a certain all-important thing called image."

I peer at the screen and use the keyboard to scroll up. My eyes alight on the peculiarly named Horny Goat Weed.

"What about this then?" I ask, deciding to wind her up. "Horny Goat Weed? It's found in –"

"Rosie, stop! I don't want to hear any more! We are *not* selling anything with Horny Goat Weed in it!"

"I don't know. It could prove popular. 'Roll up, roll up! Get your Horny Goat Weed here!'"

In my mind's eye, I picture an early morning queue of furtive, seedy-looking men in beige overcoats with upturned collars lined up outside our shop, all waiting for it to open and to make their purchase of our famous shop specialty, Horny Goat Weed Elixir. For a split second I think of sharing this image with Caroline but then think again. Anyway, she's already getting to her feet. She's heard enough.

"Let me know when you find some nice stuff, some marketable stuff," she tells me, as she takes her leave.

"Yes, boss!"

Once Caroline is gone, I decide to make myself another cup of coffee before carrying on. I'm sure I will come across more useful sites but I doubt if they'll prove quite so fascinating. My problem is, I get easily distracted from what I'm meant to be doing. It was the same in college. I'd go to the library to find some background material for a paper I was meant to be working on but quite often I wouldn't even get to the relevant section. On the way, I'd wander into another section and, next thing, I'd be sitting crossed-legged on the floor, deep in the middle of some book that had absolutely nothing to do with what I was supposed to be researching.

On first reading, the notion that men (and it is mostly men) think they'll solve their libido problems by wolfing down choice bits of animals is mildly amusing, if somewhat baffling.

What's not so amusing is the impact it has had on some unfortunate species. Rhinos, for one, are in danger of becoming extinct as a result. And while most of us look at seals and think, "How cute!" that's not everyone's reaction – rather, some are prompted to catch them and butcher them for the sake of their penis. Since the females don't have that particular organ, their carcasses are simply thrown overboard. Female turtles don't fare much better. They're poached, then cut up in order to extract their eggs which are then eaten raw with salt and lime juice. The world, I think, is a very strange place populated by some very strange people and their even stranger beliefs.

But Caroline is right. None of this is of any practical use to us. I need to stop wasting time and start focusing. But first, another cup of coffee.

Myrtle was considered to be sacred to Aphrodite, the Greek goddess of love, lust and beauty, and the tradition of brides wearing a crown of myrtle on their wedding day was common in ancient Greece.
Ancient Britons too appreciated the aphrodisiac qualities of the plant and it was always used in bridal bouquets and often planted near the home of newly-weds.

MEDIEVAL MYRTLE POTION:
2 handfuls of myrtle flowers and leaves
2 quarts spring water
1 quart white wine
Combine all ingredients. Let sit for 24 hours. Strain.

8

The following Friday evening, Caroline is standing in the middle of the kitchen, tapping her watch. "What is keeping Dana? She's late. Doesn't she know this meeting is supposed to start at 7.00pm?"

I look at the clock on the wall. It's exactly two minutes past.

"Good gracious! Whatever can have happened to her?" I ask in mock alarm. "Quick! Dial 999!"

Caroline eyes me up coolly but doesn't say anything.

"Come on, Caroline! Lighten up!" I cajole. "She'll be here. Are you nervous or something?"

"What's there to be nervous about?" She laughs but to my ear it sounds a little strained.

She goes to the cupboard now. There she takes out a glass jug and fills it with water, places it on the centre of the kitchen table, stands back and surveys her handiwork. In addition to the jug, she's earlier set out three places – each with a fresh notepad, a pen and an upturned glass, all matching and laid out just so. She picks up her briefcase and lays it down on the table beside one of the places. Not happy with the way it's sitting, she squares it up.

"All set!" she says with a fleeting satisfaction that reverts immediately to annoyance. "But what *is* keeping Dana?" she mutters. She turns to me. "Will I give her a ring?" Not waiting for an answer she picks her phone up and starts pressing buttons.

"Caroline, she's only five minutes late. Will you not hang on?"

"She knew the meeting was starting at seven."

"I know but –" I break off, hearing a key in the front door.

"Finally," mutters Caroline.

Moments later Dana breezes in with Doug following behind.

"Hiya!" she calls cheerily.

"Hi," says Doug in his quiet shy way. He always gives the impression of being slightly uneasy around people, and especially around Caroline.

Both fail to notice that Caroline is staring at Doug in surprise now and, while Dana goes to the fridge and opens it to see what's inside, he goes to the table, pushes Caroline's carefully laid things aside to make space for his bag, then sits down.

"I *am* starving!" says Dana as she carries a selection of vegetables to the counter. "Doug, do you fancy a stir-fry?"

"Ahem!" coughs Caroline.

Dana looks at her. "What? Would you like me to make some for you too?"

"No, thank you," says Caroline frostily. "I'll eat later."

"Are you sure?" asks Dana, completely oblivious to the chill.

"Dana," says Caroline sharply, "have you forgotten about our meeting?"

"No, course not. I just thought I might cook something first, if that's all right." One look at Caroline's face tells her that it is not all right, not all right at all, at all, at all. "But I guess I could wait until after . . ."

"I think that would be better," says Caroline. "Well, now, let's get cracking."

Caroline goes to the table, removes Doug's bag and puts everything back in order. She eyes up Doug for a second, like she's considering how she'll go about removing him too but then she sits down, takes off her watch and lays it out on the table. I too take a seat. Dana takes another. Doug stays where he is. Nobody says a word. We're waiting for Caroline to start the proceedings of this meeting but then I see Caroline is waiting for Doug to leave, a fact of which he is totally oblivious.

Caroline leaves out a sigh. "Doug," she says, "wouldn't you like to go and watch TV?"

"Not really – thanks," says Doug. He reaches out, picks up the jug and begins to pour some water into a glass. I glance over at Caroline. She does not look happy. She looks like she's just about managing to stop herself from grabbing the glass away from him and telling him it's for the meeting, with a capital M. I wait for her to ask him – or order him – to leave but she restrains herself, possibly regretfully reminding herself that this is a free country, not a dictatorship with her as its leader.

With a loud sigh, she takes her notes, shuffles them busily, pours herself a glass of water, takes a sip, looks at the watch on the table, and then begins. "We'll start off this meeting by recounting the progress each of us has made and –"

She's interrupted by the sound of laughter coming from the hall. It's Shane. He sounds like he has someone with him. Loretta, his girlfriend, most probably.

"Oh for crying out loud!" mutters Caroline. "What are *they* doing here?"

I think about pointing out that Shane does live here but hold my tongue.

"When I asked him this morning, he said he was going out straight after work and wouldn't be coming home," grumbles Caroline.

Shane and Loretta arrive into the kitchen and look startled to see all four of us sitting around the table so formally.

"Oh, am I missing something?" Shane asks.

"We're in the middle of a business meeting," Caroline tells them.

"Oh right!" Shane turns to Loretta. "Remember I was telling you that Caroline and the others are setting up in the love-potion business?" He's grinning as he says this. Loretta, not knowing us as well as Shane does and perhaps not wishing to offend, nods solemnly in response but something about her expression makes me suspect it's a struggle for her to maintain a straight face.

I think Caroline has noticed too. She looks insulted and for a second I think she's about to say something but she lets it go.

"Don't worry," Shane is telling Caroline now. "We'll be out of your way soon. We're just going to make a bite to eat before heading out again."

"Can it not wait until we're finished?" asks Caroline.

"Not really. We're meant to be in town for eight-thirty," says Shane.

"Caroline, why don't we go upstairs to one of the bedrooms for our meeting?" I suggest.

"Or the living room?" adds Dana.

"No, we need to be sitting around a table. It's better this way, like a proper meeting. We can't discuss things if we're lolling around on beds or on the couch."

I look at Caroline. Even for her, she's being extraordinarily regimented. Maybe deep down she is a little nervous now that all this is really going ahead, even if she'd never let on, not even to herself.

"Look, don't worry about us," Loretta tells her. "We'll be as quiet as mice. You won't even know we're here."

Accepting that she can't actually order them from the kitchen, Caroline resignedly turns her attention back to us and tries to ignore the distracting and not at all mouse-like presence of Shane and Loretta as they start preparing their meal. She reaches into her briefcase, takes out three bound documents, keeps one for herself and then hands one each to Dana and me.

"First," she begins, "I've drawn up a full business plan as you will see. This I've already circulated to five of my contacts who I've previously liaised with and who have indicated to me their interest in coming on board. Second, I've spoken with Mrs Monica Gregory and –"

"My mum?" interrupts Doug.

Caroline ignores him. "– have arranged that Dana and I will meet her at the premises this coming Thursday at 1.00 pm."

Shane has come over and is now standing by the table waiting for an opportunity to say something but Caroline ignores him.

"This meeting with Monica will give us a chance to

discuss any changes she may need to make to meet our requirements. It will also –"

"Ah – excuse me," says Shane.

Caroline breaks off. "Do you want something?"

"Sorry for interrupting but have any of you seen the soy sauce?"

"It's in the cupboard over the fridge," Dana tells him.

"Thanks."

"Thirdly," resumes Caroline.

"Shane," calls Dana, "are you making a stir-fry?"

"Yeah."

"I was going to do the same. Do you want to add in that lot of vegetables on the counter and we can all eat some of it?"

"Sure."

Dana turns back to Caroline and smiles. "Carry on."

"One thing," interrupts Doug.

"What is it now?" sighs Caroline.

"You'd better check with my mother about Thursday. Since she gave up the shop she usually meets Fay for lunch on Thursdays."

"Oh," I say, "are Fay and your mum still in contact?" When I worked in Monica's boutique, Fay was the third member of staff. I haven't seen her since the shop closed.

Doug nods. "Yeah, they meet every week."

"Ahem," coughs Caroline. "If we could just get back to business?"

"Sorry," says Doug. "I just thought you'd like to know about my mum and Fay."

"Yes, well, thank you. I will give her another ring to check. Now, where was I?"

"Thirdly," prompts Dana.

"Pardon?" says Caroline.

"You were on to, 'and thirdly'."

"Oh yes – and thirdly, last night while attending the launch of Stellar, a new perfume the marketing of which I've been heavily involved in, I met several journalists who I feel will prove useful when the time comes. There's one journalist especially –"

"How is she?" I ask Doug, my mind still on Fay. She and I have rather a turbulent history but I was always very fond of her.

"Ha? It's a he, not a she," answers Caroline.

"Pardon?" I say, a little confused.

"The journalist I was talking about," clarifies Caroline.

"No, no, I meant Fay."

"God! Can we not," demands Caroline, "just stick to what we're meant to be talking about for one moment?"

"Come on, Caroline. Lighten up! I'm just asking Doug a question."

"All right! But I just want to get through everything, you know."

I look over at Doug. "So how is she?"

Doug glances over at Caroline, then answers quickly. "Okay, I think."

"So, to continue," Caroline resumes, "I let it be known to him, this journalist, and a few others, that I was involved in a very interesting new project but did not give any more detail. I feel I did, however, generate some interest. So, now to you, Dana – what have you to report?"

Dana shuffles in her seat. "There's not a whole lot I can really do at this stage."

"Have you sourced suitable bottles?"

"No, not yet but there are a couple of companies who

might be able to come up with what we want but I still have to contact them."

"But you will?"

"Yes."

"This week?"

"Ah – okay."

"Labels? Have you looked into getting labels?"

"No. But Caroline, don't you think you're jumping ahead of yourself? We don't actually have anything to bottle or label yet."

"But we will soon. Won't we, Rosie?"

"Sure. I have come up with a lot of interesting stuff and –"

"Interesting – great! Useful even better!" snaps Caroline.

Suddenly I feel annoyed. Sure, Caroline is the brains behind this operation. Sure, she's the one looking at the bigger picture. And, sure, maybe she is more nervous than she'd ever let on *but* does she have to take on this annoyingly bossy, brusque persona and treat us like hopeless idiots? All week, I've done little else apart from going from site to site (sticking mostly, but not all of the time, to what's relevant). I've read up on dozens and dozens of herbs and spices and weeded out, so to speak, all the ones that aren't safe to use. As well, I've discovered a couple of sites that between them can supply us with a lot of what we need for the recipes I think will meet Caroline's requirements – cheap and easy to produce and attractive enough so that people will actually want to buy them.

All this is what I am about to tell her but now a certain waywardness born out of Caroline's superior attitude causes me to change my mind and instead I think of one particular site I wandered into, the contents of which I know will drive her mental. It's a site set up by a self-professed white witch written for other white witches to advise them on how to make potions the white witch way. But there's no need to tell Caroline about this aspect of the site — just yet.

"I did come across a lot of very useful information about herbs on this one site," I begin.

"Great!" says Caroline.

"This site suggests that we really need to buy them when they're in season and from our country because those that are grown in greenhouses or are shipped long distances lose much of their magical properties."

"Their what?" demands Caroline.

"Their magical properties," I repeat, then go on quickly leaving no time for further interruption. "Now the thing is, if we really want to do this properly, as I'm sure we do, we should grow all our herbs ourselves and while growing them we can augment their magical properties by channelling our positive thoughts into them."

"Are you nuts?" Caroline demands, then noticing Doug and Dana's barely suppressed smirks, she turns on them. "What's so funny?"

"I'm just imagining you," says Dana, "pottering around in that stamp-sized garden, first thing in the morning before you head to work, in your high heels, coaxing rows of herbs to grow."

All (Loretta and Shane included) burst out laughing. Caroline, however, doesn't. She's staring at Dana stony-faced.

"Very funny," she mutters.

"Anyway, the best time to grow herbs," I go on, "is when the moon is either in Cancer, Scorpio, Libra or Pisces."

"Oh for God's sake!"

"You don't," I nod towards her briefcase, "happen to have a lunar calendar in there by any chance?"

"A what?"

"A lunar calendar? Love potions should only be prepared when the moon is waxing so we'll need a lunar calendar to show us the phases of the moon and its movement through the zodiac."

"Jesus, Rosie! Where are you getting all this nonsense?"

I go to the counter, pick up my laptop, log onto the relevant site, and then bring it over to her.

"Oh, for crying out loud, Rosie!" she cries. "This site is written by some white witch! What the hell are you wasting your time on a site like this!" But then, despite herself, she begins to study the screen. There is total silence as we all watch her. Then she begins to read aloud: "*Unlucky influences can be kept at bay when preparing magical recipes by stirring deosil –*" She looks up. "What the hell is deosil?"

"I gather it's a Wicca term –" I ignore her groan "– that means in an anticlockwise direction."

"So why don't they just say that? And what unlucky influences?"

"You're most likely one," Dana remarks. "All that cynicism can only detract from the magic."

Caroline ignores her and carries on reading. "*'Herbal preparations should never be boiled in aluminium vessels but instead copper or earthenware should be used to avoid contamination.'* Oh please!" She reads on. "*'A mortar and pestle is an important tool in the making of potions.'* Hmm," she mutters but doesn't comment. "*'A good spice grinder for powdering herbs and roots and a good strainer or sieve for straining teas and brews are all essential. These tools along with traditional tools of the craft – wand, staff, etc can be powerful aids in your magical endeavours.'* Sweetest hour!"

Traditional tools of the craft! Why are you even showing me this, Rosie? We're *not* witches."

"Well, it depends on how you define witch," I point out. "What we're planning to do is make love potions – I can't think of a more witch-like activity."

Shane joins in. "If you were living in another century, the elders would probably be dunking you lot in water by now to find out whether you'd drown."

Caroline throws him an is-this-any-of-your-business look, then she turns back to me. "Have you," she says with a weary sigh, "found anything at all that's of use?"

"Well, I have come across some recipes. Here's one. It's for a love-potion tea. You take a pinch of rosemary, two teaspoons of black tea, three pinches of thyme, two pinches of nutmeg, three fresh mint leaves, six fresh rose petals, and, finally, three lemon leaves and you place the lot in an earthenware or copper tea kettle. Then you boil three cups of pure spring water and add them to the kettle and, finally, you sweeten the mixture with sugar and honey."

Caroline nods approvingly. "Now we're getting somewhere. That all sounds fairly straightforward if we tweak it a bit. We could use tap water instead of pure spring water for example – that would be more cost effective. Overall, it wouldn't be too expensive or too hard to make."

"They do have a few stipulations as to how exactly the whole process should be carried out," I tell her.

"Like?" asks Dana.

"It has to be done on a Friday night during a waxing moon."

"What's this waxing moon you keep talking about?" demands Caroline.

"A waxing moon is when it's going from nothing to full."

"Really?" remarks Loretta. "I never knew that."

"Waxing moon!" With a look and a flick of her hand, Caroline dismisses such nonsense.

I continue: "Before drinking it you have to recite the following rhyme: *By light of moon waxing, I brew this tea to make* – you put your lover's name in here – *desire me*'. Then you drink some of the tea and say: '*Goddess of love, hear now my plea, let my lover desire me! So mote it be. So mote it be.*'"

"Goddess of love! And what on earth does 'mote' mean?" demands Caroline.

"Ahh," I hesitate. "I'm presuming it means something like 'may'. You know, so mote it be – so may it be. Anyway, so then you –"

"What? There's more? I think I've heard enough for now."

"You know," says Shane, "I have a friend whose family run a fancy-dress shop." Loretta, I notice, is elbowing him in the ribs to shut him up but he pays no heed. "He could get you the right outfits. I'd say they have dozens of witches' costumes in stock."

"Right!" Caroline stands up. "This meeting is over! What's the point of carrying on when the pair of you," she glares at Dana and me, "won't take this seriously and when all these others keep sniggering and interrupting? We're trying to set up a business here so why are you all carrying on like school kids!"

"Ah, come on, Caroline!" I plead. "We were only messing. I do take it seriously. Please sit down. I have come across other stuff that will interest you."

"No! I've had enough." She begins gathering her things together.

"Enough of what?" comes a voice from the doorway.

"Mick!" Caroline cries out in delight.

We all turn to look. Leaning against the door frame is a big burly figure, with an easy grin on his face. Collectively the components of that face – the big features, the wide mouth, the ruddy complexion, plus the thatch of fair hair shouldn't, yet somehow do, make for a pleasing picture. Mick, I guess, could best be described as unconventionally handsome.

"What are you doing here?" cries Caroline. "You're meant to be down in Wicklow."

"I am, but in the words of the great bard, 'Absence from those we love is self from self – a deadly banishment'."

"What?" asks Caroline.

Switching from his perfect Shakespearian accent back to his own strong Cork one, Mick now tells her: "I was missing you so much I decided to sneak away and come and see you."

Now he comes over and pulls Caroline up from her seat, turns her fully to him, puts his arms around her waist, lifts her and plants a big kiss on her mouth. Then he burrows his face in her blonde hair and breathes in her scent. "God! I missed you!"

"And me, you," she says softly and tightly hugs him back.

But, though Mick may be a big strong fellow Caroline is no lightweight either and, pretty soon he finds he has to put her down again. Becoming aware that we're all sitting there enjoying Caroline's transformation from bossy business-woman to Mick's love thing, she now looks over at us.

"What are you all staring at?" she demands.

With the addition of some extra ingredients garnered from around the kitchen, the stir-fry has been stretched to feed all of us and now – our meeting and Shane and Loretta's plans for the night abandoned – we're squashed around the table eating. Caroline is squeezed in beside Mick and looking as happy as can be – far more relaxed than she was earlier. As we eat, the questions start coming at Mick, about this new and exciting life he's leading.

"So tell us," Dana asks, "what's Kevin North really like?" North is directing *Fate Farm*.

Mick looks up from his plate. He shrugs. "He's fine."

"Fine? That's it?"

"Yeah," says Mick. "Fine."

"And?" demands Dana

"And, what?" ask Mick.

"And what else? Tell us something more about him."

Mick shrugs. "Like what? There's not much to say about him really. I just like him, a lot. He's very good at what he does. He knows how to get the best out of people."

"What about Audrey Turner?" asks Dana. Audrey Turner is the well-known American actress who's been cast in the female lead.

"She's fine too."

"That's all you have to say?" Dana looks at him, bewildered. "You know, you really are something else, Mick!"

"What do you mean?"

"I mean this is just so like you. There you are, plucked from obscurity and thrown into the company of all these famous people and you're not in the slightest bit phased. Don't you realise just how fascinating the rest of us find it all? What's the point in you meeting all these famous people if you can't give us the inside gossip?"

"There is none."

"Sure there is, I want to hear how Audrey Turner eats

nothing but lettuce leaves. I want to hear how she keeps everyone on the set waiting for hours and hours on end."

Mick shakes his head. "Sorry to disappoint you but she's not like that at all. Quite the opposite, as it happens. She's always very professional, always mindful of the fact that she is just one cog in the whole process. She has no airs whatsoever. As for lettuce leaves? Nah – she's not a lettuce leaf kind of girl. She piles her plate as high as anyone at lunch-time," he says admiringly. "I don't know where she puts it – she's so skinny!"

"She probably spends hours working out," remarks Caroline.

"No, I don't think so and if she does she should stop. There's nothing finer than a woman with a little bit of meat on her bones." He puts his arm around Caroline's not inconsiderable waist and gives it a squeeze, leaving Caroline looking none-too-happy at this back-handed compliment, not that Mick notices. "Take Caroline here. Look at the pile on her plate. She's not worried about counting calories, thank goodness." As Caroline looks around the table, comparing her plate to everyone else's, Mick obliviously carries on in the same theme. "Anyone with a good appetite for food has a good appetite for living and, as Jackie Gleason once said, 'Thin people are beautiful, fat people are adorable.'"

The rest of us hold our breath and nervously wait.

"Are you saying –" asks Caroline after a few moments during which the only person oblivious to the tension is Mick, "– I'm fat?"

"No, you're exactly the right size. Absolutely perfect." He leans over and kisses her. "Perfect!" Then, he reverts to his original topic. "Course, Audrey has her hands full, her children are with her." Then he smiles. "One thing though, she's shocking at the Irish accent. I like her a lot but I do wonder why they didn't cast an Irish actress in the role."

"Is she as bad as Julia Roberts in that Michael Collins film?" asks Dana.

"Worse."

"As bad as Nicole Kidman in that other movie? What was it again?"

"*Far and Away?*" suggests Loretta.

"Yeah, that's the one. Is she as bad as that?"

"God, no!" says Mick with such horror that the rest of us laugh.

Mick really seems to be having the time of his life on set – I'm glad for him. It's nice to see good things happen to good people. Caroline, I notice, is quiet however. Maybe she's still bristling at Mick's 'fat' comments but she's generally pretty thick-skinned and not one to take offence, especially when none was intended. She knows Mick adores the very ground she walks on. But now, she suddenly cuts in.

"Did I tell you, Mick, we're meeting Monica to discuss changes to the shop on Thursday?"

Mick looks at her, a little taken aback at this sudden change of topic.

"That's great," he says.

"Go on, Mick," urges Dana, "tell us more about Audrey Turner."

"Well," Mick laughs, "she does have this voice coach, a strange little fellow who claims to be from Belfast but I've heard him tutoring her and to be honest I think he's only making things wor –"

Again, Caroline interrupts: "You see, we'll probably need a lot more shelving than a more regular shop would."

"Caroline," I say, "we've spent enough of the evening discussing the shop. Can't you give it a rest for a while? Can't you let Mick talk? This is so much more interesting."

"Oh, sorry. Go on, Mick, please."

"Anyway, this voice coach —" but he breaks off again as Caroline suddenly stands up.

"Does anyone want a glass of water?" she asks.

We all shake our heads. She goes to the press but then makes such a racket as she searches for a glass that it's impossible for Mick to speak now.

"Caroline," he says as soon as he gets the chance, "is there something wrong?"

"No, no — of course not." There's a couple of seconds' silence. The two of them stare at one another — Mick wearing a puzzled expression, Caroline a cross one — but then, just when Mick is about to start talking again, Caroline bursts out: "Well, actually, I would like to know why you haven't asked one single question about our new business, the one I'm risking everything for, the one I'm chucking in my job for so that I can put all my energies into setting it up? Not once since you got here have you asked how it's going. Of course I know it must be exciting for you meeting all these people but I never expected you to change, *you* of all people!"

"Caroline," says Mick, looking perplexed, "I was just answering the others' questions."

"Yes, well, you don't have to go on quite so much."

"Sorry? I didn't think I was."

"Well, you were. You should just listen to yourself. On and on and on. All you seem interested in now is yourself, your film star buddies and your precious film."

"That's not fair, Caroline!" cries Dana. "We want to hear what he has to say."

Mick is staring over at Caroline now, then quietly he says: "You know, the one thing I never expected from you – you who made all this happen in the first place – is that you'd be jealous."

"I am *not* jealous. Don't be ridiculous! Me? All I'm saying is that because you're so interested in yourself you have no interest in what I'm doing."

"That's not true."

"Well, it looks that way to me. How else would you explain the fact that you haven't asked a single question about the shop since you got here?"

Mick nods his head gravely. "Okay then, the reason I didn't ask is well, quite frankly, I don't approve."

"You don't approve?"

"No, I don't. Every time we've talked on the phone, I've listened to you going on and on and on and I haven't said anything but, Caroline, I know you. I know you're the biggest cynic in the world. I know you don't believe in any of this stuff. It seems to me that all you want to do is make money out of other people's foolishness."

"That's not true."

"It is. If you're going to start a business then why can't it be something that is really of use?"

Caroline looks around the table at all of us and, afraid I'll be drawn into this argument, I cast my eyes down at my plate. I guess Loretta isn't so quick.

"Loretta, do you think what we're doing is wrong?" she demands.

"Of course she does!" explodes Mick. "She's a doctor, isn't she?"

"Is that right? Do you?"

Loretta thinks for a moment, weighing up her words

carefully. "Well, I don't know if it's wrong *per se*. I'm pretty open to complementary medicines but love potions are just too big a leap for me."

"And you, what about you, Shane?" demands Caroline.

Shane shrugs. "I know I've been winding you up but that's because you're so intense about the whole thing but, in actual fact, I think it's a great idea."

"There!" Caroline gives a satisfied nod of her head.

But Shane's not finished yet. "People are forever being exploited – you might as well have a piece of a pie. I wish I'd thought of it."

Even though Shane's words could be Caroline's own she doesn't look too happy.

All this time Doug is sitting there, barely saying a word as usual and it doesn't even occur to Caroline to ask him his opinion but, even though Dana says that Doug finds Caroline really scary, now he draws her attention to him with a nervous cough.

"What?" demands Caroline. "Have you something to say on the matter too?"

"Ah . . ." Doug hesitates. We're all waiting. "Ah, just that I really don't understand what the problem is." Underneath his tanned skin, he looks like he's actually blushing at all the attention he's getting. I know that when they're on their own, Dana and Doug are always chatting, I hear them sometimes, but when the rest of us are about he's usually content to listen. Yet now, despite his obvious discomfort, he goes on: "If taking a potion makes people more open to the idea of love then that has to be a good thing doesn't it?"

"There!" says Caroline, triumphantly. "At least someone gets what we're trying to do. Thank you, Doug." She turns back to Mick. "You know, I expected a little more support from you, like the support you got from me when you were auditioning for *Fate Farm* but it seems you don't have it in you to give."

"Caroline, look I'm sorry but –"

She cuts him off. "I don't want to talk about it any more."

"Caroline, listen, I jus –"

"Is there any more food left?" Caroline asks Shane.

"Ah yeah – lots."

Caroline carries her plate over to the cooker and spoons out another helping.

"Anyone else want some more?" she asks.

We shake our heads. I don't know about the others but my appetite has disappeared, as has all the good in the evening. This hastily cobbled-together meal doesn't feel quite so much fun any more.

Does absinthe make the heart grow fonder?

9

I haven't seen Finn all week. I've been holed up in the kitchen experimenting. Now, pleased with the progress I've made, I've invited everyone around for a potion-tasting night. Mick is even driving up from Wicklow for it. It wasn't too hard to persuade him. I think he sees tonight as an opportunity to patch things up with Caroline. They didn't part on the best of terms that last night he was here.

The first to arrive is Finn.

"You're early," I say as I lead him into the kitchen.

"I wanted to talk to you before the others came."

"Sure. Fire ahead." But then I notice the pot bubbling on the stove. "Oh yikes! My chakra is about to boil over!" I dash across the kitchen, pull the pan from the flame and hurriedly put it down on the draining board. "Whew, that was close! Okay, where's my recipe? What's next?"

I search through the mess on the counter for the recipe I printed out from my computer, find it, and begin to read, at the same time telling Finn: "Go on, what is it you want to say to me?"

"Maybe I've leave it until later."

"I need more juice," I say to myself. "Hmm?" I say to him.

"I'll wait until you're not so busy."

Half an hour later, I ask Finn to call the others into the kitchen. Dana, Doug, Loretta and Shane come filing in, all looking keen.

"Something smells good," says Loretta.

"Where are Mick and Caroline?" I ask. "Caroline!" I shout out. "Come on, we're waiting!"

"Coming!" she shouts back, then moments later she and Mick come in, hand-in-hand, looking flushed and giddy – clearly they've made up. Caroline flops down at the table and Mick comes over to where I'm standing by the cooker.

"Hmm!" he peers into the pots.

I ladle out a glass from one and hand it to him.

"So what's this?" he asks, eyeing it up somewhat suspiciously.

"It's called Red-to-Orange Chakra Express," I announce.

"And what's in it?"

"A whole host of things – cloves, cinnamon, astragalus, star anise, nutmeg, gingerroot, fennel, bay leaf."

"Where did you find all this stuff?" he asks. "Hardly in the local supermarket?"

"Well, some I did get there but others I ordered online, like the star anise and astragalus."

It's the weirdest thing but admitting that bothers me a little. Part of me would have liked to have grown everything myself. Of course, it was never going to happen – Caroline's tight time schedule allowed no time to cultivate a little herb garden. But maybe down the line, if this thing takes off, I could look into growing some of my own. Caroline might be impressed if I told her how much we'd save by doing it that way. My parents would laugh if they knew of my recently discovered interest. They ran a garden centre for years but when the time came to retire they found that none of their children were interested in carrying on the business so they sold it. I think it disappointed them a little but that's not to say they aren't enjoying their retirement. They're home from their American holiday now but I haven't had a chance to meet them yet, I've been so busy researching and experimenting. I haven't told them about the shop so far. A couple of times when on the phone to Mum, I've been about to fill her in but dreading her reaction – the incredulity, the shock, the disappointment – I've lost my nerve each time: "You're what! You're selling love potions! Ah Rosie! After all the money we spent on your education! Your dad will be so disappointed!" She always says Dad will be so disappointed when what she really means is she will – or is – too. So for now I've held off telling them.

Mick swills the first mouthful around then swallows. "Hmm, nice!"

"So you like it?" I ask nervously.

He nods, and takes another sip.

"I forgot to mention," I add, "there's two bottles of Beaujolais in there as well."

Now Mick closes his eyes, puts his head down and stays perfectly still for ten, fifteen seconds while we all sit there, staring at him. Then, suddenly, he lifts up his head again. His eyes are wide open now. He turns his head to Caroline and begins staring at her in a weird, glassy-eyed way and then he leaves out a long, low wolf whistle.

"Wow! Baby! You are *hot!*" He leaves his glass down on the counter, hurries over to her, pulls her up from her seat.

"Hey, let's get out of here! There's something you and I need to do!" He begins nuzzling into the side of her neck.

"Stop Mick. Stop right now!" cries Caroline. "Quit messing!"

"Messing! I'm not messing. I'm deadly serious! I swear this stuff is magic. I was wrong!"

But Caroline is having none of it. "Just cut it out, Mick." She pushes him away and sits down again, glaring at him.

"Come on, Caroline. I was only having a laugh. We were getting on so well – I thought you'd find it funny."

"*Were* getting on but then you had to spoil it all by making a laugh out of it. Why did you have to go and do that?"

He stares at her for a moment. "Because this whole thing is a joke."

They're both staring crossly at one another now.

Mick turns to me. "Are you sure this is the right recipe? Or is it an antidote for love?"

This is hardly an auspicious start, I think.

"Come on," says Shane, "let the rest of us try some!"

I begin handing out glasses to the others.

Dana takes a sip. "This is really nice," she says, smacking her lips. "Well done."

"Why, thanks," I say.

"One thing . . ."

"What?"

"You said there was wine in it?"

"Yeah, wine is what's known as a psychoactive substance."

"What's that?" asks Shane.

"A substance that acts on the pysche. It doesn't mean it's an aphrodisiac *per se* but it has an effect on the mind."

"Hmm, it's certainly worked on you from time to time, hasn't it, Rosie?" laughs Shane.

"Leave it out!"

"Come on, you've donned a pair of beer goggles more often than most."

Shane may be telling the truth but that doesn't mean I want to hear him joking about my past, not in front of Finn.

"What I mean is," says Dana, getting back to her original point, "are you sure it's okay to include alcohol in the ingredients we use since we don't have a licence?"

"I never thought of that." I look at Caroline.

"I wouldn't worry," she says. "Like who's going to know?"

"I guess," I say hesitantly.

Dana looks like she's about to say something but then she shrugs and lets it go.

"What else have you got?" asks Doug.

"What?" I look at his empty glass. "You're finished already?"

"That was delicious." He smacks his lips and grins.

I pour out a glass of my next concoction. "I haven't a name for this one yet, but it's got cinnamon, spikenard and wormwood in it."

"Wormwood? Ugh!" protests Dana. "I'm not drinking anything with them in it!"

"Pardon?

"I'm not drinking anything with worms."

"Not woodworm! *Wormwood!* It's a herb and one of the bitterest known."

"A herb? Are you sure?" she asks.

"Yep and, interestingly, it's used in the making of absinthe," I say, handing her the glass. "Try it!"

"Absinthe? Isn't that what rotted all those nineteenth century French poets' and writers' brains?" asks Mick.

I shrug. "Don't worry. Your brain will be fine. This is perfectly safe."

Dana eyes up the glass distastefully. "If it's okay with you, I'll pass."

She gives the glass to Doug who shares none of her reservations and downs it in a couple of swallows.

"Great!" he says.

I smile, relieved at his reaction.

"Okay, Dana, this is one I think you will like," I say, handing her a fresh glass.

"What's in it?" she asks.

"Well, I combined milk, cloves, cardamom and cinnamon in a saucepan, scraped in some vanilla-pod seeds and then gently heated the mixture. Next I refrigerated it and, once it was chilled, I strained out the spices before blending in milk, yoghurt, honey and ice cream until it was smooth and frothy. Because there's milk and ice cream in it, we'll have to make it up in small batches and keep it refrigerated."

I hand glasses to everyone else, then wait for their response.

"Hmm. This is delicious!" says Caroline.

"Is there any more?" asks Doug.

"Yeah, sure."

I feel quite chuffed that my potions are all going down so well.

"I can't believe you made this," says Shane. "It's delicious!"

I shrug modestly. "I was only following the recipe," I say, handing out more glasses. "But I have some ideas of my own that I will try out now that I'm getting a feeling for what goes well with what."

"You're really getting into this, aren't you, Rosie?" notes Loretta.

I shrug. But she's right. I have enjoyed doing all the research and coming up with these recipes much more than I thought I would. And whether they work or not, at least people will get something tasty for the money they hand over. I guess that's my way of justifying my involvement.

Afterwards, Shane suggests we all go out. Mick says he can't, that he needs to head back to Wicklow, but everyone else bar me and Finn go.

With Finn's help, I set about tidying up the kitchen.

"So what is it you wanted to talk to me about?" I ask, now that we have the place to ourselves again.

"I'm moving out of my dad's and back to my own house."

"Oh, Finn, that's brilliant!"

"It's about time, I guess."

"Your dad will find it hard but it's probably for the best in the long run."

"I think so. The second thing is, we're going to reform the band."

"No!"

"Yeah! I've met the lads a few times lately and we've decided it's time."

"But you've no vocalist. Who's going to take Mark's place?"

"A girl called Lola."

"Lola?"

"Yeah. She was the lead singer with Griffin, you may have heard of them. They're a Dublin band that were based in London for the last few years. They were doing quite well but then they broke up a couple of months back and now Lola has just moved home. She's a fantastic singer and she writes some great songs too."

"But you're the songwriter in the band?"

"There's no reason it has to be only me. We may even collaborate on some songs – we've been talking about it. Back in school we once wrote a song together for an end of term concert."

"She was in school with you?"

"Yeah. In the same class, as it happens."

I'm a little puzzled. "But if she's so good, and if you've known her so long, how come she wasn't part of Dove, right from the start?"

"Mark was never keen on having a second vocalist. Besides he and Lola . . . well, there was some history there."

"Oh?"

"Yeah." He doesn't elaborate.

"History?"

"Yeah."

"What do you mean exactly?"

"Mark had a thing for her in school but she was too smart to get involved with him."

"Unlike, say, me?"

"Pardon?"

"She was smarter than me then?"

"I guess she knew him a little better."

"I see. So, ah, what's she like, this Lola?"

Finn thinks for a moment. "Kind of intense, kind of serious."

Good, I think, and I picture someone squat with thick glasses and short red hair like the non-pretty one, Velma, I think, in *Scooby-Dooby-Doo* but Finn quickly smashes that particular comforting image.

"But she has a pretty wild side too. She got expelled in sixth year for skinny-dipping during the school trip to France."

That would never happen to Velma. Now I see Ursula Andress but *without* her white bikini top coming out of the waves.

"Seems a stupid thing to do!" I say.

Finn shrugs. "We were just kids."

We? Why does he say *we*? *We* implies that somehow he was involved.

Finn looks at me. "You'll like her, Rosie."

"Sure, sure." Will I? Will I really? And how would he know?

"And you'll meet her soon enough. She's going to move in with me."

"Pardon?"

"It makes sense."

Sense? How? Perhaps he's mixed up the words 'sense' and 'nonsense'.

He goes on, obliviously. "Since she came back from London she's been living with her parents so she's anxious to find her own place."

Am I hearing right? Is my boyfriend calmly standing there, telling me that another woman is moving in with him? Someone who's kind of intense, kind of serious but – hey – has a pretty wild side too? The kind who gets expelled from school for skinny-dipping? Am I expected to be pleased? Isn't this the kind of thing he should perhaps have discussed with me *before* coming to a decision?

Totally oblivious to the havoc he's wreaking, he keeps on talking. "It's time I moved out of my dad's and back to my own home. It'll be good for me to have someone else in the house. It'll help with the mortgage for starters and as well it'll mean it won't be so – so, well, lonesome."

He looks a little embarrassed at this last word but I

understand exactly what he's saying. With Lola for company, Mark's absence won't be so striking.

He's still talking: "Besides, it'll be a great opportunity to work together on our music, to get really stuck into it. I think I'm finally ready for that too now."

"I see."

I do see. I really do. I'd be blind not to. All this means that Finn is finally progressing, recovering, getting back to normal. So how can I possibly object? To do so would make me the most selfish, insecure person in the world. But I'm not happy with this Lola person moving in with my boyfriend, with the pair of them working together. An image comes to me. An image that is far too cosy for my liking. This Lola and my Finn, the two of them as thick as thieves, sitting on the couch together, making up songs.

"You're okay with all this, aren't you, Rosie?"

No! No! No! I want to shout. Sure, I know Finn has a hard time getting over Mark. Sure, I can see his music career has all but disappeared. Sure, I'd like to see him moving out of his dad's and back into his own home again. Sure, I want him to be happy more than anything. Sure, I do. And, because I do, I find myself nodding.

"Sure, I'm okay with it." What else can I say?

Finn leaves soon after dropping his bombshell and I'm sitting at the kitchen table, considering the fallout. What should I do? Ring him as soon as he gets home and tell him that, on further reflection, I'm not in the slightest bit happy? But what does that say about me? That I don't trust him? That I don't want him to move on with his life? That I don't want him to move back to his own house? That I don't want him to restart the band? But I do. I'd like to see all these things happening for him. What I don't like is how this Lola seems to be tied up with them all.

"Hiya!"

I look up. It's Dana in her dressing-gown.

"Hey! I thought you went out with the others."

"No." She gives an embarrassed little laugh. "Doug – well – he decided we should stay in instead." She goes to put on the kettle.

"Oh, yeah?" I give a knowing look.

"Want a cuppa?" she asks, hastily changing the subject.

"No, thanks."

She looks at me. "Is something up, Rosie? You look very serious."

"I'm not sure. Finn has just told me he's reforming the band. Some old school friend is going to be their new lead singer."

"That's great!"

I shrug. "Some old school friend who happens to be female and who happens to be looking for somewhere to live as well so she's also going to move into his house with him."

"I see."

"I suppose you're going to tell me that there's nothing to worry about."

She shrugs. "I don't know."

I look over at her in surprise.

"What do you mean, you don't know? I thought you'd tell me to wise up, that Finn is Finn, that he's crazy about me, that I've no need to worry."

"I'm sure you don't. But I think any woman would be foolish to be complacent about any man. I mean, who knows how they tick? The way they work is a mystery. I think you should just be careful, keep an eye on things, make sure she knows you're around."

"I see." Now I feel more worried than ever.

"But," Dana continues, "if you're really not happy maybe you should tell him."

"I can't, not in the circums –"

"Dana!"

I'm interrupted by a shout from upstairs. It's Doug.

Dana shakes her head and throws her eyes to heaven. "I thought he was sleeping. He was worn out when I left him." Then she gives this sly smile. "You know, Rosie, maybe there's something to your potions after all."

One old tradition has it that swallowing a
four-leaf clover while thinking of your beloved will make
him reciprocate your love.

Maybe giving him a call and telling him how you feel
might be more effective. But, if you do go down the clover
route, it might be best to keep it quiet. You don't want him
thinking you're a complete crazy.

10

I don't ring Finn the following day but, then, when I don't hear from him by the day after I try his mobile a couple of times throughout the morning but still I get no response.

I decide to ring his dad's place.

"Hi, Mr Heelan, this is Rosie. Is Finn there?"

"Sorry, Rosie, love, you missed him. He and his friend Lola dropped by for the van first thing and loaded it up with some more of his stuff. I think they said they were calling by her parents' house as well to collect the rest of her things. They'll probably carry on to his place then. You might catch him there."

I'm taken aback. Okay, I know he said he was moving back to his own house but I kind of figured he was talking in general terms, sometime, in the undefined future. What exactly does Mr Heelan mean when he says Finn dropped by? Have they already moved in? Like, hello, where's the fire?

"Okay," I say. "Maybe I'll give him a ring there. Thanks, Mr Heelan."

When I hang up, I try his old house number but it rings out. So where is he? I try not to be bothered by the fact that I can't reach him but I am. I'm bothered by the fact that I can't reach him *and* he's with Lola. Not that I suspect him of anything untoward. I trust Finn. But this Lola? Well, what do I know of her? Not a lot. But if she has two brain cells to rub together she'll appreciate just how special Finn is.

In the end I can't stand it any longer and I borrow Caroline's car and drive over to Finn's. When I arrive there's no sign of Mr Heelan's van but parked in the driveway is an oh-so-cutsey spanking-new yellow convertible Volkswagen Beetle. Lola's? Of course. What else would someone with such an oh-so-cutsey name drive? I get out and walk up the driveway noticing as I do the bumper sticker: *Here I am! Now what are your other two wishes*? No shrinking violet then, this Lola, but I guess I knew that already what with her sixth-year expulsion for skinny-dipping. I ring the doorbell, wait, ring it again, and, when I still don't get an answer, I go to the front window and peer in.

It's been months since Finn lived here and, now, not having seen it in so long, I look at it with fresh eyes. I'd half-forgotten all the work he'd carried out on the place when he first bought it. Taking what was a very ordinary 1960's council house he managed to transform it into something special. From the front it still looks pretty standard but inside he completely transformed it. He knocked out all the dividing walls downstairs making it into one big open-plan room. He did away with most of the external back wall too at ground level and replaced it with folding glass doors that open onto a tiny patio with a little pond. The original staircase he ripped out and replaced with a sleek glass one which now descends into this ultra-modern, ultra-bright open-plan interior, all white walls with dashes of bold colour provided by the red couch, the bright green kitchen fittings and the gallery-sized paintings – marvellous paintings created by Finn. Now looking through the front window, seeing all Finn's work afresh – the changes to the house, his paintings – it strikes me how, if music wasn't his overriding passion, he could carve out a career in design or in art.

Being here again for the first time after so long brings back memories. Like of that first night I stayed here with Mark, the night of Finn's big party – the one he threw for the express purpose of having an excuse to invite me but of course his plan didn't work out quite as he'd hoped. I remember the shocked expression on Finn's upturned face in the crowd when I happened to glance down as Mark and I climbed that glass stairs hand in hand. That night, none of us – me, Finn, Mark – had a clue how tragically events would play out. God, someone or other once said, made the world round so we'd never be able to see too far down the road.

Enough of this moroseness, I think. I should go. But then I begin to notice all the little changes, little differences since Mark and Finn lived here together. Finn's drum kit now stands in the living area whereas it used to be in his bedroom, and on the couch lie two guitars. One I recognise as Finn's – he plays it in addition to the drums. The other is a shocking pink electric bass – Lola's? A picture comes to mind, of the two of them sitting there long into the night, not noticing the hours slip away, so engrossed are they in writing songs together. No, I do not like this at all. Nor do I like the other obvious signs of my boyfriend's new lodger. I've heard my mother use the expression – *he's got his feet under the table* – and by that she means someone who's well settled where they shouldn't necessarily be so well settled. What then, would she make of the shaggy boho red sleeveless jacket hanging on the back of one of the kitchen chairs and those sweet little green diamanté pumps casually abandoned on the wooden floor? Oh yes, this Lola has definitely got her feet under the table, or curled up beneath her as she sits on the couch, as she sits there all cosy alongside my boyfriend, strumming that guitar of hers.

I may not have met her yet but one thing I know for sure is that I do not like this pink-guitar-strumming, red-boho-jacket-wearing, green-diamanté-shoed, yellow-beetle-driving woman, at all, at all.

I turn from the window, go back past her cutesy car with its cutesy message (and, I notice, furry pink dice – how very droll) parked so smugly in my boyfriend's driveway and get into the car I borrowed from Caroline, suddenly acutely conscious of the fact that I don't even own a car, cutesy or otherwise. Then, just as I'm about to put the key in the ignition, a text comes through. Finn, I think, but it's not. It's from my mother – the queen of texting.

– *Rem. Dinner tonite @ 8.*

Damn, I'd forgotten. Knowing how judgmental my mother can be about my boyfriends (and in the past she's had good reason) I hadn't really told her much about Finn at all and I've put off letting them meet one another. But, when Dana bumped into Mum in town, soon after my parents got back from the States, she obviously sang his praises and, ever since, Mum's been on and on at me to bring him around until, finally, I gave in. I agreed that we'd both come to dinner tonight but, the only trouble is, I've forgotten to tell Finn. I text her back.

– Not sure if Finn will b able 2 come.

They say that when people hit their forties they lose their ability to adapt to new technology. Well, not my mum. Yes, she's in her sixties; yes, she likes to complain that she's not getting any younger; yes, she's had arthritis now for a while; yes, she's been known to moan that there's no keeping up with all these modern changes – yet, despite all this, she's as nimble-fingered a texter as any teenager and almost instantly I get a text back.

– Ah Rosie! Tell me u haven't split up already. He's so nice.

I respond immediately.

– How do u know? You've never met him! And, no, we haven't split up.

Seconds later I get a beep in reply.

– Good. Well bring him so. Ur father & I r dying 2 meet him. Dat is the whole point of the dinner.

Dat? Dat? Dat! This from the woman who'd have blown a gasket if I'd ever dared mangle the English language in such a fashion when growing up, the woman who signed me up for a childhood of Saturday mornings doing speech and drama lessons. *Dat!*

I try Finn's mobile again – no answer. I think what to do and then decide to post a note through his letter box. I find a notebook in the pocket of Caroline's car door and jot down my mother's invitation and then I think for a second and add a whole load of kisses and hearts, as much for Lola's attention as Finn's. I climb back out of the car and post the note through the letterbox.

At around five, I finally get a call from Finn.

"Hi, hon," he begins, "I've only just got your note. I've been tearing busy all day."

I think about peevishly asking if he got any of my texts but think better of it, but then think again, and do peevishly ask: "Didn't you get any of my texts?"

"No, sorry, in the middle of the chaos I mislaid my charger. I've only just found it."

"I didn't realise you were moving quite so soon."

"Once I'd decided, there didn't seem any point in hanging about."

So it seems, I think but don't say.

"So," I say instead, "are you on for tonight?"

"For meeting your parents? I guess. I can pick you up. It'd be easier. It's on my way. Dad's van is still full of the stuff I collected this morning – we got sidetracked – but Lola says I can borrow her car."

My gut reaction is to refuse but there's no logical reason to do so. He's right. It would be easier this way.

"Sure," I tell him. "See you around seven then."

When I hang up, a thought occurs to me. Just what does he mean exactly when he says 'we got sidetracked'?

The first thing I notice about Finn when I open the door are his shoes. Every other aspect of his appearance is as it always is. His curly hair is no wilder or longer than usual. He's wearing his customary uniform of jeans, T-shirt and black velvet jacket. Yes, all is as it always is except for the rather startling pair of black and white chequered plimsolls. Yes plimsolls, black and white ones, with checks, big noticeable checks.

He spots me looking at them.

"Like them?" he asks, proudly holding out one foot for closer examination.

I stare at them, then at him, then back down at the shoes again, not sure how to react.

"They're interesting," I tell him finally, settling for diplomacy.

"Interesting?"

"Yeah."

"Interesting?"

"Well, they may take a little getting used to –"

His brow furrows at my lack of enthusiasm.

"– but they're very rock-star chic," I quickly add. "I guess if you're in a band you need to look the part. And anyway, who decreed that men should stick to boring footwear?"

"Exactly. That's just what Lola said."

"Lola?"

"Yeah."

Did she now? A thought occurs to me. "Was she with you when you bought them?"

"Ah yeah – she was the one who spotted them in the window."

"You were shopping together?"

"Not exactly – just buying some groceries for the house. Lola doesn't like supermarkets. She disapproves of the way a lot of the food has such a big carbon footprint, you know, with the air miles involved and the plastic wrapping and that. And so little of it is organic too. So we went to this farmer's market she knows instead and on the way we happened to pass this little shoe shop."

Okay, I know it's not written down or anything but surely one of life's rules is that another woman should never, ever, ever help pick out someone else's boyfriend's footwear. Like, I've known Shane far longer than Loretta has, he's my oldest friend, but it would never occur to me to get involved in what he does or does not wear on his feet. What next?

Where will it all end? Picking out socks? Underwear? Grooming products? Carrying out his actual grooming?

Totally oblivious to the fact that his audience may not exactly be thrilled with what she's hearing, Finn rattles on: "When Lola saw them in the window she said they could have been made for me."

"Did she now?"

"Yeah."

The deliberately jarringly sarcastic note in my voice does not jar his consciousness one little bit. He nods his head and remains thoroughly engrossed in his admiration of his new footwear as we walk to Lola's car. When we reach it, he opens the passenger's door for me and I climb in but before I sit down I pick up the book lying on the passenger's seat and read the title: Milan Kundera's *The Unbearable Lightness of Being*. But, of course, what else? Not for our Lola the latest blockbuster. As he gets in beside me, Finn notices the book in my hand.

"Have you ever read it?" he asks.

I shake my head. I read the title again, aloud this time: "*The Unbearable Lightness of Being*" and then, lest he think I'm less knowledgeable than her, I add offhandedly: "But I have heard of it, of course. Have you read it?"

"Not yet but I'm going to. Lola says it's brilliant. It's one of her all-time favourites."

I read the blurb aloud. "*The Unbearable Lightness of Being is a rich and complicated novel that is at once a love story, a metaphysical treatise, a political commentary, a psychological study, a lesson on kitsch, a musical composition in words, an aesthetic exploration, and a meditation on human existence. Kundera draws upon his first-hand experience of the 1968 Prague Spring and subsequent Soviet occupation of his country to provide the backdrop for the story of four people whose lives are inextricably enmeshed.*" I put it down. "So what exactly makes it one of her favourites?"

"She says she likes the whole central idea behind it. She says that the unbearable lightness of being refers to the fact that because each of us has only one life to live then what happens to us might as well never happen because each life is ultimately insignificant and every decision ultimately does not matter. The insignificance of our decisions, our lives, is unbearable."

"So Lola likes a little light bedtime reading then?"

I glance over at him, expecting him to laugh and when he doesn't I feel disappointed. What's happening here? Until the other day I was totally unaware that my boyfriend even had a friend called Lola. And now, mere days later, it's become all Lola says this, Lola likes that. It's like suddenly she's the main person in his life. They're living in the same house, they've spent the day grocery-shopping together, picking out questionable shoes, engaging in existential angst and, now, he's driving us about in her cutsey yellow car complete with those bloody furry dice. How did all this happen, and so quickly? I don't get it.

And what's with Leonard Cohen on the CD player? Doesn't this woman do light?

"Do you mind if I change the CD?" I ask.

"I thought you liked Leonard Cohen?"

"No, no, not really." Not any more I don't.

"Why don't you put on something else so? Lola has loads more CDs in the glove compartment."

"Course she does," I mutter as I lean forward to open it.

"What?"

"I said, of course she does. I mean she would, wouldn't she? Being a singer and all."

I take out a handful and look through them: The Beatles' *Sgt Pepper's Lonely Hearts Club Band*; Mozart's Violin Concertos Nos. 1, 2 & 5; Nick Cave's *The Boatman's Call*; Amy Winehouse's *Back to Black*; Johnny Cash's *At Folsam Prison*. God, this women is infuriating. Could she possibly have a more rounded taste in music? I say nothing and shove the lot back in.

My parents live an hour's drive outside the city and during the journey Finn doesn't mention her again. Despite his male obtuseness, maybe he does subconsciously sense something of my antipathy towards her. Instead he asks me questions about my parents and I chat on about them telling him all sorts of stuff, a lot of which he already knows. I tell him how last year they sold the garden centre they'd run together for years and years, and then, determined to enjoy their retirement to the full they went to visit my sister who lives in Australia. How days after they returned my father became very ill and was rushed to hospital and nearly died from a perforated duodenal ulcer. I tell him how when my dad came home my mother nursed him back to health and, as soon as he'd recovered, they resumed their living-life-to-the-full resolution with a vengeance, no doubt spurred on by having come face-to-face with the mortality of one of them. I tell him how they've only just returned from the US where they spent four weeks staying in turn with each of my brothers, both of whom are married and are living with their families there.

I stick to facts. Trying to describe what my parents are actually like, my mother especially, would be too difficult and, besides, he'll meet her soon enough.

It's my mother who opens the door and, to her credit, she does so quite casually, like she hasn't been hovering for the last twenty minutes in anticipation, though I'd put money on the fact. Quickly, however, at the sight of a boyfriend, a real-life boyfriend who's lasted more than a wet weekend, a boyfriend for the daughter she feared would end up on the shelf, legs a-dangling for evermore, a flesh and blood boyfriend who she's actually meeting in the flesh and blood, a boyfriend who is her ticket to joining in boastful conversations with her bridge and golfing buddies about their twenty-something children, conversations my heretofore spectacularly unsuccessful love life and matching work life have largely excluded her from, well, suddenly, the enormity of the occasion strikes her and she loses her equanimity.

"So this is Finn!" she cries and grabs him and clasps him to her bosom. My mother is a big woman, Finn is not a big man and, when she finally releases him, he's a little winded but thankfully unharmed – no broken bones.

"Come in, come in!" she cries and then links Finn by the arm and heads off down the hall with him so briskly that his black and white chequered plimsolls barely touch the floor and all the time she's calling to my father, positively triumphantly, like some victorious warlord returning with wartime booty: "Will! Will! Rosie and her boyfriend are here!"

I follow them and as I do I meet my dad coming down the stairs.

"Rosie, love, lovely to see you," he says and holds out his arms for a hug

"You too," I say, hugging him, feeling the change in him as I do so. Since his health scare he's become very careful with his diet and has lost his pot belly. This is a good thing, I know, but I kind of preferred the way he felt before.

"So you brought him then?" he asks as we pull apart.

"I did."

"Did you warn him about your mother?"

I shake my head. "I didn't want to scare him off."

Dad laughs now, then links my arm, and we follow after them.

Mum has pulled out all the stops. She's covered the table in the seldom-used dining-room with a white cloth and set it with her good china, glassware and cutlery; she's opened a couple of nice bottles of wine, one red, one white; and she's even lit the fire in the grate – the last time there was a fire would have been Christmas and, just like at Christmas time, the room is terribly warm – the blazing fire is far too much for what is a small room made even smaller by the oversized mahogany antique furniture inherited from Dad's mother. Going by past performances, I'd give my dad until the main course before he dozes off.

"So, Finn," Mum is saying, "you sit down there opposite Rosie, and, Will, you sit at the head. Yes, that's right. Perfect. Well now, everything is ready so we may as well begin. I'll just go and get the starters."

With Mum gone from the room, the three of us sit in silence. Dad isn't great at small talk when it comes to strangers – Mum tends to do it for the pair of them. I'm happy for this little bit of peacefulness, knowing it will end the minute Mum returns. Finn is busy looking around, taking it all in. He takes off his jacket and I notice there are beads of perspiration gathering on his forehead. Moments later Mum comes back in with a tray and places a piping hot, huge bowl of thick vegetable soup down in front of each of us. She throws another log on the fire and then takes her place.

"You know, Finn, Rosie hasn't told us a thing about you

– trying to keep you a secret, I suppose. So what do you do then?"

Finn is just about to take a spoonful but now he looks up, startled. Perhaps he was expecting a little more time before the questions started, or at the least that they wouldn't be quite this direct from the outset but my mother and subtlety have never been introduced. More beads of sweat gather on his forehead. The blazing fire? The steaming soup? My mother's unwavering inquisitor's stare? All of these? His spoon remains in mid-air as he answers.

"I work with Dad. He has his own hardware business."

"Really. How interesting!"

"I guess," says Finn.

"And isn't he lucky to have you working alongside him? You know, none of our children wanted to take over the garden centre. We had to sell it after years of building it up."

Finn nods agreeably but doesn't say anything.

"Yes," Mum continues, "your dad is lucky all right to have his own son working alongside him."

I notice Finn's still nodding, like he's in total agreement, giving the impression that working with his dad is his career of choice, like he wants to do it forever.

I decide to set Mum straight.

"Finn is only working there until his music career gets off the ground."

Mum waves this piece of information away, like she doesn't really believe in such things as music careers.

"So how long has your dad been in business then?"

Finn shrugs. "I don't know. Nearly thirty years, I guess."

"And did he set it up himself?"

"Yes, he and my mum."

"And does she still work in it too?"

"No, I'm afraid my mum died when I was small."

"Oh, I am sorry." She's silent for a moment as she digests this unexpected news. "Oh dear, that is terrible," she murmurs then adds somewhat reproachfully, "Rosie never said." Suddenly she stands up and takes Finn's still near-full bowl from his place. "Here, let me get you some more soup."

Finn protests. "Mrs Kiely, I'm fine, thanks."

"No, no, there's a little left in the pot, you may as well have it. Otherwise I'll end up throwing it out."

She goes to the kitchen, then moments later returns with Finn's bowl filled to the brim. She puts it in front of him and then hovers by his chair, looking like she's trying to think of something more she can do, anything to make up for him losing his mother all those years ago. She notices the bread basket is empty and hurries off to the kitchen to fill that again too. When she returns she sets it down beside Finn. Once again she hovers.

"Do you need more wine, Finn, or more water?"

"No, no, I'm fine, Mrs Kiely."

Finn looks a little embarrassed. And very hot. He uses his napkin to wipe the sweat from his forehead.

"Mum," I say, "can't you sit down? You're making Finn uncomfortable."

"Uncomfortable! Of course, I'm not. Don't be ridiculous. I'm not making you uncomfortable, am I, Finn?"

"No, no, of course not, Mrs Kiely."

"Don't mind your 'Mrs Kiely'. Call me Nora."

Nora resumes her seat but as Finn struggles through the bowl of soup she continues to look over at him sympathetically but then, perhaps to deflect all this attention away from himself, Finn turns it to me.

"So what do you think of Rosie's new career?" he asks.

I begin shaking my head furiously at him and he looks over at me quizzically but it's too late. The words are out there now.

"Rosie's new career?" repeats my mother, looking delighted if somewhat puzzled. "What does Finn mean, Rosie? I didn't know you got a job. I didn't even know you had another interview lined up. Aren't you the dark horse? So tell us about it."

Oh God! I sit still and silent, staring at the table in front of me, knowing she's staring expectantly at me. If I say nothing, if I stay completely motionless, perhaps she'll drop it and the conversation will move on to other things. Fat chance! Like a hound dog on the scent, my mother persists.

"So, Rosie, come on. What is this new job then?"

In the absence of a better answer, I shrug.

"Will, did you hear that! Rosie has got a job!" Mum shouts at him as if he's in a different room altogether, or hard of hearing or not quite all there, mentally. "So go on," she perseveres, "tell us about it!"

"Oh, it's nothing. It's not a job *per se*, just a business idea Dana and Caroline and I are working on together."

"Oh!" My mother's brow furrows. "What sort of an idea?" she asks warily.

"An idea about setting up a business."

"Yes, dear, but what sort of business?" she asks in an overly patient voice.

I consider my words. How can I put it in terms that won't completely freak her out, in terms that she'll feel comfortable repeating boastfully to her friends.

"Amm . . . devising a range of herbal drinks," I finally answer.

I notice Finn look over at me, a little surprised.

"Herbal drinks?" repeats Mum. "What sort of herbal drinks exactly?"

"You know, with herbs," I hedge.

"Like energy drinks or something?" asks my dad.

"Yeah, something like that."

They're both staring at me, looking like they're not quite sure how they should react. To help them, I decide to emphasise the positive. "You'll be glad to know I'm using my science degree. My role is to research all the various ingredients and to come up with new tastes." My mother is still looking a little confused, as well she might, so to stave off awkward questions I quickly plough on: "We're going to sell them from our own premises, from Monica's old shop."

"I see," says Mum cagily and I can hardly blame her. Even this, though more palatable than the truth, is hardly the career trajectory she might have expected. The best thing to do, I think, is to change the subject completely.

"You know, Mick's getting on great down in Wicklow. He's having a ball of a time."

She doesn't respond immediately. She clearly has a lot more questions to ask but she's conscious of the need to be a good hostess in front of her guest and she allows the subject to drop, at least until she has me on my own.

"I guess it's time for the main course. Rosie, do you want to come into the kitchen to give me a hand?" she asks, getting to her feet.

I'm wise to her, there's no way she's getting me on my own so I pretend I don't hear and turn all my attention to Dad, telling him all about Mick. Chances are, he probably doesn't even know which friend I'm talking about. He's always confused when it comes to just who is exactly who amongst my friends and now the heat won't be helping his concentration, but still I babble on.

The rest of the meal goes okay. We get on to the safe subject of their recent holiday and they, or rather my mum on their behalf, has a lot to say on that subject. How both my brothers' wives fall short in looking after their husbands (they are of course being judged by unfeasibly high standards). How their kids talk in American accents (why this should be remarkable I don't know – America is, after all, the only home they've ever known). How Americans eat such large portions (surprising this one – the helpings she served up tonight, to Finn especially, must surely rival anything she saw on the other side of the Atlantic). How both my brothers are getting fat (which makes me wonder just what size they are now – they were hardly lightweights the last time I met them).

But, finally, it's time to go. When Finn goes to use the bathroom before we leave, my mother takes me to one side.

"Hang on to him," she whispers. "He's a good one."

I pull away, feigning annoyance, but even as I do a part of me feels pleased.

Back in the car I find myself trying to explain my mother.

"I should have warned you. She's a bit over the top."

Finn looks over at me somewhat coolly, then answers: "She's lovely."

Put so firmly in my place, I say nothing more and we carry on in silence. But then, after five minutes or so, Finn speaks.

"She's going to find out, you know."

"Find out what?" Though of course I know what he means.

"About the love potions. What was all that about energy drinks?"

"I never said energy drinks. It was my dad who said that."

"Yeah, but you never corrected him."

I shrug.

"Why didn't you just tell them?" he asks. "You should have."

"I know, all right! But I just didn't want her going on and on."

"Now when she does find out she'll think you're ashamed or something."

"I'm not ashamed! But . . ." I shrug. "I just didn't want to tell her everything all at once. The fact that I'm going into business rather than getting a well-paid, secure job is enough for now. I don't want her lying awake at night worrying about me. I'll tell her when the time is ready, when things are further along, when we're more set up and she can see how it will work."

"But Rosie, it's not fair to –"

"Just leave it, Finn! I said I'd tell her when I'm ready. Now can we drop the subject?"

When we arrive at my house I ask Finn if he wants to come in but he shakes his head.

"I'd better go home. I'll give you a ring tomorrow."

"Ah come on, just for a little while." I undo my safety belt, stretch over and kiss him. When he kisses back, I close my eyes. He begins to gently stroke my hair. "Just for half an hour?" I murmur.

He pulls away. "I'd love to, Rosie, but I can't. Ashley and Mitch are calling over. Now that the band has reformed they're keen to get down to work."

"All right," I sigh, then open the door of the car and begin to climb out.

"I'll call you tomorrow," he calls after me. "All right?"

"Yeah, all right," I say and push the car door shut. "Night!"

Yet another old tradition suggests that swallowing the heart of a white dove as you rest your hand on your lover's shoulder will ensure his eternal fidelity.

Maybe that's what Meatloaf meant when he sang, "I'd do anything for love but I won't do that."

11

When I come into the kitchen I find Dana sitting at the table, her computer in front of her, piles of books scattered all around.

"You look busy. What are you doing?"

She lets out a weary sigh and flops back in her chair. "Trying to figure out what I'm supposed to be doing."

"What do you mean?"

"I'm trying to figure out exactly what I am going to do my thesis on."

"I thought you'd decided to look into the whole area of aphrodisiacs? That you were going to try and establish if they really do work?"

"That was the plan but I don't think it's going to be a runner."

"How come?"

"Well, when I first started looking into it I thought I was really on to something, especially when there seemed to have been very little research previously done."

159

"But that's a good thing, right?"

"That's what I thought but I soon began to realise why." She picks up an open book lying on the table and holds it out to me. "Read this. There, where I've marked. It's from a report by The United States Consumer Health Information Research Institute."

I see where she's underlined on the page and begin to read aloud.

"The mind is the most potent aphrodisiac there is. It is very difficult to evaluate something someone is taking because if you tell them it's an aphrodisiac, the hope of a certain response might actually lead to an additional reaction." I look up. "So they're saying that a person's response to an aphrodisiac might not be totally physical but may relate to what they expect to happen, right?"

"Exactly. Remember Doug's reaction that night when he drank all those potions of yours?"

I smile. "Sure."

"There's no doubt that taking them influenced his behaviour but whether it was a physical response or not is debatable. He knew what he was drinking. He knew what the expected reaction was. And that's the problem with carrying out this kind of research. The minute you tell someone you're giving them an aphrodisiac substance, then their behaviour is likely to be changed by that very knowledge alone."

"Then don't tell them."

She shakes her head. "No, the problem is you can't give someone something like that without telling them what the possible impacts are. It would be completely unethical."

"Hi, guys," Caroline walks in. "What are you up to?"

Dana sighs. "Banging my head off a brick wall."

"O-kay." Caroline eyes her warily.

"Well, as a matter of fact, I'm looking into your suggestion that I carry out my research on aphrodisiacs."

Caroline nods. "Yeah?"

"At the time I thought it was a good idea —"

"I aim to please," says Caroline.

"— but I keep running into problems."

"Oh! Such as?" asks Caroline.

Dana hands Caroline the book and then waits while she reads the same underlined bit that I did.

When she's done, Caroline looks up and asks: "So why are you showing me this exactly?"

"That's why it's so hard to carry out research in this area. On the one hand if subjects know they're taking aphrodisiacs, their behaviour is likely to change but, on the other hand, you can't not tell them what you're giving them because that would be unethical."

"I see," says Caroline nodding. "So it's a Catch 22."

"Exactly. That's why the only available evidence in this whole area is anecdotal and subjective. They're impossible to test."

"So it's never really been proven that any substance works as an aphrodisiac?"

"Not at a scientific, objective level, no."

"Except . . ." Caroline reaches out her hand. "Here, show me that book again." She takes the book from Dana, scans to find where she's looking for, then reads aloud. *"The mind is the most potent aphrodisiac."* She looks up at the two of us triumphantly.

"So?" asks Dana. "Everyone's agreed on that. What's your point?"

"That's exactly my point. The only aphrodisiac experts are happy accepting is the human mind."

"And, so?" says Dana, looking puzzled.

"And so you need to change the way you're thinking. Forget trying to prove or disprove if aphrodisiacs like Rosie's really work. That's a non-starter. It can't be done for the reasons you've just given. Let that idea go. Instead, change the whole focus of your research and concentrate on the one bona fide aphrodisiac everyone is happy to accept. The mind."

"Oh, my God!" Dana leaves out a squeal of excitement. "Caroline, you genius!" She reaches over and gives Caroline a huge hug and then a great big smacker of a kiss on either cheek. "You've cracked it!"

"Hey, steady on," laughs Caroline. "You're messing up my make-up."

"What?" I look from one to the other. "What am I missing here?"

"So instead," Dana goes on excitedly, "I focus on examining how the mind influences our reactions to what it perceives to be an aphrodisiac. How in effect it, itself, works as an aphrodisiac."

"Exactly!" says Caroline, looking as proud as Punch.

"Okay, okay, let me think this through," says Dana animatedly. "How would I research it? Right, Rosie makes up a potion except she uses anything *but* ingredients that are regarded as aphrodisiacs. I then test this out on two separate study groups. I tell one group I'm testing them for – I don't know – ah, taste or something. I tell the other I'm testing out their reaction to what I've told them is an aphrodisiac. And then I compare the behaviour of both groups over a period of time, in the same controlled environment, of course. Oh my God, that's it! That's my thesis! The effect on the mind of the belief in aphrodisiacs." Face beaming, she looks from one of us to the other. "But . . ." her expression suddenly turns pensive, "there's still lots of other issues to sort out. Like where, how, would I recruit the people? And where would I carry out the experiment? It would have to be in a controlled environment."

"Like in a laboratory, you mean?" I ask.

"No, but somewhere where I could control external factors over a certain period of time. Each group would have to separately experience the same circumstances. I'd have to be sure that the participants couldn't drink alcohol – for instance, or watch or read suggestive material or listen to suggestive music."

Caroline has another light-bulb moment. "Hang on! You know Donald?"

"Yeah?" answers Dana.

Donald is Caroline's incredibly successful brother who we pay rent to every month to live in this house, his house, one of the many he owns across the city. And that's only for starters. Donald is one of the Celtic Tiger's more successful cubs: property, retail, car sales, petrol stations, anything and everything. Caroline hasn't licked her entrepreneurial spirit off the ground.

"Well," Caroline goes on, "Donald part-owns this old youth hostel down the coast. He bought it with his business partner. They're in the middle of trying to get planning permission to turn it into a luxury hotel but it's standing idle right now. It's basic but functional. We could take everyone down there some weekend. We could have the two groups come on different days and have each of them stay overnight. Would that be long enough?"

Dana nods. "Possibly. But how would I get willing participants? Who's going to volunteer? A promise of a night away at some out-of-use hostel in an off-season holiday destination is hardly likely to entice even the most impoverished of students to leave the city."

"How many students are we talking about?" demands Caroline.

"Say, two groups of forty – half male, half female."

"Eighty in all." Caroline thinks for a moment. "Okay, how about this then? Donald is also involved in setting up this thing called the Energy Weekend. It's a music festival he and some of his cronies are going to run next August. It'll be the first year but they're hoping it will become an annual thing. You could offer VIP tickets to every participant. What student is going to turn that down? Put a notice up in college looking for volunteers, tell them it involves a night away and that, as an inducement, they'll get VIP passes for the Energy Weekend. It's a sure-fire winner – you'll have them queuing up to participate."

Caroline is looking delighted with her own ingenuity. Dana still looks doubtful however.

"I don't know," she says hesitantly.

"You don't know! Why? Where's the problem?"

"It's just not the way things are done in academia."

"Academic-smackademia! Why not? There's nothing unethical in it whatsoever. People are always getting paid to undergo these kinds of trials. You're just rewarding them in a different way. The enticement of festival tickets isn't going to change the outcome of the experiment."

"I guess," says Dana doubtfully.

"There's no 'I guess' about it. It's a brilliant plan if I may say so myself."

"But do you think your brother would do all that for me?"

"Not for you, no, but for me, of course, he will. He may have something of a – how should I put this – hard reputation in business circles but he's a big softie when it comes to his little sister. Of course, he'll do it if I ask him. But, Dana, I'm not going to ask unless you're sure you'll go through with it. So are you? Yes or no?"

"I don't know . . ."

"What's there not to know? It's perfect! What have you got to lose? Come on! Say yes! I can get on the phone to him right now."

"All right then."

"Are you sure, Dana?" I ask.

"Yes, I'm sure," she answers somewhat unsurely.

"Okay, I'll give him a ring then," says Caroline.

Passion Fruit Cordial

2 cups of white sugar
1 to 2 cups of passion fruit pulp
1 cup of water
Juice of two large lemons
2 level teaspoons of tartaric acid

Put the white sugar and water in a saucepan and boil for
five minutes. Add the passion fruit pulp and lemon juice
and boil for another two minutes, Next strain, taking care
to stir the residue round and round to force the pulp
through the sieve while leaving the seeds behind.
Add the tartaric acid.
Stir well and enjoy . . .

12

"Here, taste this," I hold out the glass I've been drinking from as Dana comes into the kitchen.

"Hang on a minute!" she laughs. "Let me take my coat off first."

I take another sip while she does so. "Hmmm . . ." I smack my lips and then, as she goes into the hall to hang up her coat, I call out to her, "I was trying to come up with a drink you could use in your trials."

She comes back, takes the glass from me, takes a sip and then considers it. "It's got a kind of strange taste, hasn't it?" she says after a moment. "Quite tart, but I like it."

"Would you like a glass?"

"Okay." Then she laughs. "Is this how you've spent your Friday night?"

"Afraid so."

"Finn's not around then?"

"No, he's rehearsing."

"On a Friday night?"

"Yeah, well, what with work he doesn't get that much time. Anyway, how come you're home so early? I thought you were meeting Doug."

"I did meet him. We went to the cinema but then he wanted to go straight home afterwards. He was too exhausted to do anything else. He spent all day in the shop, painting."

Now that most of the fittings are in place, Doug has taken on the job of painting the interior of the shop.

"How's he getting on?"

"Brilliant. It's a big job to do on his own but I think he's enjoying it."

"How long more will it take?"

"He says he'll be finished by the middle of next week. You know, he's making a really nice job of it. And guess what? He may have already got some more work out of it."

"You're kidding?"

"No, some guy who owns another shop along the street popped in for a nose the other day when Doug was there and they got talking. It seems he knew Monica from the time when she ran the boutique. Anyway, I guess he must have liked what he saw because he asked Doug if he'd be interested in doing some painting work for him when he's finished in our place."

"And?"

"Doug jumped at the chance, of course."

"Caroline says he's doing a really thorough job."

Dana laughs. "She should know. She calls in every day to check on him."

"Does he mind?"

"I don't think so. He knows he's doing a good job. You know, I think he quite admires Caroline in a way. He says she's very professional, very hardworking."

"So where's Caroline now, do you know?"

"She said she'd be late home, that she had to go to some reception for work. By the way, did she tell you that she officially handed in her notice today?"

"Yeah, I can't believe she's actually finishing up in two weeks."

"It's scary how the time is flying by. The shop will be open before we know it." Dana holds out her empty glass. "Is there any more? It's really growing on me."

"Sure, there's lots."

"What's in it anyway?"

"It's a passion fruit cordial."

"Passion fruit? But, Rosie, don't you remember there's not meant to be any aphrodisiac in the trial drink? That's the whole point."

"Of course, I know, and that's the odd thing. Passion fruit is actually one of the few fruits that has never been considered an aphrodisiac. Never. Apples, pineapples, melon, watermelon, peaches, strawberries, raspberries, bananas, you name it, nearly every other fruit has been used as an aphrodisiac by someone at some time, but not passion fruit."

"So why is it called passion fruit then?"

"Well, here's the interesting thing. The name actually refers to the flower of the vine which was used as a teaching device by the Jesuit missionaries in South America. The ten petals on the flower represent the ten disciples present at the crucifixion, the thin curling tendrils are the whips that scourged Christ on the way to the cross and, the pattern on the flower is like the crown of thorns they put on Jesus and –"

I notice Dana is smirking.

"What?"

"I think you're in danger of turning into a geek."

"I think I already have!" I laugh. "I guess that's what comes of spending so much time on my own."

"Finn really is working hard lately, isn't he?" says Dana.

"I think he feels he has to – he really wants to make a success of the band. Anyway, I was thinking, on the first night of your trials, when the first bunch of students think they're there to test out taste, we should use one of the other names for passion fruit. There's loads: konyal, lilikoi, parcha, markisa, although my favourite is granadilla. And then, the second night, when the second bunch of students believe they're there to trial aphrodisiacs, we can call it Passion Fruit Cordial – to set the mood."

"Yeah, sounds good."

"So have you got any volunteers yet?"

"Any volunteers?" Dana laughs. "Too many. You know I put up notices all around college?"

"Yeah?"

"Well, you wouldn't believe the response. I've been swamped. VIP tickets to Caroline's brother's concert have proved a great incentive. I thought my phone would never stop ringing. In the end I had to turn it off."

"So when are you actually going to do the trials?"

"The weekend after next."

"So soon?"

"Yeah, between everything I've lost a lot of time. I need to crack on. Besides, when the shop opens we won't have that much time and, anyway, Caroline's brother has some people lined up to come in and strip the hostel down so I need to do it sooner rather than later."

"Is there going to be enough room for everyone?"

"Loads apparently. According to Donald there are four big dormitories which between them will have more than enough beds for the students and there's some smaller rooms on the top floor where we can all sleep. You are going to come and help me, aren't you?"

"Sure."

"Doug will too and Caroline says that she and Mick will as well. The more help the better. To be honest, I'm a bit nervous about the whole thing."

"It'll go fine."

"I guess."

She looks at her empty glass.

"Any more of this on offer?"

"Sure."

When red M and M's were temporarily removed from the market after a ban on the dye used in them came into force, a rumour spread that they were in fact so aphrodisiac that M and M workers were taking them directly off the production line and pocketing them for their own use.

So not all aphrodisiac lore stems from long ago.

13

When Caroline comes into the living-room looking absolutely stunning in a fabulous red cocktail dress, matching stilettos, and with her hair tied up high on her head, we all stare. When Doug leaves out an involuntary long low whistle, Caroline looks at him in surprise – causing him to look a little surprised himself, like he's wondering how he even dared.

"Wow!" I say. "You look amazing!"

"Why, thank you!"

"Are you going out?" asks Dana.

"You don't think I went to all this trouble to sit here on the couch with you guys!"

"Come on then," coaxes Dana. "Give us a twirl."

"Oh give over!" protests Caroline.

"Ah, go on!" urges Dana.

The normally super-confident Caroline suddenly looks surprisingly awkward as she reluctantly obliges with a twirl. "Happy now?" she snaps.

"Mick will certainly be when he sees you," says Dana. "But hang on, didn't you tell us that Mick rang to say he wouldn't be back tonight after all, that filming was going on late."

"He did."

"Oh!"

Caroline sighs. "I do have a life apart from Mick – which is just as well, given how little I see of him lately. If you must know, I'm going to the opening of the new Urbana Boutique Hotel."

"Very swish!"

"It should be. I know I'm meant to be winding down in work but I couldn't pass up on this opportunity. They're having a champagne-tasting evening at the hotel with dozens of varieties from all the best champagne houses.

"How come you didn't ask us to come along?" I ask.

"I only have one invite. I wasn't even going to go when I thought Mick would be here but since he's not – again – there seems little point in letting the opportunity go to waste. Besides, it'll be a chance to get the name of the shop out there – there'll probably be lots of press attending. I may be able to get some of them interested in doing a piece later on. Now let me see – bag, invite, phone, keys, wrap –" there comes the sound of a beep-beep from a taxi out on the road "– and there's my carriage. Now don't wait up, my lovelies!"

"Don't be too late!" Dana calls after her. "Remember, the trials are starting tomorrow. We're leaving for Wicklow first thing in the morning."

"I know. I won't be late!"

And with a wave she's gone, leaving only the scent of her favourite Chanel behind.

Soon after Caroline leaves, Doug decides he's going to

head home too. He says he's feeling exhausted which is hardly surprising. After he finished painting our place he went straight to the other job he'd lined up – the interior of another shop on the street. Even though he's been putting in fourteen-hour days and has brought his brother in to help him, he's still under pressure to finish.

Dana sees him to the door.

"Do you want a cuppa?" she asks when she comes back in.

"Okay then."

Moments later she returns with the two mugs of tea and sits down on the couch beside me.

"So, all set for tomorrow?" I ask.

"Pretty much. Thanks for all your help today."

Dana and I spent the entire afternoon in town buying food to feed everyone over the weekend: tea, coffee, milk; cereal and juice for breakfast; bread and fillings for lunch-time sandwiches; all the ingredients needed for spaghetti bolognese – all this to cater for eighty students as well as ourselves. Plus the ingredients for our Passion Fruit Cordial including bag-loads of passion fruit – we had to go to five different supermarkets to get all the fruit we needed.

"So what time are the students arriving?" I ask.

"At six, which should give us loads of time to set up the place and make sure everything is okay. I don't know what state it's going to be in since it hasn't been occupied in a good while. You're still on to come and help, aren't you?"

"Of course. So how early do you want to leave here in the morning?"

"Nine should be time enough."

"What about Loretta and Shane – are they coming?"

She shakes her head. "They'd arranged to go to London

so they won't be able to help but we should have enough hands as it is. There's you, me, Doug, Caroline and Mick."

"I'd ask Finn but he's pretty busy at the moment."

"Band stuff?"

"Yeah."

Dana takes a sip from her tea. "So how is Finn?"

I shrug. "Fine." Something in her tone prompts me to add, "Why do you ask?"

"No reason, just making conversation."

Maybe, but it doesn't feel quite so innocent.

"He hasn't been around much lately, has he?" she goes on.

"No, I guess he hasn't," I answer, then add defensively, "but he's pretty preoccupied with getting the band back on its feet. You know that. We were going to go out tonight, just the two of us, for something to eat but, then, some big-shot guy who owns a couple of late-night music places in town agreed to meet with the band earlier this evening. The same guy has cancelled on them twice before so they didn't want to miss this opportunity."

"So Finn cancelled you instead?"

"It wasn't like that, Dana. He had to go. I understand how important it is. And it was worth it. Finn rang after they met to say it had gone great, that the guy was really interested and that there's every chance he's going to book them."

"If the meeting's already over, then can't you still go out?"

I shrug. "Finn sounded pretty beat. I didn't want to put pressure on him."

"Still, it's a pity."

I shrug. "Can't be helped." Then I laugh. "I'd even bought a new top and these new earrings." I push my hair aside and show her.

"They're nice."

"Thanks."

"You must be glad to see Finn getting back to normal?"

I nod. "Course I am. He's much happier these days."

"How are he and his new flatmate getting on?"

"Fine."

"What did you say her name was again?"

"Lola."

"Have you met her yet?"

"No."

"How come?"

"Well, with me and the shop, and him and the band, there hasn't really been the opportunity or time."

"Well, you should make the time."

"Pardon?"

"You should make the time to meet her. And sooner rather than later. You don't want her to get the impression that you're never around. You need to stake your claim."

I laugh. "Stake my claim? Dana! Finn's not a nugget of gold!"

"But you happen to think he is, don't you?"

"Pardon?"

She thinks for a moment. "You really like Finn, don't you, Rosie?"

"Yes, of course I do."

"Well then, you need to make sure he knows it and —"

"He does know it!"

"— and *she* knows it too."

"What do I care about her?"

"Well, you should care. You're being a fool if you don't."

I look at her. I'm surprised that Dana would give such direct advice — it's not like her to be so interfering.

But she goes on: "Why don't you ring him now? Tell him you're calling around."

I look at her guardedly. "You sound like you don't trust him."

"I'm not saying that, not at all, but what do we know about this Lola? How do you know you can trust her? Go on. Ring him. Now." She stretches out to the coffee table, picks up my phone and holds it out to me. "Go on!"

I'm about to take it but then I hesitate. I can't help feeling that I'm being manipulated. Of course, I don't like Lola's presence in my boyfriend's life but I don't really believe anything is going on between the pair of them. If there was I'd *know* it. Finn is like an open book – a large-print one. The very idea is ludicrous.

And, yes, sure, I am missing him at the moment. I hate seeing so little of him but it is only temporary – until the shop is set up, until the band is up and running – then we'll go back to the way things were, only better – Finn is so much happier these days.

"Come on. Ring him. Tell him you're coming over."

"Dana –"

"Just picture the two of them, side by side on the couch, watching a movie together maybe, relaxing over a bottle of wine –"

"Are you trying to make me jealous!"

"Yes. Would that be a bad thing? I think it's time you took your head out of the sand and became more proactive. You're too complacent. Go on!" She's still holding out the phone. "Ring him."

Reluctantly I take it from her. I press the numbers. I hear a ring tone and then Finn answers.

"Hi, Finn."

"Hiya, Rosie."

I glance over at Dana and she's sitting there, gesticulating and mouthing at me, "Go on. Tell him you're coming over," so obediently I find myself doing exactly that.

"I was just thinking I might come over," I say.

"Now?"

"Yeah."

"Oh, right."

He doesn't sound too encouraging and I find myself adding, "If it suits."

From the corner of my eye, I see Dana throw her eyes to heaven.

"Listen, Rosie," Finn is saying, "how about another night?"

"But what's wrong with tonight?"

"Well, you know our first gig is next week?"

"Yeah?"

"Well, after I got back here we decided to work on one of the new songs seeing as how you and I had cancelled dinner."

"But I thought you were wrecked."

"I am a bit but I guess we're all a little nervous about performing in public. We haven't got some of the new stuff nailed yet."

We. We. We. Who exactly constitutes this 'we' he's talking about? I decide to ask. "Who's 'we'?"

"The band, of course."

"All of you?"

"Ah, yes, more or less."

More or less? There's a great deal of difference between more and less, more being the whole band, less being – well, less could mean just him and Lola.

As if on cue I hear the sound of a girly high-pitched laugh in the background.

"I wouldn't get in the way, Finn," I say.

"I don't know, Rosie – I feel it would be too distracting. Let's just leave it until another time. The gig is on Wednesday. That just gives us the weekend and Monday and Tuesday to get things right."

"What's he saying?" whispers Dana.

"Hang on, Finn." I put my hand over the receiver. "He says he's rehearsing for their first gig – it's on Wednesday next."

"Ask him where?"

"Stop telling me what to say!" I snap. "Anyway, I already know – the Velvet Rooms."

"The Velvet Rooms!" Dana gives a whistle. "Wow! That's pretty impressive. How did they pull that off?"

"It seems Lola has contacts from before." I hear Finn calling my name on the phone. "Sorry, Finn, Dana was just asking me something."

"Look," says Finn, "how about this? I know you're busy with the shop and helping Dana out with her trials, so why don't we leave off seeing each other until after the gig. Then we could do something special – like maybe head away for the day?"

"Yeah, I guess."

"I really wouldn't be much company for you right now. I'm a bit obsessed. I'm really nervous at the prospect of playing live again, especially with all the changes, you know, the new line-up and the new songs. I wake up in the middle of the night sweating. I've got to keep focused, to put all my energies into getting everything right."

"Yeah, sure. I know it's important. But I miss you, you know. It seems like I hardly ever see you."

"And I miss you too. But —"

Someone, someone female shouts out my boyfriend's name in the background.

"Okay! Okay!" he calls out. Then back to me again: "Look, I'd better go."

"Sure."

"Love you."

"Love you too." I hang up.

"Well?" demands Dana immediately.

"He said we should wait until after they're over their first gig before we meet up."

"I see." She thinks for a moment. "You know, you're too soft on him, Rosie."

"Ah come on, Dana! This is a big deal for him after everything he's gone through. You can't blame him for wanting to put everything he has into it. It's important."

"More important than you?"

"No, I'm not saying that. But it's still important."

"I know but nevertheless he still needs to make space for you in his life and he's just not doing that right now. Even Doug thinks so."

"What! You've been talking to Doug about me and Finn?"

"Not really."

"Yes, you have."

She shrugs. "Maybe a little."

"I'd prefer if you'd not discuss my personal life with Doug, even if he is your boyfriend."

"All I'm saying is that he's not giving you enough time."

"Ah come on, Dana. Can't you cut him some slack? He's been through a hard time. I'm only glad to see that things are coming together for him, finally."

Dana shrugs. "You've been through a lot too, you know. So, he hasn't asked you to go along to the gig at the Velvet Rooms, has he?"

"No." Which I have to say I find disappointing, though I don't say that to Dana – I don't want to add any more fuel to her fire; it's burning away nicely as it is – but I do try and explain to her why I think he hasn't. "I think I might make him even more nervous. I'd be a distraction. I come with so much baggage. I'd remind him of Mark, of the past, when he really needs to concentrate on this first night of his future."

"But would you like to go?"

"Of course, I would."

"Well, keep Wednesday night free then, for that's where you and I will be."

"I don't know, Dana. I'm not sure that's a good idea."

"He needn't know – at least not until afterwards."

In the second century, the philosopher Apuleius was accused in court of using a love potion to attract his wealthy wife but was acquitted.
Who exactly took the proceedings is not clear. His wife perhaps? It would make interesting grounds for divorce.

14

I slam the boot shut, then go to the front door. "Okay," I shout up the stairs, "we're all packed up! Are you ready?"

Dana comes down the stairs, a neat rucksack over one shoulder.

"Did you put in all the stuff we bought at the shops yesterday?" she asks.

"Yep. It's all there. There's barely room enough for it all in the boot."

Dana looks concerned. "I still think we should have cooked everything here. What if we find we've forgotten some ingredient or whatever?"

"Dana, stop fretting! We have everything we need. I've checked and rechecked. It'll be easier to prepare everything once we're there. We couldn't have travelled down with big vats of liquid or huge pots of bolognese."

"Did you remember to take the mince for the bolognese out of the fridge?"

"Yes, yes. It's in the boot."

"And the milk?"

"Yes, in the boot too, all forty litres of it. Now will you please go and get in!" I turn to the stairs again. "Caroline!" I call up. "Come on! What's keeping you?"

"All right, all right, keep your hair on." She appears at the top with a suitcase.

"Caroline! Where are you going with that? We're only going for two nights."

"Stop giving out. It's not that big."

"But where's it going to fit? The boot is full."

"We'll squeeze it in somewhere."

We finally leave the house at nine. Caroline is driving, I'm in the passenger's seat, Dana is in the back with Caroline's suitcase on the seat beside her. When we stop off at Doug's house en route to collect him, it's Monica who opens the door and while Dana goes inside to get Doug, she comes over to the car.

"Hi, Monica!"

"Hi, girls! You've a big weekend ahead of you. How many students are coming?"

"Forty today and forty tomorrow."

"Rather you than me!" she laughs. "So Doug tells me the shop is coming on a treat?"

I nod. "Sure is. Only a week to go now."

"You wouldn't recognise the place," adds Caroline.

"That's what I'm afraid of!" Monica laughs. "I remember when I was setting up the boutique I had to work around the clock getting everything in order. I thought I'd never get the place finished on time. But you know, looking back now, it was probably one of the most exciting times of my life. One of the best times even." She gives a wistful laugh. "I had so much energy back then. God, it all seems such a long time ago now." She notices Doug and Dana coming back out of the house. "Here come the lovebirds. I'd better let you go – you've better things to do than to be listening to me going on and on."

Doug gives Monica a kiss, then he and Dana get into the back – but it's a bit of a squeeze and Doug ends up with Caroline's suitcase on his lap but he doesn't complain. As we pull out, Monica stands there watching us go and though she's smiling as she waves, I'm struck by how lonely she looks. When I worked with her in the shop she seemed like superwoman to me. Widowed early, it always amazed me to see how she coped with everything – running the shop, supporting a family – managing their needs all on her own. Her boys are older now, only Tim is still at school, and she no longer has the shop to occupy her. She seems a little lost standing there this morning. I wonder if she regrets letting the boutique go.

I turn to Caroline. "You haven't forgotten to invite Monica to our launch?"

"Taken care of – her invitation's in the post. She should get it on Monday." She calls back, "Did you hear that, Doug?"

"Yeah. Thanks, Caroline."

As we drive on, Doug and Dana soon become engrossed in their own conversation in the back and after a while it strikes me that Caroline seems uncharacteristically quiet in herself.

"You're very quiet today, Caroline."

She looks over. "Am I? Just tired, I guess."

"Had you a good time at that hotel thingy you were at last night?"

"What? Oh that? Yeah, it was okay."

"What time did you get home?"

Caroline shrugs. "Twelve maybe."

"Liar!" I laugh. "Dana and I were still up at that time."

"Well, one then. I can't remember." She shrugs.

"Anyone interesting there?"

She looks over at me. "What's with all the questions?" she snaps.

"Sorry! I was only making conversation."

"Well, don't feel you have to on my account." She reaches over and turns on the radio. "There, that will keep you company."

"Okay, I can take a hint."

"Look, sorry. Rosie. I have a headache."

"Do you want me to drive then?"

"No, no, I'm fine. I just don't feel like talking, that's all."

After an hour or so, Caroline takes a turn off the main road and heads down a long narrow winding potholed lane.

"Are you sure you took the right turn?" I ask as we bounce along the overgrown track, with grass all down the middle.

"I'm sure."

"Em — how long has it been since this hostel was up and running?"

Caroline shrugs. "Dunno. A year, eighteen months maybe."

"If the entrance is this neglected, what's the place itself going to be like?"

"Let's just wait and see, all right?"

We come to a clearing and pull up outside a big old building. We climb out.

"Is *this* it?" asks Dana in astonishment, mirroring exactly what I'm thinking.

"Ah yeah," says Caroline, defensively. "What were you expecting? The Ritz?"

I don't know what I was expecting but I know it wasn't this. I've never seen anywhere so unwelcoming, so foreboding, so desolate! Like the *Psycho* house, it's perched high on a cliff overlooking a grey windswept beach. There's not a single other building in sight; I didn't think there were places as remote as this in Ireland.

"Are you sure?" asks Dana.

Caroline nods. "Of course, I'm sure. Come on. Let's go!"

We let her lead the way but when Caroline goes to put her key in the door with its peeling red paint, she finds it's unlocked. "Oh! That's strange." She pushes the door open and shouts out, "Hello!" a couple of times but when she gets no answer she goes to walk in.

"Caroline!" Dana reaches out and grabs hold of her arm.

"Jesus! What?"

"You can't go in. What if there's someone in there?"

"If we don't go in, how will we find out?"

"Aren't you nervous?" asks Dana.

"I'm sure there's nothing to be worried about."

As Caroline sets off down the dim dreary hall, Doug, Dana and I anxiously follow her.

"We'll need to give the place a good airing before the students arrive!" Caroline calls back to us. She flicks on a switch and the lights come on or, more specifically, one naked forty-watt bulb hanging from the centre of the ceiling. It impacts on the dimness only marginally and makes the place no less dreary, maybe even more so.

The first room we arrive into is the kitchen. The first thing we notice is that there is a little portable radio sitting on the counter, playing away to the empty room. The second thing we notice is that on the big wooden table stands a Weetabix box, a carton of milk, and a bowl with a spoon and the remains of breakfast sitting in it.

"Is there someone living here?" asks Dana, looking around nervously.

"There's not meant to be," answers Caroline, sounding puzzled. She picks up the milk carton and sniffs. "It's fresh."

A voice on the radio is singing that strange old song, 'Video Killed the Radio Star'.

"Oh, God," I say, "this place is weird."

"It gives me the willies," adds Dana. "Are you absolutely sure we're in the right place, Caroline?"

"Yes! Will you stop asking me that!"

"It's just like the *Marie Celeste*," says Doug quietly.

"The what?" asks Dana

"The *Marie Celeste*. It was a famous ship that was discovered drifting off the coast of Portugal hundreds of years ago. When the crew from another ship boarded it they found it was completely deserted even though there were untouched breakfasts and cups of tea on the cabin table and washing hanging out to dry."

"Where had all the people on board gone?" I ask.

"No one knows. None of the crew or passengers were ever seen again."

"Stop!" cries Dana. "You're giving me the creeps!"

"You mean *this* place is giving you the creeps," says Doug.

The radio sings on about video killing the radio star and and how we can't rewind we've gone too far . . .

I shiver.

"Turn that blasted thing off!" Caroline demands.

I go over and flick the switch and then all of us stand in the kitchen looking around.

"Maybe there's a caretaker," says Caroline. "Donald never mentioned one but he could have just forgotten to." She steps back into the hall and we follow her and stand clustered together as she begins to call out loudly. *"Hello! Hello!"* When there's no answer she begins darting from doorway to doorway, sticking her head in every room. She calls up the stairs, *"Hello!"* and we all stand with ears cocked but there's no answer.

"We'd better take a look upstairs."

"Are you sure that's wise?" asks a worried Dana.

"We can stick together," Caroline answers back, already halfway up the stairs.

We hurry after her. We take a peek into all the rooms on the second floor and then on the top one. When we're done with the last room, she turns to us and shrugs. "Nobody. Maybe I'll just phone Donald." She takes her mobile from her bag and tries his number but after a while she hangs up. "He's not answering. I'll try him again later. In the meantime, we need to get ready for the students. Okay, let's start getting this place into some shape!" She heads back down the stairs again.

"What! You have got to be kidding!" cries Dana, following after her. "We can't stay here! The place is dirty and downright spooky. We didn't come here to carry out endurance tests. And, oh yeah, there's still the little matter of our unseen fellow resident. What if he shows up?"

"Look, he's probably just some old squatter who legged it the minute he saw us coming. He's probably out on the main road now, thumbing to get as far away as possible. And if by chance he does turn up again there's enough of us here to deal with him. As for this place, I grant you it's pretty basic but –"

"Basic!" erupts Dana.

"Yes, basic, but it *is* functional. We just need to give it a good airing and to tidy it up a little."

"You're joking!" protests Dana.

"I brought all the cleaning stuff we need," Caroline says. "We've got hours yet before the students start arriving."

"Hours!" laughs Dana, a little hysterically, and I notice Doug quietly take her hand. He begins to pat it reassuringly but with little effect. Dana is pretty wound up. "We'd need days, weeks, months!"

"So what are you saying then, Dana?" demands Caroline. "That we simply get back into the car, drive home to Dublin and forget all about this. Fine. It's you not me who all this matters to. I've plenty of things I could be doing with my time. I'd be quite happy not to spend the day cleaning or the weekend helping you to supervise your students. You want to walk away then, fine, why am I arguing with you? We can leave right now. We can tell the students it's cancelled. I can drop the keys into my brother's office on our way home and that'll be the end of it. You just tell me now if that's what you want."

"No, I'm not saying that but . . ."

"But what?"

"It's just . . ." Dana looks around. We're back in the kitchen now. "Well, look at the place!"

"Come on, Dana," says Doug. "It's not as bad as all that. Like Caroline says, it's just neglected. We may as well give it a go now we're here."

Caroline nods approvingly. "Listen to the man, Dana! He's talking sense."

"But where would we even start?" Dana looks around hopelessly.

"First things first," says Caroline. "We'll need to sort out the kitchen. Rosie and I will tackle that. Next, you two," she points to Doug and Dana, "go back upstairs and check out the bed situation, make sure there's enough room in the dormitories for the students. Next, go up to the top floor and pick out rooms for the rest of us to sleep in and air them out. Then we'll need to decide on which reception rooms we're going to use and give them a going-over. Rosie and I can do that while you," she nods again to Dana and Doug, "check out that we have everything we need in the dining-room. Like I said, I brought all the cleaning stuff we could possibly want but if there is anything missing we can give Mick a ring and he'll bring it with him when he comes at lunch-time. Okay, I think that's it, so let's get started." She takes her bag off her shoulder, opens it, and pulls out a pink apron and a pair of pink rubber gloves. She puts on the apron, one glove, then the other, but then notices us three, standing there, looking at her.

"What?" she demands.

"Where did you get those?" asks Dana, pointing at the apron and the gloves. "I never saw them before. I never knew you even possessed such items."

"I bought them especially. I may as well have the right outfit for the job."

Since a top, skirt and heels make up the rest, it seems to me that the only job she's dressed for is appearing in a TV advert, holding up some cleaning product for the camera, in an unfeasibly clean and shiny kitchen, with 2.5 unfeasibly clean and shiny kids in the background. What her outfit is *not* right for is the dirty job ahead of us.

Dana is thinking along the same lines. "Maybe a tatty old pair of trackie bottoms and a sweater would be more in order?"

Coolly Caroline looks Dana up and down, taking in her old tracksuit bottoms and her worn jumper. "For some, maybe."

"But heels, Caroline?" asks Dana. "How are you going to manage in them?"

"You should know by now I don't do flats. I function better in heels. I'm used to them." She reaches into the bag of cleaning supplies she brought with her and takes out a cloth and a bottle of Cif, then stands there, looking around, deciding where she should start. "What?" she demands when she notices that we're all grinning at the absurd figure she makes.

"What was that film again," I ask, "where the husbands had all these perfectly made-up, perfectly dressed wives who worked like robots?"

"You mean *Stepford Wives*?" says Caroline.

"Yeah."

"Yes, well, the one thing those Stepford Wives could do was clean." She pats her own perfect hair and straightens her pink apron, "*And* look good at the same time. There's no crime in that. Just because I don't look like a skivvie doesn't mean I won't work like one. So come on, you lot. Let's get started!"

Dana and Doug head upstairs while Caroline and I tackle the kitchen grime, and there is a lot of grime but, true to her word, Caroline puts her back into it from the start. She's like a whirlwind.

After twenty minutes or so, Dana comes back into the kitchen. "Okay, I think we have a problem with the beds."

"What do you mean? Don't we have enough?"

"There's plenty but I'm afraid the mattresses are really manky. I did tell the students to bring their own sleeping bags but they're going to baulk when they see the state of the mattresses. I guess I should have told them to bring sheets as well but I never thought. Do you think there's any chance Mick could get his hands on forty or so sheets?"

"I'll text him," says Caroline. "I guess he could rent them out or something. Don't some hotels get fresh laundry brought in from outside everyday?" She puts down her cloth, picks up her phone from the counter and immediately starts texting.

"And tell him to bring down about twenty sets of knives and forks as well," says Dana, "and about the same number of plates. There aren't enough here."

"Sure, sure." She finishes texting but, almost immediately, before she puts her phone down, it rings. She looks at the screen. "It's Mick." She answers it. "Hiya," she says brightly, then listens, then disappointedly says, "Oh! I see." She sighs. "Well, when do you think you'll get here so? Aah, Mick! But that will be too late! What? I guess I'll have to work something else out, won't I? What? Yeah, love you too." She hangs up. "Okay, we have a problem. Mick's not going to be able to get here after all, at least not today. Filming is behind schedule again."

"Hell!" cries Dana. "What are we going to do so? The students will run a mile when they see the mattresses!"

"And what are they going to eat with?" I ask.

"Oh for crying out loud!" says Caroline. "Why are you all looking at me, like I'm the only one who can sort things out?" Then she thinks for a moment. "Okay, I'll try Donald again. He might be able to help."

We stand there, waiting, while she rings but once again she doesn't get through. "Damn, where is he? I can't even leave a message. He must have his phone switched off or else he's out of coverage."

"Maybe one of us should take your car and drive back to Dublin and try and get our hands on all the stuff we need," I suggest.

"No," says Caroline. "That would take up the whole morning and we have too much to do here."

"What are we going to do so?" asks Dana.

"Look," says Caroline. "I have an idea. I'm not sure it'll work but leave it with me. I just need to make another phone call."

"To who?" I ask but she's already on her way out to the hall.

As she's going out, Doug comes back in. "There's definitely someone staying here," he tells Dana and me.

"How do you know?" asks Dana.

"I found a dirty old sleeping bag on one of the beds on the top floor."

"But that could have been there for ages. It doesn't mean whoever owns it is still around."

"But I also found some wet clothes drying in one of the bathrooms."

"Oh!"

Caroline comes back in.

"Doug found some clothes drying in one of the bathrooms upstairs," Dana tells her.

Caroline considers this. "Okay, so there is definitely someone using the place but, look, they're not here right now, are they? We just need to keep an eye out for them and make sure to lock up properly tonight." Then she changes the subject. "As for the sheets, everything is sorted. A friend of mine will be here as soon as he can with all the sheets we need, and all the knives and forks too."

"What friend?" asks Dana.

"His name is Niall Wallace."

"Niall Wallace? I've never heard you mention him before," I say. "Who is he?"

"I've known him for years but I met him again last night for the first time in ages at that champagne party in the Urbana Hotel. He's one of the backers."

"You don't mean Niall Wallace, the rugby guy?" asks Dana.

"As it happens I do."

"Pit Bull Wallace? He used to be on the Irish team?"

Caroline looks annoyed. "He doesn't like being called that but yes, he was on the Irish team."

"Is he still playing?"

"No, he had to pack it in because of a knee injury. These days he's concentrating on his businesses."

"Isn't he, like, a millionaire now?' Dana asks.

Caroline nods her head. "Yes."

"I never knew you knew him," I say.

"I did some marketing work for him some time ago but I hadn't seen him in a while until I bumped into him last night."

"And what?" demands Dana. "This Pit Bull Wallace is –"

"Niall, his name is Niall."

"– is going to drop everything to come down here to deliver some sheets and stuff to us?"

Caroline nods. "Like I said, he's a friend. Now come on. We'd better get back to work."

But even if Caroline is finished with this conversation, Dana isn't.

"A very good friend if he's prepared to do all this at a moment's notice," she observes but Caroline doesn't respond.

Maybe she doesn't even hear. She's already down on her

knees and has her head and half her body stuck in the oven. We watch as the part that's still outside moves from side to side with the effort of her cleaning.

"Who'd have thought?" says Dana in wonderment. "I think I've seen it all now."

After many hours' grafting, the place starts to look fairly okay and, at Caroline's suggestion, I go out to the overgrown garden to gather bunches of flowers to make it more welcoming. As I'm doing so, a brand-new silver Mercedes comes tearing up the driveway and pulls up right outside the front door. I walk over.

Out of the car steps a heavy-set guy in a dark suit and a dark open-necked shirt that reveals a thick gold necklace nestling on a crop of thick black hair. Though the day is overcast, he's wearing shades. He's got a deep tan and his shoes are as well polished as his thick black curly hair is oiled.

"Hi!" I call out as I go over.

"Hi! I'm not sure if I have the right place. I'm looking for Caroline Connolly?"

"Yeah, sure. Come in." I lead him inside.

"Wow! This place sure is a dump," he says, looking around.

"Caroline!" I shout. "Your friend is here!"

Caroline appears out from the kitchen.

"Niall! Hi!"

"Hi, Caroline." He goes over to her and, as he kisses her on either cheek, I notice the oversized gold signet ring and the gold cuff links. This guy has more jewellery than I do.

"Well, don't you look yummy!" he says, taking in her outfit.

197

"Are you kidding! I must look a right state!" she says – a little flirtatiously, I notice.

But she doesn't look a state at all. I'm not sure I'd choose the word 'yummy' to describe her but while the rest of us are completely dishevelled, Caroline hasn't a hair out of place.

"I brought everything you need," Niall goes on now. "The minute you hung up I rang the Urbana and got one of my people there to get the stuff you wanted – then I drove over, collected everything, and came straight here."

"I hope I'm not putting you to too much trouble?"

"For you, nothing is too much trouble," he says, then quickly adds, "I did have to cut short a meeting and blow off some guys that I'd arranged to meet for a business lunch, but, hey, for you, not a problem."

"So you've already met Rosie?"

"Hi there, Rosie."

"Niall, isn't it? Listen, thanks for helping us out."

"Not a problem."

"So, Rose, do you want to get that stuff out of the Merc?" he asks and throws me his keys but, caught off guard, I fail to catch them and they fall to the floor. "Ho, ho, Miss Butterfingers!" he laughs.

I bend down and pick them up. Miss Butterfingers! I don't suppose he ever called one of his team members that but, before I can think of a fitting response, he's already moved on from me.

"So, Caroline," I hear him saying, "are you going to show me around?"

"What's with this Niall anyway?" Dana asks as we dress one of the dormitory beds. "How come none of us have ever heard her talking about him before?"

I shrug. "I don't know any more than you do."

"Doug swears he saw a photofit of him on *Crimeline* the other night," Dana jokes.

"What? Complete with shades?" I laugh and, thinking of all the gold he's wearing, I ask, "What was he on for? Robbing a jewellery shop? Here," I hold out the sheet to her, "catch this end, will you?"

"I mean, has Mick ever met him?"

"Dana, you know as much as I do! Now come on. Catch the sheet. The students will be arriving soon and I still have to cook spaghetti bolognese for all of them, and Caroline and you and Doug and me. And Pit Bull too, I guess. He doesn't look like he has any intention of heading away."

"Tell Caroline to make him get some of 'his people' down here pronto with food for everyone!"

I laugh. "He does seem kind of taken with her, doesn't he?"

Now she laughs. "I'll say. He can't keep his eyes off her."

"How can you tell? He hasn't taken his shades off since he got here. Look, will you finish off here and I'll go down and start on the cooking?"

"Welcome, everyone!" calls Dana as the students climb down from the bus.

"Welcome! Welcome! Welcome!" choruses Caroline at her side.

By the time the students arrive, the place is looking much better, superficially at least, and the students' own high spirits combined with Caroline's diversionary over-the-top welcome prevents them immediately appreciating the shortcomings of the place. Fussing loudly, she corrals the lively crowd inside and straight up the stairs and to the dormitories. There, she directs them to put their sleeping bags on beds (now covered with clean white sheets which make all the difference) and tells them to come back down as soon as they're ready.

At around six, Dana, with difficulty – even with our help – gathers the students from where they've scattered and directs them into the dining-room. She's already complaining that she's beginning to feel like a shepherd but once she's finally managed to get them sitting at the tables we've set up for dinner, Caroline, Doug and I begin serving up. As we're doing so, Niall goes out to take a phone call and Dana goes to the top of the room to outline what's in store for the students.

"Hi, everyone," she begins. "I just want to say thanks again for coming and to tell you a little about why you are here."

Hardly anyone is paying Dana much heed. This random selection of forty students, strangers to one another, are more interested in getting to know each other than listening to Dana. I look around. Yes, there are a few sitting silently, paying attention, but these are by far the minority. Mostly the students are talking animatedly, laughing, some are flirting already and one couple are even arguing, but in a flirty kind of way – their attraction mounting by the second. And the noise level is something else. How can they be so loud!

"It's like a bloody crèche!" shouts Caroline over the din.

Though I'm not that much older than them, being here in this position of 'authority,' does make me feel years and years older. Not that we seem to have much authority right now.

Dana raises her voice: "*The reason you're all here is to –*"

The rest of the sentence gets drowned out and I look to see her standing at the top of the room, looking around in despair.

"It's not nice to ignore her like that," says Doug who is now standing beside me. "They really should pay her more attention."

He's right. She needs to get everyone's attention, and soon.

"Right," says Doug with a grim look on his face. "Enough!" He hurries off and I see him go over to the light switch. He flicks it off, leaving the place in near darkness.

Shouts of "Hey!" and "What's going on?" go up around the room.

It's a good thirty seconds before Doug puts it back on again but, when he does, he's got everyone's attention. He looks a little flustered to suddenly find himself in the spotlight but then he shouts out: "Right! Now listen to the lady!" He points in Dana's direction. "She's got something to say."

The room is silent now. All eyes turn from Doug to Dana but she's staring at him in surprise. Then she gathers herself together.

"Okay, well," Dana begins, "the reason you're all here –" She breaks off for a second when Niall comes back in and noisily makes his way back to his seat. When he sits down, she begins again. "The reason you're all here is to allow me to carry out a comparative study on people's taste. After you've finished eating, I'll be handing out glasses of a drink called Granadilla Cordial. Now, feel free to drink as much of this as you want. Tomorrow morning I will ask you to fill in a questionnaire. To state the obvious, taste refers to the ability to detect the flavour of substances such as food and drink. However, many factors affect taste perception such as vision impairment, hormonal influences, genetic variations, amongst others. Because each of you has a particular make-up, you may experience taste differently. That is what we are here to investigate. We may also find that some of you suffer from certain taste disorders such as hypogeusia, that's a partial loss of taste, or even dysgeusia which is an inaccurate taste perception. By partaking in this trial and filling in the questionnaire tomorrow, you will be helping me to learn a little more about how people experience taste differently." She pauses for a moment and looks around the room. "Is everyone with me so far?"

It seems they are, so she goes on. "There are a few small rules you'll need to follow: a) no alcohol, b) no food after dinner, c) no drugs, d) no smoking – all these could impact on your taste perception, and, e) you have to stay within the grounds." She looks around again. "Well, that's about it really. In the meantime, just enjoy yourselves. We have laid on some things for you to do. After dinner there'll be a film playing in the TV room – and we have others lined up too, for the rest of the evening. Also, we'll set up some board games and card games here in this room, and we'll have music to dance to in the reception room down the hall for anyone who's interested."

With the students all served, the five of us, Caroline, Niall, Doug, Dana and I begin our own meal. Niall has finally taken off his dark glasses and I can see now why he's so fond of them. With them on he looks like he could be handsome but without them there's no question but that he isn't – he has small eyes that only serve to emphasise how big the rest of his features are.

"So far, so good," says Dana looking around.

"So, Dana, I'm confused," says Niall. "I thought you were testing out aphrodisiacs?"

"And we are."

"So what's all this about taste then?"

"Well, tonight's group are really just the control group."

"The what?"

"The control group. They believe that we're interested in examining taste so their behaviour will not be influenced by what we're giving them to drink. However, tomorrow's group will be told that that exact same drink – the Granadilla Cordial, also known as Passion Fruit Cordial – is an aphrodisiac and we expect this belief will influence their behaviour. So it's the mind not a particular drink I'm testing. One group will be under the impression that they've been given an aphrodisiac, one won't, so I'll be able to compare the behaviour of both groups, see if, or how, tomorrow's crowd act differently compared to tonight's."

"I see. I didn't realise the experiment was going on that long but I guess I could juggle a few things, get some fresh clothes brought down and try and stay on."

"You're going to stay the whole weekend?" Caroline asks in surprise.

"Yeah. No offence but I think you could do with a man and –"

"Excuse me," interjects Doug.

Niall goes on as if Doug never spoke, "– and remembering back to when I was a student, things could get out of hand pretty quickly."

"I think we'd be able to manage," says Doug in his quiet way.

"Anyway," Dana comes in, "Mick will be here tomorrow."

Doug sighs, "I'll be here too, remember."

"Oh yeah, Mick – I forgot about him," says Niall. "Mick's an actor, isn't he? Tell me, what movies would I have seen him in?"

"Well, none yet," admits Caroline. "He hasn't been at it long but –"

"I have a sister who's an actress," Niall interrupts, and then he laughs. "Or at least that's what she likes to say when anyone asks."

"Actually Mick is in the middle of a film shoot right now," Dana informs him. "He's playing the part of Lenny – it's the lead role in *Fate Farm*. Kevin North is directing it. Isn't that right, Caroline?"

Before Caroline can get a chance to answer, Niall cuts in again. "Oh yeah, I've heard of Kevin North. You know, I've often thought of investing money in the movies. I've heard it's a good tax break but I don't know, I'm happier putting my cash into something more solid. Film-making is a risky business. Even with a big name like North behind a movie there are no guarantees." Right then his phone rings again and he picks it up and checks the number. "I've got to take this." He gets up. "Stevie, my boy," he shouts into his mobile as he walks to the door, "what's the story?"

"So?" Dana turns to Caroline the minute he's gone.

"So?" asks Caroline.

"Never mind what's the story with Stevie, my boy – I want to know what's the story with *him*?" She nods in the direction Niall went.

"What do you mean? There is no story."

"Yeah?"

"Yeah. He's a friend."

"A friend?"

"Yes."

"So *you* say."

"Because that's what he is. That's all he is."

"Does he know that?"

Suddenly Caroline gets annoyed. "Look Dana, if it weren't for him, half of us wouldn't have knives and forks to eat with tonight and the students mightn't have been so happy unrolling their sleeping bags on pee-stained mattresses as opposed to freshly laundered sheets. So why don't you lay off and stop with all your innuendos, all right!"

"All right, all right. I'm sorry."

Despite Niall's concerns, everything is going well but it's hard work keeping an eye on everyone. When recruiting them, Dana specified that they had to be single but many, it seems, are determined not to stay that way for long. Now Dana comes back into the kitchen where Caroline and I are just finishing the last of the washing-up.

"You know, I've just come from the TV room and there are a couple in there, snogging! Already! I mean they hardly know one another. Like, what's the world coming to!"

"Is one of them that cute blonde, the little one with the purple top and black leggings?" asks Caroline.

"Yeah? How did you know?"

Caroline laughs. "Haven't you noticed? She's been flirting with just about every guy here this evening. She's even been flirting with Doug."

"*Even?*" Dana looks annoyed. "What do you mean *even?*"

"Also. I meant she's *also* been flirting with Doug. Not that she got anywhere. He was totally oblivious."

"If this is how they behave tonight," I think aloud, "what's it going to be like with tomorrow's crowd when they believe they've taken an aphrodisiac?"

"I guess that's what we're here to find out," says Dana. "Look, if you two are okay with finishing up here, I'll just go and take some notes, okay?"

At about twelve, I decide I'm going to go to bed. I find Dana and Doug sitting in the TV room – Dana is writing up some more observations. There's no sign of the girl with the purple top or her companion but there is another couple snuggled up on a couch, watching the movie – it's an old one with Tom Hanks – *The Green Mile*, I think. Dana was at pains to pick ones with no sexy stuff. Maybe it's no coincidence then that all the movies tonight seemed to have Tom Hanks in them.

"Are you two coming to bed?" I ask. "Caroline is going now. I think I will too."

Dana shakes her head. "We'll hang on. I want to wait until everyone else has gone first and I know they're all asleep."

"Okay, see you in the morning."

Caroline, Niall and I climb the stairs to the top floor. My room is at the end of the hall, Caroline's is next to it, then Niall's and then Dana and Doug's. It's pretty chilly so I undress quickly and hop into bed with the book I brought with me – Samuel Pepys, which I'm finally getting into. Burying myself as far into my sleeping bag as I can to protect myself from the cold, I begin reading where I last left off. That Pepys is a chronicler of an age past is interesting but much more so are the details of his private life. What a navel-gazer he is, and quite the Romeo – no detail is too sordid or private to write down. At this point in his life – January, 1665 – there's the ongoing relationship with his long-suffering wife, plus his dalliances with a Mrs Bagwell, *and* a Jane Welsh – his barber's servant, *and* a Sarah (second name unknown but she works at the Swan Inn) *and* another woman called Betty Martin. The man has absolutely no qualms flitting from one woman to another. It would be hell to be with someone like that. Then I think of Finn and how lucky I am and I decide to text him goodnight. Braving the cold, I reach from my sleeping bag to where my phone is lying on the ground by my bed. I pick it up. I see there's an unread text from Finn sent an hour ago but that I hadn't noticed.

– *Sleep well. XXX.*

I text back:

– *I'd sleep better if I had u here 2 share my sleeping bag. Then again, maybe not!*

I wait for a reply but none comes and I decide he's probably already asleep so I put the phone back down, switch off the light over the bed, and snuggle deep into my sleeping bag.

I'm not sure how much later – it could be five minutes, it could be fifteen – but I'm not yet quite asleep when I hear a soft tapping on my door. Or at least I think it's my door but, before I answer, I hear Caroline call out, "Who is it?" and I realise the knock was on hers. I don't hear the answer but I do hear the bedroom door open and then there comes the sound of Caroline's voice and a male one – Niall, for sure – in conversation. I sit up. And I listen. One part of me doesn't want to be hearing them, but the other part of me wants to know what's going on. Is there something going on? Does she like this guy? No, the idea is crazy. Caroline is mad about Mick. Mick is mad about Caroline. That's how it is. We all know that.

But Mick hasn't been around much lately and, when he has, Caroline and he haven't exactly seen eye-to-eye. And as for Niall, well, I might not like him but he's a successful businessman with oodles of money and all the trappings of wealth. Everything Mick is not. Everything Caroline used to say she admired and wanted in a man before she got together with Mick. Maybe deep down, she still does. Maybe she welcomes this nocturnal visit.

If something is happening or is about to happen, should I go barging in there on some pretence, like I can't sleep? But is it any of my business? Probably not. But Caroline is my friend. Mick is my friend. Damn it! I can make it my business. I'm not going to let this happen. Caroline is *not* going to throw away what she has with Mick for someone like Niall, not if I have anything to do with it. I sit there listening until there comes a short lull in the conversation. What are they doing now? That's it. I'm going in. I unzip my sleeping bag, swing my legs over the side of the bed, stand up, go to the door, and creep out onto the hall. There's no light on and as I'm trying to work out where the switch is, I get the feeling someone else is there. I look around and see the outline of a figure at the top of the stairs.

"Hello," I say. It's male, I think. "Is that you, Doug?"

But already I know it's not Doug.

He – whoever he is – turns and quickly runs down the stairs.

"Hey!" I call after him. "Come back!"

Immediately, Caroline comes to her door. "Rosie, what's the matter?"

"There was someone standing out here in the dark." I find the light switch and turn it on. "He ran downstairs when I spoke to him."

"Relax. It was probably one of the students."

I shake my head. "No, I don't think so. He seemed too

furtive. Why would he have run away if he was a student? Maybe whoever was here this morning has come back."

"Maybe. But the doors are locked and all the downstairs windows are shut – I checked before I went to bed."

"Maybe he came in before you locked the door . . . or maybe he has a key . . . the door was open when we arrived . . ." Then I hear a sound. "Hush," I whisper. "Someone is coming up the stairs." But then I hear the soft murmur of Dana's voice.

"Hey," says Dana, looking surprised to see us. "What's up? I thought you were gone to bed."

"Did one of the students just go downstairs?" I ask.

"I don't think so," said Dana. "I didn't see anyone. As far as I know, they're all in their beds – well, they're all in *a* bed. Though not necessarily their own."

"I think we've got a prowler," I tell her.

"Are you serious?"

"He was standing there when I came out and then he ran downstairs."

"Maybe I'll go down and have a quick look around?" says Doug.

"I'll go with you," says Dana.

"Why don't we all go?" asks Caroline.

I look at her. I feel like telling her I know why she wants us all to go – so that Niall can sneak back into his room undetected.

"Will I go and wake Niall, ask him to come as well?" asks Dana.

A look of anxiety crosses Caroline's face and I find myself saying, "There's enough of us to deal with whoever it is. Leave him. He's probably asleep." And then I add pointedly, "Isn't that right, Caroline?" Caroline looks at me, and I look at her. I know she knows I know, and I'm glad she does. "Anyway, haven't we got Doug?"

"That's right," says Doug, looking pleased.

"Besides, it's probably nothing to worry about."

In the end, all four of us – Doug, followed by Dana, followed by Caroline, followed by me, go back down the stairs and take a look around but all seems in order until we hear Dana call out from the kitchen:

"Hey guys, come look at this!"

We file in. The window over the sink is wide open and the high wind from outside is causing the flimsy curtains to dance about.

"That was definitely closed earlier when I checked," says Caroline, leaning over and pulling it shut.

"I'll take a quick look around outside," says Doug.

"Maybe it's better if you don't," I say, thinking how, in the movies, people always say something like that, that they're going to take a quick look around outside, and then go and walk themselves straight into whatever danger is out there. Next thing you know, they're found with their throats slit, or a bullet in their head – *if* they are ever found again.

"I'll go with you," says Dana.

Yep, just like in the movies, one goes, and then another. But Dana and Doug are determined.

"Be careful!" I shout after them as they head off.

So there's just me and Caroline. I know she's looking over at me but I steadfastly ignore her.

"Rosie?" she says eventually.

"What?" I snap.

"Nothing happened, you know."

"Good," I say, and then I turn to go. "I'm going to see how the others are getting on."

In the end, we find nothing either inside or out.

"Whoever it was is long gone," says Dana, as we climb back up the stairs. "Anyway, goodnight, you two," she calls going into her own room. "Sleep tight!"

"Yeah, goodnight," says Doug, following after her.

When they're gone, I turn to Caroline and say pointedly. "Hopefully Niall's all tucked up in his own bed by now."

I leave her standing on the landing and go back into my own room.

The word 'honeymoon' comes from the ancient practice of guests giving honey to newly-weds before their wedding night to – ahem – pep up their antics.

When I was little, I thought the reason it was called a honeymoon was because the bride and groom headed to the moon after the wedding where they would get to eat honey from morning to night. It sounded pretty exciting and entirely plausible to me. After all, how else would they pass the time?

15

The following morning I'm tired. When I went back to bed I didn't really get much sleep. In the light of day, I'm pretty sure that if it was an intruder then he'd fled into the dark of the night, never to be seen again but, last night, lying in the darkness in a strange bed in an even stranger building, I wasn't quite so confident. I kept imagining I could hear all these sounds. One sound I'm glad to say I didn't hear however was that of Niall paying Caroline any more night-time visits.

But he's still every bit as attentive to her as he was yesterday.

"When is Mick getting here?" Dana hisses in my ear at breakfast. "The sooner the better if you ask me. Maybe then Romeo here will sling his hook."

At ten, Dana gets all the students to fill in her questionnaires.

At eleven, the bus comes to take them back to Dublin

At eleven-thirty, Mick rings to tell Caroline that he won't be able to come at all.

At one, a van with the Urbana insignia on the side arrives to deliver a bag with a change of clothes for Niall and an Urbana picnic basket.

At one thirty, Niall arrives down, showered and dressed more casually than yesterday in an open-necked shirt and jeans with razor-sharp pleats down the centre of each leg.

At one thirty-one, Dana spots him and whispers, "Doesn't Caroline know the golden rule? Never trust a man who irons pleats into his jeans?"

At one thirty-two, Niall calls out, "Hey, you guys, fancy going down to the beach for a picnic?"

To which Dana replies, "Yeah, sure," then whispers to me: "There's no way I'm leaving them on their own."

Somehow Niall orchestrates it so that Doug is carrying the picnic basket as we clamber down the steep incline to the beach.

"Call them back!" wheezes Doug when he reaches the bottom and sees how far ahead Caroline and Niall have gone. "Do they think I'm a pack mule?"

"Hey, you guys!" I shout. "Come back! Here's perfect!"

Niall, or rather whoever packed the picnic for him, has thought of everything including a tartan rug, and Niall unfolds this now and begins laying out the food. And there is one hell of a lot. There's a huge array of sandwiches, all sorts: home-cooked ham, cheese and pickle, roast chicken with stuffing. There's some gourmet Italian sausages with fennel, chicken goujons with lime and coriander, and there's meat loaf and chicken satay skewers.

"Wow!" I say, looking at the spread.

"What's that?" asks Doug as Niall takes off the lid of a container of pale green liquid.

Niall reads the handwritten label on the lid. "Chilled cucumber and mint soup."

"Chilled soup?" repeats Doug, sounding doubtful.

"Yes, a gazpacho," explains Niall, sounding rather condescending.

"Actually," says Doug, going on to sound satisfyingly knowledgeable, "I think gazpacho specifically refers to a cold Spanish soup made from tomatoes and peppers."

Dana gives a little smirk, then looks over at Doug proudly.

To wash down all this food there's an array of drinks to choose from: still and sparking water, home-made lemonade, red wine, white wine and even champagne.

"Oh my God!" cries Caroline. "This is just incredible!"

Dana shakes her head in wonder. "And I thought picnic meant a few rounds of ham and cheese sandwiches and a flask of tea shared while standing around the bonnet of the car, or inside the car if it's raining. At least that's what it was in our family."

"Tuck in, guys," urges Niall.

"I couldn't eat another bite!" says Caroline, flopping back on the sand.

"What a pity!" says Niall. "I guess these brownies and the peanut-butter cookies and the banana nut bread will have to go to waste then."

Caroline sits bolt upright. "Maybe I could squeeze in just a little more." She picks up one of the cookies and takes a bite. "Hmmm, delicious!"

"Tea or coffee?" asks Niall.

"Coffee, please."

"It was good, wasn't it?" says Niall as he pours. "Compliments to the staff at the Urbana!"

"It must be cool running your own hotel," observes Dana. "Imagine being able to ring up on a whim and have them deliver all this."

"Well, I don't run it *per se*. I'm just one of the backers. But yes, owning a hotel has its advantages." Niall turns to Caroline, patting his stomach. "When you're through with your coffee, do you fancy walking off some of those calories?"

I look at Dana and she looks at me, and raises an eyebrow but whether it's at Niall's concern for his waistline or at his invitation to Caroline I'm not sure. It could be either.

"I don't think so," answers Caroline.

Dana gets to her feet. "I guess we should be getting back – the second lot of students will be descending upon us soon."

Caroline stands up next. "Come on!" she says to Niall.

He holds out a hand, "Pull me up then!"

She takes hold of his hand and starts to pull but then he suddenly pulls against her and she ends up falling on top of him.

"Ooops! Sorry!" he laughs.

"Niall, let me go!" she snaps. She gets to her feet and straightens up her clothes.

"Hey, sorry, Caroline!"

"It's all right. Just forget it."

Again, somehow, Doug gets lumbered with the picnic basket. With so much of the food gone it's lighter but he's struggling with it on the steep slope. He's not complaining but Dana is furious.

"Caroline," she calls out, "can you come here a second?"

"Yeah, what is it?"

"Don't you think Niall could give Doug a hand carrying the basket?"

"He would except he can't with his knee injury."

Dana snorts.

"Excuse me?"

"I didn't say anything."

"But you snorted."

"Snorted?"

"Yes, snorted, in that way someone does when they want you to know that something is annoying them, but don't want to say what, but do want you to ask."

Dana snorts again. "I don't know what you're talking about."

"Okay, Dana, if you have something to say, why don't you just spit it out?"

"All right then. I would like to know what you think Mick would think of all this."

"All *what*?"

"Niall being here for the whole weekend."

"Well, let's ask him. Oh, hang on a second! We can't! Because he's not here. Silly me! That's right – he's not here. First he said he'd be here by lunch-time yesterday. Then he said he'd be here this morning. And then he said he wouldn't be here at all. So we can't ask him after all, now can we?"

"Don't be cross, Caroline. I'm just –"

"Minding your own business? Good!"

"Caroline, don't be so angr –"

"Dana, listen to me. Niall is a friend. He knows that I have a boyfriend. Nothing is going on between me and him, so you can stop worrying, all right? And maybe you could even start being a little more civil to him, considering all he's done."

Tonight's dinner is spaghetti bolognese, same as last night and, after we've served it out, Dana stands up and gives her welcome speech but this time more confidently and the crowd are more attentive.

"Hi, everyone, thanks for coming." As she did the previous evening, she lists out all the rules: no drinking, no drugs, no food other than dinner, no smoking, no leaving the grounds. Like before, she informs everyone that, after dinner, there'll be board and card games in one room, DVDs to watch in another, and music to listen or dance to in a third. And then she comes to the big difference.

"Okay, at this point I need to tell you that there's a slight difference to this evening from what you're expecting. When you signed up I told you that the trial you were partaking in was concerned with taste. Now that isn't actually the case and in fact what I want to do here tonight is to test aphrodisiacs." Suddenly the room begins to buzz but Dana carries on. "The reason I misled you was to ensure that you didn't tell this to yesterday's group, the control group, who were, and still are, under the impression that this trial is concerned with taste. Now I'll understand if any of you want to pull out, you're fully entitled to, and even if you decide not to partake you won't lose out on your VIP passes for the Energy Concert." She looks around. "Okay, so does anyone want to opt out? Raise your hand to let me know." There's a hum in the room as they all consult one another but nobody raises their hand. "Okay," says Dana, looking around. "Great! So I'll take it you're all happy taking part. I will, of course, need you to sign forms after dinner, indicating your consent."

"What happens then?" asks one bookish, bespectacled, worried-looking male student who's sitting near the front. I imagine he always sits near the front at lectures too, looking worried, asking questions.

"I'm just coming to that," Dana tells him. "After you've finished eating and have signed the forms, I'll be handing out glasses of a drink called Passion Fruit Cordial. Feel free to drink as much of this as you want. Now you have mine and the college's assurance that the cordial is absolutely safe to take and all ingredients are natural. There are no chemicals of any sort involved or even permitted additives. Again," Dana goes on, finding that she has to raise her voice over the heightened noise level, "if any of you feel that you wish to opt out at this stage, then please do. There is absolutely no compulsion on you to participate. Oh yes, I will be asking you to fill in a questionnaire tomorrow morning. So, any questions?"

"How soon can we start?" calls out one of the girls, causing the room to erupt with laughter.

"Straight after dinner," answers Dana.

"How will this cordial affect us?" asks the bookish guy.

"That's what we're here to find out!" Everyone laughs. "But don't worry – as I said, it's safe and there are no chemicals involved."

When they finish their meal, I start clearing away the tables when one student who I noticed earlier – a dark-haired, good-looking guy with a very pronounced chin dimple, who's wearing a black leather jacket – reaches out and takes hold of my arm.

"So are you taking part in this trial then?" he asks, raising an eyebrow flirtatiously .

I look at him properly now. He is *very* good-looking – not unlike John Travolta in his heyday *Grease* days.

"Afraid not."

"Sure I can't tempt you?"

Another time, another place, I'm about to answer but then decide that in the circumstances that would be totally inappropriate. Plus I'm years older. Plus I don't want Dana writing me up in her notes. Plus I have a boyfriend.

As I head back to the kitchen with a stack of dirty plates, it strikes me that even the mention of the word aphrodisiac has changed the atmosphere and tonight's crowd are even more animated than last night's.

As the evening goes on, the difference becomes more and more pronounced. Fewer of the students are watching DVDs. Only two are playing cards – the bookish guy with a girl just as bookish-looking, who wears matching specs. Tonight it's the room with the music that proves to be by far the most popular and whereas last night there were just a few girls dancing, tonight nearly everyone takes to the floor at some stage. I notice too they're drinking an awful lot more of the cordial and I'm kept busy serving it out and noting down for Dana who I give it to and how much. I'm also the subject of quite a lot of male admiration, different too from last night. John Travolta has now set his sights elsewhere however – a pretty blonde girl with half a dozen eyebrow rings – but two other guys, one beefy-looking fellow and one skinny guy dressed all in black with deathly pale skin, have been vying for my attention.

"Seems you're proving your hypothesis," I remark to Dana as we pass one young couple kissing in the hall on our way to the kitchen to fill up with more cordial. Already I've handed out three times as many glasses as I did the previous night.

As the end of the evening draws, there are more loved-up couples than there are singles.

"Isn't the mind a wondrous thing," remarks Dana. Then she notices one couple about to slip out the front door. "Hey!" she calls out. "No going outside, all right!"

It's near two by the time we finally get to our own rooms leaving Dana and Doug downstairs to keep an eye on things until she's satisfied everyone is asleep, and to write up her observations.

It's near three when a shout – from Caroline, I think – wakes me. It takes me a second to get my bearings but then I disentangle myself from my sleeping bag, hop from my bed and go running out into the hallway.

"Caroline!" I knock on her door which is ajar. "Are you okay?"

But before I get a response, I push the door fully open and immediately turn on the light. I'm not sure what I was expecting but it's certainly not what I do see. Caroline is sitting up in her bed, a terrified look on her face, her sleeping bag pulled up around her. But the truly surprising thing is the figure crouching under the bed, like he's looking for something. And the figure is not Niall, nor anyone else I know, as far as I can tell from this angle – from what I can see, he's far shabbier than any of the students.

"What's going on?" I ask Caroline. "Who the hell is he?"

"I don't know. All he'll say is that he's looking for some photo he left under the bed."

By now Dana and Doug have joined us.

"What's happening?" asks Doug. "Who is that?"

The figure comes out from beneath the bed and stands up. The first thing I notice is how small and slight he is. The second thing I notice is his beard which sits oddly on his childish face and, the third thing I notice is that I recognise that face underneath the beard. It's Seán. I know him from before. He used to sleep in a doorway opposite our shop, back when it was Elegance Boutique and I used to work there with Monica and Fay.

"Seán?" I say.

He looks surprised that I should know his name. He stares at me nervously but then he grins in recognition. It's a grin I remember well. He always had a nice smile, and nice white even teeth with a gap in the middle.

"Ah, Rosie, my friend! The coffee lady!"

"You remember me then?"

"Course I do."

"You know him?" asks Caroline dubiously.

"Yeah. You must remember me talking about him. Seán used to sometimes sleep in the doorway opposite Monica's shop when I worked there."

They're all looking at him now.

"Yeah," says Caroline, a little more kindly now. "I remember."

Every morning when I worked in Elegance, I used to bring in coffees and doughnuts for Fay, Monica and myself. Then, one day, Monica was late in so I was standing outside the shop waiting for her to arrive with the key when I became aware of someone watching me. It was a homeless guy lying in the doorway opposite, in his sleeping bag. To begin with, I ignored him but then he started talking to me. It seems he'd noticed my late arrival to work on other mornings. In the end, deciding he was harmless and feeling sorry for him, I gave him one of the coffees and we ended up talking. I don't know that you'd call us friends exactly but I did grow very fond of him, and I did get into the habit of chatting with him and bringing an extra coffee for him each morning. But then, one day, he disappeared.

222

"Look, I'm not trying to cause trouble," Seán is saying now. "I just came back to look for my photo. It was in the sleeping bag I left here but that's gone now – it's been taken away – but I was thinking that maybe the photo fell out and that it's still here somewhere, maybe under the bed."

I look at Doug. "Did you notice it when you were cleaning out this room?"

Doug shakes his head. "No."

Seán is agitated now.

"Seán," I say, "look, maybe it is here. Let me help you look." I kneel down beside him and peer under the bed, as he too is doing again.

It's Seán who spots it, stuck between the leg of the bed and the wall. "There it is!" He worms under the bed, reaches in, gets it, comes back out and stands up.

It's a photo in a thick wooden frame. Without even seeing the image, I know what it is. Seán showed it to me before. He used to always keep it in his sleeping bag. It was – still is, I guess – his most prized possession. I hold out my hand now and he passes it to me. I look at it. It's of Seán – all clean-shaven, and barely looking fourteen though I know he was around seventeen, eighteen maybe, when this was taken over a year ago. With him are his young girlfriend whose name I don't remember and their two young daughters.

A name comes to me. I point at the older, dark-haired girl.

"That's Julia, isn't it?"

Seán smiles and nods and looks pleased that I remember.

"And what's this little one called again?" I ask.

"Queenie."

He takes the photo back from me and strokes Queenie's blonde hair.

"But, Seán, what are you doing here?" I ask him.

He shrugs. "I was staying here. I wasn't doing any harm. Now that I have my photo I'll go."

Before I can ask any more questions, there comes an interruption.

"What's going on?"

We all look to the door. Niall is standing there, looking in at us. We must make an odd picture. Caroline still in her bed. Seán in his filthy clothes standing in the middle of the room, clutching his photo. Dana, Doug and myself, pyjama-clad, gathered around him.

"Who is *that*?" asks Niall, not bothering to disguise his distaste.

"This is Seán, an old friend of mine," I tell Niall and, despite the oddness of the situation, I momentarily find myself enjoying Niall's obvious surprise.

"Look," repeats Seán, "I have my photo. I'll leave now."

"But you can't!" I protest. "It's pouring rain outside!"

"Rosie, hang on a min –" begins Caroline.

"We're *not* going to throw him out on a night like this," I tell her straightaway. Then a thought occurs to me. "Where did you sleep last night, Seán?"

Seán looks around at the crowd of us all looking at him, then admits: "In the car out front."

"The silver one?" demands Niall.

Seán nods. I smirk.

"You slept in my car!"

Quickly I intervene. "Don't worry. You won't have to do that again. Look, you can sleep downstairs on one of the couches." I look at Caroline. "Can't he? Seán isn't going to cause any harm, I know him. I trust him."

Caroline hesitates for a second then she nods. "All right,

all right, but he'll need to be gone first thing in the morning. This is my brother's place. I'm responsible for it."

"Sure," says Seán. "Course I will. I'll be gone before you're even up. Look, thanks very much – I appreciate it. I do, really," he tells Caroline. "You're very kind."

Momentarily disarmed, Caroline tells him: "You're welcome." She even smiles at him.

"Come on, Seán. Let's go downstairs and get you sorted," I say. "One of yesterday's students left their sleeping bag behind. I'll see if I can find it."

When I got to know Seán, in the days he slept in the doorway opposite the boutique, he once told me the heartbreaking story that saw him end up on the streets. He told it in a matter-of-fact way, without self-pity, but it was no less tragic for all that. He and his young girlfriend, Hilda – I now remember her name – shared a little flat with their two young daughters. He did most of the childminding while Hilda brought in some money by cleaning offices. But then, early one morning when she was on her way back from a cleaning job, she had the gross misfortune of running into two drunks who hadn't yet gone home from the drinking session they'd started the previous afternoon. These two scumbags set upon her, robbed her, and beat her up. Back then, Seán gave the impression that as soon as Hilda recovered, then they'd all move back home again, and their family photo would be back up on their mantelpiece where it belonged

But this is where Seán's version of the story differed from the reality, as I subsequently found out after he went missing. Concerned when I hadn't seen him around for some time, I began making enquiries and two other homeless guys told me the truth: that Hilda was never going to recover but was in a permanent vegetative state and would spend the rest of her life in care, that Seán's kids were in foster care, and that Seán had probably gone back to the mental institute where he'd been a patient before when he found his reality too difficult to cope with.

Seán doesn't know I know any of this and now I consider telling him I do but, in the end, I decide not to.

I look at him now. Do I feel threatened by this young man who lives rough and who has mental problems? No, not in the slightest. I remember now how he intervened when Mark was hassling me on the street one day. I trust Seán. He's one of the good guys who just happened to be dealt an especially crap hand.

"So, Seán," I ask him as he settles down on the couch, "how come you're staying out here in the sticks? I'd have put you down for a city boy."

He shrugs. "Too many drugs, too many lowlifes – it's safer out here." But then he quickly adds, "But I understand how your friend feels and I'll be gone in the morning – tell her not to worry about that."

"But where will you go?"

He shrugs. "There's always somewhere to go." He turns over onto his side. "Well, goodnight now and thanks again."

"Goodnight, Seán," I say. "It was good to meet you again."

"You too."

"Sleep tight." But still I don't go. I stand there watching him. "Seán," I say, "can I give you my phone number just in case you ever need it?"

"Sure."

I go into the kitchen, find a pen and some paper

226

belonging to Dana and write out my number. When I go back in to Seán, he's already sleeping, his precious photo clutched to his chest. As quietly as I can, I slide the sheet of paper into the pocket of his jacket. He stirs a little as I do so but doesn't wake. I turn out the light and leave him be.

The Greek Thessalonian witches combined belladonna root
with wine to make powerful love drinks.
Did they know that belladonna or deadly nightshade is
one of the most toxic plants found in the western
hemisphere with the root generally being considered the
most toxic part? Symptoms of belladonna poisoning include:
dilated pupils, tachycardia, hallucinations, blurred vision, loss of
balance, a sense of suffocation, paleness followed by a red
rash, flushing, husky voice, dry throat, constipation, urinary
retention and confusion.
Perhaps they confused these symptoms with those
of falling in love?

16

When we come downstairs the following morning there's no sign of Seán, apart from the sleeping bag I gave him last night which is neatly folded on the couch. I should have told him to take it with him, seeing as how Doug threw out his old one plus the clothes he found in the bathroom the day before.

"I wonder where he's gone?" asks Dana.

I shrug. "I don't know. I wish I did."

"Morning all!" I hear Niall calling as he comes down the stairs. He arrives into the room. "So, has our little visitor vamoosed then?"

I don't bother to answer, neither does Dana.

"I'd better go and get the students up for breakfast," says Dana.

I follow her.

After breakfast, Dana hands out the questionnaires to the students for completion.

"Okay!" she calls out. "I'm missing two of you. Are

Geraldine McWilliams and Eoin O'Brien here?" She looks around. There's no reply. "Were they here earlier – for breakfast?"

The students are craning their necks, checking each other out. No reply.

"Were they still in bed when you came down?"

There's a general but uncertain shaking of heads.

"Has anyone seen them this morning?"

More headshaking.

"Okay," says Dana, beginning to sound worried, "who was in the bed beside either?"

One of the girls calls out: "I was next to Geraldine!"

"And was she there when you woke up?"

The girl shakes her head. "No, but she was there when I went to bed."

Then the bookish guy speaks up, giving the impression he has only just tuned in to what's going on. "Eoin O'Brien? He's the guy with the black leather jacket, isn't he?"

"Yes."

I now realise we're talking about John Travolta.

"I heard him slipping out early this morning – a girl came in to get him. Is Geraldine blonde, with a whole load of eyebrow-rings?"

"Yeah, that's her," one of the others replies.

"Have you any idea where they were going?" Dana asks the bookish guy.

"I think I heard her say something about the beach."

"The beach? In this weather?"

"It sounded like they thought it might be fun."

"Fun! Oh sweetest Jesus!"

The overnight rain may have eased off but the sea is wild

this morning with massive, crashing waves. Most of the beach is underwater including the spot where we picnicked yesterday and, as we walk along the cliff, the spray from the most ferocious waves hits us. Doug says something but I can't hear him over the noise of the thunderous waves and the high winds.

"What?" I shout.

"Keep well back from the edge!"

"Do you think anything's happened to them?" shouts Dana.

I shrug and shout back, "We'll probably meet them walking along, hand-in-hand, oblivious to all the excitement they're causing!"

But we don't meet them walking along. No. But would that we had.

It's Caroline who spots them first. I hear her scream out:

"There they are!"

We look at her first and then to where she's frantically pointing, out to sea, to two little figures battling against the waves, desperately trying to make their way to shore.

"Oh my God!"

"Jesus!" cries Dana.

Already Caroline has taken her phone out and is pressing 999. I hear her describing the scene in a breathless rush and, even as she does, the two figures are being carried further, the distance between them increases, as does the distance from the coast — their battle against the waves looks hopeless.

Caroline hangs up, then shouts at us: "They're contacting the coastguard. They're going to send a helicopter. The guy I was talking to said that we're not to even think of going in, given the conditions!"

But Dana is over at the cliff edge, looking like she's trying to find a way down and just as a huge wave comes crashing over, Doug pulls her back.

"Dana! Careful! Or you'll be swept away too!"

Some of the students have joined us now.

"Oh Jesus!" one of them standing right behind me cries out hysterically. "We're going to watch them die!"

Two others girls are hugging one another and crying softly.

"The guy on the phone said not to lose sight of them!" Caroline shouts.

But that's easier said than done. One of the figures – Geraldine – goes under for a second.

"Oh God!" cries Dana.

"Look! There's someone else in there now!" one of the students calls.

We look and see a third figure battling his way out to them. Immediately I know who it is and my heart sinks. It's Seán. What hope has he, I think, such a skinny malnourished little scrap? But we watch him fighting against the odds and the waves, against a large swell, the strong current. It seems like he's not getting anywhere but little by little, despite the constant knock-backs, he inches nearer to Geraldine and then we watch as he grabs hold of her and begins swimming with her towards the shore. They both go under for a moment but then resurface. We run along the cliff-top to where he's struggling towards the only bit of beach above water – all the time keeping our eyes on them. They go under again. They resurface. The incline down to this sliver of beach is less than along the rest of the coast and Doug, who's ahead of us, has already gone clambering down and when the pair are still some distance from shore,

Doug begins swimming out to help Seán bring Geraldine the rest of the way.

"Come on," I say and begin making my way down the cliff, and Dana, Caroline and a couple of the students follow after me.

All three have reached the shore now and as we're climbing down, I see Seán turn as if he's about to start out again but Doug pulls him back. The pair struggle with one another but then Seán manages to pull away from Doug and plunges back into the water. Doug doesn't hesitate for a second: he follows after him.

"Doug!" shouts Dana.

"Watch it, Dana!" I say when in her rush to get down she nearly loses her step.

We reach the bottom. Caroline goes immediately to Geraldine who's lying on the sand. She kneels down beside her and straight away begins CPR on her.

"Doug!" Dana is shouting. "Doug! Come back! He's going to drown!"

"Jesus! Dana! It's not going to help if you get swept in. Stand back, will you!"

"But Doug is going to drown!" she cries hysterically. "They're all going to drown."

"They'll be okay. He'll be okay. Don't make things worse! Stay where you are!"

I hold onto her and she clings to me. We watch as they reach Eoin and begin trying to bring him in but they make little progress. Everything is against them. Eoin has no strength in him. He's heavier. His leather jacket is weighing him down. The current seems stronger now. Seán has less power in him second time around. They look like they're losing their battle. They are losing the battle. They're being dragged out to sea.

233

"They're all going to drown!" cries Dana. "Doug is going to drown."

I don't say it but I'm beginning to think she might be right. Dana tries to push me away now but I keep a firm hold of her.

"Dana, don't!" I shout and then I hear a noise overhead. I look up. "See! The helicopter is here!"

"Thanks be to God!" she cries.

The helicopter passes over us and then begins hovering over the three. We see the figure of a rescuer being lowered down by rope until he reaches the water. We wait, then he gives the signal and we watch as he and Eoin are lifted out of the water and slowly pulled up into the body of the helicopter. Two more times we see the exercise being repeated. Seán is lifted up. And then, finally Doug, is lifted up to safety. With everyone on board, it heads off again, inland.

Back in 1994, US plans for a so-called 'love bomb' envisaged an aphrodisiac chemical that would provoke widespread homosexual behaviour among enemy troops, causing what the military called a 'distasteful but completely non-lethal' blow to enemy morale.' Let's hope the US doesn't decide to dust off this particular plan and put it into action.

17

"Rosie!"

"What?"

"You're not listening to a word, are you?"

I turn from the window and towards Dana who's sitting beside me in the back of a taxi.

"Sorry," I say. "Go on – what were you telling me?"

"I wasn't *telling* you anything. I was asking if you thought Geraldine McWilliams and Eoin O'Brien will sue?"

"Well, have you heard anything from them since?"

"No, but it's early days. I don't think Eoin will but I swear I've never met such an angry man as Geraldine's father." Not noticing my lack of interest, Dana goes on. "If you ask me he could do with talking to someone – professionally, I mean. There's so much rage locked inside. It's not healthy. When he was screaming at us like that, out in the corridor in A and E, all I kept thinking was that he and not his daughter would be the one who'd end up being kept in for overnight observation but in the coronary care unit, if you know what I mean. You know . . ."

Dana goes on and on but I don't hear much of what she's saying. I'm feeling anxious. Maybe I should have told Finn we were coming to see him and his band. But how, when I know in my heart he doesn't want me there?

"Rosie!"

"What?" I snap.

"I was asking, what did you do with Seán's jacket in the end?"

After they were taken to the hospital by helicopter and the ambulance had collected Geraldine, I found Seán's jacket and the photo on the beach. When we followed in the car, I brought them with me to give him but, by the time we got to the hospital, he'd already left.

"I still have them," I tell her. "I don't know what I'm going to do with them."

Everything will be so different at tonight's concert. The last time I saw Finn on stage was with Mark fronting the line-up and now Lola will be taking his place.

"Maybe you should wrap them in something waterproof and leave them back where you found them?" suggests Dana.

"Maybe. I thought about that but what if someone else were to find them first?"

"I take your point."

We pull up outside the Velvet Rooms.

"Oh, are we here already?" asks Dana.

The Velvet Rooms isn't a big venue but it is a very popular one and tonight it's packed. There's nobody on stage when we arrive but once we've got our drinks from the bar, Dana begins to "Excuse me! Excuse me!" her way through the crowd towards the front with me following behind.

"Dana!" I call after her. *"Dana!"*

But she doesn't hear me over the noise so I grab onto her sleeve and give it a tug. She swings around.

"What?" she shouts.

I lean in close and shout into her ear. *"Don't go too close to the stage! Remember I don't want him to know I'm here, at least not to begin with!"*

"Yeah, sure. Is here all right then?"

I nod.

Small talk is too difficult to be bothered with and so we settle for sipping our drinks and defending our small patch from encroachment on every side. Then a guy, the support act – some comedian I've never heard of before – walks onstage with the cocky, laid-back gait of someone keen for the audience to assume he's a funny guy. He walks up to the microphone, pulls it in close to his mouth and begins talking in a confiding manner to us all but I can't hear a word – the microphone is too close to his mouth. Every few moments he laughs at whatever witty insight he thinks he's sharing with us but, as he gradually begins to notice how few are joining in, his own laughter grows less confident, his jokes more rushed and even less audible until, finally, with unadulterated relief, he bellows out: "Now it's time to give it up for the reason you're all here, for the new line-up of your old favourites – the extraordinarily talented band that is Dove!"

First on are Mitch and Ashley, the two guitarists, and they run on to the stage, waving to the crowd, looking like they're thrilled to be back, just as the crowd sound like they're thrilled to have them back. Judging by the intensity of the clapping and the volume of the cheers and whistles, the break-up didn't obliterate their fan base – they've turned out tonight as loud and as vocal as ever I've heard them.

Next comes Finn. Dressed in his trademark black velvet jacket, he walks on slowly, casually, one hand buried deep in his jeans pocket, the other waving to the cheering crowd. His demeanour is casual, not overly confident, but quite relaxed in fact. If he is as nervous as I suspect he must be, he's managing to hide it pretty well. God, how I love him! I want to turn to those around me and proudly tell them, "Hey! That's my boyfriend up there!" I watch him climb up behind his drum kit and, once seated, he raises both his hands high up in the air, forming V-signs with his fingers. And then it starts, the thumping of feet from somewhere up front, and, gradually, it spreads right through the room, and as the force increases I begin to understand what it's about. It's the crowd's way of telling Finn, Mitch and Ashley that they're glad to have them back, that they're sorry about Mark too. I'm so glad I'm here to witness this. If Dana hadn't talked me into coming, I'd have missed it.

Gradually the thumping begins to die down and then an expectant hush fills the room and for what seems like five, even ten, minutes but in reality is probably less than one, nothing happens but, just as the crowd begins to grow a little restless, a petite figure, who I can only assume is Lola, comes running barefoot onto the stage, keeping her face turned from the audience and towards Finn and the boys. She stops mid-stage and, with her back still to the crowd, she gives the band the nod and they launch into the opening strands of a slow tune I've never heard before. Slowly she turns around, keeping her head down. Staying absolutely still, she begins to sing, ever so softly, and in order to hear this little figure clad in leggings and a skin-tight black T-shirt, the crowd is compelled to keep completely silent. Not until the chorus does she finally look up at the crowd.

So this is Lola. Is she as I expected? Unfortunately yes, and more. She is absolutely stunningly, even shockingly beautiful, in an edgy rock-chick way; cheekbones sitting impossibly high, dangerous pouty lips, eyelashes heavy with black mascara, brash platinum-blonde hair cut tight into her delicate, beautiful little face. Even if this Lola hadn't a note in her head, she looks like she was born to be a rock star, right down to her delicately tattooed ankle and her silver-painted toenails. I search for something, anything, to criticise.

"I mean, like, what's with the bare feet?" I shout over at Dana.

"What?" cries Dana.

"Why isn't she wearing any shoes?"

Dana shrugs but doesn't reply.

"Like does she think she's so above convention?" I demand, knowing I'm being jealously petty but unable to stop myself.

And what about her voice? I would like to say that it lets her down but no, that's not so — it is in fact quite extraordinary. It's both angel *and* devil. One minute it's light, tinkling, sweet and as innocent as an angel's but it changes in an instant so that she sounds like a devil, a cigarette-puffing, vodka-drinking, staying-out-all-night devil infusing the words she sings with dirty suggestion.

I drag my eyes away from her and look around at the crowd and I see that any initial ill-feeling this loyal crowd might have had towards Mark's replacement has been blown away by Lola's looks, talent and extraordinary stage presence. And, now that Lola has them where she wants them, she moves without pausing onto one of the band's old songs, a sad song about lost love, one that Finn wrote, one that Mark used to sing, but tonight she manages to make it totally her own. The crowd is literally stunned into silence until she comes to the end of the song. And then they react in the most spectacular fashion. The clapping is thunderous, and like the cheering and the whistling, it goes on and on. This is the start of something big, I can feel it.

I see the band members looking at one another, I see Lola looking at Finn, all of them amazed by the reaction. Probably anticipating a certain resistance to their new line-up, I don't imagine they ever expected such an over-poweringly positive response but, happy to run with it, they launch straight into the next song.

Song after song, it's the same thing, except the level of support continues to grow. And then, finally, they come to their last song. It's another new one, one Lola tells us is penned by her, but no surprise, the crowd love this too. At the end of it, when the cheering finally settles down, Lola walks over to Finn, gives him a kiss full on the lips, then takes him by the hand, pulls him from his seat behind his drums and drags him up to the front of the stage. Hand-in-hand, they bow. I see them look at one another, smiles beaming and eyes sparking with the excitement of their enormous success and then Lola throws her arms around him and gives him an almighty hug. The crowd erupt again. Still hand-in-hand, they take another bow, as do Mitch and Ashley.

After all Finn has gone through, I should be sharing in the goodwill the rest of the crowd feel towards him, to all the band, but I'm not. There's a nasty, hard lump of jealousy sitting in the very pit of my stomach. Suddenly all I want to do is get out of here.

"Dana!" I shout. "I've got to go!"

"What?" shouts Dana.

"I'm leaving!"

241

I turn and let it up to Dana to follow me out.

Dana catches up with me as I come out onto the street.

"I suppose you'll say I'm a mean jealous cow but I couldn't bear watching them a moment longer," I explain.

She doesn't say anything, just looks at me with this odd kind of pitying look.

"I mean, I know all that kissing and hugging and holding hands is just a professional kind of thing, isn't it? It's not like it means anything."

"I guess," she answers tentatively.

"You guess? What? What do you mean? Don't tell me you think it's more than that?"

"No," she shakes her head, "no, I'm sure it's not. But, well . . ." she trails off.

"But what?"

"Look, I should have told you . . ."

"Told me *what*?"

"Okay." She takes a deep breath. "I saw the pair of them together the night you and I and Caroline went to that disco, ages ago, around the time Caroline came up with the idea for the shop but I just assumed it must be innocent – I didn't think Finn would be that type."

"What *type*? What do you mean? What were they doing exactly?"

"That's just it. They weren't actually doing anything but I don't know, the way she was acting towards him that night when I saw them made me a little uneasy. She seemed – you know – so touchy-feely around him. Now I guess that could be her way but . . ." She trails off.

I stare at her. "That night you insisted we all go home because you had a headache? Is that the night you're talking about?"

She nods her head.

"And did you have a headache?"

She shakes her head.

"No, I just didn't want you to get hurt. I didn't want you to see them. Look, I'm sorry, Rosie. I probably should have played things differently but I just reacted on the spur of the moment. I'm sorry. I should have told you sooner."

"Yes, you should have! Instead she's been like this with him for months now and I never knew. If I had, I don't think I'd have been quite so understanding when he told me she was moving in with him!"

"Rosie, I think it's all on her side. Like I say, I don't think Finn would be like that."

"Look, I've got to go home, I need to figure this out." I begin marching off.

Dana hurries after me. She grabs my arm. "You're not going anywhere! We're going to stay here and wait for them and, wherever they go to celebrate afterwards, we're going with them."

"No, no!" I try to pull away from her. "I couldn't bear that!"

"Yes, you could. You have to. You're right. I should have told you from the outset but now you know what she's like you need to stick around. You need to let her see you and Finn together."

"Oh Dana, no!"

"Rosie, get a grip! You've never been as happy with anyone else. We don't know there's anything between Finn and her – yet. But you saw the way she was acting with him – she's going to do everything she can to make something happen. Now you've seen her, are you just going to stand aside and allow it?"

"No, I guess not."

"Exactly."

"So we're going to stay right here and wait for them to come out. Okay?"

After what seems like ages, the departing crowd eventually slows to a trickle and then we hear them before we see them or hear her rather, her musical, girly, infectious laugh that sounds like nails on a blackboard to me. When we do finally see them, the first thing I notice is that she's linking his arm.

Finn spots me immediately and, despite my worries, he gives me a great big smile. "Rosie! Hi!" I'm pleased to notice he looks happy to see me and even more pleased when he disentangles himself from her, comes over and kisses me, a warm gentle kiss. Then he draws away.

"What are you doing here?" he laughs.

I laugh too. "We thought we'd come down to see you. I know you said you didn't want me here so I figured I'd just come without telling you."

"So you were there for the whole thing?"

"Yeah – you don't mind, do you?"

He shakes his head. "I guess I'd no need to be so nervous after all. Wasn't it amazing? What a reaction! The crowd loved us. Or should I say loved Lola!"

"Hey, it was a team effort," says Lola modestly, false modestly I presume. "It took all of us." She steps forward. "Hi, I'm Lola." She holds her hand out to me.

With no choice, unless I want to appear downright rude, I shake it. "I'm Rosie," I say.

"Finn's girlfriend," Dana adds, a little unnecessarily I think, but I'm quite pleased that she does. "And I'm Dana, her friend."

Finn laughs. "I forgot. None of you have met, have you?"

"No!" Both Lola and I say in unison, looking at each other, weighing each other up.

Now Mitch and Ashley appear.

"Hi, Rosie! Long time, no see!" cries Ashley. "Damn! You're looking well."

"You too, Ash!"

"Rosie! Hey, it's good to see you again," laughs Mitch. "Were you here all evening?"

I nod, finding myself unable to speak. I'm feeling a little emotional all of a sudden. I like Mitch and Ashley. I always liked hanging around with them before everything happened and the original band fell apart.

"Hi, you guys!" I finally manage. "You were brilliant this evening. What a reaction!"

"It was amazing, wasn't it?" says Mitch. "Listen, we're going for a drink. Are you coming?"

"Sure we are," answers Dana.

"I was so nervous going on stage, I really thought they were going to hate me." Ever since we sat down, Lola has been going over and over the details of their glorious triumph. "I mean they loved Mark so much that I thought they'd never accept me so I figured that if I could just catch them off guard, that if I started singing straight off without any introductions then, maybe, I'd have a chance of winning them over. But I never dreamed it would work so well! And it did, didn't it, Finn?"

Finn nods over at her, a big smile on his face. "You were brilliant!"

"Brilliant! Yeah! We all were!" She hops up from her seat. "Okay, I need to use the Ladies'. Be back in a mo."

"So is Lola Love really her name?" Dana asks the guys while she's gone. "It doesn't seem like a real name to me."

"Well, her parents aren't Mr and Mrs Love," answers Mitch. "And no, I don't think she was, like, christened Lola."

Ashley joins in: "Isn't it something like Charlotte Louisa Cunningham? Do you know, Finn? You know her best."

"Charlotte Louisa Olivia Clara Cunningham, to be precise," answers Finn.

"What a handful!" says Ashley. "I think Lola suits her better."

For a second I think of asking Finn if he remembers what my second name is (I don't have a third or a fourth) but change my mind. I don't want to be humiliated if he doesn't know.

Soon Lola comes back.

"I hope you guys weren't talking about me!"

"I was asking them about your name," says Dana. "Where does it come from?"

"Since you ask, I chose it in homage to The Kinks and, in a roundabout way, to my dad. I grew up listening to their music. Dad was really into them and they've been, like, a huge influence on me – musically. You know the song, 'Lola'?"

Dana is looking at her blankly but I know the one she's talking about. It's about this guy falling for someone called Lola in a club. Some of the lyrics come to me – how girls will be boys and boys will be girls and how it's a mixed-up, muddled-up, shook-up world.

A thought occurs to me. "But didn't Lola turn out to be a man in that song?" I ask.

Lola laughs. "I know, I know, but even so my dad used

to call me Lola all the time. His Lovely Lola. I guess he just liked the sounds."

"Okay, you guys, what was The Kinks' first hit single?" Ashley suddenly asks.

"'All Day and All of the Night'?" Mitch guesses.

"Fraid not! That was their second. Try again."

"'You Really Got Me'?" shouts out Lola.

"Spot on! Ten points to Lovely Lola!"

"Okay," says Mitch. "I have one for you. What famous band did a cover version of 'All Day and All of the Night' back in the late eighties?"

"The Stranglers!" shouts out Lola.

"Another ten points for the lovely lady!"

"Come on," teases Lola. "Give us a hard one this time."

"Okay." Mitch thinks. "What were The Stranglers originally called?"

"Ah, ah . . . " Lola squints her eyes as she thinks hard. "I know this one. I know it. I do."

Mitch decides to give a hint. "Think of a place name in Britain, somewhere connected with the band."

"Guildford!" cries Lola. "The Guildford Strangers. That was where they came from, wasn't it?"

"Well done, Lola!"

"Now think hard this time, Mitch," coaxes Lola. "Give us something difficult."

Dana is evidently as bored as I am and when she thinks the others aren't looking she gives me a big false yawn but Lola spots her.

"Here, these two girls are getting bored. Not everyone finds rock 'n' roll trivia as fascinating as we do." She turns to me. "So, anyway, Finn tells me you're going into business. Love potions or something?"

"Yeah," I say defensively. "Love potions."

But it seems I have no reason to be defensive.

"That sounds fantastic," Lola gushes. "I'm really into all that sort of thing. I think we've all become far too removed from nature."

"You do?"

"Yeah, I mean like, why is alternative medicine called alternative medicine? Calling it alternative suggests that it's not really medicine if you know what I mean. I think we're losing a lot of the knowledge our forefathers and mothers took for granted. You know, like all the different uses of wild plants. I have this niece and nephew, right, and they've never even spent an afternoon picking blackberries. Can you believe that?"

I shrug. "Well, I guess that is har –"

"They've never, ever," she interrupts, "ever had the experience of doing something as simple as picking blackberries. Instead they spend most of the time stuck in front of their computers – I mean that can't be right."

Sure, Lola may have a point but this self-righteousness of hers is getting on my goat, as well as just about everything else about her, if I'm honest. "Maybe they're happier on their computers," I find myself arguing.

"Only because they don't know any different."

"Not necessarily – some kids aren't terribly outdoorsy. My sister Sarah was always happier inside with a book than playing outdoors."

"No offence to your parents but maybe they were at fault. Kids need the right encouragement."

"Excuse me!"

"You were asking about the shop," interrupts Dana, playing the peacemaker. "Well, we're due to open officially on Monday but we're having a launch party this Saturday evening if you'd like to drop in. You'd be very welcome. Finn will be there, won't you, Finn?"

"Yeah, of course," answers Finn.

"Then I'd love to come."

"Great!" I say and remind myself to throttle Dana on the way home.

But it seems nobody is thinking of going home any time soon and, at closing time, we find ourselves standing around outside the pub.

"I know, let's go to a club?" suggests Lola.

"Yeah! Why not?" agrees Ashley. "It's way too early to go home yet. Especially on a night like this."

"Sounds good to me," says Finn. "What do you think, Rosie?"

I hesitate before answering. I look around. Everyone seems sold on the idea, even Dana. But I've had enough of Lola's company. I want to be with Finn but, if I want to be with him, then it looks like I'm going to have to tag along and go wherever the group decides we should go.

I shrug. "I guess . . ." I say half-heartedly.

Finn must sense my lack of enthusiasm. Now he draws me closer and whispers in my ear. "Then again, we could just go home."

I smile and whisper back. "Yours or mine?"

"How about yours?"

"Hey, you two love-birds!" laughs Ashley. "Are you coming?"

"Well –" begins Finn.

"Course he is," laughs Lola.

"– actually, I think we'll give it a miss."

I have to admit to being more than a little pleased to see

the obvious disappointment on Lola's face. Round one to me

"Is it okay with you, Dana, if I don't go?" I ask.

Dana grins. "See you tomorrow. Have fun."

"We will," Finn answers.

"Let the sky rain potatoes."
Falstaff's call in 'The Merry Wives of Windsor' stemmed from his belief that potatoes were an aphrodisiac.
When it was first brought back to Europe, the potato was treated with distrust and fear as some thought it was dirty, unholy and primitive but its popularity grew as belief that it was a powerful aphrodisiac caught on.
For a while herbalists insisted that the potato could cure everything from diarrhoea to tuberculosis.

18

The next morning, I reluctantly leave Finn sleeping and get up early so that Dana and I can catch the bus into town to be in the shop at nine as ordered by Caroline. When we do get there, she's already standing at the door, directing two guys who are struggling under the weight of a huge cardboard box.

"Careful now, yep, that's it. Right, you can leave it down there." She points to a spot in front of the counter.

"There's another twenty of these," one of the men tells her.

"Well, just keep them coming."

"What's in them?" Dana asks.

Caroline doesn't answer but slits open the top of the box with a knife, reaches in and pulls out a ball of white paper and unwraps it to reveal a delicate, beautifully shaped octagonal little bottle with a glass ball on top for a stopper.

I take it from her. "It's really beautiful."

"Isn't it?" agrees Caroline. "You chose well, Dana."

Dana nods. "I thought these looked the classiest."

Caroline unwraps a few more and then lines them up on a glass shelf in the window. Suddenly these bottles make everything seem more real. I can get a real sense of the products we're going to be selling. I think of the potions I've come up with, especially the more colourful and, for the first time, I can really see this whole thing working, I can see people wanting to buy what I've created.

"Course these bottles cost us more than the actual potions we'll be filling them with," says Caroline, admiring the one she's holding in her hand, "but in this game presentation is everything." She puts the bottle down on the counter. "Come on into the back for another surprise."

We follow her.

"Oh my goodness!" I look around. "When did they finish the kitchen?"

"Yesterday. Doug will need to touch up some of the walls again. He says he'll do it tomorrow."

I look around, admiring what was once the old stockroom. Along one wall there's a brand new cooker, fridge and sink. On the other there's a huge workspace facing a wall of shelves.

"So, what do you think?" asks Caroline.

"It's fantastic!"

"We're all set up now. Or we will be when the bulk quantities of the ingredients you ordered come in. I checked with the company yesterday and they should be here this morning. Oh, yeah, and the labels Dana ordered for the bottles should be ready today too, as well as the bags with our logo. I'll pop around to the printers this morning to get them and I'll pick up some tissue paper too while I'm there. I was thinking pink tissue and purple too. Anyway, come on, let's get some more of these bottles unpacked."

Around noon, another delivery truck pulls up. This time it's those ingredients we sourced online. Caroline has gone to collect the labels and the bags so I direct the men into the kitchen. When they're gone, I start unpacking and I try to organise everything on the kitchen shelves. I'm beginning to feel really excited at the prospect of cooking in this new little kitchen and I work as quickly as possible to get everything sorted.

At one, the three of us go to get some lunch and when we get back, we start cooking up the first patch of potions. Caroline may be in charge of almost every other aspect of this project but this little kitchen is now my domain. These are my recipes. I can't help feeling quite proud. We don't talk much, just listen to the Rick Montague talk show on the radio as the girls prep and I cook. Dana hums as she slices and dices. I realise I'm feeling happy, really happy. On impulse, I put everything aside and go to my handbag hanging on the back of the door to get my phone to take a picture. When I take my phone out, I see there's a message from Finn:

– *Did you have to leave so early! Missing you already. Love you loads.*

I text back:

– *Love you too.*

Then I hold it up.

"Smile!" I say to the girls.

They both look up from their work. Wearing broad smiles and the blue and white stripy aprons Caroline has outfitted us with, they put their arms around each other's shoulders and wait for me to take the picture.

But then Dana cries out, "Hang on a second. We need all three of us in the photo!"

"You're right." I go over, step in beside Dana, put one arm around her shoulder and then hold the camera at arm's length from us.

"Say cheese!"

In unison, they cry out, "Cheese!"

All three of us look at the shot.

"Oh no! I look like I've a squint," moans Dana.

"Give over," Caroline tells her. "You look great! We all do."

And we do. We look so young and excited. And happy. I think of Monica. She must have gone through all the same emotions when she was setting up the boutique in these same premises. I think what a special time this is for us three.

"You know, I'm going to download this photo, print it off and stick it up right here."

"Ah, Rosie," moans Dana, "I look terrible!"

"You're fine, lovely. You know, we're like the Three Musketeers. What is it they used to say again?"

And then, at the exact same time, all three of us shout it together: *"All for one and one for all!"*

"If anyone heard us," laughs Caroline, "they'd think we're crazy!"

All afternoon we work away.

"Did you know," I say, thinking back to something I read, "that potatoes are considered aphrodisiacs?"

"No!" laughs Dana. "The humble spud! You are joking!"

"It wasn't considered humble back in the sixteenth century. No, when it was first introduced into Europe, it was viewed as very exotic and had a rarity value that made it very expensive. It was only as it became commonplace that it lost its allure."

"Have you found any recipes that include it?" asks Caroline.

I shake my head. "No."

"Maybe you should try coming up with one of your own," says Caroline. "Especially since they're so cheap. Think of the mark-up. I have it! We could market it as a special Irish love potion. The city centre is crawling with tourists during the summer. They'd be climbing over each other to buy it. Americans would love it. And just think of all the Spanish students."

"Don't you think Spanish students are loved up enough as it is?" laughs Dana.

"Hey, don't knock it!" laughs Caroline. "I say we make our money wherever we can."

Dana laughs. "You know, you could make that your motto: Make your money wherever you can!"

Caroline shrugs but doesn't take offence.

"By the way," says Dana, "where did you go to yesterday afternoon?"

"Yesterday afternoon?" Caroline pretends to think for a second. "Nowhere special."

"Yes, you did. Shane said you loaded up your car with bags and bags of groceries and then took off without saying a word."

"Well now, isn't he quite the snoop."

"So where did you go? Come on, what's the big mystery?"

Caroline is silent for a moment. She looks like she's considering whether she should answer.

"So?" Dana is looking at her expectantly

"Okay, I went back down to the hostel to bring some things to Seán."

"Seán!" I look at her in surprise. This certainly wasn't what I was expecting to hear.

"Yeah."

"But he wasn't there, was he? After all, you told him he had to leave."

"No, he wasn't. But, I don't know, I just figured that if he were still around, then I'd like to do something for him, even if it was just something small."

"You've certainly changed your tune," I laugh.

"Why, you big softie!" laughs Dana.

Caroline shrugs, then she smiles and puts her finger to her lips. "Just don't tell anyone. I wouldn't want to ruin my reputation."

"You know," I say, "I'd really like to know where he's gone. I still have his jacket and his photo. I'd really like to be able to give them back to him."

"Maybe you should try ringing around some hostels and the like."

"I have tried but no luck. I'll keep trying."

A little while later, Caroline's phone rings. She picks it up and checks the number.

"Are you going to answer it?" I ask.

She shrugs. "Nah."

"Who is it?"

"Niall."

"So why aren't you answering it?"

Caroline shrugs. "I don't want to get side-tracked. He'll keep me talking for ever."

Ten minutes later, Caroline's phone rings again. "Oh for crying out loud!" she snaps. She picks it up but when she sees the caller's name her frown disappears.

"It's my brother," she says, then answers the phone. "Hiya, Donald!" She listens. "Yeah, yeah. What? Now? Brilliant! Sure, no problem. Okay then, see you in half an hour." She hangs up and grins at us. "Let's lock up here. We need to go and collect something."

"What?" the pair of us demand.

She taps her nose. "Just come with me and you'll soon see."

When we get to Caroline's car, parked in a multistorey carpark around the corner, she throws me the keys. "Will you drive? I just need to send a couple of texts."

"Sure."

A minute later I'm sitting in the driver's seat, Caroline's beside me and Dana's in the back.

"So where exactly are we going?" I ask as I drive out of the carpark.

"Just turn left."

"But where are we supposed to be going?"

"All will be revealed." She doesn't look up from her phone.

"Why can't you just tell me?" I demand. "If I don't know where I'm going, how am I supposed to drive us there?"

"Okay, well, yes, head for the Stillorgan Dual Carriageway to begin with."

"And then?"

"And then I'll let you know."

I sigh in exasperation.

Twenty minutes later, we're on the dual carriageway.

"So where now?" I ask.

"Just carry on for a while."

I carry on for a while.

"Where now?"

"Just keep going straight ahead."

I keep going straight ahead.

"Do a left at the traffic lights," directs Caroline suddenly.

"What? These lights?"

"Quick! Before you miss it."

"Caroline! Jesus! I'm in the wrong lane – I'll never make it! You could have given me warning."

"Go! Quick! Now!"

Somehow I manage to cross over to the left-hand lane without incident and take the turn as directed.

"Now where?"

"Straight on."

I carry on for another five minutes.

"Now pull in here," she tells me.

"Here?" It's a car showroom. "Is this your brother Donald's place?"

"Yep, that's right."

I find a spot to park.

"Stay there," she says, and climbs out.

We sit there waiting.

"What do you think she's up to?" Dana asks from the back.

I shrug. "Heaven only knows."

"Do you think it's something to do with the shop?"

I shrug again. "Don't know. I guess. Why else would she drag us along? Though just what, I have no idea."

There's another pause.

"Caroline's worked incredibly hard, hasn't she?" remarks Dana suddenly.

"Yeah, she's been brilliant."

"She's really given it one hundred per cent."

Another brief silence.

"Rosie?"

"Yeah?"

"Do you ever worry that it won't work out?"

I think before answering. "At the start I guess I did, a little, but not any more. We've a great location. The shop is looking fabulous. We've a really nice selection of potions that are costing us so little to produce yet have a great mark-up." I consider all this, then add, "I think it will work."

"Yeah, so do I."

"Here she is now," I say spotting Caroline walking towards us.

She gets in.

"What are those for?" I ask, noting several sets of keys in her hand.

"You'll see. Okay, drive around to the back."

So I do, and there I spot them: three pink Mini Coopers each emblazoned with *LOVE POTIONS* on the side, with the address and phone number in smaller writing.

"Oh my God, Caroline! They're amazing!"

I park and we all climb out.

On the bonnet of each car is a deep pink heart. I walk around. *LOVE POTIONS* is printed on the other side as well and on the rear is the name and address of Donald's garage.

Caroline explains: "Donald's given us the loan of these for a month. Everywhere we go, we go in these. We'll make such an impact. They'll really get people talking about the shop."

"Caroline, you're a genius!" I tell her and give her a hug. "You know, I've always wanted a Mini Cooper. I was thinking of a little bright red one, but hey, I can cope with this." Then I notice Dana is not quite so enthusiastic. "Dana, don't you like them?"

"Yeah, sure, I do."

"Good!" says Caroline.

"But Caroline, you don't really think I'm driving one of these into college. What would people think?"

"Come on, Dana. What's the problem?"

"What's the problem? Do you even have to ask? How would my colleagues ever take me seriously again? Or take my research project seriously?"

"You don't have to park it right outside your building. Park where the students park their cars."

Dana still doesn't look happy but Caroline has moved on.

"Donald is inside at some business meeting. He's going to bring my car home for me and afterwards I can run him back here. Here, catch!"

She tosses us each our key. I catch mine and try it in the door of the nearest car. It fits and I climb in. Caroline comes over.

"Right," she says, "we'll drive along in convey for maximum impact. I'll go first."

As we drive along the strangulated dual carriageway, I notice that everyone is staring at us. It's a funny feeling. We're definitely attracting attention. Despite, or maybe because of the heavy traffic, we manage to stick together. When we're stopped at traffic lights I notice someone in the other lane gesticulating at Caroline who's in front of me. She opens her window. I see her talking. I see she's doing the hard sell already.

The minute we get back, she's on the phone, asking when the flyers she's arranged will be ready. From now on, she tells us, we'll always carry flyers with us and we'll give them out where and whenever we can.

And now she has another idea. She asks Dana to try and

source some potpourri cheaply. It would be a nice touch, she says, to line each bag with it before putting in the tissue-wrapped bottle of love potion every time we make a sale.

"What do you think?" she asks us.

"I think you're brilliant," I tell her. "I do, really."

"No, about the potpourri?"

"That's brilliant too."

"There is but one genuine love potion – consideration."
When were those words written? Not today or yesterday but
way, way, back in 342 BC by Menander of Athens,
the ancient Greek dramatist and poet.

19

Finn rings me early on Saturday morning. "So, are you all ready for the launch tonight?"

"We sure are. Caroline didn't want any last-minute hitches so we were in the shop until about three last night. I'm wrecked but it was worth it. Everything is set up now so I will be able to spend the day with you as promised. After all the hard work, I think I deserve it."

"How about going for lunch so, somewhere in the country? What do you think?"

"Sure, sounds good. Why don't I collect you?"

"That'd be great."

It occurs to me that I should tell him that I'll be collecting him in a pink heart-emblazoned vehicle as opposed to Caroline's car which is what he probably assumes but then I decide not to. He'll find out soon enough. Instead I tell him I'll see him in an hour's time.

As I ring off I notice Caroline has come into the kitchen.

"Was that Finn?" she asks.

"Yeah."

"Are you heading off somewhere?"

"Yeah, we're thinking of going for lunch somewhere out of town. Maybe Wicklow."

"Sounds good. It's a nice day." Then she has an idea. "I know. Why don't we make a day out of it for all of us?"

"All of us?"

"Yeah. I'm sure Doug and Dana would be on for it, and Loretta and Shane too. And we could collect Mick. He thought he'd get back yesterday but after all the rain the director wants to make the most of the fine weather we've been having so he's decided to shoot some extra scenes today."

I hestitate before answering.

"Come on, Rosie," coaxes Caroline. "It'd be great fun. And it could be our last chance to do something like this for ages. We've been working like crazy but we finally have everything under control. Everything is set for tonight's launch. We deserve a break. And once the shop opens our weekends are going to be really tied up. We can stop off somewhere fancy for lunch. What could be nicer? Come on. Say yes. It'll be great."

"All right," I agree.

"We can go in the minis. Think of the publicity!"

All the others are still sleeping so Caroline roots Loretta and Shane and Dana out of their beds, tells them the plan for the day while brooking no arguments and orders them all to have showers and get dressed.

So we head off in convoy, Caroline in the lead with Loretta and Shane, next comes me and bringing up the rear is Dana. Our first stop is Doug's house. It's Monica who opens the door and when she sees the three cars lined up, she gets very excited.

"Girls! They're brilliant! What a fantastic idea! You'll definitely get noticed in these."

"That's the plan," laughs Caroline. "So are you coming tonight, Monica?"

"I wouldn't miss it for the world." Then she walks over to me and leans in the window. "Rosie, would you mind if I brought Fay with me?"

"Fay? Would she want to come?"

"Yes, to be honest I'm a little surprised given what happened between you and her but when I mentioned I was going she asked me if I thought you'd mind if she came too."

"No, of course I wouldn't. Tell her she's more than welcome. I'd love to see her there."

What Monica means is that when Fay and I were working together in Monica's boutique we had a huge falling out. She was having a relationship with a married man who, years before, had dumped her in the most appalling circumstances. Of course, none of this was my business yet I decided to make it, but my interference resulted in him dumping her for the second time. To this day, I cringe when I think of what an interfering busybody I was and how my interfering ruined Fay's relationship with the only man she'd ever loved. I can't believe she'd want to come tonight but I am glad she does.

"Class!" laughs Doug when he comes out and sees the three matching cars parked along the pavement.

Next stop is Finn's house. This time I hop out and ring the doorbell. It's Lola who answers, in an old pyjamas, not a scrap of make-up on her face, but – I really hate to say it – still managing to look so very lovely.

"Hi, Lola," I say. "I'm here to collect Finn. Do you know if he's ready?" I see her notice the cars but she doesn't comment.

"Hi! It's Rosie, isn't it?"

"Ah, yeah." How rude! There's no way she doesn't know my name.

"I'll just go and tell him you're here." And she goes in, leaving me standing at the front door. Dana gives a blast of her horn and I look around. She makes a shooing motion, urging me to go inside, so I follow Lola.

As I come down the hall I hear her telling Finn, "Your friend is here – that girl, Rosie."

"Oh, great!"

Why doesn't he correct her, I wonder – point out to her that I'm his *girl*friend?

"Hi, Finn," I say and I pass by her and go over to where Finn is standing at the counter, eating a bowl of cornflakes. I take the spoon from him, lay it down and then give him a long kiss. At first he's taken by surprise but then he begins to respond and I'm the one who ends up pulling away.

"So are you ready?" I ask.

"Ready for what?" he laughs.

I give him a knowing look, hoping that Lola is taking all this in. "Not *that*," I laugh. "Unfortunately all the others are waiting outside."

"All the others?"

"Yeah, Caroline overheard me talking on the phone to you and decided she wanted to tag along too. And Doug and Dana are coming, and Loretta and Shane, and we're collecting Mick en route. I hope you don't mind."

"I guess not. I'll just go and get my jacket." He goes bounding up the stairs, two at a time.

That leaves just me and Lola.

"So are you set for tonight?" she asks.

"Pretty much."

"What time do you want us to come?"

I hesitate for a second. What's with the 'us'? I asked him to come. Dana asked her to come. No one asked 'them' to come. I see she's waiting for an answer. "Well, it kicks off at eight."

"That should suit, shouldn't it, Finn?" she asks him, as he comes back down.

"Yeah, I guess," he answers, struggling with his jacket.

"Well then, I'll see you later this evening so," says Lola to me.

"See you later, Lo!" says Finn as we head out.

When we reach the front door, Finn lets out a cry. "What the hell!" He points at the three minis. "Where did they come from?"

"From Caroline's brother's garage. We have them on loan for a month. Caroline arranged it. She thought it would be good publicity."

Everyone – Caroline, Loretta, Shane, Dana and Doug – are all grinning and waving at Finn.

"Bloody hell!" he laughs. "Are we really going in these?"

"Sure, why not? So, what do you think?"

"Well, they'll definitely get attention."

"That's exactly what we want."

We drive out of the city. As directed by Caroline I tell Finn to pass out flyers to any car that pulls up alongside us. At first he's reluctant but I point out that if they were for his band, he'd have no problem doing so. He begins handing them out.

Fifty minutes later we arrive at where shooting for *Fate Farm* is going on that day – at an old farmhouse. Lining the lane to the house are lorries and vans and cars, all associated with the film. Each of us pulls our mini into wherever we can find enough space, get out, and begin making our way over to where the action is.

Mick has already spotted us. He shouts out a cheery hello and, wearing a big grin on his face, he comes over to meet us. He gives Caroline a big hug and a kiss. Then she steps back and looks him up and down, taking in the stubble, the messy hair, and the torn old clothes he's wearing.

"I'm hoping you're in character," she laughs.

Mick laughs too. "We're just about to shoot a scene – I hope you don't mind waiting."

"Not at all," says Caroline. "What's it about?"

"Well, I'm on the run, you see, and I've been living rough for a couple of nights but now I turn up at the house of my old girlfriend. You can watch if you like, if you promise to be quiet."

"Really?" asks Dana excitedly.

"Sure."

Someone calls out Mick's name, he looks around, then shouts out, "Coming!" He turns back to us. "Okay then, see you afterwards. It shouldn't take too long."

So we stand and watch as shooting commences. The scene opens with Audrey (yes, *the* Audrey Turner, in the flesh) coming out of the house. She's wearing a tatty yet short dress, has her hair tied up in a messy yet sexy fashion, has a laundry basket balanced sensibly yet provocatively on her hip and she's humming to herself. She goes to the washing line and begins hanging out the washing, stretching up as she hangs each piece of clothing so that her own clothing rides up revealing the full length of her long and very shapely legs.

"The hussy!" whispers Dana.

Mick emerges from the trees, and then stands there silently watching.

"Well, he's certainly enjoying the view," Caroline notes dryly.

"Remember he *is* acting, Caroline," Dana reminds her.

"Hmm, well, then, he's an even better actor than I gave him credit for."

Suddenly seeing Mick standing there, Audrey gives a yell.

"Anthony!" she cries in her version of an Irish accent. "What are you doing here! You'll be caught! Everyone is searching for you!"

He doesn't answer. He looks too weary.

"Jesus! Look at the state of you!" she cries.

"I need help, Minnie," he finally manages. "I have no one else to turn to. I haven't eaten for days. If there was just somewhere I could rest for a little while."

"Oh, Anthony! They were here only this morning looking for you!"

"Please, Minnie. I won't stay long but I'm dead with exhaustion and with the hunger."

Audrey/Minnie looks him up and down. "Stay here!" She glances around furtively. "I'll see if I can find something for you to eat."

Mick/Anthony wearily rests himself on a window ledge of an old outhouse. He closes his eyes. He looks like he's nodding off.

Audrey/Minnie calls back to him. "Go take a wash if you want," she points to a hose lying on the ground, "but be quick. I'll bring you some clothes – some of Martin's old ones might do you." She leaves Mick and goes into the house.

Mick starts taking off his clothes, and I mean *all* his clothes, every last stitch. Embarrassed, I look away, wondering why we haven't been asked to leave. Everyone, at least the professionals, seems unconcerned by the fact that Mick is now totally naked but Caroline, Dana and Loretta's eyes are all out on sticks (and mine too now, if I'm being completely honest). Dana leaves out a low whistle and gets an elbow in the stomach from Caroline.

"Stop staring!" hisses Caroline.

"How can I?" Dana hisses right back.

Audrey/Minnie comes out from the house once more and, quietly, she walks over to Mick who is now showering himself with the hose. She lays the tray of food she's carrying down on the ground and then carries on slowly towards him, taking out a bar of soap from her pocket as she does so. Seeing her, he smiles shyly. She smiles shyly but flirtatiously back. Then, ever so gently, she begins to soap his back.

"And, cut!" shouts the director.

I look at Caroline. She looks a little taken aback by the scene she's witnessed. I look back at Mick. He's putting on his clothes again but, even as he does so, Audrey Turner is talking to him. Then he nods in our direction, says something to her and, as soon as he's dressed, they both make their way over to where we're standing.

"Audrey, this is my girlfriend, Caroline."

"Hi, Caroline!" She's speaking in her own American accent now. "How lovely to meet you!"

"You too."

Caroline smiles back at her somewhat warily, but it

occurs to me that Caroline has no worries on the Audrey front. This open pleasant woman who greets Caroline in such a friendly manner has no designs on her Mick.

As if confirming my theory, she adds. "I've heard all about you! Mick never stops talking about you!"

"Really?"

"Oh yes. It's all 'Caroline this,' 'Caroline that,' with Mick."

"I'm glad to hear it," laughs Caroline.

Mick introduces the rest of us and Audrey shakes each of our hands in turn.

Then Shane digs Mick in the ribs. "I know we haven't seen much of you lately but I certainly didn't expect to see quite so much of you today!"

"Oh, give over!" laughs Mick.

Audrey is talking to Caroline again. "Mick says you're about to open your own business. How exciting!"

"Yes, it is." Then a thought occurs to Caroline. "Listen, we're all going for lunch. Mick may have told you. Would you like to join us?"

Mick looks surprised. As am I. I never expected Caroline to be quite so friendly to the woman her boyfriend is acting with in such intimate scenes. She's being surprisingly mature.

"Sure," says Audrey. "I'd like that. Just give me a moment to get changed."

"Yeah," says Mick. "I'd better go and get changed too."

Audrey walks away but Mick hangs on to give Caroline a kiss.

"What's that for?" she asks a little surprised.

"Just so that you know I love you."

"I know that!" Caroline laughs.

Mick hurries off and soon catches up with Audrey and we watch the two of them walk off together.

"Well," says Dana to Caroline, "you're certainly being very mature about all this."

"You think?"

"Course, you've no need no worry," I say. "She has no interest in Mick. You can see that."

"Well, she is an actress, isn't she?" says Caroline. "Even if she has she's not going to let it show."

"So why are you being so friendly then?" I ask.

"Haven't you ever heard the expression 'Keep your friends close, but your enemies closer'?"

Sometimes there comes a day that turns out to be just perfect. This is turning out to be one of those days. The lovely little hotel we stop at has a beautiful garden-room-cum-dining-room, filled with lush green plants and tables covered in crisp white cloths and we eat there, luxuriating in the warm sun. Lunch itself is positively delicious. Everyone is in great form and having a really lovely time.

After eating, Finn and I leave the others – three happy couples and Audrey who proves to be a very entertaining addition – chatting animatedly around the table and we go for a walk by ourselves in the grounds. When we come across a bench we sit down. At first we simply enjoy the quiet pleasure of being here together in these lovely surroundings and, with Finn's arm around my shoulders, we sit there companionably, feeling little need to speak.

"So, are you looking forward to tonight?" asks Finn after a while.

I nod. "But I'm a little nervous. I just hope a good crowd turns up."

"Well, I've asked everyone I know."

"Great! The more the merrier."

"I've even asked my dad."

"Really?" I laugh. "And is he coming?"

"Sure. He wouldn't miss it for the world. Though I can't guarantee he'll buy anything. He's really only going to show his support. You know how much he likes you."

"And does he like Lola?"

"Pardon?"

"Nothing, nothing, silly question." Where did that come from? Why did I have to bring her up?

"Dad doesn't really know Lola," says Finn, looking a little nonplussed at my non sequitur.

"Good," I say.

I notice that Finn is still looking at me strangely but then he laughs, leans over, and whispers in my ear: "I love you, Rosie Kiely. You know that."

"Course I do." I laugh. "And I love you too."

We lapse back into silence, sitting hand-in-hand now, until, eventually, somewhat reluctantly, I get to my feet.

"Come on."

"Ah, no, it's perfect here! Sit back down."

"But the others will be wondering where we are. We have to head back to town soon. We need to go down to the shop early to do the final arrangements for tonight. So come on! Up!"

"Oh, all right – but only if you give me one last kiss!"

"Ah, Finn!" I laugh. "That's blackmail!"

"Come on, one last kiss!"

Up to that point, the day has been perfect but then everything changes. When we get back to the garden room, to where the others still are, it's immediately apparent that the earlier good feeling between Caroline and Mick has disappeared. They're wearing faces like thunder and everyone else seems very ill at ease.

I sit down beside Dana and whisper: "What's going on?"

"Oh God," she mutters. "World War III has broken out."

"What are you talking about?"

"Come with me to the bathroom."

She gets up and I follow after her.

"So, go on," I say, once we're behind closed doors. "Tell me what happened."

"Caroline only went and put her foot in it."

"How?"

"She only asked Audrey would she come tonight and pose for some photos."

"And? So? That sounds like a great idea."

"And so Mick got very annoyed, said she'd no right to put Audrey in a position like that and accused Caroline of only asking Audrey to lunch so that she would have an opportunity to ambush her."

"Well, I was kind of wondering what she was up to."

"To be honest, Mick is more annoyed than Audrey. If he hadn't lost his temper with Caroline, I think Audrey might have been quite happy to do it. But now Caroline and Mick aren't talking to one another. I swear one of them is as bad as the other. Maybe Caroline shouldn't have put Audrey on the spot like that but I think Mick could have handled it better – there was no need to give out to her in front of everyone."

When we come back out of the bathroom, we learn that Caroline has already left on her own, so Mick and Audrey travel back with me and Finn. To leave Audrey off at the pretty little coastal cottage she's renting while filming, we detour through Dalkey and then we carry on and drop Mick at his apartment in the city centre. As we pull away from Mick's place, a message comes through on Finn's phone.

I look over at him quizzically as he reads it.

"Lola," he explains. "She wants to know if I'll be home for dinner before the opening."

What is she, your mother? I think to ask, but hold my tongue. There's been enough fallings-out for one day.

"So what time is the opening again?" he asks.

"Eight."

"Do you want me to come down early to give you a hand?"

"No, I think we'll be okay. We're pretty well organised. You know how Caroline is."

He nods. "Sure."

We pull up outside his house. Lola's car is in the driveway, of course.

"See you at eight then," he says, leans over, kisses me and then climbs out.

As I pull away, I see Lola opening the door to let him in. If not his mother, then who does she think she is? His bloody wife?

"I took my troubles down to Madam Ruth."

The Searchers

20

"Love Potions!" From across the street Caroline reads the sign over our shop door. "Well, girls, we did it! We created all this!" Under one arm she's holding a package but with her free hand she waves to indicate the newly-erected sign, the walls painted white, the pink door, the matching pink framed window featuring a kaleidoscope of bottles beautifully illuminated in the early evening sun and, parked outside in a row, the three pink Mini Coopers. "This is it, girls! We've created this! Doesn't it look fantastic! Haven't we done a great job! Come on!"

She darts across the road, weaves her way through the stalled traffic, reaches our shop, turns the key in the door and we file in after her.

"Okay, we have an hour before everyone starts arriving." She opens the package she's been carrying. "Here, Dana, put this on." She throws a pink-coloured bundle to her.

"What is it?" asks Dana, as she unfolds it.

"It's your uniform."

Dana holds it up to examine. It's a pink version of a doctor's coat with a little heart embroidered on the breast pocket.

"And here's yours, Rosie. Now we'll look the part." She puts on her own, then stands back. "Well? What do you think?"

"You look great, Madam Ruth. All you're missing is the gold-capped tooth."

She looks at me blankly. "What *are* you talking about?"

"Finn played me this old song by The Searchers about a gypsy called Madam Ruth who has a gold-capped tooth and who sells Love Potions." I begin singing it.

"No, you've got the words all wrong," interrupts Dana. "You mean Madam Rue." Now she sings: "*'I took my troubles down to Madam Rue. You know that gypsy with the gold tattoo.'*"

"No! It was Madam Ruth and she had a gold-capped tooth!"

"No, it was Madam Rue and she had a gold tattoo!"

"Gold tattoo! But that doesn't make sense!"

"Sure it does."

"Girls! Girls!" intervenes Caroline. "It doesn't matter. Please! We need to focus."

We let it go. I look at Caroline again. Okay, she's no gold-cap-toothed gypsy but with her blonde bob, pink hair band, white dress, white stilettos and pink coat, she's certainly convincing as the proprietor of a modern-day shop selling love potions.

"Okay then," she says, "let the games begin!"

Tonight we're expecting quite a crowd. Caroline has invited all her PR and press contacts and all three of us have invited all the friends and family we can muster.

The ping-ping of the door signals the first of our arrivals and immediately I see that I've mustered more 'friends' than I anticipated. Here come my mum and dad accompanied by what looks like Mum's entire golf club, all their bridge club, all their neighbours, as well as all my aunties and uncles. I'm not sure they're quite the glittering set Caroline was aiming for but one thing I am sure is that this is not at all what Mum or Dad were expecting – how could it be when I never actually told them what to expect. I see Mum now, looking around, a gay smile fixed firmly on her face but, knowing her like I do, I know there's nothing real about that smile. Oh dear! Time and time again, I was *going* to tell her and Dad that it was love potions and not energy drinks we'd be selling in the shop but again and again I chickened out and, then, as D-day drew nearer, I decided it would be easier to hang on, to let them see it for themselves, rather than try to explain. That way, I reasoned, they wouldn't have the chance to worry but would be able to appreciate how good a job we'd done when they could see it for themselves. Now I wonder if I was wrong. Maybe I should have told them. It was unfair not to do so.

I go over to them.

"Hi Mum, Dad, Mrs Lamont, Auntie Joanna, Uncle Dave, everyone. Thanks for coming."

"Well," says Auntie Joanna, "your mum certainly kept us in the dark. This is not what we were expecting at all!"

My mother manages to keep her smile firmly on her face and nonchalantly shrugs her shoulders, managing to give the impression that perhaps she wasn't letting on everything she knew. But then, when Caroline comes over to say hello to everyone, when Mum gets the opportunity, when she thinks nobody is looking, she grabs me by the arm.

"You told me energy drinks!" she hisses. "That's what I told everyone."

"What?" I decide there's nothing for it but to play dumb. "No, you must have misunderstood."

"I know what you said to me. Ah, Rosie! You might have warned me. Why didn't you tell me what you were really up to?"

I give it to her straight. "Because I knew you'd worry and I knew how disapproving you would be."

"That's not fair. I've always been very supportive."

"Only when what I'm doing is what you want me to do."

She looks hurt but before she gets a chance to say anything, Caroline – who I notice is now linking my father's arm – interrupts.

"Mrs Kiely, I was just telling your husband that you'll have to avail of this opportunity to spice up your love life." Then she gives a wicked laugh. "Not that I'm saying it needs to be spiced up, of course!"

I cringe. I do not want one of my friends making any reference to my parents' love life, in front of me, not even in a jokey way.

"Ah, now," says Dad, "love-life indeed!" Then he laughs as if the idea is utterly ridiculous, like all this time he might have been living under the impression that I and my siblings – the tangible evidence of his love-life – were found beneath a cabbage leaf.

My mother hastily changes the subject altogether. "I must say, Caroline, you've done wonders. You must have worked very hard. The place is a credit to you, to you all. Isn't it, Will?"

"It certainly is," Dad agrees.

"Do you really think so, Mum?" I ask, feeling very pleased, not to mind relieved.

"Yes, I do – actually. Of course I do. Come here to me!" She reaches out and gives me a hug and I hug her back – tightly. I realise how much it means to me that she should feel proud.

"I'm sorry I didn't tell you."

"Well, yes, so you should be. I'm not some ogre, you know."

"I do know."

"So is Finn here?" she asks, once we pull apart. She looks around expectantly.

"No, but he's coming."

"So Mr Kiely," I hear Caroline saying, "what can I interest you in? What about some Heart's Warmth?"

"And what is that then when it's at home?" asks Dad, showing a little too much interest for my liking.

"Just a very tasty concoction, something that will – you know – put you in the mood for a little loving." She reaches up to one of the shelves, takes down a little pink bottle and holds it out to him. "How about it, Mr Kiely?" She gives him a wink. "What do you say?" Has Caroline any limits? Is she actually flirting with my dad? And worse, is he actually enjoying it as much as he appears to be?

"A little loving?" he says. "Let me see it." He takes the bottle from her, finds his glasses and begins to read. "Hmm," he looks up, "this sounds like powerful stuff."

"Well, why don't you take it home and try it and then I can ask Mrs Kiely just how powerful it is the next time I see her." She winks at him. Again.

Enough, I think. "Caroline," I take her by the arm, "did

I tell you there's a guy looking for you. I didn't catch his name but I think he's a journalist."

"Really? Where?" She scans the room.

"Over by the window," I lie. "Behind that group there."

She drops Dad like a hot potato and goes hurrying across the increasingly crowded room.

I'm kept busy rushing to and fro keeping people's glasses topped up with wine and soft drinks. We've restricted everyone to a single free love potion which we recommend they take home with them – otherwise, as Caroline tells everyone, we'd risk having chaos on our hands. But people, as she keeps reminding everyone at every opportunity, are free to buy as many as they like when leaving.

Dana comes over to me. "Have you any idea how much this evening must be costing?" she asks.

I shake my head.

"I'm guessing we've had well over two hundred people in here so far tonight."

While she's talking, I notice Mick arriving. I look around to see where Caroline is, to see if she's seen him yet. She has. She promptly air-kisses the woman she's talking to and immediately takes her leave and then, defying the height of her heels, she practically gallops across the room to Mick. I see him lean towards her and they kiss. Clearly they've managed to put this afternoon's fight behind them. At least neither of them is the kind to hold a grudge which is just as well – considering how tempestuous their relationship is. They pull apart now and I see him looking around. He looks pretty impressed as well he might – the place does look absolutely fabulous.

And then my own heart soars. I see Finn at the door.

And then my heart plummets again when I see Lola following in after him. But at least they're not on their own – Mitch and Ashley have come too, and Finn's dad.

I go towards them. "Hi, guys! Hi, Mr Heelan!"

"This place looks amazing," gushes Lola, who also looks amazing I'm annoyed to notice. "Well done, you!"

"Thanks."

She goes to kiss me but I back away before she can. I'm not trying to be rude but I just don't think I could bear it.

I look at Finn. I don't care what Lola thinks about the place. I want to know what he thinks.

"Yeah," he says, looking around and nodding, "congratulations. You've done a fantastic job, Rosie."

"So, Rosie, do these potions work then?" asks Ashley.

"You'll have to try one to find out!" I joke.

"Hi, Rosie!" It's Shane with Loretta.

"Hi, Shane! Hi, Loretta! Thanks for coming."

"As if we'd miss it!" laughs Shane.

"Hi, Rosie!" Now I look around to see Monica standing there with Fay.

"Monica! Hi! And, oh my goodness, Fay. It's lovely to see you!"

"Hi, Rosie. Congratulations!"

I don't think Fay could have any idea just how much her presence here means to me but it means a lot. Maybe she's finally forgiven my unforgivable interference in her life. But now is probably not the time to go into all that with her. Instead, I settle for saying: "Thanks for coming."

Then I notice Monica take a hankie from her bag.

"Monica, are you okay?"

"Oh, silly me! I was hoping I wouldn't react like this!" She dabs her eyes. "There! All better now," she says, with forced cheeriness. "I guess seeing you starting off like this brings back memories of when I opened the boutique. It all seems such a long time ago. Another lifetime."

Doug comes over and puts his arm around her. She pats his arm. Then she laughs. "Maybe we should go and look at some of the produce. What do you think, Fay?"

"Whatever about you, Monica," says Fay, "there's not much point in me buying love potions, now is there? It's not like I have anyone to give them to!"

If it was anyone but Fay, I might suspect she was taking a dig at me but Fay's not like that, yet her words remind me once again how I am responsible for the fact that she has no-one.

Monica pulls away from Doug and then leans in towards me in a conspiratorial fashion. "Has Doug told you I'm seeing someone?"

"No!"

"Yes," she says, as excited as a love-struck teenager. "It's early days, but you never know. Things are going very well so fingers crossed. But I can tell you now, I'll definitely be stocking up here tonight." She leans in even closer now. "Doug tells me your potions are incredible!"

I have to leave them when, from across the room, I notice a stressed Dana calling and gesticulating for me to come give her a hand with the queue that's forming at the cash register. Telling them I'll catch up later, I go to help Dana.

When there's a rare quiet moment, my mother comes over to me.

"Rosie, you know I hope this goes well for you. I really do."

"I know, Mum."

"Good, I hope you do. I just worry for you, that's all. What kind of a mother would I be if I didn't?" She reaches across the counter and gives me another big bear hug and I hug her back. "I'll just have to get used to the fact that you're grown up, that you're old enough to make your own decisions."

"Thanks, Mum."

I spot Mr Heelan across the room, standing, chatting to Lola.

"Have you met Finn's dad?" I ask, nodding in his direction.

"Who? That very distinguished-looking gentleman talking to that girl with the dyed-blonde hair and that dreadful red shaggy jacket?"

"Yep."

She studies Mr Heelan for a moment. "Well now, why don't you introduce me, Rosie?"

"I will when it quietens down more but I'd better stay here for now."

"Maybe I'll go and introduce myself."

I'm about to protest, to tell her hang on a while, but then I realise, with Lola for an audience, it couldn't be better.

"That's a great idea. Make sure you tell him you're my mum and what a wonderful daughter I am and how Finn and I are a match made in heaven."

My mother looks at me strangely, then laughs. "Of course. Isn't it the truth?"

I watch her go over but then I'm distracted when I notice Niall coming in. I see him looking around, then he spots Caroline and goes straight up to her and gives her a kiss on the cheek. And then they begin talking animatedly. I notice his hand resting on the small of her back as they do so.

I'm not the only one.

"So who's Caroline's new friend then?" asks Mick, coming up behind me.

"Who?" Of course I know who he's talking about, but I pretend not to.

"That sharp-eyed guy in the sharp suit talking to Caroline."

"Oh," I laugh, "you mean Niall?"

"Do I?"

"He's just some guy Caroline knows."

Mick studies the pair of them, watching how they interact. Niall is still standing right by Caroline's side in a proprietorial manner. But however it might look, I know she has no interest whatsoever in him. She's told me. I believe her. But why is he always hanging about of late? Why doesn't she tell him to get lost?

I glance at Mick. He looks annoyed.

"From where I'm standing it looks like he's pretty fond of her."

I don't blame him for feeling annoyed. Even I feel annoyed looking at her. What's she playing at? I decide to have a word with her but, before I get a chance, Audrey Turner walks through the door, looking every inch the film star.

A hush descends on the room. I notice people nudging one another. All heads turn to Audrey.

"So she came after all?" I say to Mick.

Mick nods. "I wasn't sure she would. She said she'd try as a favour but she's got young children so she wasn't sure if she'd be able to make it. She's finding it hard having them here with her in Ireland during the shoot when their real home and their dad are in America."

"But I don't understand. Why did you get her to come? I thought you were mad at Caroline for trying to get her involved?"

"And I was. I didn't like her putting Audrey in a spot like that when she'd just met her but I probably overreacted. Audrey is used to people asking her to do things – I didn't need to jump to her defence like that in front of everyone. Caroline was only making use of a good opportunity. I mightn't approve of this business entirely but I do know how important it is for Caroline and I do want it to succeed so, when I got home, I rang Audrey and asked her to come. Caroline's right – having her in a couple of photographs would be great publicity."

Mick leaves me. I watch him walk over to Caroline. I see him butt in between Niall and Caroline without so much as a nod in Niall's direction. He gives Caroline a kiss on the lips and then he takes her arm and I see him guiding her across the room to where Audrey is standing. Already the few photographers that are here are clustered around Audrey and are getting ready to take some shots. Mick takes command and places Caroline beside Audrey. That done, he tells the photographers to hold on a second then comes to the counter, takes one of our glossy bags, fills it with some love potions and brings it back to Audrey. Obliging, she takes it, and stands posing with it, with Caroline at her side, Mick smiling from the sidelines. Noticing him, Caroline smiles back and blows him a kiss. He grins back at her now. This, I think watching, is real love. Sure they argue, sure they're each as volatile as the other, but there's a real warmth there.

Dad interrupts my thoughts when he comes up and puts three of the potions on the counter. I look at him in surprise.

"I'm only buying them to support you," he grins sheepishly.

"Sure," I say and laugh. "I believe you."

I begin wrapping the three bottles individually in alternate sheets of pink then purple tissue paper and then place them carefully in one of our paper bags already lined with potpourri. Though I protest, he insists on paying for them. He takes the bag from me, then looks around.

"I'd better look for your mum. It's time we were going home. If I left it up to her, she'd never leave."

"Did you enjoy yourself?" I ask him.

"Very much. I had a great time. You've done a brilliant job."

"Thanks, Dad."

As he's walking away, Mick comes hurrying over to him. "Mr Kiely, will you come with me?" Allowing no protest, he takes Dad by the arm and leads him over to Audrey and stands him in beside her.

Ignoring the photographer's cry of "Cheese!" Dad keeps staring up at Audrey like he's wondering how on earth he got to be standing beside this fabulous creature.

Before long, Mick shouts out my name and I make my way over. The photographer takes some shots of Caroline, me and Dana with Audrey, and then one with just the three of us, then one with the three of us together with our boyfriends. As the six of us stand there posing, I notice Lola looking on from the sidelines. She's staring at me with such undisguised dislike that I know at that moment, without a shadow of a doubt, just what her feelings for Finn are and there is nothing platonic about them whatsoever.

Gradually the crowd begins to thin. Audrey has gone home. As have my mum and dad. I notice Finn's dad is still here and somehow he's got talking to Fay. They look, I think, like they could be a couple, two fine-looking people in their fifties.

When Dana comes over to me, I say as much.

"Don't even go there!" cries Dana immediately. "You stay out of Fay's life. You've done enough damage."

"Dana! I wasn't going to do anything."

"Good!"

"I was just remarking."

Dana leaves me again and as I continue looking around I spot Caroline. She's talking to Niall *again*. She's waving her arms all over the place and yapping excitedly but then when she throws her head back and laughs I see him reach out and stroke her neck. Suddenly she looks stunned. I wait for her to slap him in the face or something but no, instead she shakes her head and takes a step backwards. He takes a matching step forward, grabs hold of her hand, then leans in and whispers in her ear. She frowns as she listens, then I see her shaking her head. Now Niall reaches out and strokes her cheek. She doesn't brush him away but stands there and lets him. What the hell is going on? Why is Caroline, of all people, putting up with this creep's unwelcome attentions?

Just as I'm thinking I should go over, Lola comes up to me.

"So," she asks, "can I test one of these famous potions then?"

"Now?"

"Why not?"

Why not, indeed? I think to myself. "Ah, sure," I say. I think for a moment and then from the shelf behind me I take down one of the last I came up with. Running out of names we called it 'Fool for Love'.

"Try this," I say.

Lola takes off the stopper and drinks it – all in one go.

"Hmm . . ." She smacks her lips.

I look back to where Caroline and Niall are. He has a hand on her shoulder now and is talking to her very intently while she stands there, listening to him, a very serious expression on her face.

"What exactly is in this?" I hear Lola demand.

I turn back to her. "Oh my God!" I cry. "Your lips! They're going all puffy."

"What's in this," repeats Lola, sounding panicky. "There was banana in it, wasn't there?"

"Ah yes, strawberry, raspberry, banana and –"

"Jesus! I'm allergic to banana!" gasps Lola.

"To banana?"

"Yes! Oh my God! I'm going into anaphylactic shock!"

"But you can't be! People only get those from fish!"

"What? You think I'm joking?" wheezes Lola. "Are you some kind of expert!" She shoves her handbag at me. "My EpiPen!"

"What?"

"My EpiPen!" she repeats. She's wheezing hard now. And her lips are even puffier.

"Okay, okay."

"Quick!"

I open her bag and throw the contents out on the counter. Now people around are beginning to notice.

Dana comes rushing over. "What's going on?"

"Lola has had an anaphylactic reaction to some banana in one of the potions!"

"Where's Loretta?" Dana scans the room. "Will I see if I can find her? She'll know what to do."

"I think she and Shane have just left."

"Oh God! Will I call an ambulance?"

"Yes!" shouts Lola. "Quick!"

"I'm already on it," says Doug, stepping out from the crowd gathered around us. He's holding his phone to his ear and he talks into it now. "Yep, that's right. What? Yeah, there's a big sign over the door – 'Love Potions' – you can't miss it. One thing, it's a one-way street."

He hangs up, then pulls out a chair from behind the counter and helps an already doubled-over Lola to sit down.

"Has she an EpiPen?" he asks.

"Is this it?" I ask, holding what I presume is it out to him.

He takes it from me and uncaps the needle. "Okay, Lola, I'm going to stick it into your thigh, through your leggings, all right?"

Lola nods.

"Are you sure you know what you're doing?" asks Caroline, looking very doubtful.

Doug ignores her.

"Now don't worry," he says to Lola. "Everything is under control. Everything is going to be fine. The ambulance is on its way." He talks softly and, then, swiftly, without fuss, he jabs the needle in. "There, all done!"

Lola leaves out a scream. Then, spotting Finn close by, she reaches out for his hand, takes it, and she sits there, holding it tightly. All the while, Doug keeps up a flow of soothing conversation, breaking off every now and then to tell people to keep back and give Lola some space.

"He's full of surprises lately, isn't he?" comments Caroline who's standing beside me.

"Who?"

"Doug."

"How so?"

"You know, jumping into the roaring ocean to help save those students. Coming to Lola's rescue. I mean, most of the time he goes around being all Clark Kent-ish – all quiet and inoffensive and, then, when a hero is needed he morphs into action, like some kind of Superman."

I look over at Doug. It is odd to see him in command like this. "Hmm, I wonder if he has a Superman costume stashed away in his wardrobe?" I joke.

"Maybe we should ask Dana," says Caroline with a wink, then she gives a loud laugh, causing everyone to turn in our direction to see who's acting with such impropriety.

Finally, after what seems like a very long fifteen minutes, the ambulance arrives. I guess presuming Finn is Lola's boyfriend, one of the paramedics suggests that he goes in the ambulance too and, as he leaves with her, I shout out that I'll meet him at the hospital but I don't think he hears me. He's occupied with Lola.

At Accident and Emergency, Lola is seen to immediately and, by the time I get there, Finn is able to tell me that everything is under control, that Lola is fine, that she'll be able to go home in an hour or two. All there is for us to do is just sit and wait.

I guess I could have picked a better moment but I didn't. Maybe it's the sudden relief from hearing that she's fine again, I don't know but, suddenly, I find myself saying what I've been wanting to say from the very start.

"Finn, I don't like you living with Lola."

"Pardon?"

"I don't like her. I don't like the way she's all over you. I don't like the way she seems to be coming between us. I want you to ask her to leave."

"Pardon?"

"I'm asking you to ask her to leave."

"Asking me or telling me?"

"All right then, telling you."

"You sure pick your moments! Here we are in A and E all because Lola drank one of *your* bloody potions and, as if you hadn't done enough damage to her in one night, now you're telling me you want me to ask her to leave! To throw her out on the street! I'm not thick, Rosie. I know you dislike her, even she knows you dislike her – you've done little to hide it but –"

"Excuse me?"

"– but she's an old friend of mine and I'm not doing that. Sorry, no can do."

"*No can do*! Ah, come on! It's not like she's going to find herself homeless! She can go back to her parents, can't she?"

"Why should she? She has a home."

"So you won't ask her to leave?"

"No, absolutely not."

"I see."

"Rosie, look. You've got to learn to trust me. I'm not going to cheat on you. I'm not that kind."

But I'm not listening. "Okay, if you don't ask her to leave then I don't think I have much option but to end our relationship."

He looks stunned. "You're joking me!"

Even as I'm saying it I know there are so many ways I could have handled this better. I know I'm being hasty but I don't turn back.

"I'm not," I say.

"Fine then, have it your way. I guess this is the end so."

"I guess it is."

And just like that it seems our relationship is over. This was the best thing I had and I've just thrown it away. How could I be so stupid!

The Kama Sutra has it that an ointment made of the flowers of the nauclea cadamba, the hog plum, and the eugenia jambolana, and used by a woman, causes her to be disliked by her husband.

Unfortunately, there are so many other ways this can be done.

21

I wake to the sound of Caroline yelling from downstairs.

"Come quickly! You've got to see these! There are some brilliant photos in the paper!"

"Already?" I hear Dana shout back.

"Yeah, can you believe it? I never expected them to be out this soon!"

And then it hits me. I remember. I have just broken up with the best man I've ever gone out with. Why? Because I found him in bed with another woman? No! Because I realised that he wasn't really the man I thought he was? Ah, no. So why then? Because I am a jealous, rash, stupid, stupid cow!

I get out of bed but instead of going downstairs, I climb into the shower and I let it run and run until the water begins to get cold. Then I dress and make my way down to where the others are. Everyone is in the kitchen and Shane's in the middle of cooking up a big fry.

"Here!" calls Caroline, excitedly passing me the paper. "Take a look at these."

I study the photographs. Audrey features prominently which isn't surprising. There's one with Audrey holding our bag with the logo plainly visible standing alongside Caroline. There's one with Audrey and Dad, and Mum – though only those in the know would spot her face, in the grainy background, looking on disapprovingly. There's one with Fay and Mr Heelan, close together, smiling for the camera. If circumstances were different I might pay more attention to this one but instead I focus on the final photo, the one of Finn and me. I study his lovely face, the happy expression, his smile that stretches from ear to ear, his eyes crinkled up so much they're almost closed. I notice the way our heads are angled fondly towards one another. I see his arm draped around my shoulder. How could I have left him – all this – go?

"That's a good one of you and Finn, isn't it, Rosie?" says Dana, looking over my shoulder. "Maybe you should call up the newspaper and get a copy."

I give a bitter laugh. "Or call them up and tell them that we've broken up. There might even be a story in it for them! *Love Potions Do Not Work – Proprietor of Love Potions Splits From Boyfriend!*"

"What?" cries Caroline. "You're kidding! Right?"

"Wrong."

"But I don't get it," says Caroline. "What on earth happened? I thought you two were love's young dream!"

I shrug. "I kinda did too."

Everyone is looking at me. I can feel their surprise and – worse – their sympathy. Suddenly, I feel the tears begin to well up but I force them down.

"Has this anything to do with that Lola?" asks Dana.

"Yes and no."

"What do you mean?"

"He didn't dump me for her if that's what you're thinking."

"Did something happen between them?" asks Caroline.

"No, not as far as I know."

"Well, what then?" she demands. "What happened?"

"In a nutshell: I told him I didn't want her living with him any more. Then he told me that he wasn't going to ask her to leave. So then I told him, fine, that I didn't want to go out with him any longer."

"So that's it?" asks Caroline. "You're history?"

"Seems like it."

"Come on. You can fix this. Ring him up. Tell him you're sorry, that you didn't mean it."

"But the thing is, I did mean it. I hate him living with her. I'm jealous every time I think of him and her together in that house. I don't want to feel jealous all the time. Besides, I know she fancies him. All along she's been biding her time, waiting for her opportunity."

"So, what? You just hand him to her on a plate?" asks Dana.

I shrug. "I just don't understand why he can't see the obvious."

"Ah, Rosie, come on. Where's your fighting spirit?" demands Caroline.

"Okay then, how do you think Mick would react if Niall moved in here?"

"Niall? What's he got to do with anything?"

"Ah come on, Caroline. We can all see the way he's coming onto you all the time. I don't know why you don't blow him off."

"Just stop it! You don't have a clue what you're talking about!" she shouts angrily.

"And you don't have a clue what you're talking about so back off!" I shout at her.

"Hey, you guys, calm down," says Dana. "If it's any consolation to you, Rosie, I think you're right about Lola. She is dangerous. Finn had no business getting her to move in with him without asking you first. It wasn't fair."

"Thank you, Dana."

"But maybe you could have handled this a little better and –"

"You think I don't know that!"

"– and maybe you could ring him up now and talk to him about it all."

"And what would I say? Tell him I'm sorry I flipped, that I take back everything, that on further reflection I'm quite happy for Lola and him to go on living together? The fact is, I'm not."

"That's understandable but don't you think splitting up with him is a little drastic?"

"I didn't mean for that to happen! I just wanted him to see how annoyed I was. I didn't expect him to go, 'You want to split up? Fine. See you around!' I thought he loved me. He could have put up more of a fight."

I hear Shane give a laugh. I look over. He's standing at the cooker frying, his back turned to us.

"Did you just laugh?" I ask.

He looks over his shoulder. "Me? Heavens forbid! What's there to find amusing? That when you told Finn you were dumping him you wanted him to plead with you and try to make you change your mind? No, that all sounds perfectly reasonable."

"Exactly."

"Perfectly reasonable. If anyone is being unreasonable it's

Finn. Imagine believing that someone means it when they say they're breaking up with you!"

I look over at him, but he's turned back to the cooker again.

"Are you being sarcastic?" I ask him. "Or do you actually mean what you're saying?"

"Maybe you should have asked yourself that when you were busy dumping Finn."

"Pardon?"

Shane picks up a plate, comes over and puts it down in front of me. "Here, tuck in. You'll feel better. Look, all I want to say is that as long as I've known you, and that's longer than anyone here, remember, I've never seen you so contented with anyone. I don't want to see you give all that up."

"I don't want to give all that up!"

"Well then, don't," says Shane. "Go back and tell him you're sorry. Try and talk to him. Try and tell him exactly how you feel about Lola."

"Aren't any of you people listening? I tried that. It didn't work. He wasn't interested." I push away the plate of food. There's no way I could eat a bite. I get up from the table, leave them all there, and go back to bed.

When I come down again at eleven, it's just Caroline in the kitchen. She's sitting at the table, a cup of tea in front of her. She looks up.

"Feeling better?" she asks.

I shrug, and sit down opposite her.

"Caroline, I've been thinking about a lot of things."

"About Finn and Lola?"

"Yes, but also –"

"Do you know how she is, by the way?"

"Fine, I presume. I'm sure we'd have heard otherwise."

"So are you going to ring him?"

"Finn?"

"Yeah."

"I don't think so. I don't want things to be over between us but I really hate him living with Lola. Why can't he understand that? He just thinks I'm being completely unreasonable. I guess my mistake was not making my feelings clear from the start. I shouldn't have let things go on this long without saying something."

"I wouldn't rule out ringing him and talking with him. He might see things differently this morning."

"Maybe. Or maybe he has Lola comforting him, telling him that he's better off without someone who makes such unreasonable demands. You know being the shoulder to cry on is always a good tactic to ultimately get the one you want."

Caroline picks up her empty cup, then pushes back her chair. "I'd better get moving, I need to sort out some new labels, ones that will list all the ingredients so we won't have a repeat of last night."

"Caroline, I want to talk to you about that, about the shop."

"Go on."

"The thing is, I m not sure I want to be part of the shop any more."

She looks at me in alarm. "No! No! Tell me you're kidding. You can't do this to me, not at this late stage."

"Someone ended up in hospital last night because of my recipes. It made it clear to me that I don't really know what I'm doing."

"Sure you do, as much as anyone. Look, Lola is fine. You know, people are allergic to all sorts. I'll get the new labels with a health warning sorted and we'll just have to remember from now on to advise people to read them."

"But, Caroline –"

"Look, nobody would manufacture anything or sell anything if they worried about all the things that don't suit all the people in the world. Rosie, you can't just walk away. We have too much money riding on this. Think of our investors. If we fail, how are we going to pay them back?"

"Yeah, but you'll manage without me. You can have all the recipes. I'm not going to be asking for a cut. Now that the shop is as good as up and running, you don't really need my help any more."

"Yes, I do. Dana and I can't do everything on our own. And, anyway, what about you? What would you do if you gave up the shop?"

"Try to go back to a career in science?"

"Don't you think you've burnt those bridges?"

I shrug.

"And how would you account for this particular period of your life on your CV?"

"Get you to lie for me again?" I say, jokingly. "You've done it before."

Caroline laughs. "And if I say I won't then you have no option but to stick with us. Look, Rosie, I can't help thinking this is about other things as much as the shop, that you've been affected by what happened between you and Finn. You're just feeling down about everything."

I shrug. "Maybe."

"For sure. And maybe things will work out between you and him."

"I can't see it happening, not as long as Lola is hanging around like a bad smell."

"Look, don't leave the shop. We need you. Remember: *All for one and one for all*."

"Yeah, yeah," I say.

"So no more talk of leaving then?"

"No."

"Good!" She gets to her feet. "All right then, we have work to do. First things first – we'll need to replace all the labels on the bottles and –"

"But it's Sunday. We won't be able to get new ones printed today."

"I thought Donald might be able to help but he's out of the country again so I was just about to give Niall a ring."

"Niall?"

"Yeah. I'm sure he'll know someone who'll be willing to do it, especially if he rings them up on our behalf."

"Caroline, don't you think you'd be better staying away from him?"

"I beg your pardon?"

"I saw him last night at the launch. The way he was acting with you."

"Why don't you mind your own business?"

"It is my business. Or do you like him, is that it? Did you like him stroking your face?"

"Jesus!"

Suddenly she runs from the kitchen and up the stairs. I hear the door of her room slamming.

I go out into the hall. "Caroline?" I call out but there's no answer. I bound up the stairs and as I go to open her door I hear the key turn in the lock. "Caroline, let me in!"

"Go away, Rosie."

"No, I'm going to stay here until you come out and tell me what's going on."

"Fine."

Five minutes pass and not a sound comes from her room but then the door is unlocked and Caroline steps out and smiles at me, as if nothing was amiss.

"Right, let's get those new labels sorted out. We'll need them if we're going to open tomorrow as planned. I'll ring Niall. Like I said, he's bound to have some contact that will do him a favour."

"Caroline!"

"Rosie, I'm sorry but you're blocking my way."

"Why can't you talk to me, Caroline? Tell me what's going on? Whatever happened to *All for one and one for all*?"

"Well, this *one*," she says, pointing to herself, "needs to sort things out, if we *all* are going to open tomorrow. Now, if you'll excuse me."

"Caroline! Why won't you talk to me?"

She shrugs. "I am talking to you. Or was. But now I'm finished – I have a lot I need to do."

One of the ocean's ugliest creatures, not to mention most deadly, is the fugu fish. The danger is in its high content of a poison called tetrodotoxin considered to be over 1,000 times deadlier than cyanide. In Japan, chefs must be specially licensed to prepare this deadly delicacy. The sense of danger surrounding a fugu feast ensures that it rates among the best-known aphrodisiacs in the world.

22

D-day has finally dawned, or should I say it will in an hour or two for it's still so early it feels like predawn when we leave our house and make our way in convoy into the city centre. The traffic is already beginning to build up but we arrive early enough to park the three minis in a row in parking spaces outside the shop, exactly as Caroline planned, all for maximum impact. First task completed, Caroline decides we should head around the corner for a big breakfast.

Both Dana and I sit there, not touching our plates piled with rashers, sausages and eggs. Just the smell is making me feel queasy. Caroline – on the other hand – has no such problem and, bar a single sausage, she's cleared her plate when she looks up and notices for the first time that neither of us is eating, but we are just sitting there, watching her.

"Come up, girls. Eat up," coaxes Caroline. "We have a big day in front of us. I bet we're going to be tearing busy. After the success of the launch, we're bound to be run off our feet."

Dana pushes her plate away. "I can't. My stomach is in bits."

"Mine isn't the best either," I admit.

Caroline reaches for her mug of tea and takes a long drink.

"Aren't you at all anxious?" asks Dana, watching her.

"Anxious? Me?" she asks, then shrugs. "What's there to be anxious about?" She stabs that last sausage with her fork, brings it to her mouth and takes a big bite. I study her as she eats it. Maybe, despite all her bravado, she is, like us, suffering from nerves but I can't see any sign as she munches away, like she hasn't eaten in months. Yep, she's her usual cool, calm and ever-so-collected self this morning.

"Anxious about the shop, of course," insists Dana. "What if it all goes belly-up?"

"Why on earth would you say that? It's going to be a great success."

"How can you be so sure?"

Caroline shrugs. "How can it not succeed? Look, you've just got last-minute jitters. Everything will be fine. You know it will. Are you going to eat that rasher?"

Dana shakes her head and Caroline reaches over and picks it up with her fork and then we sit there in silence watching as she cuts it up and eats it. When she's finished, she looks around for her handbag, gathers it up, then gets to her feet.

"Alrighty. Are we ready then?"

The first hour drags. We don't sell a single potion – not one. But how can we when not a single person steps through the door?

After all the build-up, this feels like the greatest let-down ever. I really, really wish it was busy, for the sake of the shop, of course, but, also, it would take my mind off things, and by things I mean Finn. I keep checking my phone to see if I've missed a call from him but no, nothing – not a dickie-bird.

"You could phone him, you know," says Dana, noticing.

I pretend I don't hear her.

The minutes continue to crawl.

"I can't believe this. We're never going to make a sale," moans Dana, growing increasingly despondent.

"Quit moaning. It's early days yet," snaps Caroline.

Finally, at exactly ten minutes past ten, the first customer arrives in. When Caroline calls out a cheery hello to her, she looks around nervously but avoids making eye contact. Just as I'm wondering if one of us should go over, Caroline makes a move, but Dana takes hold of her elbow.

"Give her space," she whispers. "She looks like she needs it."

The woman, I'd guess she's in her early thirties, walks around the shop, picking up bottle after bottle, and inspects each of them, carefully reading every label. She does this for over fifteen minutes until she must have examined every bottle in the shop thoroughly. I'm feeling uncomfortable. I'd be happier with gaggles of teenagers coming in for a laugh but this woman really looks like she's desperately searching for a solution to her problems whatever they might be.

"Why don't the pair of you go for coffee?" whispers Dana.

"But it's too early," I protest.

"Look, the three of us standing here like this is probably quite intimidating."

Dana has a point. Caroline and I head out.

On our way back in, we meet the lady leaving.

"So, Dana," Caroline demands immediately. "Did you manage to sell her anything?"

"No, afraid not!"

"You're joking? But she was here for ages."

"Nothing suited her."

"What do you mean? She was obviously looking for something."

"Yes, but we got talking and, to be honest, one of our love potions isn't going to solve her problems."

"What?" Caroline looks perplexed. "I don't understand."

"Look, that woman is going through some serious marital difficulties. She's been married for five years and she and her husband have been trying for a baby almost from the word go. They've gone to all the doctors, done every test, had every treatment, and nobody has been able to tell them what's wrong nor have any of the treatments worked. She still loves her husband and believes that he loves her too but she feels he's beginning to give up on their marriage, that he's had as much as he can put up with. She's afraid that if things go on the way they are, they'll end up splitting. When she spotted the shop this morning she came in on a whim, thinking that maybe a love potion would help her somehow. She's that desperate. But you know, I hadn't the heart to start flogging her one in the middle of her spilling her guts out to me."

Caroline sighs. "Dana, I have no problem with you giving her all the advice you like but you could at least have had her leave here with a purchase. How do you think we're going to repay all the money? Dana, this *is* a business."

"I know, I know, but that woman really just needed someone to listen, to help her. She'd lost all perspective."

"So you spent the last half an hour sorting her life out?"

"I don't think I quite managed that but yes, I did spend the time talking to her. What's the big deal?"

"Dana! You don't get it! We've got to start making money on this place, and soon!"

"Look, Caroline, I will work hard here. I will, you know that. I'm as anxious as you to make this place succeed but –"

"Are you? Are you really?"

"Yes, of course I am. You know I am. But I'm not flogging stuff to people who need a lot more."

The two of them are really angry now. They're both standing there staring at one another but then the door goes ping and a gaggle of girls come in. I breathe a sigh of relief.

"Hiya," one of them says as she comes straight up to the counter. "We're in Dublin for our friend Miriam's hen and we're hoping you might be able to spice it up for us."

"Well, you've come to the right place," says Caroline beaming and goes immediately to one of the shelves and picks up a bottle. "Ladies, I think this might interest you. We call it Liquid Love and I have to say it's one of our more delicious potions and one of our most effective. You girls take this before you go out on the town and it will have the effect of making you attractive in the eyes of any man you fancy."

One plain, low-sized, serious-looking girl picks up the bottle and reads the label on the back. She looks up. "It sounds like it's very strong."

"Oh, it is," says Caroline. "Very strong."

"But I don't want a whole bunch of ugly fellows falling for me."

"It doesn't work like that."

"How does it work then?" the girl asks.

"Well, what you do is this," Caroline begins to explain.

"Before you even start to get ready to go out tonight, you all gather in one of the bedrooms in whatever hotel you're staying. Then you leave the curtain open – moonlight is very important, you know, and –"

"Ah, come on! You're having a laugh!" cries one of the girls.

"Sshhh!" urges her serious-looking friend.

Caroline goes on. "*And* in the moonlight you imbibe three-quarters of this, no more, no less – exactly three quarters and then you recite: '*Light of moon, let me my one true love see, and when I do he will fall for me.*'"

"'*Light of moon, let me my one true love see, and when I do he will fall for me*'," repeats the girl like she's committing it to memory.

"Don't worry," says Caroline. "It's all in this little leaflet."

I can hardly believe this girl is being so gullible. I look at Dana, to see what she's thinking of all this and I see she's looking on at the proceedings with a very intense look on her face.

Caroline goes on, "Later on in the night, when you spot the man you like then you take the rest of the potion and say: '*My one true love I see, now let him be with me.*'"

"And that's it?"

"Yup. Now, shall I wrap it up for you?"

"Yes, please."

The girl stands at the counter as Caroline wraps the bottle. I study the girl. She is quite plain and I can't help feeling a little guilty that we're giving her false hope, that we're raising her expectations, letting her believe that she'll be lucky tonight – especially when all of the girls she's with are so much prettier?

Then I hear Dana address her: "Can I ask you something?"

"Sure," replies the girl.

"Well," Dana thinks for a second, "have you ever thought about wearing your hair down?"

I fully expect the girl to take umbrage but she doesn't – maybe it's Dana's manner, she speaks so gently. Instead the girl's hand goes to her hair and she fingers it.

"I don't know. It tends to go a bit frizzy."

"Take it down now, and let me have a look."

She does, and she's right. It doesn't do her any favours. Suddenly I feel sorry for her. Caroline has convinced her to place her hopes in a potion and now Dana seems to be suggesting that she wear her hair down in a most unflattering way.

"What do you think, Rosie?" Dana asks. "Up or down?"

Put on the spot, I feel I have to give an answer. "Have you thought about getting it cut?" I ask. "I think it would suit you better at neck length. It's lovely and thick but maybe there's just a little bit too much of it?"

"Cut it? Oh no, I don't think so."

"Maybe you're right," I concede. The last thing I want is to be responsible for making this girl do something she's uncomfortable with.

But then one of her friends joins in. She speaks directly to me. "You're right. We're always at her to cut it."

"You really think it would look better shorter?" the girl asks.

Clearly she takes more notice of advice coming from a stranger.

I shrug. "That's just my opinion. You should do what you think is best."

"Maybe cutting it a little would be best."

"Could you recommend anyone?" her friend asks me.

"Well, there's a very good stylist in Davide's," I tell her.

"It's just around the corner. Jack's his name. He might not be able to fit you in, but you could try him anyway."

When they finally leave the shop, each of them is carrying a bag with a potion for herself, and one – at Caroline's suggestion – even has a little something for the bride and groom too, for their wedding night.

Now Caroline leaves out a sigh. "Our first sales! I hope we don't have to work so hard for all of them."

As we head towards noon, sales pick up. We sell a potion to a woman for her unattached sister's fortieth birthday. Not that I said as much to the woman but I think I'd be pretty peeved if someone gave me a love potion for my fortieth. A crowd of southside-sounding ("Oim, loike, so loike, kool, roysh!") teenage girls come in to buy something for their friend's eighteenth and in the end leave with a bottle each. Our first male comes in. He rejects all offers of help from Caroline and we assume he's not going to buy anything but eventually he leaves the shop with one of everything.

"Let's hope they're for his wife," says Dana as we watch him walk past the window.

"I didn't notice a wedding ring," I tell her.

"Well, for his girlfriend then. I don't like the idea of him going around doling them out to every girl he meets."

"Maybe they're for himself," suggests Caroline.

At the end of the day, we find we've made over five hundred euros.

"Not bad for a first day," says Dana.

"But nowhere near good enough," says Caroline.

Shakespeare too understood the aphrodisiac quality of danger. Wasn't Juliet's love for Romeo heightened by the sense of danger, of violence, of death that surrounded the young couple?

What would be the modern-day equivalent? Gangs of youths beating one another up outside the chippy while their girlfriends stand watching, holding their jackets for them?

23

I'm busy fixing up the window when I happen to glance up and see Lola crossing the street.

"Oh no!" I mutter. Surely she doesn't intend coming in? No, please God, no! I move away from the window in case she spots me but then, almost immediately, the door opens and in she breezes.

"Hiya, Rosie!" she smiles, like we're the very best of friends.

"Hi, Lola," I reply. Determined not to let my feelings show, I even manage a smile. This is my shop. She is a member of the public. I will be courteous. "I'm glad to see you're well again."

"Thanks."

"We've labelled all the contents of each potion so nothing like that will happen again."

"Good. Good. You don't mind if I look around?"

"No, of course not," I say but manage to stop myself from adding that it *is* a shop.

As she browses, I pretend to occupy myself tidying behind the counter but out of the corner of my eye I watch as she picks up one bottle after another. What's she doing in here anyway? Is she actually interested in buying?

"Can I help you with anything?" I ask as brightly as I can.

She puts the bottle she's holding down, then casually walks over to me. All the while she's looking at me, smiling at me. She stops in front of the counter. She drops her smile.

"You? Help me?" She gives an unpleasant laugh.

I bristle but manage to answer evenly: "Ah, yes, that's my job."

"Well, I'm not buying something for myself – heaven forbid! In fact, I was thinking of getting something for a friend – as a joke really. She's just split up with her boyfriend. She's feeling kind of low, poor thing." Then she gives another nasty little laugh. "How insensitive of me! Of course, you'd know exactly how she must be feeling now that you and Finn have split up."

I shrug but otherwise don't respond.

"But it can't have come as much of a shock to you – I guess it was kind of inevitable, wasn't it?"

"I beg your pardon?"

"People who are in love, truly in love, want to spend every moment they can together – you could hardly say that about you two."

"It's not that we didn't want to, we couldn't, at least not in the past couple of months, what with the shop and the band, but now –"

She interrupts: "Did you ever think that you both might have been using these – the shop, the band – as excuses?"

"No! You don't know what you're talking about. Finn and I are – were – close. But the band is important to Finn. I understood why he needed to put time into it."

"You're right. The band is important to Finn. Music is such a big part of his life, isn't it? What he needs is someone who can understand that. I don't know you well but I do know Finn and, I have to admit, it was always a puzzle to me what the pair of you could possibly have had in common."

"We had plenty in common, as a matter of fact."

Why am I even bothering to defend Finn's and my relationship to this . . . bitch!

"Really?"

"Yes, really."

"But Finn is so creative – with his music, his song-writing, his painting. Whereas you . . ." she looks around disdainfully, "well, you work in a shop."

"Excuse me?"

"You were hardly soul mates, were you? No, it would never have worked . . . even if I hadn't come on the scene. If not me, he'd still have found someone more suitable than you."

"Are you trying to imply that you and Finn are together now?"

She thinks for a moment, then answers, "I wouldn't say I'm trying to imply, no."

"Good."

"I'm more like actually telling you." She smiles when she sees the shock on my face and then casually she looks around the shop again. "You know, I think I've changed my mind. I won't be buying anything. Anyway, I'd better go. I told Finn I'd stop off and pick up something tasty for dinner, maybe a bottle of wine too to go with it. I'm thinking a nice Pinot Grigio. We don't have a gig tonight so we've decided to have a quiet night in." Then she adds with a wink, "Maybe have an early night – if you know what I mean."

"Power," said Henry Kissinger, "is the ultimate aphrodisiac." Maybe it could be said to work for him and other male leaders regardless of how challenged they are in the looks department. As for women leaders, I don't think it increased Margaret Thatcher's, Indira Gandi's or Hilary Clinton's appeal to the unfairer sex one iota.

24

A few days later I come into the shop to relieve Dana but she's in the middle of talking to a customer. She looks over, tells me to come back in half an hour or so, and then goes on talking. The potions aren't exactly flying out the door so I have no new ones to mix up and I decide to go for coffee.

On my way out I bump into Caroline.

"Where are you off to?" she asks. "I thought you were starting work at two?"

I'm about to tell her that Dana is in the middle of giving advice to a customer but then, knowing how much Dana's propensity to get so involved in the customers and their problems annoys Caroline, I think again.

"Dana's going to hang on while I nip out for a quick coffee. Want to come?"

"I guess," says Caroline but with a distinct lack of enthusiasm.

We walk around the corner to a new little place. We go in. I notice some free seats by the window.

"Why don't you go and sit down and I'll order."

"Yeah, okay." She begins walking over to the empty table.

"Hey!" I call out. "You never told me what you want!"

She looks back and shrugs. "Whatever."

"Whatever?"

"Yeah."

Whatever? But there's never been any place for whatever in Caroline's life. That's what makes her Caroline. She's a black and white kind of girl.

I order two coffees and when they're ready I bring them down with me to the table, then slide into the bench opposite Caroline. "Here you go," I say.

"Thanks," she says, barely looking up.

We sip our coffee in silence. She sits there staring out the window. I sit there, trying to figure out what's up with her. I know I haven't been in great form lately but I realise she's not been her usual self either. She's like a bottle of Coke with the fizz gone out.

"Caroline?"

"Yeah?"

"Are you all right?"

"Yeah, sure," she says but not very convincingly.

"Are you worried that the shop isn't busier?"

"No, it's early days yet. It's bound to take time to get established."

"Are you and Mick okay?"

"Course."

"Good."

"When I get to see him."

"Is that's what's up with you? You're missing Mick?"

"No, well yes, partly. I just really wish the film was at an end. I wish Mick was around more. You know, you're right. I do miss him. But . . ." She thinks for a moment, then sighs and suddenly changes the subject. "Anyway, what about you? How are you doing?"

I shrug. "Well, you know."

"Any more visits from Lola?"

"No, thank God."

"Do you think she and Finn really are together?"

"I don't know what to think."

"Have you thought about ringing him?"

I shrug. "I've thought about it but I'm not going to. He knows where to find me."

"I hate to say this, Rosie, but he doesn't seem inclined to come looking. You need to find out exactly how things stand. Either he and she are together or they're not. If they're not, then maybe you can patch things up with him. If they are, well, then, you need to make up your mind to move on."

"Sure," I nod despondently.

"Come on," Caroline stands up. "Let's go back to work."

I glance through the front window as we're passing on our way back to the shop and I see Dana is still engrossed in conversation.

"Is that the same woman she was talking to when we went for coffee?" asks Caroline.

"I don't think so." It is but I see no point in adding fuel to the fire.

"It is. I'm sure of it. Sweetest hour! What does Dana think this is? I swear she's not living in the real world. What's with all the chatting? Does she not realise that we're up to our tonsils in debt? Doesn't she know she's meant to be selling?"

"Caroline, please don't go flying off the handle with Dana. Look, the shop is quiet. It's not like she's spending time with this woman when she could be selling to other customers – there are no other customers right now. Just calm down, all right!"

"All right! All right!"

When we do go in, Dana is saying goodbye to the woman and we stand aside to let her pass.

"Bye now, see you soon!" Dana calls out to her. Then she smiles over at us. "Hi guys, guess what? Did you see that woman who just left? You might remember her. She came into the shop on the very first day we opened. I don't know whether I told you about her at the time but she and her husband were going through a very hard time – they'd been trying for a baby for years and had finally given up." Unaware that Caroline's face is darkening with every sentence, Dana goes on. "She was worried that the strain was too much for her husband, that he was going to walk out on their marriage. Anyway, that last time she was in, she started asking me what I thought she should do so I told her that the best thing was to just concentrate on her husband, to try to get back to being one another's friend, to start talking, start doing things together, and to leave all the baby stuff alone for the time being. Well, she did all that and she says the transformation has been amazing. Now they take the time to have breakfast in the morning together. They meet for lunch in the middle of the working day. They sit down together at night with a glass of wine. She says these little changes have made all the difference. Everything is starting to improve. They've stopped obsessing about babies and are learning to simply enjoy one another's company again. This week is their sixth anniversary and he surprised her this morning by announcing that he's booked a two-week holiday in the Maldives! She came in to tell me. Can you believe that?" Dana finishes, looking dead chuffed.

"Did you actually manage to sell her anything this time?" asks Caroline.

Like she's been slapped on the face with a wet fish, Dana's smile instantly slips. "Why do you have to go and ruin the moment?" she says.

"Forgive me but it would be nice to see people actually walking out the door carrying our bags in their hands when you're looking after the place."

I hold my breath. Please let there not be a fight.

Dana looks at her, with a face like thunder. Without a word, she takes off her pink coat, lays it down on the counter, finds her bag, slings it over her shoulder and marches to the door. She opens it but then stops and turns around.

"For your information, Caroline, the reason that woman came in wasn't so much to update me on the state of her marriage but to buy some potions to take with her on her holiday, to make it that little bit special. If you look at the till roll, you'll see she spent a grand total of €189.80. In fact, she bought so much I suggested that she leave her bag here until she'd finished the rest of her shopping. She's coming back in later to collect them."

The artichoke was not introduced into England until the reign of Henry VIII. Catherine de Medici's promotion of the vegetable and its purported aphrodisiac properties are said to have accounted for Henry's personal interest in it.

Henry VIII + artichoke = six wives ???

And so the power of the artichoke changed the course of history . . .

25

The days that follow are mixed and the takings are up and down but never up enough to satisfy Caroline. The look on her face this evening as she does the till means she's not happy with today's takings either. She breaks off counting and looks over at me.

"Rosie, why don't you head off?"

"I don't mind hanging on for you. It's not like I have much else to do."

"Thanks but I'm going to stay on in town for a little while. I have to meet someone."

"Oh, right. Who?"

"Jesus, Rosie! Can you just give me some space! We work together, we live together but we're not joined at the hip, you know!"

"Okay, keep your hair on. Fine, I'll see you at home then."

When I get home, I find Dana sitting at the kitchen table,

surrounded by piles and piles of books. She has her glasses on. Her hair is up in a messy bun, with a couple of pens sticking out of it. She's wearing the same clothes she had on this morning, one of her oldest tracksuits and a pair of thick socks – her study clothes – which probably means she hasn't been out of the house all day.

"Hiya," I say. "Have you been here all day?"

She gives a big stretch. "Sure have."

"Working on your thesis?"

"Yep."

"How's it going?"

"Good, good. I'm back on track again. How was the shop today?"

"So–so."

"I wish it was a bit busier."

"Don't we all?" I sigh.

"You know, I love working there and despite what Caroline might like to say my sales are every bit as good as either of the two of you but sometimes I wonder if it can ever support all of us. I know Caroline talks, or at least used to talk, about opening another branch, and then another, but we have to get the one we have operating profitably before that can happen. What if it doesn't?"

"Look, let's just take each day as it comes."

"I'm not very good at that. I like to be able to plan. I like to know where I'm going. I'm not sure I'm cut out for the vagaries of business." She pats one of the piles of books. "Maybe I'm better suited to academia."

"No reason you can't combine both,' I say. "Want a cup of coffee?"

"Nah, I've had about a hundred already today."

I go to the kettle and put it on.

"Rosie?"

"Yeah?"

"I meant to tell you that when I met Monica the other day she told me that when she and Fay last met for lunch, Fay was making discreet enquiries about Finn's dad."

"Really?"

Dana nods. "Yeah."

"I just knew they were getting along so well that night at the launch of the shop."

"Seems you were right."

I think for a second. "If I were still going out with Finn I could orchestrate things between them."

Dana laughs. "You never change, do you? Always wanting to meddle!"

I shrug. "Maybe it's just as well I can't, considering the damage I did in the past where Fay is concerned. But what if it turned out they were perfectly suited? Now they'll never get that opportunity to find out."

"But they have already met. She or Mr Heelan could have said something that night if either one of them felt that strongly."

"Maybe, but people don't always find it so easy to say what they want in that kind of situation."

"I guess. But it's out of our hands now – we can't do anything about it."

I sigh. "I suppose."

The heat in garlic is known to stir sexual desires.
Perhaps this recommendation should be qualified with a
warning: only effective if taken by BOTH parties.

26

The shop is quiet when I arrive in to work to take over from Caroline at two. The first thing I notice is that Caroline is listening to a talk show on the radio which is unusual. She normally insists that we keep it tuned to Lyric FM to maintain a nice gentle atmosphere for the customers.

"How come you're listening to Rick Montague?" I ask.

"Sshhh! Just listen."

"To what?"

"The radio, of course."

"But why?"

"Sssshhhhhhhh."

". . . a sudden drop in temperature is all that's required to cause that chip in your windscreen to start cracking but you can save yourself time, money and trouble by ringing us on . . ."

"Why do I need to know this?" I ask.

"You don't. Just keep listening."

Just then a trio of well-dressed, thirty-somethings come in and Caroline changes her mind.

"In fact, don't! Take care of them instead. I'll keep listening."

I do as she says and manage to make quite a nice little sale. When I'm done, Caroline still has her ears glued to the radio.

"You know," I begin, "I think our Sweet Delight is turning out to be one of our best sell –"

"Sshhh!" Caroline urges again.

"So this text goes," says Rick Montague, " *'Hey Rick! Has anyone else seen those pink Mini Coopers with the hearts and with love potions or something written on them? What's the story with them?'*"

"Caroline!" I squeal. "They're talking about us!"

"I know. Now ssh!"

"If anyone has any information," Rick goes on, "let us know."

Suddenly it all becomes clear to me. The expectant air, her satisfied smile and, the smoking gun – the mobile she clutches in her hand.

"You!" I cry. "You're the one who texted in! Aren't you the sly one!"

"Sly? Well, I prefer the term 'clever' myself!" Caroline laughs. "There may be no such thing as a free lunch but we're bagging ourselves some free publicity. I just needed to get the ball rolling somehow and now it has. If all goes according to plan, somebody else will soon text in with an answer."

We go on listening. Rick calls out other texts he's receiving. Someone warns about a fifty-minute delay on the N7. Someone wants to know what's the best way of getting rid of a broken fridge. Someone complains about being charged ten euros for a pot of tea for two in some city centre café. And then:

"Okay, more on the subject of those mysterious Mini

Coopers. This text from Anne goes, *'I've seen those pink minis too. Aren't they advertising that new love potion shop in town?'"* Montague laughs. "Love potion shop! I've heard it all now! So does anyone know anything about this place? Has anybody been in there and bought one of these potions? Come on, people, let us know!"

Caroline claps her hands in excitement. "Do you have any idea how much this kind of publicity would cost? Okay." She goes over and turns up the radio. "Let's see what happens next? Let's see if anyone else takes the bait."

But nobody does. Instead the charge of ten euros for a pot of tea seems to have caught the imagination of Montague's listeners and they're keen to beat it with their own accounts of being ripped off. €1.50 for a glass of tap water in a city centre pub! €1.00 to use the toilet in a popular shopping centre!! €5.00 for a glass of Coke in a restaurant in the leafy suburbs!!!

Caroline begins to grow impatient. "What a nation of moaners! Is he going to read out every single whinge-bag's text? Here, give me your mobile!"

"What? Why? You have your own."

"I don't want to text in twice on the same phone in case they remember the number."

"But what are you going to say?"

"Listen and you'll find out."

I take my phone from my bag and hand it to her. Quickly she thumbs in her message and then sits back and listens but the whingeing texts keep coming. €3.45 for a single scone that wasn't even fresh and came without any jam . . . €8.00 for one hour and five minutes' parking . . .

"Moan, moan, moan that's all they're doing!" moans Caroline.

But, then, he reads out Caroline's second text.

"More on these love potions," says Rick. "This text has just come in – '*Boyfriend bought me a present from the love potions shop last weekend. It was their Red to Orange Chakra. Delicious! And, boy, does it work!*' Hmm, interesting," laughs Rick. "Maybe I should pay them a visit."

We go on listening but when nobody has any further comment to make on the subject of the shop, Caroline decides to take matters into her own hands once again. She goes to the shop phone this time and dials.

"Hello, my name is Caroline Connolly. I'm the proprietor of Love Potions. One of our customers happened to mention that someone texted in about our shop." She listens for a moment. "Would I come on air? I guess I could. Okay, yeah, I'll stay on the line." She sits there with the phone cradled to her ear. Seeing me looking at her, she gives me a thumbs-up.

I shake my head and throw my eyes to heaven. She really is unbelievable. But I am impressed.

"Hi, hi, Rick! Yes, I'm Caroline Connolly. That's right, I'm one of the proprietors of Love Potions."

I take the radio and go to the far end of the shop and listen.

It's funny hearing Caroline on the airwaves like this but she sounds good – confident, friendly, and not at all nervous.

"Yes, we opened three weeks ago," she's telling Rick. "Myself and my two best friends, Dana and Rosie."

"So the three of you are running it together?"

"Yep, that's right, Rick."

"And business is good?"

"Business is booming!" she lies. "The shop is packed even as we speak. We can hardly keep up with demand."

"But love potions, come on! You don't really believe in this stuff?"

"Of course, I do. I wouldn't be selling them if I didn't. All our recipes are made from ingredients that have been considered aphrodisiacs throughout history. We're just taking traditional recipes and making them available in a modern world."

"I have to admit to being a bit cynical about all this, Caroline."

"Don't knock it until you try it!"

"Okay, why don't you put on one of your customers – let's hear what they have to say."

"Ah, sure. You can talk to Simone. She popped back in to give us an update after buying one the other day." Caroline gestures to me to come over but I shake my head, leaving her no choice but to go on talking. How could she put me on the spot like this! "Yeah," Caroline goes on, "Simone's fancied one of her colleagues for months now and last week she invited him over for dinner." All the time she's talking, she's beckoning me over. "So, anyway, Simone started the evening off with one of our potions and then she followed it up with a meal. She says the evening was a tremendous success. They're going out again on a date this weekend."

"Well, that sounds like a result! So put Simone on. Let me talk to her."

"Sure." Caroline puts her hand over the mouthpiece. "Rosie, come on! Get on the phone! *Now!*" She holds it out to me.

I walk over to her slowly and take the phone reluctantly, throwing her a filthy look as I do. "Hi."

"Is this Simone?" booms Rick.

"Ah, yes, that's right."

"So you're a satisfied customer of Love Potions?"

"Ah, yes, I am."

"Caroline says you've used one of her potions on a colleague and that it worked?"

"Ah, yes, that's right."

I notice Caroline is gesticulating furiously. I cover the receiver. "What?"

"You could try being a little more animated, chattier."

"Chattier? You're lucky I don't tell him the real story!"

I missed whatever question Rick is asking me. I ask him to repeat it.

"So, Simone, tell us what happened after you gave your colleague the love potion."

I manage a laugh, though to my ears it sounds like a very false one. "I'd rather not say!"

Caroline pulls the receiver from me.

"I think what Simone means is that an afternoon radio show may not be the appropriate place to divulge such – ah – intimate details."

"So, Caroline," Rick begins winding up, "maybe you'll send us in a couple of these potions?"

"Yeah, sure, I'd be delighted to."

"Maybe we'll even test them live on the air."

Caroline laughs. "Sounds a little risky. Are you sure you're up for it?"

"We'll chance it. Be sure to send them in. Nice talking to you, Caroline."

"Well," says Caroline, looking as pleased as Punch as she hangs up. "What do you think? Am I a genius or what? Think how many people heard that!"

"Yeah, think how many people heard that and knew it was me!"

"Only people who know you and they don't matter. We're trying to reach people who don't know us or the shop."

"How could you put me on the spot like that?" I ask, feeling really annoyed.

"Jesus, Rosie! What are you so mad about?"

"Because you got me to lie on radio, to pretend to be someone else. How could you do that to me?"

Now it's Caroline's turn to be cross. "Oh, so it's all right for me to stick my neck out to get this place on the map but not for you!"

"You could have warned me!"

"How? Did I know he was going to ask to speak to a customer? Did you want me to tell him we didn't have any?"

"Don't *ever* do anything like that to me again!"

We don't talk much for the rest of the afternoon, partly because we're both mad with one other but also because we're run off our feet. We've never been so busy and there's no doubt that it's due to our exposure on the radio – several of the customers mention that they heard it.

Towards closing, when the shop is empty for the first time all afternoon, Mick calls in.

"This is a surprise!" cries Caroline. "I wasn't expecting to see you! Guess what?"

"You were on the radio?"

"Yeah, so you heard it?"

"Me and half the country."

"That's what I'm hoping."

Mick looks over at me. "Whatever about Caroline, I'm surprised at you – *Simone*." He turns to Caroline again and looks at her keenly. "Did you phone in that original text?" Caroline doesn't answer straight away. "You did, didn't you!" He turns to me. "Did she, Rosie?"

"What are you asking her for?" demands Caroline.

"Because she might give me an honest answer."

"So what if I did? It's got people talking about the place. We've just had our best day so far."

"What are you like!"

"Come on. It's business! Where's the harm? It's not like I shot someone."

"It's just all a big pretence!"

"Pretence? On the contrary, it's all very real! This is a real business, with real money invested in it. If we fail we'll owe thousands upon thousands of *real* money. Can't you understand that? I don't see what your problem is. So we bagged ourselves a little free publicity. Big deal! Now I've had a long day and I'm going home. We're closing up. So do you want a lift? Or would you prefer to travel by high horse?"

Nutmeg was highly prized by Chinese women
as an aphrodisiac.
Another note of warning: in large quantities nutmeg
can produce a hallucinogenic effect.
However, a light sprinkling of it in a warm pumpkin soup
can help spice up a cold evening.

27

The surge in business we experience in the days following the publicity doesn't last too long. True to her word, Caroline did send Rick Montague a basket of love potions, and then rang the station again and again and again, hoping to remind Rick of his idea to try the potions on air. But no such luck. Rick and his show had moved on to other topics and Caroline never got any further than the receptionist whose initial cheery response gradually gave way to an icy professional politeness whenever she heard Caroline's voice, like she was now – as Caroline put it – dealing with one of the station's regular crank callers.

But something very exciting does come out of the *Rick Montague Show* after all, as Caroline is telling us now, having arrived home after spending the afternoon in the shop. The only problem is that she's so excited it's hard to follow what she's trying to say.

". . . so he says his name is Felix and he's ringing on behalf of Andrew Marsh and so I say something like, oh, but

I didn't make an appointment, and so he says that, yeah, he knows that but he's keen to have all three of us come in, and so I say I didn't think you two would be interested, and I tell him that you have your own hairdresser, Rosie, and that you, Dana, hardly ever get your hair done, and so he says something like, hairdresser? What are you talking about hairdressers for? And so I say, but you're the one ringing from the hairdresser's and so he says something like, oh, you think I'm ringing for Andrew Marsh, the hairdresser, no, no, I'm ringing on behalf of Andrew Marsh, the TV presenter, and so I say, oh really? And so he says, yeah, you know from *Topical Ireland*, I work on the show and then –"

"Okay, hold it there," I interrupt. "Are you telling us that Andrew Marsh wants all three of us to come on his show?"

"Isn't that what I just said? They'll be recording on Monday morning so we'd have to get someone to cover for a couple of hours. Monica might be –"

"Andrew Marsh?" Dana interrupts now. "Is he the guy on after the news on Mondays?"

"Yeah, that's right."

"I don't think I've ever watched it."

"You should. It's a great show."

"What kind of show is it exactly?" asks Dana.

"It's quite broad," I tell her. "He deals with anything that's topical really – hence the name."

Caroline goes on. "Sometimes he interviews people who have a new book or film or whatever coming out. Other times he deals with issues with a panel in the studio. And he goes out and about too and talks to people right around the country."

"Yeah," I add. "People protesting against some new motorway. Asylum seekers unhappy with the treatment they get here. Tidy Town committees. All sorts really."

"But how did he even hear about us?" asks Dana.

"This Felix guy who rang said he heard the piece on the *Rick Montague Show*," explains Caroline.

"But why does he want us to come on exactly?" asks Dana.

"He's interested in the idea of three young women, three friends, going into business together."

"And that's what we'd be talking about?"

"Yes," confirms Caroline.

Dana looks to me. "What do you think, Rosie?"

"I think we should go for it. That mention on the radio did us a lot of good. This would even be better."

"So, will I ring him back and tell him we're on for it?" asks Caroline.

"Yeah. Go on then," I say while Dana nods in agreement.

Asparagus is reputed to have aphrodisiac properties so strong that during the Renaissance it was banned from the tables of most nunneries.

28

Dana leaves out a big sigh. "How long more are we going to have to wait? My stomach is all queasy. God, I am so nervous."

I glance over at her and see that she does look a little green despite the heavy make-up the in-house experts applied to her face when we first arrived at the television studios.

"Don't be. There's no need," says Caroline. "You can just sit there, looking pretty. Leave all the talking to me. Then, as soon as this is over, we can go and have a big breakfast."

"Breakfast! Ugh!" Dana pulls a face. "Don't talk to me about food."

The door opens and I look up expecting it to be someone coming to tell us it's time but it's not. Instead it's two women who I presume are also guests. One, in her late sixties, is rather bohemian-looking with long flowing grey hair and long flowing colourful clothes. Her eyes are ringed in dark kohl and her lashes are thick with black mascara. The other is a pretty-looking woman around the same age as ourselves. She shares the older woman's bohemian air – same style of clothes, same heavy make-up, same long hair but with one difference, it's pitch black.

Both, but the older woman especially, have a confident air. She doesn't deign to so much as glance at us while the younger woman nods somewhat regally in our general direction, like we should know her. The older one sits down first.

"Adeline," she says, patting the seat beside her and when Adeline sits down too, the older woman begins talking unselfconsciously, like it's just the two of them in the room.

"Adeline, dear?"

"Yes, Nana?"

"Tell me, what's the rest of our schedule for today?"

Adeline lifts her large carpetbag onto her lap, roots around in it, then takes out her electronic diary. She switches it on, waits a moment or two, then begins to read: "11.00am: flight to London. 3.00pm: lunch with publishers. 6.00pm: return flight. 8.30pm: Dinner in Howth with Dixie Duggan."

"Excuse me," pipes up Dana, "can I ask if you're the wo –"

Suddenly Caroline cuts in, "– if you're going on *Topical Ireland*?"

Adeline nods. "Yes, we are."

"So are we," Caroline tells her. "It's our first time on television. We're a little nervous."

"What are you –"

Caroline ignores Adeline's interruption. "We were afraid we'd be late. Wasn't the traffic horrendous coming in? But it's always like that when it rains – much worse than on other days. I heard on the early morning news that it's set to clear up later on, thankfully. But I guess we can't complain.

345

Overall the weather has been quite good this year, hasn't it? I mean, compared to last year we're doing okay. Remember, there was hardly a dry day in the whole of . . ." She babbles on.

Dana is looking at her, puzzled. As am I. Maybe, despite what she'd like us to believe, she is nervous after all. Why else would she be rabbiting on like this?

"The rest of Europe is getting its share of rain, isn't it? My brother was in Spain recently and he said that –"

Just then, the door opens and Caroline breaks off from her rambling monologue. It's Felix again – we already met him when we first arrived. Early twenties, he's a very natty, retro-looking guy with a quiff and an American baseball jacket with '*Stanford*' embossed across the back, who seems to be permanently clasping a clipboard.

"Okay, ladies," he announces, "the other guests are done in make-up and we're ready to start filming the second half of the show. Would you come with me?"

We all get to our feet and follow. Already with him are two other guests. The first is a slight man, in his forties – I'd guess, with a bony face, a furrowed brow, freckled skin and sparse, lank, sandy-coloured hair. He's wearing brown socks, brown sandals, brown slacks (there's no other word for them), and a brown shirt teamed with a vertically striped sleeveless sweater and a horizontally striped tie. The second is a woman who I'd say is in her late sixties/early seventies who has big white hair in the style of Barbara Bush, Senior. She's dressed in a baby-pink suit, matching shoes and handbag. For a second I'm thinking maybe she actually is Barbara Bush but then I think again, maybe she's no longer even alive and, if she is, whatever would she be doing on such a show here in Ireland?

All of us follow Felix down along a long narrow corridor and then out on to the set. Centre stage, facing the studio audience, is a row of armchairs with a high stool a little distance apart on which, I presume, Mr Marsh will be sitting.

"Okay, guys, take your seats," Felix tells us. "We're running a little late so we'll start straight back into the second half. Mr Marsh is on his way."

Caroline, Dana and I sit down first, then the Barbara Bush lookalike, then Mr Stripy-Tank-Top, then Adeline and the woman who is either called Nana, or is Adeline's grandmother. It's probably the latter, I'm thinking.

I smile at the Barbara lookalike in the seat beside me. "Have you just started up your own business as well?" I ask.

She looks at me. She seems puzzled. "Whatever gave you that idea?" she says dismissively, then turns away.

Before I can even begin to figure out what to make of this strange exchange, the studio audience starts clapping and I look around to see Andrew Marsh walking on to the set. He climbs up onto the high stool.

"Welcome back," he talks into one of the cameras. "In our second half, we have an interesting line-up." He begins introducing us one by one. "We're joined on this week's show by Mina Butterfield and her granddaughter Adeline Winston, probably two of Ireland's best-known psychics." Mina and Adeline smile to the camera. Adeline even gives a little wave. "Next, we have John Duggan, a prominent homeopath." John nods solemnly, again to the camera. "Also with us is Celeste laRue, an angel adviser. Welcome, Celeste."

"Lovely to be here, Andrew."

"And last but certainly not least we have three young women, Caroline Connolly, Dana Vaughan and Rosie Kiely who are the proprietors of the recently opened city centre shop, Love Potions. Welcome, ladies!"

Oh! My! God! Suddenly it's clear to me. Today's topic has *nothing* to do with setting up in business. What all of us guests have in common is that we represent some facet of what is 'New Age'. I see Dana is looking absolutely horrified. She's clearly just reached the same conclusion as I have.

"Thank you for having us," I hear Caroline answer.

I look over. I see her smiling. But how can she be so calm? She must realise too that we've been brought on under false pretences.

Suddenly the bright studio lights feel unbearably hot. I begin to sweat. I think I'm going to faint. How the hell did we end up here? This is like a living nightmare from which there's no escape. I look around. At Andrew Marsh on his high stool, at the other guests, at the camera operators, at Felix and the other studio people, at the studio audience who are all clapping now, ready to be entertained.

The clapping dies down and Marsh climbs down from his high perch and walks over. He stops beside Celeste.

"We'll begin with you, Celeste. You call yourself an angel adviser, I believe."

I think I'm getting palpitations. I look to see how far away the nearest exit is.

"That's right, Andrew," Celeste smiles sweetly.

"Tell us a little about yourself. How did you become an angel adviser?"

"Actually, Andrew, I didn't become one. The gift was there since birth," Celeste answers, still smiling sweetly.

I wish I had the courage to simply get up and walk away but I don't. I can't. Not before all these people. I'm trapped.

"I see. So tell me a little about your – ah – gift?"

"Well, Andrew, everyone has an angel watching over him or her but most of us have lost our ability to communicate with the angel assigned to us. And that's what I do. I act as a communicator for people who want to get in touch with their angel."

"You say angels are assigned to us. Who exactly does the assigning?"

"Why, God, of course."

"God?"

"You've heard of guardian angels, haven't you?"

"Of course. But I thought they went out of fashion." He gives a short laugh. "Like Hell."

"Now, Andrew, just because they're out of fashion that doesn't make them any less real. They're still there but modern life is so busy people have simply forgotten how to commune with them."

"But you can."

"Yes. That is my gift."

"The gift you were born with. Tell me, when was the first time you remember actually knowing you possessed it?"

Celeste thinks. "Well, even as a young child I displayed powers of perception that extended far beyond the normal range of the five senses and by the age of three, maybe four, my family remember me telling them that I could see these visions standing beside them."

Marsh laughs. "They didn't presume you were talking about imaginary friends, like kids of that age so often do?"

Celeste looks at Marsh like she genuinely pities him. She shakes her head sympathetically. She really does seem like a very sweet lady, like the kindly (albeit wacky) granny in a children's story.

"Andrew, my powers were clear for anyone to see. These

visions, these angels, told me things, things from the past, warnings about the future, things that were already true or soon became true. By the time I was ten, people were queuing outside my house in my little home town. They came from far and wide because they knew I was speaking the truth, that I had the gift to communicate."

"And you charged them, of course."

"Not at first, no."

"But you do now?"

"Andrew, I feel you're sceptical and I un —"

"What?" Marsh looks around. "Is my angel here? Is he telling you that?"

"I feel you're sceptical and I understand that. Many people are and that, of course, is their right. You asked me to come on your show as a guest and I did. I'm not here to try and convince you or anyone of my gift."

"Yes, but —"

"To answer your question, I devote my life to interfacing between people and their angels and because I do that I don't hold down an ordinary job. So, yes, I do accept a small donation. I have to live too, Andrew."

"So you take money from people and tell them what their angels want them to hear?"

"Yes. Andrew, I can see you're trying to make this out to be a bad thing but that is exactly what I do and I make no apologies."

"At least you haven't caused anyone to die."

"Pardon? No, of course not!"

"On that note, let's turn now to Mina and her granddaughter, Adeline. Let's start with you, Adeline. Why don't you tell us a little about yourself? You call yourself a psychic. Why?"

"Because I am one, of course," she answers defensively. Clearly Adeline is not going to be as amicable as Celeste. "I'm psychic and so is my nana. She was the one who first realised I shared her gift."

"And your mother is not psychic?"

"No, but she accepts that both her daughter and her mother have the gift. I think she'd prefer it if we were normal but accepts the way we are."

"I believe you've worked closely with the police?"

"Yes, that's correct."

"And I believe they have redirected resources in response to your advice?"

"Yes."

"Some might object to the taxpayers' money being used in this fashion considering –"

Mina cuts in. "Andrew, I'd like to know where you're going with this?"

"I thought with your psychic powers you'd already know!" laughs Marsh. The gloves are off. No more pussy-footing. "Something has always puzzled me when I see people like you in action. When you're looking for, say, a missing person, you say things like: 'I see water.' Or 'A man with a name beginning with M is significant.' Now the thing that's always puzzled me is this: how come you always give such sketchy detail? How come you can't just simply say, 'I see water. It's a lake. In fact it's Lough Neagh.' Or, 'I see a man. His name is Michael Murphy.'"

Mina looks angry but she manages to respond calmly. "I'm not sure how you expect me to answer. I can't pretend that I know more than I do."

"But maybe that's just it. Because you are pretending, you have to keep it vague. The vaguer you keep it, the more chance you will stumble upon something in your wild guesses that approximates to the truth."

"I beg your pardon!"

Marsh ignores her and begins walking over to a big screen. "I'd like to show the audience a clip of you in action." An image comes on the screen. It's Mina sitting on a couch with a man and woman both of whom are poorly dressed and have tired, terribly sad faces. The woman's bottom lip is trembling. The man is tightly holding both her hands in his.

"Water is significant," we hear Mina telling them, "and a wood."

"You think that's where our son is?" asks the sad-looking woman in a voice that's barely above a whisper.

Mina nods.

"Is he alive?" the man asks with anxious hope.

On the big screen, the camera closes in on Mina. She doesn't respond for what seems like ages. I forget my own current prediction as I wait for her answer. Very slowly Mina shakes her head. "No, he's not." Off camera, there comes a wailing sound. The screen goes dead.

Marsh walks back over to her.

"Mina, I have one question for you. A simple yes or no will suffice. Is it true that days after this was filmed the couple found their son in a hospital, in a coma?"

Mina looks as if she'd like to chew him up and spit him out but Marsh is unconcerned.

"When you were telling them that their son was dead, was he in fact alive, yes or no? Is it true to say that neither water or woods had any significance in this case, yes or no?"

"Stop badgering me like this!" shouts Mina. "Only God can get it right one hundred per cent of the time. I am not God!"

"No, you are not God. You and your granddaughter are in fact con artists, charlatans with no conscience who prey on the vulnerable, yes or no?"

"No, we are psychics! You're distorting things! You could have shown any of the people we have helped but you chose to show those people instead. The information they gave us to work on was inaccurate."

"Oh, please! You're blaming these poor people – can you get any lower?"

"I'm not blaming them. I'm explaining!"

But Marsh is done with Mina and Adeline and now he moves on to John Duggan.

"Most of those who set themselves up as alternative medicine practitioners are able to satisfy customers because their medicine is generally harmless . . ."

As he goes on, all I'm thinking is how the hell can we get out of here before it's our turn? If we stand up and try to walk away no doubt it'll only add to the drama. I glance over at Dana – she looks as pale as a ghost (which is fitting, considering the company). I look at Caroline. She still seems quite composed. How can she be? A thought occurs to me: could she have known beforehand what this show was going to be about?

". . . the real danger from such practices," Marsh goes on, "comes not from the practice itself but from the patient avoiding conventional treatment that could save his or her life. Usually when the . . ."

Did she lie in order to get us to come on? Could she really have done that to us?

Now Marsh gets up from his stool and walks over to the homeopath.

"Mr Duggan, two years ago, thirty-three-year-old Sadie Hurley came to you having being diagnosed with breast cancer but you told her that her illness was the result of gangrene and mercury poisoning in her teeth. You advised her not to undergo chemotherapy. She agreed and put herself in your hands instead. She died after six months of treatment by you. Is that correct?"

John Duggan doesn't say a word. He gets up from his seat and walks off the set.

"I think that says it all," Marsh tells the camera.

I'm seriously thinking about following John Duggan but before I can find the courage to mobilise myself, Marsh finally turns his attention to us.

"And our final guests are these three young women, Dana, Caroline, and Rosie who, as I mentioned in my introduction, have recently set up a business in Dublin's city centre – in their shop called Love Potions." He smiles at us. "So, can you tell me a little about this."

Immediately, Caroline begins talking. Her voice is strong and sure.

"Can I say first of all, Andrew, that all we do is sell love potions, that's all, and the ingredients we use have all historically been considered aphrodisiacs. We don't purport to communicate with the dead, or with angels, or put people's lives in danger. There's nothing in our potions that would harm anyone."

"We'll come back to that."

"Pardon?"

"But first, aren't you guilty of feeding on people's insecurities to make a profit?"

"No, our potions do nothing but good," insists Caroline.

"So are you telling me they work? That people who take one of your potions will find love?"

"No, but they can, for example, give a person a sense of

confidence that he or she might not otherwise have and that can have a positive impact on their love life."

"So in effect you're selling placebos?"

"No, we're selling what are commonly and historically considered aphrodisiacs."

"So you say. But, Dana, what I –"

"Caroline. I'm Caroline."

"I beg your pardon. Which one of you is Dana then?"

"I am," Dana says weakly.

"Dana, as a psychology postgraduate student, is it true you recently carried out a study on the placebo effect of a substance that you led the participants in the study to believe was an aphrodisiac?"

"Andrew," Caroline cuts in, "I'd like to –"

"If you don't mind, Caroline, I'm talking to Dana. So Dana, did you recently carry out a study on the placebo effect of a substance? Did you lead the participants in that study to believe the substance was an aphrodisiac?"

Dana looks bewildered. "Yes. But –"

"And what did your study tell you?"

"I don't understand. This has nothing to do with our shop."

"But surely it has. People are entitled to know a little about you in the circumstances. So this study didn't involve using aphrodisiacs at all, is that correct?"

Dana nods.

"Why was that?"

"Because such a study would be too difficult to administer."

"Would it be true to say that there has never been a scientific study that has conclusively shown that aphrodisiacs work, yes, or no?"

"Well, yes, like I said it would be too difficult to administer. There are too many ethical issues."

Marsh laughs derisively. "You sit there and talk to me about ethics! Where are your ethics? You engage in academic research to prove that people will react positively to something that is not an aphrodisiac *if* they are told it is. *And* at the same time, you churn out unproven substances and sell them to make a profit. It looks to me like you're having your cake and eating it. I'm not defending any of these others but at least they seem to genuinely be deluded enough to believe in what they peddle. You, on the other hand, do not!"

"Mr Marsh, the ingredients we use in the shop are considered aphrodisiacs, have been regarded by people throughout the generations as such. Just because they've never been scientifically proven to be so doesn't mean they're not. Yes, they may have a psychological impact too but that doesn't mean they don't also have a physical impact."

Andrew Marsh looks at his notes.

"Is it fair to say that your recent study was poorly supervised?"

"No!"

"Then can you explain how two young people almost drowned while under your supervision?"

"But that was —"

"And they're not the only casualties of your carelessness. One of the potions on sale in your shop resulted in another young person, this time a very talented singer, also ending up in hospital. Is that correct? Yes or no?"

"Yes, but both were very minor incidents."

"Minor? Two people nearly drowned under your supervision —"

"But they didn't! Both are —"

"— and one of the potions resulted in another going into a life-threatening anaphylactic shock. You call these minor incidents?"

"That couple were expressly asked to stay away from the beach but they ignored our instructions. As for the other woman, she's fine now. She was discharged within hours. And for your information, we've changed the way we do things in the shop — all the ingredients are clearly listed — there's no reason why the same thing should ever happen again."

But Marsh is now finished with Dana. He walks over to his stool, sits, and begins to wind up the programme.

"In this show, we've seen the different faces of the people who prey on the vulnerable, on susceptible people who, when faced with life's challenges, turn to these charlatans and willingly hand over their money. These fraudsters are . . ."

I'm not listening. Dana is shaking like crazy. Caroline reaches out to take her hand.

"Get away from me!" Dana snaps.

The minute the programme ends, Dana stands up and runs to the exit.

"Dana!" Caroline shouts and is about to run after her.

"Jesus, Caroline!" I catch hold of her arm. "Let her go! Don't you think you've done enough damage? What the hell were you thinking? How could you!"

"I didn't know."

"You didn't know *what*? Did you really think we'd been invited on to talk about our experience of setting up in business, like you told us?"

"Yes . . . kind of."

"Kind of? Caroline! You either did or you didn't!"

"Okay, I didn't, all right!"

"So what did you think we were coming on to talk about?"

"Okay, I knew the show was going to be about all this New Age stuff but –"

"So you lied to us?"

She doesn't answer my question. "Look, I just thought any publicity would be good publicity. I thought we'd be able to turn it to our advantage, that *I'd* be able to turn it to our advantage. There was no way I could have known Andrew Marsh was going to zone in on Dana like that. I did try to stop him. And like, how did he even know any of that stuff anyway? About Dana's trials? About those students nearly drowning? Or about Lola? I had no idea the whole thing was going to pan out like that!"

In 1590 a Jesuit priest by the name of Jose de Acosta warned that chilli was "prejudicial to the health of young folks, chiefly to the soul, for it provokes to lust".

Perhaps he believed that if chilli were banned, as asparagus was banned for the nuns, then that might put a stop to youthful shenanigans.

Hadn't they heard of hormones back then?

29

Caroline and I drive home in her car. We don't say much. In fact we don't say anything. I'm still so mad I'm afraid to even talk to her for fear of what I might say. Once or twice I do glance over at her but though it's an overcast day she's wearing sunglasses so I can't see her eyes but her tensed shoulders and the rigid set to her jaw tell me she's not feeling too happy either.

As we're nearing home, when she has to pull up at a red light, she takes off her sunglasses, turns to me, and speaks for the first time since we sat in.

"Do you think Dana will forgive me?" she asks in a tiny little voice that sounds nothing like her own.

"I doubt it."

"What about you?"

I glance over at her again. This apprehensive Caroline with her big Bambi eyes is one I've never met before. I almost find myself feeling sorry for her. Almost.

"Let's just say I'm not in a very forgiving mood right

now," I say coldly. "You should have told us the truth. You should have given us the opportunity to decide for ourselves if we wanted to go on the show knowing what it was really about."

"But you'd have said no."

Would I have said no? Okay, what we do is 'new-agey' but it's a world apart from what these others do. Maybe the homeopath and those two psychics and that angel woman believe in their own powers, or maybe they don't. I don't care – I personally have no faith in them. We peddle love potions, that's all. We don't pretend to grieving parents that we know what happened to their son. We don't advise the terminally ill to come off their medication.

"You know," I tell her, "you're right. I would have said no. I don't want to be lumped in with these people. I hate what they do."

"But, Rosie, it's not all that different to what we do."

"Yes, it is. It's worlds apart."

"That's not how others see it. We're just one end of the spectrum."

"We're *nothing* like – like those psychics for instance. What they do is morally bankrupt. That poor couple, telling them that their son was dead!"

Caroline sighs. "Look, I'm not going to argue. I'm sorry you're so annoyed. I should have talked to you beforehand."

"Yes, you should have. You seem to forget we're meant to be a team."

"And we are."

"A team! We were like lambs to the slaughter and worst of all you knowingly led us into that slaughter. A team, don't make me laugh!"

"I thought the exposure was too good an opportunity to

pass up. We need to take the shop up a level if it's ever going to be viable."

"I understand that but not at such a high cost. Poor Dana, she was humiliated."

Caroline sighs. "I know, I know. I really never thought it would turn out like that."

We've pulled into the driveway now. I get out of the car and, as I do, a taxi pulls in behind us.

The taxi driver rolls down the window, "Taxi for Vaughan?" he calls out.

Before I have a chance to answer, the front door opens and Dana comes out, wheeling a large suitcase behind her.

"Dana, what are you doing?" I ask her.

"Doug says I can move in with him at Monica's for the moment."

"Dana!" Caroline rushes over to her. "Hang on, don't go. Can't we talk about this? You've no idea how sorry I am. I never imagined it would turn out the way it did! I thought I'd be able to do all the talking, that you two would be able to just —"

"Can you excuse me, please? You're blocking my way. I have a taxi waiting."

"Dana, please!"

"Get — out — of — my — way!"

She pushes past Caroline, hands over the suitcase to the taxi-driver and hurries into the back of the car.

Together Caroline and I stand there and watch her pulling away.

"She'll be back, won't she?" asks Caroline. "When she's calmed down?"

If Caroline is expecting me to offer her any comfort, then she must be disappointed. I'm still too annoyed. Okay, maybe she could never have foreseen how bad it would be but if she'd been more honest to begin with, it would never have happened.

"How should I know?" I snap, turn on my heel, and head into the house.

As I go into the kitchen, I hear Caroline going straight to her room. I think to make myself something to eat but then decide against it. I haven't the stomach for it. Instead I stand there, leaning against the counter, thinking over the events of the morning. What a mess! It's almost surreal – I can hardly believe it actually happened.

And there's still more to come, worse to come.

At nine-thirty this evening, the country will be able to tune in to watch our humiliation. I think of Finn. To think there's a chance he will see us on television tonight – him, my parents, everyone else we know. It's going to be awful. How are we going to live this down?

Caroline comes back into the kitchen. She smiles anxiously at me.

"Hi," she says timidly.

"Hi," I answer coldly. Then I notice she's changed her clothes. "Are you going somewhere?"

"I'm going to go into the shop. Monica is only covering until twelve. I need to take over from her."

"You're joking me! After all that's happened!"

"What am I supposed to do, Rosie? There's no point in chasing after Dana. She needs time to calm down – she wouldn't listen to a word I had to say if I went after her now."

"So instead you're calmly heading into work like nothing's happened?"

"No, I'm *not* calmly heading in like nothing's happened! But someone has to do it. I don't actually want to."

"That's all you care about, isn't it? The shop?"

"That's not fair. What do you want me to do, Rosie? Tell Monica to lock up so that I can sit here in the kitchen with you and have you throwing me filthy looks all day making sure I don't forget for even a second what I've done? But whatever's happened, we still have a business to run. Letting that fall by the wayside isn't going to do Dana any good."

"I don't think Dana could give a toss about that right now."

"Not right now, no. But she's still invested an awful lot of time and effort in it. We all have. Letting it fall apart now is just plain stupid."

Caroline is right of course. I can see that. But I'm feeling a little too raw right now to be all mature about this.

"Well, you'd better go then. Don't let me delay you."

"Rosie, come on. Don't be like this!"

"Don't tell me what way to *be*!"

Caroline sighs. "Okay, well, I'm heading. I'll see you later."

When she's gone, I try ringing Dana but she doesn't pick up so I leave a message asking her to call me. And then I wonder what to do with the rest of this horrible day. If only I had Finn to talk to about things. God, how I miss him! If I could ring him now I could persuade him to take a few hours off work to meet me for lunch and tell him all about the events of this morning and then, maybe, in the afternoon we could skive off to a movie, some comedy that would cheer me up. But I don't have Finn to ring any more.

In the end I get the bus into town and mope around for a few hours. I think about calling into the shop to see how Caroline is getting on but decide against it and, as the shops are closing, I head to the cinema – on my lonesome-ownsome.

I get home five minutes before Andrew Marsh is due to air. I can hear the television on in the living room. I stick my head around the door. Caroline is sitting on the couch on her own. I go back out again before she sees me. I don't want to watch it. I couldn't bear to. I climb the stairs and go to bed. I try to read my book but I can't concentrate. I can hear the murmuring voices on the TV below. I think I can hear Caroline's voice. I can definitely hear Dana's. Finally I hear the theme music but it goes dead almost immediately. Then I hear Caroline coming up the stairs. I sense rather than hear her standing outside my door. I wait for her to knock and call out my name but she doesn't. Instead she carries on to her own room.

On Crete, folklore medicine used olive oil as an
aphrodisiac and many newly-weds had to eat bread
soaked in the first olive oil of the year. There's even
an old Greek saying:
"Eat butter and sleep tight. Take olive oil and play all night."

30

The next morning when I get up, the house is quiet. I come downstairs and find a note on the kitchen table.

Hi Rosie,

Gone to work. You're scheduled to come in at two but if you don't feel up to it, don't worry. I'll do your shift for you.

Caroline X

I feel a twinge of guilt. Caroline did lead us on. She did let us go on the show with completely the wrong idea of what it was going to be about but I find now I'm not as mad as I was with her yesterday. Her intentions were good if misguided. As well, I can't help feeling a grudging respect for her. I couldn't even bring myself to watch the programme last night, yet she did, all on her own and now she's gone off to the shop, with none of us to support her, to face whatever the day will bring.

In the end, I don't even wait until two. Instead, as soon as I've finished breakfast, I get showered and dressed then catch the next bus into town. It's just coming up to eleven when I get there.

I don't know what I was expecting. Most likely Caroline sitting forlornly in a deserted shop. At worst, an angry crowd gathered around her, berating her. What I did not expect is what I see – the shop is busier than it's ever been and for the first time since we opened there's an actual queue at the counter, all waiting for service. Without saying a word to Caroline, I go and get my pink coat from the back, put it on and join her at the counter.

"Thanks," says Caroline.

"No problem." Then I call out. "Next please!"

As Caroline has said, all publicity is good publicity and, in the days that follow, we're busier than we're ever been. It doesn't help that there are only two of us to cope with this increase in business. We haven't heard from Dana since. I've tried ringing but she's not answering. Why she can't talk to me I don't understand exactly. Caroline was the one who hoodwinked her into going on the show. Andrew Marsh was the one who grilled her in front of the nation. What did I do?

This morning, I'm first in the shop since Caroline has stopped off to collect more paper bags from the printers on the way. I've just finished a couple of big sales but now the shop is quiet. I hear the door open but before I look around, I hear a familiar voice:

"Excuse me." I turn to see Finn standing at the counter, grinning sheepishly. "I'm looking for a love potion, one that will make someone, a girl I used to go out with, a girl called Rosie, fall in love with me again."

At first, I'm too taken aback to say anything. I just stand there, staring.

"Well," he says, "do you think you might have anything suitable?"

Finally, I find my tongue. "Isn't that just a bit cheesy?" I ask and can't help but smile back, but then, I stop myself.

But that brief smile is encouragement enough for Finn. He turns, goes to the door and pushes across the bolt. Then he comes back over.

He shrugs. "I guess I'm a cheesy kind of guy."

I don't say anything now, just stare at him.

"I've been a fool, Rosie. Lola is gone."

"Gone?"

"Yeah."

"What do you mean? That you're not going out with her any more?"

"Going out with her? I was never going out with Lola! I mean she's moved out of the house."

"You were never going out with her?"

"No, of course not! Are you crazy? Where did you get such a ridiculous idea?"

"From her. She came in here and told me so."

"Are you sure you heard her right?"

"I'm sure. She made it perfectly clear."

He sighs. "I wouldn't put it past her!"

"So you were never going out with her?"

"God, no!"

"I see." I think about all this. "So she's moved out?"

"Yep, lock, stock and barrel."

"Did you ask her to leave because I wanted you to?"

"No, not exactly," admits Finn. "I asked her to leave because you were right all along. She was hoping for more out of our relationship but I was too stupid to realise it at first. But since you and I spilt up, she upped the ante. She was only too keen to comfort me."

"I see."

"So what do you say, can we try again?"

I don't hesitate for a second. I reach over and kiss him.

Suddenly there comes a loud banging on the door.

"Rosie! Are you in there? Open up!"

"Oh my God! It's Caroline. She'll kill me! Quick, unlock the door!"

"Maybe it'd be safer if we didn't," suggests Finn jokingly.

"This is no time for joking. Open it quickly before she knocks it down."

"Rosie!" Caroline is shouting. "Open up right this minute!"

Finn unbolts the door, then jumps aside as Caroline comes charging in.

"How the hell are we meant to make any money if you have the door locked in the middle of the day!" But then she looks at Finn. "Well, well, we haven't seen you for a while." Then she eyes us both up suspiciously. "What's going on here? Why was the door locked?"

"Locked," says Finn. "No, no, it was caught in the mat."

"Do you think I came down in the last shower? So what is going on here? Are you two back together again?"

"Yep!" I give a huge grin. "We sure are."

"It took you long enough. But I'm glad. Not least because now I won't have to put up with any more of Rosie's long faces."

"Excuse me!"

"Why don't the pair of you head off, go celebrate," suggests Caroline. "I can manage."

"Are you sure?'

She smiles. "Sure I'm sure! Now go, go!"

"So, what shall we do?" I ask, once we're out on the street.

Finn digs his hands in his pockets and stands there thinking. "I know. Let's have one of those movie days."

"What do you mean? Like spend the whole day at the movies?"

"No, no." Then he explains: "In the movies they always show couples having one fabulous day. You know, walking along a boardwalk, riding a carousel, eating ice-cream cones, buying hot dogs from a hot-dog stand, or colourful balloons from some stall manned by some equally colourful character – that sort of thing. Let's have one of those days."

I look doubtfully around at the busy street full of shoppers. "Ah, sorry to burst your bubble but there aren't too many people selling balloons or hot dogs around here."

Finn laughs. "I'm not saying it has to be that exactly. I'm just giving you a flavour. We can do our own version." He grabs hold of my hand and starts walking quickly through the crowds. "Come on!"

"Where are we off to?" I laugh.

"Off on our day of fun. To find our hot dog equivalents."

"Right then, show me the way."

At the top of Grafton Street, when we come to the horse-drawn carriages and their owners touting for business, Finn comes to a stop. I reluctantly come to a stop too. Oh no, I don't want to go in one of these! They're for tourists! They're about as cheesy as it gets! What if someone I knew saw me, high up, with a tartan blanket over my knees?

"So what do you think?" asks Finn, nodding his head in the direction of the nearest one.

But if Finn really wants to then maybe I could. What does it matter what we do, as long as we're together?

"Yeah, sure," I say, faking a smile.

"Ha! Only kidding you! I wouldn't be caught dead in

one of them." He gives me a playful dig in the ribs. "You should have seen the look on your face!"

"That was mean!" I protest.

"Come on!"

We cross under the stone arch into Stephen's Green and, leaving the bustle of the city, we join other strollers in the relative calm of the park.

"It's been ages since I was here," I think aloud as we stop to watch a group of little kids throw bread to overfed, lazy-looking ducks.

"Mark's mum and mine used to bring us here all the time when we were little."

"I remember you telling me. Didn't you both strip off and go swimming once?"

"Not quite. We did go behind a bush and take off all our clothes while our mothers were sitting close by on a bench but then some passer-by alerted them and they caught us before we ever got to the water. Boy, were they mad!" He laughs. "We can't have been more than two or three."

Finn catches my hand again and we walk on.

"Did you know that this park was once a hanging ground?" he asks.

"No!" I shiver. "I think I like it better as a park."

We come to the gate by the famine memorial – three abstract, emaciated figures with their dog.

"I'm not sure I like all these reminders of harder times," I say aloud. "Anyway, where to next?"

"Just follow me."

"Right, let's go."

We walk down Dawson Street until Finn stops outside a red door. "Here we are."

"What is it?"

"The smallest pub in Dublin."

I go first and climb down a vertigo-inducing flight of steps that lead to a subterranean pub little bigger than a living room but, even this early, it's packed full of people – but then, it probably only takes about thirty to fill it to bursting.

I spot two of the thirty getting up to leave so squeeze my way in to take their seats.

"What are you having?" Finn asks.

"A Coke is fine for me."

I watch as Finn tries to make his way through the crowd to the counter. This, I think, looking around, is not a place to come if you suffer from claustrophobia, have private matters to discuss, or have issues as regards personal space. Or suffer from BO – for the sake of the other customers.

I spot Finn coming back, holding our drinks high over his head. He squeezes in beside me.

"You weren't joking about it being the smallest pub!" I laugh.

"Would you believe they actually play live music here sometimes?"

"No way!"

We each take a sip of our drink. Then Finn turns and suddenly gives me a kiss.

Laughingly, I ask: "What was that for?"

"Just because I missed you."

He kisses me again.

"And that?"

"Just 'cos I can."

He kisses me a third time.

"And that one?"

"Just because you're so lovely."

I laugh again. "You charmer!"

"It's easy to be charming when I'm with you."

"It's nice to see you so happy."

"Why wouldn't I be? I have you back!"

"For what it's worth, I'm happy too. Very."

"Good!" He takes another sip of his pint. "So tell me, how's the shop going? Any busier?"

"It sure is. It's tearing ever since our appearance on television."

"What appearance?"

"You mean you didn't see it?"

He shakes his head.

"Just as well, it was awful! It was Caroline who agreed to go on but she told us it was going to be about friends setting up in business together but it wasn't. In fact, we were part of a cast of various 'new agey types'. It was so awful – the presenter was gunning for us all and gave Dana a really hard time. She took it badly. She went storming out of the studio straight after and by the time Caroline and I got home, there was a taxi pulling up and, next thing, Dana was loading up her suitcase and telling us that she's moving into Doug's. She was really mad at Caroline. Who knows what's going to happen now? I mean if Dana can't even bear to be in the same house as Caroline, she's hardly going to want to come back to working in the shop. Andrew Marsh humiliated her but even so –"

"Andrew Marsh?" asks Finn.

"Yeah?"

"From *Topical Ireland*?"

"Yeah. So you know it?"

"Very well." Finn looks uncomfortable. "Lola used to watch it all the time."

"I wouldn't have thought it was her kind of thing."

"I'm not sure it was. The reason she used to watch it was because her brother Felix works on it."

"Felix? But we met him!" And then the significance of this strikes me. "Oh my God! That's how they knew so much! About the students nearly drowning, about Lola and her anaphylactic shock. That's how they knew everything. She must have told her brother."

"I guess this was her way at getting back at me, and at you."

"How will I ever tell the others that it was my fault?"

"It wasn't your fault. You couldn't have known."

"Caroline thought the TV people asked us on because they'd heard us on the radio that time but that mightn't be so. Lola could have suggested us to her brother."

"I'm guessing that's what did happen, or maybe a combination of both." He shakes his head. "I never thought she'd be so devious."

"What a cow!"

"That's putting it mildly."

"I can't believe it!"

We both sit in silence, considering this new development but then, after a few moments, Finn says:

"Hey, let's not let Lola spoil this day."

"Yes, but how could she have done that?"

"Come on. Let's get out of here."

"Sure."

We collect our things and leave.

"Where are we going now?" I ask as Finn takes my hand and we start walking down the street.

"You'll see."

"You know, I still can't believe Lola did that."

"Rosie, let's not think about her. Let's just enjoy ourselves."

Next stop turns out to be the Guinness Storehouse. We don't bother with the exhibits but take the lift straight to the top, to take in the 360-degree view of Dublin. We stand there for ages picking out all the well-known landmarks – Croke Park, Lansdowne Road, the Spire on O'Connell Street. We can even see as far as the Dublin Mountains.

"Rosie, you know Fay who used to work with you?" asks Finn.

I nod. "Sure, what about her?"

"I think Dad was quite taken with her the night he met her at the launch."

"Really?"

"They were talking for ages that night and he has that photo of the pair of them, the one that was in the paper, stuck on the fridge. He's brought her name up a couple of times too which is a first in itself. I've never heard him talking about a woman before. Do you know if she's seeing anyone?"

I shrug. "I don't think so." And then I add, "I think Fay was rather smitten with your father too. I know she's mentioned him to Monica."

"Maybe we should do something to try to get them together?"

I hesitate. Of all the people I know, the one whose love life I least want to interfere with is Fay's.

"Oh Finn, I don't know. I really don't think I should get involved."

"Come on! Where's your sense of romance?"

I shrug. The idea of Fay and Mr Heelan getting together is a nice one but I've caused Fay enough trouble in the past with my meddling. "I'll think about it, all right?"

"But what's there to think about?"

"Look, I've interfered in her life enough as it is."

"Yeah, so now you have a chance to make it up to her."

"Look – I don't know." I shrug. "Let me think about it, all right?"

We walk through Temple Bar, stopping for ice creams and to watch a teenager strumming his guitar and mangling "Stairway to Heaven". We cross over the Ha'penny Bridge, stroll along the boardwalk and then stop by the entrance to the narrow Italian Quarter.

"Fancy something to eat?" asks Finn.

"If it means we can stop walking, yes."

We sit at a table outside, overlooked by a huge photographic re-interpretation of Leonardo da Vinci's *Last Supper* but with a modern-day Jesus and his disciples.

"I wonder who all these people are?" I say, studying them.

"Well, from what I remember, one of them is a tattoo artist. And," he points, "I think that woman works at the Pavee Point Travellers' Centre, or at least she did."

I laugh. "How can you know this?"

He shrugs. "I'm always storing up information, especially when it comes to art. I like knowing these things."

"You don't say!" I joke. "You're like some magpie, always storing away little nuggets of useless information."

"Useless!" He laughs. "I beg your pardon!'

The waiter comes out to take our order.

Sitting there, waiting for my food, holding Finn's hand across the table, it occurs to me that I've never felt happier and, perhaps experiencing somewhat similar emotions himself, Finn leans over to me.

"I wrote a song about you last night."

"You did?"

"Well, actually it's more to do with how I feel about you.

In fact what it is actually about is how I don't want to be just one of the boyfriends in the story of your life but I want to be . . ." he shuffles awkwardly in his seat – he's actually blushing, ". . . well, I want to be the one who's there at the end, in the final chapter."

"Why don't you just sing it," I suggest.

He laughs nervously. "Okay, maybe I will do just that." He leans across the table to me and begins to sing in a low voice.

"Who remembers Bonnie and Thornton?
Where was he the day they cut Bonnie and Clyde
From their bullet-ridden Ford?
Don't want to be your Thornton, I want to be your Clyde.
You and me, baby, side by side, 'til the end.

Who remembers Mrs Simpson and Earl Winfield?
It wasn't him she meant when she said:
'You have no idea how hard it is to live out a great romance.'
Don't want to be your Winfield, I want to be your Edward.
You and me, baby, side by side, 'til the end.

Who remembers Cathy and Linton?
'If Linton loved you with the power of his soul for a whole
lifetime,
He couldn't love you as much as I do in a single day.'
Don't want to be your Linton, I want to be your Heathcliff.
You and me, baby, side by side, 'til the end,

You and me, baby, 'til the end.
You and me, baby, 'til the end.
Side by side, 'til the end.
No end, no end, no end, no end.

He sits back in his seat. "Well, what do you think?" he asks with an apprehensive look on his face.

I can't answer with the lump in my throat so I simply nod and smile foolishly at him. This is the second song Finn has written about me. I love that first one – "Just a Glimpse of You to Fall in Love" – but this is way better. That first was just about a girl he spotted in the audience at one of his gigs, a girl he fancied, but this song is about me and him, and our future.

I lean over to kiss him. "I love you, my Heathcliff, my Clyde, my Edward!"

"And I love you, my Cathy, my Bonnie, my Mrs Simpson!"

I smile at him again. "Thank you," I say.

"For what?"

"For the song, stupid! I love it." And then a thought occurs to me. "It'll be funny seeing Lola sing that song, knowing that the words are about you and me."

"She won't be singing it."

"What do you mean?"

"She's not just moved but she's left the band too – did I not say that earlier? There was no way I could go on working with her."

"Oh! That's brilliant." But then I think of the band. "So you're back to having no lead singer again. What are you going to do?"

"We've already sorted it."

"You have?"

"Yep, You're looking at Dove's new lead singer!"

"Seriously?"

"Yep, Mitch and Ashley persuaded me to give it a go. I've always felt more comfortable having someone else singing my words but, I don't know, now that I'm older and more experienced it doesn't seem so scary any more. I mightn't be as sexy as Mark or Lola but these are my songs and I feel I'm ready to sing them. Mitch and Ashley seem to think I'm up to it."

"But that's fantastic!"

"Besides, we've worked hard at getting gigs lined up for the coming months. I didn't want to cancel them. We'd get a reputation for being unreliable. And I'm on a real creative streak lately. I've lots of material I want to try out." And then he grins. "You, know, there's nothing like your girlfriend dumping you to get the creative juices flowing."

"Well, you'd better make the most of this creative streak then."

"Oh?"

"Because I don't intend dumping you again any time soon." I hold out my glass. "Here's to your new career as a singer!" I take a sip. "You know, you just never know when you're going to get the gift of one of life's perfect days."

"Quick," laughs Finn. "Give me my pen – there could be a song in that."

"I think it's already been done."

In the Middle Ages, chicken soup was believed to be
an aphrodisiac.
Chicken soup? Come on, could there be a less sexy food?
It calls to mind stuffed noses, balled-up hankies,
Vick's lozenges . . .
I think I'm seeing a theme here – just about anything was
declared an aphrodisiac in the Middle Ages. And the
Greeks weren't far behind.

31

Caroline and I may be working alongside one another but relations are still a bit strained. There's just not the same easiness between us and I don't really understand why. I'm not angry with her any more but even so we're not talking much. Part of that is to do with the fact we're so busy but that's not the whole of it. Caroline is just quiet in herself, withdrawn. It's like she's avoiding real conversation though I don't understand why. Since Finn and I got back together I'm in great form yet even still I can't cajole Caroline out of the bad one she's in.

Though the shop is doing better than ever it seems a hollow success. Dana still hasn't been in contact. She knows nothing of the unfortunate link from me to Finn to Lola to Felix to Andrew Marsh to our national humiliation (and the somewhat extraordinary side effect of a huge increase in business).

I've tried phoning her lots of times with no luck but then, finally, during a quiet moment, when Caroline's nipped out on a break, I try again and this time Dana actually picks up.

"Dana! At last! Is it really you?" I kid.

"Hi," she responds but she doesn't sound very cheerful.

"So, how are things?" I ask.

"You know," she answers ambiguously.

"I don't, that's why I'm ringing you. That, and because for some reason you've decided not to return any of my calls."

"Ah look, Rosie, I didn't decide not to. It wasn't like that. There's just been such a lot of other stuff going on."

"Like?"

"Well, the heads in the Psychology Department aren't exactly happy with me right now."

"Why not?"

"Okay, for starters they're annoyed about my appearance on Andrew Marsh's show – they feel I brought the department into disrepute. And then – given the nature of my thesis, they consider my involvement with the shop as representing a conflict of interest. What else? Oh yeah, they're concerned too about the way I conducted the trials, particularly how it came about that two of the students nearly drowned. Oh yes, and did I mention the parents of one of those students have made a complaint against me too? So, between one thing and another, I've been pretty preoccupied."

"But what does all this mean for you?"

"It means they've asked me to reconsider carrying on with my thesis."

"You're kidding!"

"What do you think?" she asks dryly.

"But they haven't told you that you can't do it?"

"No, they haven't but, since they are going to be involved in deciding whether I pass or fail, it kind of makes sense to listen to them. There's little point in carrying on if they're all set against me."

"So what are you going to do now?"

"I don't really know." She sighs. "I'm not sure if I have it in me to start over again. For the *third* time."

"Well, why don't you think about coming home for a start?"

There's a pause. I hear her sigh.

"Dana?"

"I don't think so. Not for now anyway. I'm happy where I am. Staying with Doug feels right at the moment and Monica has been really good to me."

"Are you still mad at Caroline?"

There's another pause, longer this time.

"Dana? Are you still there?"

Then she answers. "Am I still mad with Caroline? Well, I was furious with her at the start. I think it was really high-handed of her to get us to go on the show like that without telling us what it was going to be about. She did know, didn't she?"

"She did."

"But after a while I began to calm down. I guess I could understand why she did it – I know how important it was to her to make the shop succeed. And there was no way she could have known that Andrew Marsh was going to focus in on me, rather than on her, or you."

"True."

"I think if she'd rung me in the days following the show I'd have been willing to talk to her, to let her apologise, but she didn't."

"What? She never rang you after the show?"

"Well, she did twice, on the day, but that was it and I was far too wound up to talk to her then. After that I didn't hear from her. That really annoyed me – that she didn't try a bit harder. It annoyed me even more when I started getting all this hassle from the department. The thing is, if it wasn't for the show, I wouldn't be having all these problems now. All this current hassle stems from my appearance on TV, even down to the complaint from Geraldine McWilliam's parents. Seeing me on telly and hearing Andrew Marsh talking about their daughter's near-drowning mobilised them into writing. They even mention the show in their letter. Here I was getting all this flak because of that show, yet Caroline couldn't be bothered to even ring me."

"But she didn't know."

"She would have if she'd rung. By the way, I bumped into Mick in town. He told me all about Lola's involvement. What a bitch!"

"You don't know the half of it." But that's for another time.

"So go on," Dana is saying. "Tell me, how is she?"

"Who? Lola?"

"No, Caroline?"

"She's pretty down."

"Did she tell you why she did it?"

"You know Caroline. 'All publicity is good publicity'. She expected –"

"No, I don't mean the TV programme. I mean Mick."

"Pardon?"

"I was really surprised to hear it. I never expected them to break up."

"Break up? Mick and Caroline? Are you kidding me?"

Caroline comes back into the shop now. She waves to me, and I nod back to her but carry on listening to Dana.

"I'm afraid I'm not," Dana is saying.

"Are you absolutely sure?"

"Absolutely. Mick told me when I bumped into him."

"But I don't understand."

"Neither does he. He's gutted. Listen, I'd better go, I'm in the queue at the supermarket and my turn is coming up."

"What? Oh right. Well, give me a ring again soon, okay?"

When I hang up, I look over at Caroline. She's busy straightening out the bottles on one of the shelves after the last rush.

"Who was that you were talking to?" she asks without looking round.

"Dana."

"Oh! How is she?"

"Not great. The Psychology Department have advised her to consider pulling out of her research."

"Why?"

"Because they feel she brought the department into disrepute by appearing on Andrew Marsh's show. Neither are they too pleased with some of the things they learned on the show, like her involvement with this shop, for one, and those two students nearly drowning, for another."

"Oh?"

"Oh, is right." I nod my head.

"Poor Dana!" says Caroline. "What's she going to do now?"

"She doesn't know. You know she's mad because you never rang her to apologise."

"But I did ring her."

"Only on the day of the show."

Caroline shrugs. "Yes, but I left two messages for her then, telling her how sorry I was about everything."

"Yeah, but maybe you could have tried again – when she had time to calm down."

Caroline looks at me for a second before speaking. "The thing is, Dana's the one who walked out on the shop – she left us high and dry – she's never once bothered to ring and find out how we're coping."

"Yeah, but she had her own problems."

"And I had mine."

"You mean the shop?"

"Yeah, we've had to cope without her help."

"Or do you mean Mick?"

"Pardon?"

"Why didn't you tell me about Mick and you?"

"Oh, that!"

"Yes, 'Oh that!'."

"Did Dana tell you? Does she know?"

"Yes."

Caroline considers my answer for a moment. "You know, if she and Doug had split up, I'd have been the first on the phone to tell her how sorry I was. She could have rung me, don't you think?"

I think she has a point but this is between the two of them. I am not taking sides. I go back to the subject of her break-up.

"So why didn't you tell me? I thought we were meant to be friends. Friends talk to one another."

"There's not much to tell. We've split up."

"Why?"

She shrugs. "These things come to a natural end sometimes. We'd grown apart."

"You and Mick, come on! I know you haven't seen much of each other lately. I know you've had your moments, but not for a second did I think things had got this bad!"

Caroline shrugs. "Look, let's just get back to work."

"But Caroline —"

"Look, Rosie, there's nothing else to say about it. It's over, that's all there is to it, all right!"

"Caroline!"

"Now just leave it! All right?"

When the Science Museum in West London opened up its vast storerooms to the public, one of the 170,000 objects that went on display was a bottle of pills labelled 'Aphrodisiac'. Bizarrely it also carried a warning in small print: 'Poison'. As one of the curators put it, "I guess you have to pick your priorities."

32

Things change little in the following days. Dana's still living over at Doug's. Caroline's mood hasn't lightened at all and she refuses to tell me what happened between her and Mick. The only positive is that business is booming.

But then, Caroline comes back from lunch.

"Caroline! I'm glad you're here. I need to go and make up some more batches of potions."

"Don't bother."

"But I have to. We're down to the last couple of bottles of Fool for Love and we're running low on –"

"Didn't you hear me? I said, don't bother. There's no need." She goes and turns the sign on the door.

"Caroline what are you doing?"

"We're closing."

"In the middle of the day?"

"I don't mean for the day. I mean forever."

"Pardon?"

"Here, read this." She pulls out an envelope from her

bag, looks at it, goes to hand it to me but then snatches it away again. "Actually there's no need to read it. I can tell you what it says. It says we're in breach of the licensing laws."

"What?"

"We're breaking the law by selling alcoholic substances from an unlicensed premises. And that's not all." She pulls out another two envelopes from her bag. She holds up one. "This one says we're in breach of health and safety regulations and, ah, this one," she holds up the other, "says we're in breach of planning regulations."

"What? Why? What are you talking about?" I take all three envelopes from her, open them, and then glance through the letters, trying to make sense of them. "What's all this about the kitchen?"

"In a nutshell we shouldn't have one on the premises. We don't have permission for it – it contravenes both health and safety regulations and planning regulations."

"When did you get all these?"

"Let me see, the licensing one I got on Friday last, the planning one at the start of this week and the building regulations one yesterday."

"But how do they even know about the kitchen? Or about the alcohol content? Nobody ever came to inspect the place."

"I'm not sure about the licensing people – maybe one of them came in and made some purchases without letting on who they were. But someone from the council did call. You weren't here."

"Why didn't you tell me? And why did you wait until now to show me these letters?"

"I was trying to figure out how we should deal with it all. I rang the council the day we got the letter about the lack of relevant planning and the person on the phone told me that we could apply for retention of the kitchen."

"Well, that's something."

"Except she reckoned that even if we put in an application immediately, the soonest we'd find out if we got permission to retain would be three months. Of course there's no guarantee. In the meantime, if we keep using it, we're breaking the law. I was also trying to get hold of the health inspector but he's away on holiday." She shrugs. "But there's no point to any of this now."

"Sure there is."

"Rosie, there isn't!"

But I'm not listening. "Okay, this one about the licensing laws – well, that's easily fixed. We can simply stop selling all the potions that have any alcoholic content. There's only a handful. In fact we wouldn't have to stop selling them – I could substitute some other ingredient for the alcohol. As for the kitchen, there's no reason why we can't make the potions at home. Okay, so it would be more hassle having to bring them in to the shop but –"

"Rosie, our kitchen at home isn't a commercial kitchen and anyway –"

"Well, then we can rent out a commercial kitchen in some industrial estate."

"With what, Rosie?"

"What do you mean?" I ask.

"Rosie, we don't have any money."

"What? What do you mean? The shop is doing brilliantly. We've never been so busy. We're taking in more than ever."

"Just shut up, Rosie! And read this."

She hands me yet another letter. It's a bank statement for

our current account. I study it, then look up. "What's the problem? The balance looks healthy enough."

"Jesus! You're not reading it properly!" She begins prodding the page with her finger. "Look! Look! OD means overdrawn. We're that much overdrawn!"

I look at it again. "Oh!"

"'Oh!' is right."

"I don't understand. How can this be? We're taking in lots of money right now. Didn't you say we'd soon be in a position to start paying back our investors?"

Caroline sits down. "I've been a fool."

"What do you mean?"

"Our investor has pulled out and has taken every penny in our account with him and everything he could get on our overdraft."

"Who? Why?"

She takes a deep breath. "The who is Niall Wallace? The why is me."

"Niall Wallace? Your friend, the hotel guy? I didn't even know he was one of the backers."

"The main backer. In fact, the only backer, aside from Monica."

"But I thought we had several investors."

"We didn't. We never had."

"You're winding me up!"

Caroline shakes her head. "Of all the people who agreed to invest, Monica was the only one who came up with the money straight away but her share was only a tiny per cent. All the others who'd promised to get involved weren't quite so forthcoming. It was all taking too long with them. I was going to tell you but then I met Niall at the launch of his hotel and we started talking and I told him how I was having trouble raising the finance as quickly as I wanted so he offered to stump up all we needed, and I thought, hell, why look a gift horse in the mouth?"

"Why didn't you tell us?"

"I was going to but it didn't seem important. We still had all the money we needed."

"So where is it now?"

"In one of Niall's accounts, I presume."

"But why? Surely if he realises we need the money to make the changes we need like an alternative kitchen he'll put it all back in again. Isn't it in his interests to make the shop work?"

"He doesn't care about that." She sighs. "It's no coincidence that we suddenly came to the attention of the planning people, the health people, and the licensing people – all at the same time. Niall was the one who put them on to us. All he cares about is getting back at me."

"What do you mean getting back at you? For what?"

"Okay, where do I start?" She thinks for a moment. "When I took the money from Niall I thought it was purely a business arrangement. That's what we'd agreed. There was nothing between us. He knew I had a boyfriend. Even so, every now and then he'd ring me up to find out how things were going. I liked having him to talk to. He was interested in the whole thing. I met him a couple of times too. For the odd drink or meal. I enjoyed his company and I guess I was foolishly impressed by how rich he was, and how successful. I was impressed by his car, the clothes, the foreign trips he took, the whole package really. But it wasn't just that. To have someone like that take me seriously, well, I guess I found it flattering. Then one night when we were out, I let him kiss me."

"Ah, Caroline!"

"I did know Niall was interested in me, he made that pretty obvious, but I thought I could handle it."

"Ah Caroline, why –"

"I didn't even want that kiss. He took me off guard. For all his faults, it's Mick I love. But I felt so guilty. There I was worrying about Mick fancying his co-star when all along I was the one who couldn't be trusted. After that, Niall acted differently, like there was something between us. I avoided him as much as I could but I couldn't cut ties with him completely, not when he was so heavily involved in the shop. I was afraid he'd take out all his money and the shop would never get off the ground."

"But how was he able to take the money out of our account?"

"Foolishly I let him be a signatory. The money was all his anyway to begin with. I didn't see it as a problem."

"You said it was just a kiss?"

"Yeah, that's all it was. Like I said, I tried to avoid him as much as I could but that made him pester me even more until finally I lost my temper with him and told him I had absolutely no interest in him, that if it was a choice between him and Ozzy Osbourne, I'd pick Ozzy Osbourne – no contest."

"Did you actually use those words?"

"Yes," confesses Caroline. "Yes, I did."

"Caroline!"

"I was mad at him. As you can imagine he wasn't impressed. I may have wounded his ego but he certainly got his revenge. This morning, when I went to make a lodgement, I found that all the money had been withdrawn. The game is over, Rosie. The shop is finished. I don't even know how we're going to pay off our overdraft."

"So that's it?"

"I'm afraid so."

"Can't you talk to Niall?"

"Talk to him? You have no idea what he's like. The only way I'd get any money back from him is if I went and told him I was wrong, that I do really care for him. And though I might desperately want this business to succeed, even I'm not that desperate – despite what people may think."

"Does Mick know any of this?"

"No." Caroline shakes her head.

"Has it got anything to do with you and him splitting up?"

Suddenly Caroline gets up. "I think I need a strong coffee. Want one?"

"Yeah, I guess.

She goes into the kitchen to make the coffee and as I stand there waiting I look around at the shop. I can't believe this is all really going to end, after everything we put into it, when we were finally getting off the ground. I hear a knocking on the door. I look up. A customer is peering through the glass and waving to catch my attention.

"We're closed," I mouth. "We're closed."

Looking disgruntled, the customer turns away.

"Here," Caroline has come back and is holding out a cup to me.

"Thanks." I take a sip. "Caroline?"

"Yeah?"

"So why did you break up with Mick?"

She sighs. "We're just too different."

"But you knew that from the outset. That didn't stop you getting together."

Caroline shrugs. "It's complicated."

"Go on, I'm listening."

She sighs, pushes her hair behind her ears, then takes another sip.

"Okay then. Ever since we first started talking about setting up the shop, Mick has been so disapproving. Remember the night we had that business meeting and he showed up and I got cross because he wasn't showing any interest and he said it was because he didn't approve? Well, he was like that all the time. It really annoyed me. I really wanted him to support me, like I'd supported him. I guess he did try a bit. I know he turned up for the launch, and got Audrey to show too, and he tried to make a pretence of listening whenever I talked to him about the business but it was always there, in the background, his disapproval. I wanted him to be proud of me but I kept feeling that he was ashamed of what I was doing. Can you understand that?"

I nod.

"I guess I wanted him to be more supportive too."

"Sure."

Like she's always been so proud and supportive of Mick, she could but doesn't say. She was the one who got him his big break. She was the one who dragged him off to London to meet Kevin North in the first place. I guess she could have hoped to get the same in return.

She goes on: "He was already acting like he was ashamed of me, disappointed in me. I couldn't tell him I took the money from Niall. I couldn't bring myself to tell him that I'd kissed him. How would it look – snogging our investor? He'd be hurt. He'd be disappointed in me. He'd start thinking I'd do anything for money. Everything is so black and white with Mick, so uncomplicated, he'd never get himself into such a ridiculous situation. I felt so guilty about that bloody kiss. Each time I met up with Mick or talked to him on the phone, I kept thinking how much more disapproving of me he would be if he knew the whole truth. I couldn't bear to tell him, I couldn't bear him thinking that I was a complete lowlife but I couldn't go on the way it was, knowing what I'd done, knowing how Mick would feel if I told him. So I decided to get in there first, not to let him have that opportunity to look at me as if I really was rubbish." She gives a laugh. "I guess I dumped him before he could dump me."

"Without even telling him why?"

She shakes her head. "I couldn't bring myself to. I'm such a fool. Everyone thinks I always know what I'm doing, where I'm going but," she shrugs, "well, they're wrong. I've messed everything up. I've let everyone down. I still think the shop was a good idea. It could have worked but now I've messed it all up, for you, for Dana – all of us."

She looks so vulnerable sitting there. I go over and hug her.

"Come on, Caroline. We'll get through this."

"Will we? The shop certainly won't. Mick and I are already finished. Dana isn't even talking to me. I've ruined everything for everybody."

Afghani tribesmen must hold the record for the worst drink ever thanks to a concoction known as "khoona". This alcoholic beverage is traditionally taken by men on their wedding night (ah-ha, another obsession, one spanning history and geography: that everyone should perform well on the big night).

The key aphrodisiac in khoona is – wait for it – recently extracted bull semen.

33

From my seat on the bus, I see the *To Let* sign. It's only been a week since we closed the door for the last time but, looking at the shop as we pass by, I notice it's already taken on a neglected look. The glass panes in the window and in the door have been whitened over. The wind has blown the street's debris into the recess of the doorway: a plastic cup, a McDonald's burger box, a crumpled cigarette pack, all sitting amidst a heap of leaves.

That's it, then, I think, no last-minute reprieve. The dream is over. No chance now that Caroline will come bursting into the kitchen to announce that she's come up with a brilliant plan that will save the shop and the day for all of us. But then, there is no 'all of us' any more.

I turn from the window and pick up the stapled sheets of paper on my lap. *Curriculum Vitae of Ms Rosie Kiely, B.Sc.* My CV. My true CV, not Caroline's version and how much duller it is now that I've removed her little embellishments. Just like my life will be duller now without the shop. That exciting little chapter is closed.

But the factual version of my CV served me well today. For the first time ever I left an interview with the impression that when they said they'd be in touch it wasn't a polite brush-off but that they might actually offer me a job. Maybe it's because I came across as more serious – I guess I am, disappointment can do that – but a more likely reason is that the company are taking on a hundred new scientists as part of a big expansion. As my mother put it, they'd probably even offer her a job if she showed up.

The bus pulls up at a stop and as the people are still trying to exit, others start getting on.

"Would ye just hold on a minute and let the people off first!" I hear the bus driver giving out.

"You can't blame us for rushing to get on given how long we've been waiting!" I hear someone call back.

I look up. The voice is unmistakably Caroline's. And then I see her. She's standing by the driver now, tottering on her heels, obliviously holding everyone up. "We've been waiting over half an hour for a bus and now two of you come together. Were you and the other driver keeping one another company over your tea break? Was that it?"

"Careful now or I won't let you on at all," he tells her.

"Don't even think about it!" She holds out a note.

"Twenty euro! You think I'm going to give you change for that?" snaps the bus driver. "Don't you know it's exact fare only?"

"But that's ridiculous! I don't have the exact fare."

"You can give me the twenty if you like, but you won't be getting any change."

"You're joking!"

"Do I look like I'm laughing? I don't make the rules, love."

401

"Will you bleedin' well hurry up!" the old man standing behind Caroline urges her.

"I beg your pardon?" Caroline swings around to him. "I'm not the one who's causing the delay. If the driver would just take my money and give me my change then there would be no hold-up."

"What part of 'exact fare only' don't you understand?" asks the driver.

"Look here, I don't have the patience for this," Caroline tells him.

"And neither do I!" moans the old man.

"Nor I. Will you pay the fare or get off!" demands the driver.

A tiny part of me wants to sit here and see what the conclusion to all this will be. Would the driver actually try to eject Caroline and what would be his fate if he did? But the better half of my nature wins. I pull out my purse, sift through the change, pick out some coins and then quickly make my way to the top of the bus.

"Here." I drop the coins into the little slot.

"Rosie!"

"Now will you give her a ticket?" I ask the driver.

I go back down to my seat and Caroline follows behind me.

"Can you believe that fellow!" she says at the top of her voice.

"Will you keep it down if you don't want to get kicked off?"

"I'd like to see him try!"

"You know, I kinda would too."

She slides into the seat beside me. "I can't believe how crowded these things get."

"These things. What? Buses, you mean?"

"And they could really do with being cleaned more often." She points to the graffiti scrawled on the seat in front and reads it out loudly. "Gina is a slag!" I mean, do we really need to know that? Tell me, are your feet sticking to the floor? Because mine are."

"Caroline, why are you even on this bus? Where's your car?"

"I sold it."

"Ah no! But why? You've always loved that car. It's your pride and joy!"

"My savings didn't clear all our debts from the shop so I had to sell it."

"Oh, Caroline, you must be heartbroken! You loved that car!"

"Look, stop going on about it and stop looking at me like you feel sorry for me. I can't stand that. It's done now. It's no big deal. I'll just have to get used to doing without it. And it won't be forever." Then she notices my dark suit. "So where are you coming from dressed like that? A funeral, or something?"

"No. In fact, I've been for an interview."

"Oh, why didn't you tell me? I could have helped you prepare for it."

"That's exactly why I didn't."

"Thanks a lot!"

"I don't mean it like that. I just didn't want to make a big deal out of it."

"So, how did it go?"

"Okay, I think. I could be in with a chance. The company are undergoing a huge expansion and are taking on over a hundred scientists."

"Ah but, Rosie, is that what you really want?"

"Yes, it is. It's a job, I need to get a job, any job."

"But, Rosie, maybe you should think of other things?"

"Stop right now, Caroline! Don't even think of trying to talk me out of it."

"I'm not, really. But I just want to see you happy."

"A steady pay cheque every week will go a long way to making me happy, very happy, thank you."

"Will it? Will it really?

"Yes. Yes, it will really."

"But —"

"Just leave it, Caroline." I decide to turn the conversation back to her. "So, any more thoughts on what you're going to do?"

"Well, I have a bit of money left over from the car so I'm not on the breadline just yet. But I'm not sure. I have a few options. My old company would take me back, I think. I know they're not too happy with my replacement. And through the grapevine I've heard of a few other openings that are coming up." She shrugs. "I'll see. There's no hurry. So, tell me, have you seen Dana?"

I think before replying but then I decide to tell her: "I'm meeting her tonight as it happens. We're going to go for a drink."

"Oh!"

I can feel it. I know she's waiting for me to ask her to come along.

"Where are you meeting?" she asks.

"Hardy's."

"I see. Well, that will be nice."

"Yeah, it will."

"Is it just the two of you?"

I nod. "Oh, and Doug too."

"Well, I hope you have a good evening."

"I'm sure we will."

"I wonder how she's getting on?"

I shrug. "Not great – all the hassle with college is really bothering her."

"Does she mention anything about coming home?"

"No."

"Maybe you could ask her. You could tell her that her room is still there for her but that she needn't worry about the rent for now."

"What do you mean? Your brother is hardly going to let her off it – is he?"

"No, but now I've sold the car I can cover it for a while, until she's ready to come back."

"But Caroline, what if she doesn't come back? You can't keep paying for it forever."

"I know that. But I've been thinking a lot about things since the shop closed down – I guess I've had the time. Losing the shop is one thing but I'd really hate to lose her. I've been friends with her forever."

I think for a moment and then, before I can get a chance to change my mind, I ask, "Why don't you come along tonight?"

"Okay then," she replies without a moment's hesitation.

We lapse into silence for a while but then I think of my other exciting news.

"You'll never guess who called into the hardware store when Finn was working yesterday."

"No, I guess I wouldn't ever guess."

"Only Fay!"

"Fay who you used to work with?"

"Yep."

"She doesn't live anywhere near there, does she?"

I shake my head. "No, but she came in to buy some picture hooks."

"Very odd. Did she just happen to remember she needed them when she just happened to be in the area?"

"No, no – she came in to see Mr Heelan. Finn is certain of it. Remember they were chatting all evening at the opening night of our shop? He said that when she first came in and saw that it was only Finn behind the counter she looked really disappointed and was about to leave without buying anything but, then, Mr Heelan arrived back in. Finn says it was a pantomime to watch them. One was more nervous than the other. They both kept talking at the same time, then breaking off and apologising and telling the other one to go ahead. He said they were blushing like a couple of lovelorn teenagers. In the end, Finn said he decided to get out of there and leave them on their own so he went off to get some lunch. When he came back in, Fay was sitting on a stool behind the counter, sipping tea from Mr Heelan's old mug while he was serving a customer."

"That's so sweet."

"It is, isn't it? I get a really nice feeling when I think of the pair of them together."

"Maybe there's hope for me yet."

"What do you mean?"

"Well, Fay's in her fifties, isn't she? So maybe there's still a chance that I might meet someone, someday – maybe." Then she thinks for a moment. "Although I'm not sure I want to meet anyone else."

"Ah, Caroline. Don't talk like that."

"Rosie," warns Caroline, "take that look off your face!"

"What look?"

"That pitying one. You know I can't stand that!"

A hint of perfume

A beautifully prepared meal

Music, but not Barry White - too clichéd by now

Light touches on soft skin - under the hair at the base of
the neck is an underrated spot

Champagne, of course

And kisses too - a bad kisser never makes a
good lover

A kind word

A smile

A poem

A backrub

Freshly laundered sheets

Rays of sun

A midnight dip

Laughter

34

That evening, sitting alongside Caroline on the bus on the way to Hardy's Pub, I get a text from Dana.

 — *Just to tell you, Mick is coming along too.*

I consider her message. Should I text Dana back and forewarn her that Caroline is with me? Should I tell Caroline that Mick is coming too? I weigh up these two options. If Mick knows that Caroline is coming, chances are he won't hang around. If Caroline knows that Mick is there, chances are she'll change her mind and will be clamouring to get off at the next stop. I reject both these options in favour of a third. I decide to say nothing, and let the evening take its course.

When we arrive at the pub, it's Caroline who spots Dana and Doug first.

"There they are!" And then she spots Mick. "Oh no! What's he doing here?"

She looks like she's about to bolt but I take a firm hold of her arm. "Caroline, you can't avoid him forever. Just because you've dumped him, that doesn't mean we're all going to stop being friends with him. You're going to have to meet him sometime and now is as good a time as any. Now come on."

"Oh no, Rosie, I'm not sure I can do this." She turns to go but I keep hold of her.

"You have to. You can't just walk away now. Besides, he's already spotted you."

"Has he?"

"Yes."

"Is he looking over?"

"Yes." With a look that is something akin to horror but I see no reason to tell her this. "Now come on."

Reluctantly she comes with me.

"Hi, everyone," I say breezily, ignoring the surprised expressions of Dana and Doug, and Mick's one of shock.

"Hi, Dana," says Caroline cautiously.

"Hi, Caroline," says Dana as cautiously

"Hi, Mick," says Caroline even more cautiously.

"Hi, Caroline," says Mick awkwardly.

"Hi, Caroline, good to see you," says Doug warmly.

"And you too," says Caroline with obvious relief.

But then, silence.

There are two seats free, one between Mick and Dana and one at the other side of the table beside Doug. Caroline is about to make for that seat but I get there first, leaving her no option but to sit down between Dana and Mick.

"Well now, isn't this nice?" I announce rather stupidly.

Nice? No. More like terribly, awfully, most horribly awkward. I feel sorry for Caroline. She looks so nervous. Almost immediately, she stands up again.

"I'm going to the bar – does anyone want anything? Rosie?"

"I'll have a white wine, please."

"Doug?"

"I'll have a pint of Guinness so, thanks, Caroline."

"Mick?"

"I'm fine, thanks."

"Dana?"

"I'm fine too," she answers, despite the fact that her glass is completely empty.

"Are you sure?" asks Caroline

Then Dana reconsiders. "Okay, I'll have a white wine, thanks."

I take this as a positive sign. Not quite an olive branch but maybe a little shoot.

"Right then."

Caroline heads to the bar and immediately Dana turns on me.

"Why didn't you tell me you were bringing her?"

"Come on, Dana! The way you're both carrying on is just stupid. At least she was big enough to come here tonight. Now you need to meet her halfway. This quarrel between you has gone on far too long."

"Hush," says Doug, "she's looking over."

We all look up. Awkwardly Caroline turns around again.

"Come on," I say. "This is hard for her. You've been friends for so long. She's lost without you."

"I hardly think so! I think she might have made more of an effort if that was true."

"Okay, at the start she just wanted to give you some time to calm down and then, well, things went crazy, the business was so busy, she was upset about Mick," I look over at him and see he's listening – good, "and then, all that hassle with the shop and winding it up. It's been a crazy time for her."

"Still, she could have rung. You told her about my thesis, didn't you?"

"Yes, I did, but, like I said, she had her own problems." Then I shrug. "You could have rung her too, you know."

"But I wasn't the cause of any of her problems."

"And she wasn't entirely the cause of yours either."

"I know that but –"

"And you did walk out on the business – whatever your reasons were. "

"I know. I know." Dana sighs. "Maybe I should have rung her. I guess I was preoccupied with my own worries. I know the shop was important to her but college is important to me too."

"Do you know, she told me today that she's going to keep paying your rent for the time being, so that you still have the option of coming back."

"Really?" Dana shifts uncomfortably in her seat.

"Yes."

"Well, I never asked her to," she says defensively and then decides on an even better defence – attack. "And isn't she lucky to have the money to be able to do it?"

"Only because she sold her car."

"What?"

"What she had in her saving account didn't cover all our debts – *our* debts, Dana – so she sold her car to clear the rest and now she happens to have a little left over – some of which she's put aside to keep your room for you."

Dana is looking extremely unhappy and embarrassed now.

"But she loved that car," says Mick. "How will she manage without it?"

And then, despite everything, I find myself smirking. "We got the bus in together. You should have seen her. She's just not cut out for public transport. At any moment I was expecting her to take out an antiseptic wipe and give the seat a good clean."

I see Mick is smiling at the thought.

"So come on, Dana, she's trying – can't you met her halfway?"

"All right, all right," snaps Dana.

I see Caroline coming back down, I decide to change the subject. "So, Mick, how's filming?"

"We've just finished shooting."

"Here you are, Doug, Rosie, Dana." Caroline puts the drinks down and slips back into her seat.

There's another awkward silence.

"So what are you going to do now?" I turn again to Mick.

"Well, I have another role lined up – it's a support in a new Irish film but it's not starting for another three months so I'm going to head to Australia and do some travelling around there. I've always wanted to go."

"What?" Caroline looks at him with something akin to shock. "You're going to Australia for three months?"

"Yeah, that's the plan."

"When?"

"As soon as my visa comes through. The sooner I go, the more time I'll have."

"Oh!" Caroline looks completely disconcerted by the news and, noticing this, Mick himself looks a little disconcerted by her reaction.

"I will be back," he reassures her.

"Yes, I'm sure you will." Caroline gathers herself together and quickly changes the subject. She turns to Dana. "So, how are you?"

"Okay."

Doug interrupts. "Tell her about the course you're starting."

Dana shrugs but doesn't say anything.

"What course?" asks Caroline.

"I'm starting a new course. I'm going to become a relationships counsellor."

"Really?" I say. "How come you decided to do that?"

"It's just something I'm interested in."

Doug comes in: "When Dana was working in the shop, she found that the part she liked most was talking to people, helping them. Isn't that right, Dana?"

Dana nods non-committally.

"So," Doug goes on, "some good came out of working in the shop for you after all. Isn't that so, Dana?"

"I guess."

"But Dana, that's brilliant!" says Caroline. "You'd be fantastic at it."

For a moment, all awkwardness between Caroline and Dana disappears.

"Do you really think so?"

"Absolutely. It would suit you down to the ground. You'd be brilliant. I know you would."

I notice Mick keeps looking over at Caroline, like he can't help himself but Caroline doesn't notice. She's too engrossed in Dana's good news.

"I can't think of anything you'd be more suited for," she goes on enthusiastically. "I always thought you'd be wasted in academia."

"Well, you helped put paid to that particular ambition," says Dana. Oh God, I think, there goes the peace treaty. But then she laughs. "Maybe I'll be thanking you one day. Look, Caroline, I'm sorry things didn't work out in the shop."

"I know. And I'm sorry for making you go on Andrew Marsh's show, and sorry that it had such repercussions for you." Caroline looks nervous as she speaks. As if looking for support, her eyes go automatically to Mick but, although he's been watching her all along, now he quickly looks away.

"You couldn't have known," says Dana.

Mick is looking at Caroline again, his heart on his sleeve, or rather on his lovelorn face. He is still crazy about her, that's plain to see – except when Caroline happens to look in his direction and then the shutters quickly go up. Clearly he still loves her, and she him, but neither of them is going to do anything about it which leaves it up to – I decide – me.

"Dana, can I ask you a question?"

"Ah, yeah?"

"Say you were working as a relationships counsellor and you had this couple, right?"

"Right?" she says warily.

"Say you had this couple and, say, they were going out together for a while. Now this couple, even though they were complete opposites, were really mad about one another but they had their ups and downs because they were both – well – she was at any rate, rather a fiery character. And say she then split up with him but she really regretted it but, then, she learnt he was going away for a while so she was afraid she wouldn't get the chance to put things right again. Now my question is this, do you think she should go to him and tell him she's sorry?"

"I don't know," Dana answers. She looks over at Caroline and then at Mick "It depends. For starters, does she really want him back? What do you think, Caroline?"

"She does." Caroline is looking directly at Mick as she answers.

"And do you think he would go back to her, Mick?" Dana asks.

Mick is looking at Caroline now but his answer is slow in coming. "I don't know. I mean if he had no idea why she decided to break up with him then he might be worried she'd do it again. I think he might be reluctant to put himself in that situation again."

"So why do you think she split up with him, Caroline?" Dana asks.

Caroline shifts uneasily in her seat. "Because she's a fool?"

"Yes, well, we're all agreed on that but there must have been a particular reason. What do you think it was?"

Caroline thinks for a long time before answering. "I think this girl was very foolish. She really loved – does love – this man but circumstances meant they hadn't been seeing a lot of one another. When they did meet, they always seemed to end up fighting. She felt a little jealous. His new career was going so well while she was really struggling to set up a new business. To make matters worse, he made it obvious that he didn't really approve of her new business. And then along came another man, let's call him Niall and –"

"Caroline," I say warningly. Even though I started all this, I'm not sure she needs to go this far, here, now, in front of everyone, but she ignores me.

"Let's call him Niall. Niall Wallace. This Niall Wallace is a successful businessman who decides to invest in this woman's business and the woman is thrilled because the original backers aren't coming up with the money. What's more, he's really interested in it, and they start meeting up occasionally and he listens to her when she talks about her new business. The woman enjoys talking to him because he's so interested in what she's doing and not at all disapproving. But then one day, he –"

"Caroline!" I warn again but she ignores me.

"But then one day, he kisses her and she feels guilty. She wants to tell her boyfriend but she's afraid of how he'll react. He's already made it clear that he thinks she's a hard-hearted businesswoman with no conscience who's intent on taking money from foolish people, so how would he feel if he knew she'd been carrying on with her main investor? He'd think even less of her than he already does. He'd probably say 'enough is enough' and would break it off with her. So she decides to take matters into her own hands and break up with him, rather than give him the chance to do it to her." Caroline stops talking, then looks nervously over at Mick. "I think that was the reason why she broke up with him."

Nobody says anything. We all just sit there, anxiously, waiting to see how Mick will react but for a long time he doesn't respond at all. Caroline is looking increasingly uneasy.

Then, finally, Mick answers.

"You know, I'm thinking that this boyfriend of hers is rather a sanctimonious type."

"What?" Caroline looks bewildered.

Clearly this wasn't the reaction she was expecting at all. Nor I.

Mick goes on: "There he is, riding the waves of his own good fortune, while she's struggling to realise her own dream after having helped him so much and, instead of giving her the support she might expect, he makes her feel so isolated that she turns to someone else."

"Oh!"

Mick goes on. "But I'd have one question, was it really just a kiss?"

"Oh, yes."

"Just one?"

"Absolutely."

"I would have to question her taste however. The one Niall Wallace I know is a thuggish fellow with mean little eyes, who's full of his own self-importance, who wears sunglasses indoors and jeans with neat creases down the legs and more jewellery than a WAG and goes about –"

"All right, all right! Enough!" interjects Caroline.

"But if it was just a kiss, one kiss –"

"It was –"

"And if the reason she broke up with her boyfriend was because she was afraid of how he'd react well, then, I think that boyfriend would have to say that, maybe, their relationship is worth another go."

"But what if he's heading to Australia for three months?" asks Caroline.

Mick thinks for a moment. "That's a difficult one. I guess he could stay at home and not go but –"

"Would he do that for her?"

"He'd do anything for her. On the other hand, however, he could say to her, 'Look, after the rollercoaster ride of the last few months, maybe you should think about taking an extended holiday to recharge your batteries. Maybe you should think about going to Australia with me.' He might try to convince her that she's as likely to come up with another great idea for a business while lying back on a white beach looking out on an azure sea as she is at home. You see, he knows she will come up with another idea. She's smart, she's resilient, she's tough, so it's only a matter of time. But, then again, maybe he's afraid to ask her to come with him, maybe he's afraid she'll say no."

"She says yes!" Caroline shouts.

"She does?"

"Yes, she does. I do. I will come with you."

In the words of Dr Ruth Westheimer,
"An aphrodisiac is anything you think it is."

35

I come down for breakfast to find Doug and Dana sitting at the table.

"Look at you!" cries Dana, taking in my suit.

"Do you think I'm overdressed?" I ask. "I'm not going to wear this all the time but I thought I should look smart on my first day."

"Well, you look very professional," remarks Doug.

"Thanks – I think."

I find myself a bowl and pour out some Cheerios.

"Are you excited?" asks Dana.

I shrug. "I guess I will be when I get my first pay cheque. Not that I'll be keeping much of it. I owe so much money. I still haven't paid this month's rent."

Dana holds out a postcard. "This came this morning from Caroline."

"So she hasn't totally forgotten about us then?"

I take the card. This is the first we've heard from Caroline since we saw her and Mick off at the airport two weeks ago. I begin to read aloud.

"Hi guys, having a whale of a time! Have left Sydney after a brilliant week – even did the Sydney Harbour Bridge climb – unbelievable – 134 metres high!"

"Isn't Caroline afraid of heights?" I ask.

"Terrified."

I read on:

"Spent today scuba diving – fantastic, first day of a four-day course. Renting out a four-wheel drive next and going walkabout, or drive-about rather, all the way up to Cape York at the very tip of Australia."

Dana laughs. "So much for Mick's plan of kicking back on white sands."

"Miss you all, love you loads, Caroline X

PS: Came up with the most BRILLIANT idea for all of us – can't wait to tell you about it – you'll love it!"

"What do you think she means?" I ask.

"It doesn't matter," says Dana resolutely. "We're doing fine as we are."

"Yeah. I've just started work."

"And I've just started my counselling course."

"And we're all friends again."

"Yeah."

"No need to rock the boat."

"No."

"No matter what she comes up with, we can just stay firm and say no."

"That's right. Stay firm. Say no."

"Besides she won't be home for ages yet."

"Exactly. And she can't make us do anything when she's so far away, now can she?"

"No."

"No matter what she comes up with, we won't be tempted."

"Absolutely not. No way."

"Still, I wonder what it is?"

THE END

If you enjoyed *Love Potions* by Anne Marie Forrest
why not try *The Love Detective*
also published by Poolbeg

Here's a sneak preview of Chapter one.

The Love Detective

Anne Marie Forrest

POOLBEG

1

"I want to know what lo♥e is . . ."

"I'm telling you, weddings are just one big swiz. You'd have to wonder why anyone would be foolish enough to go through with one, you really would."

It's Sunday night and I've just picked up my friend and flatmate Caroline at the airport after her flight home from the wedding of one of her colleagues in London, and we're driving back into the city in her car which she let me borrow for the weekend. Or rather, we're stuck in a line of stationary cars pointed in that direction. We haven't moved in over fifteen minutes and all the time I have Caroline yap-yap-yapping into my ear. She hasn't paused for breath since she hopped into the passenger seat and there's no sign of it happening anytime soon. She's in one of her famous rants.

"Till death do us part!" She's practically spitting with indignation. "You mean until the next bit of skirt do us part – bridesmaid skirt in this instance!"

I glance across at her. "What *are* you talking about?"

1

"Don't you ever listen, Rosie? I'm talking about the groom and bridesmaid – *obviously*."

"And what? Are you trying to tell me the groom went off with the bridesmaid?"

"Yep." She nods emphatically. "I sure am."

"On his wedding day?"

"Oh, yes."

"Oh, come on! That sort of thing only happens in movies."

"Hah! That shows how little you know. In actual fact, it happens all the time."

"And you know this. How?"

"I just do."

"No, you don't."

"Yes, I do."

This could go on all night but, not wanting to feel like a character in a pantomime, I drop the matter and revert to our original topic. "So go on, tell me, what *did* happen between the groom and the bridesmaid?"

"Like I said, they went off together."

"I still don't believe you!"

"I'm not lying! I saw them!"

"You saw them – what?"

"You know . . ." She raises her eyebrows suggestively.

"No, I don't *know*! Like, what are you saying? That you saw them having sex together, is that it?"

"Yeah –"

"No!"

"– or as good as."

"Caroline! You either did or you didn't. Which was it?"

"I saw them going up the stairs in the direction of the honeymoon suite. *Together.*"

I wait to hear more but, when there's nothing else

forthcoming, I glance over at her again. She's sitting there, a smug Hercules Poirot look on her face, like she's just delivered the most conclusive proof imaginable.

"That's *it*?" I demand. "That's the sum total of your evidence?"

"Well, yes."

"Oh, for crying out loud! There could be dozens of explanations."

She throws me a dismissive look. "Sure!" She brushes away a non-existent speck of dust from her immaculate cream trousers. Who else but Caroline would choose to wear a cream suit when flying? *And* how can it be still so spotless, and totally creaseless?

"They could have been putting presents away for safe-keeping," I go on. "Or freshening up. Or fetching something. Who knows?"

"God! Rosie! You are so naïve! If there's one thing I know, it's human nature and –"

"And I don't?"

"Well, come on, you're not the most perceptive. No, those two were definitely up to something, believe me."

I let the dig pass. That's just Caroline. She speaks without thinking but I know her well enough not to take too much offence and, anyway, she has a point. I may not be the world's most perceptive but, then, she won't be lining up anytime soon to collect her award for sensitivity. In fact, she's just the kind who would go up to a bride on her wedding day and –

"Oh God! Please don't tell me you said anything to the bride."

"What do you take me for? Of course I didn't."

"Good."

"Well, not exactly."

My heart sinks. "Well, what *exactly* did you say?"

"I don't really remember. Come on, Rosie, can't you start passing some of these cars out?"

I don't know what she's seeing out through her side of the windscreen but all I'm seeing is two lanes of bumper-to-bumper traffic – nothing is moving. "We're never going to get home at this rate," she grumbles.

She's avoiding the subject, of course, and if she's embarrassed enough to do that then I fear the worst. This must be bad.

"What did you say to her?"

"Nothing – nothing much."

"Nothing much?"

"I just warned her to look out, that things aren't always as they seem."

"Caroline! You sound like you were threatening her!"

"Funny you should say that; she said exactly the same thing."

"That's all a bride needs on her wedding day – unhinged guests going around making threats." I love Caroline, I really do, she's one of my best friends, but sometimes I have to wonder about her. "Remind me not to invite you to my wedding."

"Your wedding!" She laughs.

"What's so funny?"

"Rosie, you can't keep a boyfriend for any length of time so don't you think talking about your wedding is just a little premature?"

"That's not fair!"

"But it's true!"

"No, it's not!" I protest though, of course, she's right. It is true. I've never gone out with anyone for more than a few months. What am I saying? Not even that long – my dismal average is about a month.

"What was it Shane said about you the other night, before I went to London?"

"Shane? *Shane*?" I explode. "Like what does he know?" Then I mumble, "Anyway I don't remember." But again, I lie. Of course, I remember. How could I not?

"You must remember," Caroline insists. "You went storming off in a huff!"

I stormed off, yes, but not in a huff. I stormed off because I was afraid of what I might say if I stayed. Like, what the hell gives Shane the right to say things like that? What makes him so sure that when everyone else has settled down, I'll still be lurching from one disastrous relationship to another? And does he really think it's by choice? Does he really think I like starting off each new relationship full of hope, full of that excited feeling that – maybe – this could be the one – and then to see it all fall apart – just like all the others before it?

"Rosie, what's the matter?"

I shrug. "Nothing," I snap.

The thing is, all I really want in life is to fall in love, live in a wonderful house, work in a fulfilling career, have two perfect children, and to live happily-ever-after. Is that too much to ask for? Okay, maybe it is quite a lot but I don't believe it's that much different from what most people want. But to live happily-ever-after with my perfect man in our perfect life, I first have to meet him. It's fine for Shane. He may have struck lucky by finding the love of his life but not all of us have been so fortunate and we end up – or at least I have – kissing an awful lot of frogs in the process.

"Come on," coaxes Caroline, "don't get into a puss on me."

"I'm not in a puss!"

"Good.

I try explaining: "Shane's wrong, you know."

"About what?"

I shrug, then I look over. The thing about Caroline is that she has the attention span of a goldfish and I see I've lost her. She's moved on. She has her phone out and she's checking her texts.

I sigh. "It just seems – well – you know – you have to kiss a lot of frogs to find out that they are just that – frogs."

She laughs. "Haven't you learnt by now that all men are frogs?"

Now she's just being stupid. I look over at her again. Her eyes are glued to the little screen and her fingers are going like the clappers. I sit silently and stare out at the depressing sight of the tail-lights of the car in front of me. It begins to drizzle. I flick on the wipers. And then I begin to think of Killian and I smile to myself. Now here's a man who I've good reason to suspect may not turn out to be a frog. Part of me wants to tell Caroline all about him, but another part of me is reluctant to; I should just keep the thought of him to myself for a while, dwell on it, enjoy it, savour it.

"Actually," I blurt out, like there was ever a chance I wasn't going to, "I met someone nice at that party Shane and I went to last night."

"I don't believe you!" she cries.

"What?" I glance over at her. Swish, swish, swish goes her blonde, shoulder-length hair as she shakes her head in disbelief. It looks so sleek, so glossy that it could be the hairdresser's I collected her from, not the airport. But then, that's Caroline. She likes to be in control of her appearance,

6

of work, of every aspect of her life. I guess that's what makes her so successful. "Rosie," she goes on now, "the reason you were going to that party was to catch up with Shane. Your plan was to spend some quality time with him, remember?"

That's true and I am embarrassed by the way things worked out but I didn't know that, as soon we arrived in the door, I'd literally bump into someone like Killian.

"Yes, well, plans are made to be broken."

"I think that's promises, actually. Anyway, go on, tell me about him."

At first I'm reluctant to but then I start thinking about him and that gets me talking.

"Okay, he's tall, good-looking –"

"So far so exactly the same. Rosie, you don't go for any other kind!"

I ignore her. "– and smart and creative. He works as an architect. He has a cat and – "

"But you *hate* cats."

"I don't hate them – I just find them a bit spooky. You know, the way they stare at you, like they can see into your very soul. But at least it shows Killian has a caring side. Plus he's musical. He plays the trumpet."

Caroline laughs.

"What?" I demand.

"You really think you could stick someone who plays the trumpet? When Dana started on the violin you never gave over moaning about the racket."

"A trumpet is different. It's not whiney and screechy."

"Okay, but you still haven't told me what makes him so special."

I think. "Well, he has this great smile and these eyes, these gorgeous, really gorgeous big bright blue eyes."

"So what are you saying? That if his eyes were a fraction less blue or a fraction smaller then you wouldn't fancy him, that he wouldn't be special?"

"No, I'm not saying that. I just – just – just, oh forget it."

All the things I said about Killian are true but what I really liked about him was the fact that he was so easy to talk to. From the moment we met we never stopped – it was like we'd known each other for years. There was none of the usual awkwardness; we were tripping over one another with all we had to say. I kind of felt this guy got me, *really* got me. He even laughed at my poor attempts at humour. But I know if I try to explain all this to Caroline it will come out all wrong.

I shake my head. "I just like him, all right?" I leave it at that and change the subject. "Anyway, apart from your belief that the groom ran off with the bridesmaid, did you enjoy the wedding?"

"What was there to enjoy?" she grumpily snaps.

"It was a wedding!" I snap right back.

"Exactly. Cringe-making from start to finish. Everyone doing 'a little bit of this and a little bit of that and shaking their ass, da, da, da da'! All the single lay-deez scrumming like rugby players for the bouquet. Crabby old relatives moaning at the end of the night how the music's too loud, the cuppa tea's too cold, and how there's nothing but cheese sandwiches left to eat. Enjoy it? I don't think so. Especially when the whole thing is a farce anyway, a big sham, a big celebration of love when everyone knows there's no such thing!"

"No, they don't!"

"Well, they should! They should know that love's just a delusion to keep us all procreating in order to ensure the survival of the human species."

"Rubbish! Just because you've never been in love doesn't mean there's no such thing. Of course, there is."

"All right then, give me an example of two people you know who you really and truly believe are in love with one another."

"That's easy," I say as the traffic *finally* begins to move.

"Go on so."

I think for a while. I must know dozens. Mentally I go through all the people I know but find that surprisingly few are in serious relationships. When I think of those closest to me, the situation is even worse. I've known Dana and Caroline since our first year in college and their love lives could best be described as non-love lives. As for our other good friend Mick, as an actor an on-stage kiss is the nearest he's got to romance in the time we've known him. That leaves Shane. Shane and Loretta.

"So?"

"I'm thinking."

"See, I told you!"

"Okay then, Shane and Loretta."

She laughs. "They're the best you can come up with! Oh please! You don't think they're in the least suited!"

"I never said that."

"No, but you've made it pretty obvious."

"*If* I do think it, it doesn't make it true. They've been going out together for a while now. They seem to get along."

"Is it because you don't like Loretta? Is that why you think they're unsuited?"

"I said I thought they *were* suited. Aren't you even listening? God! You can be annoying! Now, can we just drop this whole stupid conversation?"

9

"Fine by me."

"Good."

"Good."

Her phone beeps and after reading the incoming message, she begins texting a reply. The traffic is moving nicely now and, finally, some fifteen minutes later, I pull into the drive of the 1960's semi-d Caroline and I share with Shane and Dana.

"One couple, that's all," she repeats as we get out of the car.

"Just give it a rest," I answer crossly.